# VENGEANCE OF THE
# DEMON

## DIANA ROWLAND

**DAW BOOKS, INC.**
DONALD A. WOLLHEIM, FOUNDER
375 Hudson Street, New York, NY 10014
•
ELIZABETH R. WOLLHEIM
SHEILA E. GILBERT
PUBLISHERS
www.dawbooks.com

First Printing, April 2015

1 2 3 4 5 6 7 8 9

DAW TRADEMARK REGISTERED
U.S. PAT. AND TM. OFF. AND FOREIGN COUNTRIES
—MARCA REGISTRADA
HECHO EN U.S.A.

PRINTED IN THE U.S.A.

*For my completely awesome readers! Seriously, do you even know how surreal it is to go from being an unpopular bullied nerd to having fans? So, yeah, Petey and Carrie and Angela and you other jerks in junior high who picked on me to hell and back,* suck it! *Ha!*

# ACKNOWLEDGMENTS

Huge quantities of grateful appreciation are due to everyone and everything that made this book possible. Many thanks to Jack Hoffstadt, Tara Zeller, Charlie Watson, @notaalanister, Riv Hellington, Gerard Bultman, the Twitter hivemind, Mary Robinette Kowal, Anna Hoffstadt, and Sherry Rowland for vast quantities of help, support, and useful information. Praise and awe go out to my brilliant cover artist, Dan dos Santos, and of course the people who take care of all the pesky details: Matt Bialer, Lindsay Ribar, Betsy Wollheim, Joshua Starr, Marylou Capes-Platt, and everyone at DAW and Penguin. You all make my life much more fun.

# Chapter 1

*Accessory after the fact. Principal to murder in the first degree. End of life as I know it. Death row.*

Those thoughts ricocheted through my mind as Detective Vincent Pellini arranged a half-dozen photos on the diner table between us. I took a sip of iced tea in an attempt to cover my shock. It didn't matter one bit that Pellini pointed to a man front and center in one of the photos rather than the hazy figures in the background. My entire focus locked onto the distant blurry image of *me,* caught on camera seconds before the execution-style murder of James Macklin Farouche, as I stood shoulder to shoulder with the equally blurry killer.

My eyes slid to the other photos—all most likely taken with cell phone cameras. Watery ripples of distortion or jagged bands of color marred each one, but a few aspects were clear enough. People running. Faces full of panic and fear. Strange purple fire on rubble.

And then there were the details that only someone who'd been at the scene would be able to identify. A circle twenty feet across of charred grass. A pond steaming after being boiled away. The melted remains of a tablet computer.

Pellini tapped the man in the photo—powerfully built, with fading red hair and a ripple of photographic distortion through his face. "Angus McDunn," he said. "He's still at large with no sightings."

I pushed aside my half-eaten cheesy fries and clung to the hope that Pellini couldn't possibly recognize me in the blurry picture. "Farouche's right-hand man," I said, oh-so-coolly. "I've seen him on the news." Up close and personal, too. Only a few weeks ago McDunn had held a MAC-10 submachine gun on me as motivation to have a conversation with his boss.

The booth seat creaked beneath Pellini's bulk as he shifted. "Yeah, but here's the kicker," he said. "McDunn is Boudreaux's stepfather."

"You're shitting me." I stared at Pellini and pushed down my selfish worries about pesky murder trials. Detective Marcel Boudreaux was Pellini's partner, a weaselly piece of work I'd had the displeasure of knowing for years. Yet even though Boudreaux ranked right below Pellini on my asshole list, in this moment I felt for him. With his slight stature and surly attitude, he already caught more than his fair share of crap from other cops. Add in a felon stepdad in a high-profile case, and things were sure to get ugly.

"Serious as a heart attack," Pellini said. He swiped a piece of sausage through the mustard on his plate and popped it into his mouth. A speck of yellow bobbed on his mustache as he chewed and swallowed.

"Damn. How's he holding up?"

"Coping by concentrating on finding Farouche's killer," Pellini said. "He's obsessed."

I sucked down more iced tea. I'd never known either Pellini or Boudreaux to be *obsessed* with a case. Why the hell did his first obsession have to involve me? "It's not in Beaulac PD jurisdiction," I said. "Is he assisting the sheriff's office?"

"He's restricted from the official investigation because of his stepdad's involvement, but it's not stopping him from doing whatever he can." Pellini picked up his napkin and, to my relief, wiped away the dab of mustard.

"Yeah, but why is he so worked up over this?" I frowned down at the photos. "I mean, the news reports say Farouche was involved in organized crime. Clearly, he wasn't the saint everyone thought he was."

"I guess Boudreaux thinks otherwise," he said then exhaled. "His mom's the head trainer out at Farouche's horse farm and has worked with his thoroughbreds for over thirty years. Boudreaux grew up working with horses and still lives out there." He paused to take a sip of water. I strained a few neurons in my attempt to picture scrawny, cigarette-smoking Boudreaux around horses. Nope. Couldn't see it. Had to be an alternate universe.

"He's always been private about his past," Pellini continued, "but he claims Farouche saved his life and didn't deserve to die like that. He's pretty torn up."

Great. It was bad enough having the FBI and sheriff's department all over the Farouche Plantation incident, but now an unpredictable Boudreaux joined the mix. "Are these the only pictures of what happened out there?"

"The sheriff's office has a few others, but they're so distorted they're useless." His dark eyes sharpened on me beneath shaggy black eyebrows. "You have any idea why that might be?"

I could have said, "Probably because a crap load of arcane potency flies around when demonic lords battle it out over a passageway between worlds," or, "Maybe it was from the lightning Lord Mzatal summoned in rage—right before he almost incinerated everything within a mile radius," but instead I opted for, "No idea."

His mouth tightened. "I get it. You can't tell me."

I scrambled to read his expression. Did he *know* I knew more or was he simply fishing for information? Neither possibility appealed to me. "I don't have anything to tell," I said, keeping my face composed.

"Sorry," he said and sounded as if he actually meant it. "With Kristoff on the case, I thought it was worth a shot to ask, but I shouldn't've pushed it."

Relief flooded through me. Agents Ryan Kristoff and Zack Garner led an FBI special task force that dealt with weird stuff, and after I resigned from the Beaulac PD they brought me on as a civilian consultant. It made perfect sense that the task force would be assigned to the plantation case considering all the bizarre crap that had occurred there. It was natural for Pellini to assume I'd have more info.

"I was out of town for a while and haven't been updated," I said. It wasn't even a lie as long as the demon realm counted as "out-of-town." I didn't bother to mention that Zack and Ryan were both as neck-deep in the plantation fiasco as I was. Or that Zack was totally out of commission, and Ryan hadn't bothered to answer his phone or reply to any of my messages since I'd arrived back on Earth a couple of weeks ago.

"Boudreaux and I went out to the plantation the day after all the shit went down," Pellini said. "Kristoff got us in before Boudreaux got banned because of his stepdad." He pulled a file folder from his briefcase and placed it on the table beside the photos. "You think you might have time to go out there with me tomorrow?"

What was his game? Had he recognized me in the photograph after all? And did he think I'd break down and confess if I returned to the scene of the crime? Out of habit I mentally reached for Mzatal, like turning to share with a friend, but only felt the barest hint of him. He'd walled off his emotions after he wreaked havoc at the plantation. While I understood the necessity, I still ached with the muting of our connection. Beneath the table, I ran my fingers over my ring—Mzatal's Christmas gift to me. Though the stone had been destroyed, I couldn't bring myself to stop wearing it.

"I saw that you left messages for me while I was away," I said. "Were they about this plantation incident?"

Damned if Pellini didn't look guilty. Or maybe ashamed? "Yeah," he said then paused. "And a few other matters."

Other matters? Yeah, that wasn't at *all* ominous. But my thoughts derailed as Detective Marco Knight of the New Orleans Police Department stepped into the East Shore Diner and headed straight for us.

Why in blazes was he in Beaulac? I'd known him for close to a year, ever since he helped out with one of our task force investigations in New Orleans. He was clairvoyant—at least as far as I could tell—which made him a perfect fit for the strange shit we dealt with. On the other hand, his talent for knowing more than he should unnerved most people. In fact, Pellini had once pulled me aside to warn me that secrets didn't always stay secret around Knight. At the time, I was more shocked that the typically abrasive and unpleasant Pellini had my back than worried that he thought I had secrets that I wanted kept secret. Later, the NOPD detective admitted that many years ago he'd shared one of his revelations with Pellini and hurt him in a way he didn't deserve.

By the time Knight reached our table I'd recovered from my surprise at seeing him. "Hey, Marco," I said with a friendly lift of my hand. "What brings you to our neck of the woods?"

Knight gave me a quick smile and a "Hey, Kara" but then turned to Pellini. "Need to talk to you. *Now.* Outside."

My bafflement increased. "Is something wrong?"

Knight shook his head and hooked a thumb at Pellini. "Nothing this ugly sack can't handle."

"Kara, I'll be back in a few," Pellini said. He pulled himself out of the booth and headed toward the door with Knight following, leaving me to stare after them in disbelief. Why on earth would Pellini jump to do Knight's bidding when he distrusted the man so much?

Knight slowed and stopped, then he pivoted back to me. "Twelve," he murmured, eyes unfocused. "The twelfth is a radical game changer." He drew a deep breath and took a step closer. "Spawned of fierce cunning. Beauty and power exemplified. Beware the twelfth."

Time stopped as the echoes of his words reverberated in the air. In the next heartbeat he staggered and blinked, shattering the moment. His face paled as he met my eyes, then he muttered an apology and hurried after Pellini.

The lunchtime din of the restaurant rushed back in his wake. My heart pounded as I pulled my notepad out of my bag and wrote the words exactly as he'd said. The small of my back tingled as I reread the seemingly prophetic warning, and I had a feeling I knew exactly what "twelfth" he'd referred to.

Whether by design or dumb luck, I'd spent my first decade as a demon summoner naïve in my worldview and ignorant of the machinations of the demonic lords. The last couple of years had changed all of that. I now sported eleven complex and hideously beautiful scars—sigils carved into my torso by the demonic lord Rhyzkahl during a failed ritual intended to strip my identity and make me his tool. Only a few weeks past, Ryan—a.k.a. Lord Szerain— completed and activated the twelfth sigil in a risky bid to save me from being enslaved by Rhyzkahl.

*But was that his only purpose?* Knight's warning rekindled simmering doubts, and the sigil pulsed warm on my skin as though it knew my thoughts. With a shudder I dragged my attention back to the immediate issue: my freaking picture at a murder.

I tweaked the faded green curtain aside to peer out at the back parking lot. Beyond it, sun shimmered off Lake Pearl, silhouetting the two men in deep conversation while also making it annoyingly impossible to read facial expressions. Then again, Knight's arrival gave me the perfect opportunity to give the other photographs a more careful perusal. To my relief, other than the one with me in it, I didn't see anything damning to me or my posse.

Casually, I flipped open the folder Pellini had left on the table. More photos. Five pictures of the ravaged plantation, likely taken by Pellini when he visited.

A copy of Jerry Steiner's driver's license. I bared my teeth in automatic response at the sight of the hard-faced man. Steiner was the sadistic piece of shit who'd done wet work for Farouche and liked it.

A photo of Leo Carter, Farouche's head of plantation security. I didn't know much about him, but he'd obviously piqued Pellini's interest.

And finally, several photos of the eighteen wheeler where the body of Amber Palatinq Gavin had been dumped. The sister of fellow summoner Idris Palatino, she'd been raped, tortured and murdered to create an arcane trap for me. I glanced back at the driver's license with unmasked venom. Jerry Steiner had been one of her attackers.

The waitress approached with a pitcher of tea, and I quickly closed the folder before she could see the contents. I spotted Knight leaning against his car and puffing on a cigarette. A second later Pellini came back inside and returned to the table, but didn't sit.

"Everything cool?" I asked.

"Something came up," he said tersely, then gathered the photos and stuffed them into the folder. "I've got to go, but I want to head out to the plantation with you tomorrow," he continued, snatching up his briefcase. "I'll call."

"No problem," I replied, acting nonchalant and not at all completely perplexed.

Pellini fumbled a ten from his wallet and dropped it on the table. "If that doesn't cover it, you're shit out of luck." With that he hurried out.

At least that hadn't changed. Pellini still knew how to act like a dick. I peered out the window again and watched the two men get into their cars. A few seconds later Knight pulled out with Pellini following right behind him.

*What. The. Fuck.*

# Chapter 2

Heat shimmered off the hood of my car as I crawled through downtown Beaulac at approximately three miles an hour. I cranked the air conditioner up as high as it would go, then glanced in the rearview mirror to see my demon bodyguard Eilahn a few cars back, astride her sleek new motorcycle. She didn't appear to mind the oppressive Louisiana summer heat and sported a vivid green tank top that accentuated the rich olive tone of her skin. I thought I heard a distant wail of sirens over the blasting AC but had no desire to turn down the air to find out.

The line of cars moved forward a few more feet before stopping again. This was more than the usual post-lunch traffic jam, but whether the cause was an accident or the ubiquitous road construction, I wasn't going to let it stress me out. I had nowhere I had to be anytime soon. Besides, it gave me a chance to ponder the weirdness of my lunch with Pellini.

What the hell was up with him? For years he and Boudreaux had been nothing but pricks. Annoying, but generally harmless. Then, gradually, Pellini had begun to show traces of humanity, from warning me about Knight, to asking me to grab a beer with him, to this invitation for lunch—which I'd only agreed to because he'd mentioned the strange happenings at the plantation.

As soon as traffic moved again I capitulated and turned down a side street to find a detour around the jam. Three blocks away the congestion eased, and I proceeded to mull over the photos Pellini had shown me. If the blurry one was the only piece of evidence that tied me to the plantation and the murder, I had no reason to worry. There was no way to make a positive identification from that even if someone suspected it was me.

*So why am I worried?* My grip tightened on the steering wheel. Because I was guilty in the eyes of the law, and any physical evidence I'd inadvertently left at the plantation had the potential to implicate me. It didn't matter that I hadn't pulled the trigger on James Macklin Farouche. One of his former hit men, Bryce Thatcher, had taken care of that detail. But Bryce had been part of our team—all of us acting as judge, jury, and executioner. Believing there was no other acceptable option, I'd stood by when Bryce put two bullets in Farouche's head. *What does that make me?*

Responsible.

Things had been a lot simpler when I was a street cop. Ignorance was underappreciated bliss, and my work ended along with my shift. A twinge of loss went through me, though I knew it hadn't been all sunshine and roses. Besides, I was a demon summoner with talents, knowledge, and experience I never could have imagined back then. With both Earth and the demon realm at risk from demonic lords with dangerous agendas, I had a responsibility to use my rare expertise to do everything possible to assure the safety and stability of—

I snorted. What a crock of shit.

Sure, those noble goals and ideals were there, but only because the alternative was catastrophe. I had no real choice in the matter. But it *was* my choice to act as responsibly as possible given the circumstances. Earth laws didn't take into account otherworldly schemes that put humans at risk. J.M. Farouche had committed unforgivable crimes against humanity, but we hadn't executed him as punishment. We'd executed him because, with his ability to influence others, human laws weren't enough to stop him. One hell of a responsibility.

That said, I had to admit it felt good to make a difference. Didn't matter that most of humanity remained clue-less that a ragtag band of demons and humans fought tooth and nail for their right to remain blissfully ignorant. My posse had kicked ass at the plantation and prevented the Mraztur—the demonic lords Rhyzkahl, Jesral, Amkir, and Kadir—from establishing a permanent gate between the worlds.

Though not without cost. Another member of our team, Paul Ortiz, had suffered horrific arcane burns and now clung to life in the demon realm. Idris Palatino was there as well, recovering from the backblast of an arcane explosion.

Thoughts somber, I pulled into the driveway of a dusky blue, skinny two-story house owned by my best friend, Jill Faciane. She was currently almost nine months pregnant and living in a mobile home on my property until this whole demonic conflict settled down. Her boyfriend and father of her child lived here now: Zack, my favorite demon FBI agent.

Yet another casualty of the plantation battle.

As I walked up to the porch, I checked out the condition of the place. Though the lawn needed mowing, the potted plants looked perky enough to indicate they'd recently been watered. However, the blinds of the living room and the upstairs bedroom were closed tight, and a hand written *Do Not Disturb* sign hung on the porch rail. My worry rose in an aching wave. Zack had turned the tide of the battle at the plantation when he broke ancient oaths and severed his *ptarl* bond with Rhyzkahl. The act had shattered both of them, but Zack suffered an added blow by being ostracized, locked in human form, and cut off from the beyond-telepathy connection with the others of his kind, the demahnk.

I'd put off pestering Zack with questions so he could rest and recuperate. I truly hoped to find him strong enough to interact again, if only through insights and advice. But even beyond my need for him, he *deserved* to recover.

The door swung open a few seconds after I ignored the sign and knocked. Sonny Hernandez offered me a fleeting smile. "Hey, Kara. I didn't know you were coming over."

Sonny was a former Farouche henchman, one who had a

talent for keeping people tranquil in highly stressful situations—such as being kidnapped. That same talent turned out to be equally useful for easing Zack's trauma, and Sonny had been grateful for the chance to use his ability in a positive way.

"Surprise inspection," I said congenially as I peered into the gloom beyond him. "How's everything going?"

Sonny stepped back and looked away. "Everything's good."

He was full of crap, but I didn't challenge him on it. I moved past him and into the semi-dark living room. A lump shifted on the sofa.

"Sonny is overly optimistic," the lump said—Zack, his voice thin and frail, as if each word lost its strength in the effort to come out. "Somehow I manage to put up with him."

"Too soft for you, huh?" I said. "I'll see if Moonlight Temp Agency can find an angry, bitchy nurse to babysit you. Whatcha think?"

Zack let out a breathless laugh and struggled to sit up even as Sonny swept in to assist. "I think I'd be an idiot to agree," he said then murmured thanks to Sonny. My worry kicked up another notch. I'd spoken to Zack on the phone a few times since my return to Earth but hadn't seen him before now. He'd managed to keep much of the weakness out of his voice when we spoke. Or maybe I hadn't wanted to hear it.

"Damn straight." I rested a gentle kiss on Zack's cheek then sank to sit beside him. "You ever let any light in?"

"Not lately. It hurts too much."

A lighter rasped, and Sonny lit a fat jar candle on the coffee table. "This is all he can tolerate. Sorry, Kara."

"I don't mind," I said. "Candlelight's fine." Usually that was true, but in this case it only emphasized Zack's pale, gaunt face—so unlike the robust surfer dude I'd known. My hope that he'd soon be ready to rejoin the posse dribbled away. I felt as if I was visiting a hospice patient rather than someone in recovery. "I won't stay long, but I wanted to see you."

"I'm not ready," he said with such sorrow and understatement it tore my heart out.

"It's okay," I murmured, throat tight as I took his hand. It was so cold it seemed to pull the heat from mine. "You take all the time you need. Everything's okay." I abandoned all thought of updating him on the overall situation. His universe had collapsed to near nothing, and I felt as though I could scatter him to oblivion with a puff of breath.

He dropped his head back against the sofa and closed his eyes. "I'm sorry."

I squeezed his hand, willed him to take my warmth if it would ease him. "What about Jill? Maybe she could help you to—"

"No!" His eyes flew open, wild and desperate. "Kara, I cannot. *No.*"

"But she loves you—" I intended to add *and needs you as much as you need her*, but the panic that flashed across his face stopped me.

"No. Please, Kara," Zack said, breathing unsteadily. Desperation bled through the words. "Trust me. It's not her. But I can't. Please don't bring her here. I *cannot* see her as I am now."

Was it because of the baby? I didn't dare ask him, though. He looked as if any more stress would shatter him. Damn good thing I *hadn't* brought Jill over—as I'd seriously considered doing. "Zack," I said gently. "It's okay. I trust you." A tiny amount of the tension eased from his grasp. "What about the Demahnk Council? Can't they help?"

"They won't." He paused and flipped me the bird with an unsteady hand. "They can't."

The middle finger was his signal that we'd ventured into territory he couldn't talk about. He was bound by agreement and mandate to both the Council and unnamed ones he obliquely referred to as "the others." Apparently, breaking his bond with Rhyzkahl hadn't negated his other contracts. "What about the demahnk who aren't on the Council? Surely I can rally at least a—"

"Kara. The demahnk *are* the Council."

I shook my head, confused. "Wait. Are you saying that every demahnk is a Council member?"

"All but one, now," he murmured. "The other ten remain united."

I sat in stunned silence. Only eleven Elder syraza in the whole of the demon realm and Earth? I fished through my memory for anything that contradicted his information and came up with nothing. I'd assumed the Council was comprised of a handful of the eldest demahnk, never guessing that there were less than a dozen demahnk in total. Questions rose, but as I opened my mouth to ask, Zack flipped me the bird again. I swallowed my questions back. Obviously that tidbit of information was all he could give me, and I wasn't going to push the issue while he was so weak. "Rest, Zack."

He focused on me with effort, pain he couldn't hide reflected in his eyes. "What of . . . Rhyzkahl?"

In those three words, Zack managed to express profound grief and frustration. Considering Rhyzkahl's betrayal and torture of me, I was inclined to do a happy dance to celebrate the lord's downfall. But Zack had been ptarl bound to Rhyzkahl, as his chief advisor and advocate, for *millennia*. His concern outweighed my anger.

"I haven't heard anything new," I said gently. "When I left the demon realm he was cloistered within his palace. According to Mzatal, he's debilitated to the point where he can't take care of his plexus, so the other lords are pitching in to cover it, like they do for Szerain." Each of the eleven lords had a plexus, a chamber dedicated to monitoring and adjusting the arcane potency flows of their planet. Without constant attention, the flows would tear the world apart. Preventing that end was the one thing the lords agreed on unanimously. "I promise I'll let you know as soon as I have any new info."

Zack slumped into the cushions with a long sigh as though he'd never draw another breath. Candlelight glimmered in a tear on his face. Though I couldn't hear the words, I read them on his lips. "Thank you." His hand went slack in mine, and my heart thudded in dread until I spotted the shallow rise and fall of his chest.

I untwined my hand from his and kissed his cheek again. "No," I whispered as I stood. "Thank *you*, Zakaar." I looked down at him, struck by the eerie sense that I might never see him again. Aching, I finally turned away, caught Sonny's eye and nudged my head toward the door. With a last glance at Zack, I exited to the heat and blinding light of the afternoon sun. I wiped away tears and cleared my throat as Sonny followed me out and closed the door behind him.

"He's fading," I said hoarsely. "And I have no idea what to do for him." I wanted to thrash the rest of the demahnk and all the demons who'd turned their backs on him. Stripping his innate connections to the others was like pulling a fish out of water and leaving it to die slowly, gasping for breath.

"Every day it's as though less of him is here," Sonny said, grim. "I can barely get him to eat or drink anything, and he only moves when he has to. It's not good."

"Keep doing what you're doing," I said. "Let me know if there's anything, *anything*, that you need and I'll take care of it." My brow furrowed. "Has he had any contact with Ryan . . . Szerain?" The cagey demonic lord Szerain had recently freed himself from his horrific imprisonment as Ryan Kristoff. He continued to maintain the persona of Ryan, but I didn't know where he was or what he was doing.

Sonny shook his head. "Zack's had me call him a few times, but it always goes to voicemail."

"I know Ryan's working, but he's not answering my calls either." It was one thing for Szerain to snub me, but blacklisting Zack was beyond the pale. Szerain wouldn't even be here if Zack hadn't kept him sane in his hellish prison for over fifteen years. "Let me know if he calls. Anything else I should know?"

"He talks in his sleep at times," Sonny said with a small frown. "Not a lot, but there are a few words and phrases he repeats. Jill, Rhyzkahl, and Szerain I recognize, but the others must be a different language." He paused, clearly trying to recall the sounds. "Ekeeree akar is the most frequent," he finally said. "Sovilas mir nah shey. Zarbeck. Ashava."

"I've heard a couple of them," I said. "Nothing alarming, but I'll keep them in mind." I didn't know what "akar" meant, but the Ekiri were an ancient race that abandoned the demon realm thousands of years past. Xharbek was

Szerain's demahnk ptarl, though he was deep in hiding for reasons unknown to me. I didn't recognize Ashava or the longer phrase. "You have my number. Keep me posted on how Zack's doing, please."

"You got it, Kara."

"You're the best," I said. And I meant it.

With that I headed for my car. Nearby, Eilahn leaned on the seat of her new Ducati motorcycle, her helmet under one arm, and her foot propped on the curb. With her sleek multiethnic look and hot chick body, she might as well have been posing for a motorcycle pinup calendar.

Her gaze slid to the front door of the house, and her face tightened into an expression of disdain. "I tolerate phone communications," she said as she turned her glare on me, "but I do not approve of in-person consort with the *kiraknikahl*."

I matched her syraza glare—hell, I doubled it. "Get. Over. It." In the eyes of demons, Zack was a kiraknikahl, an oathbreaker, having openly shattered the most sacred and hitherto unbreakable oath—his ptarl bond to Rhyzkahl. I, however, wasn't blindly stuck in bullshit custom. "Let me be clear," I said. "I get that you disapprove of him because of his actions, and that's your prerogative. No one's asking you to sully yourself by *consorting* with Zack. But I absolutely will *not* tolerate anyone disrespecting him in front of me. Everything will be cool if you keep your hostile opinions about Zack and me to yourself. He's no threat. To anyone."

She pursed her full lips then nodded. "Your conditions are understood and accepted," she said with only a trace of petulance in her voice. "Agreed."

I smiled. "Agreed." She believed what she believed, but in the end all she wanted to do was protect me. "Out of curiosity, how old does a syraza have to be to become an Elder syraza, a demahnk?"

"Your question is nonsensical and has no answer."

I tamped down my amused annoyance. At times my demon bodyguard seemed to enjoy being a smartass. "Then help me understand. How does a syraza become an Elder syraza?"

"That is like asking how a *faas* becomes a *reyza*." She lifted one shoulder in a so-there shrug. "Or how a hamster becomes a crocodile."

"No," I said. She obviously didn't understand what I was asking. "Those are different entirely different spe—" I stopped and did an open-mouthed gawk. "Hold on. Syraza and Elder syraza aren't the same *species?* Elders look like big syraza with a few extra ridges and stuff. And you call them Elder syraza!"

Her hair flowed over her shoulders as she shook her head. "No, the demon designations are syraza and demahnk," she said. "Syraza simply translates to shapeshifter. All demahnk are syraza, but not all syraza are demahnk. The ten demahnk are ancient. The oldest living syraza has lived less than one thousand years." She gave me a sweetly patronizing smile. "To keep it simple for humans, we designate younger and Elder syraza."

Demon logic. "I'm human and, speaking for all humanity, that's *not* simpler."

"Have you had difficulties with the terms before now?"

"No, but—" I stopped myself before I plummeted further down the logic hole. I got it. Most humans wouldn't need more of a designation than younger and Elder.

Her smile turned smug. "There. All cleared up."

"Ten demahnk? Zack is still demahnk, even if you shun him."

"Yes, that is immutable. But Xharbek is no more."

"Oh. Right." No point in telling her she was likely wrong, especially when I had no solid evidence to support my belief. The demahnk Helori had told me that most demons considered Szerain's ptarl to be dead, yet he believed Xharbek was alive and in hiding. Moreover, Zack's count of demahnk had been eleven, not ten. I'd side with the demahnk on this one. But why was Xharbek in hiding? Szerain could sure as hell use the added stability. And why did the demons think Xharbek was dead?

Eilahn's smile faded and she closed her eyes. My concern rose at the stress lines on her brow and around her eyes, and the slight tremor in her hands. "We need to get you back to the house," I said. Before Rhyzkahl had revealed himself as a lying, treacherous scumbag, he'd placed Eilahn with me, which meant her ability to remain on Earth depended on arcane support from him. With him stricken, that support was virtually nonexistent. Instead she was forced to spend time on the "mini-nexus" on my property, drawing what power she could. It seemed to be working, at least so far.

"That would be most wise," she said and donned her helmet. In a graceful movement she mounted the Ducati and zoomed off, the throaty Italian purr of the bike fading as she receded in the distance. I wasn't worried that she'd ditch me. She'd drop in behind my car as soon as I got on the road.

Indeed, within a tenth of a mile she and her bike slipped behind me. I cranked up the air, turned on the radio, and tried to pretend I was a normal person on a normal day.

That lasted less than five minutes. Mocking banter on the Terry & Kerry afternoon show riveted my attention, and I turned the AC down a notch in order to better hear. The traffic jam earlier had been the result of a fender bender, one caused by a black "devil dog" that had bounded over the hoods of several cars with animal control in hot pursuit. The hosts entertained themselves and listeners by baiting a caller who insisted the animal wasn't a dog because it had double rows of teeth and spoke. Amidst gales of laughter, Kerry latched onto that one. "Speak, boy, speak!" and "Never heard a dog speak before. Woof!" That bit of fun complete, they cracked jokes about pink elephants and officers needing glasses since, not only did tranquilizers fail, but after cops shot the beast they couldn't find a body. The consensus of the hosts and callers was that obviously the shots missed the dog and it remained at large.

I listened, palms sweating on the steering wheel. The "devil dog" nickname was very possibly closer to the truth than they knew. I was willing to bet Eilahn's new bike that the "dog" was a *kzak*, a vicious demon species that could easily pass for a large dog at a distance. I'd had up close and personal experience with one that had been sent after either me or Ryan. Zack had brought it down with several well-placed shots, and it had discorporeated upon death, as did any demon killed on earth.

Fortunately, today's unwelcome visitor hadn't hurt anyone, but that didn't put my mind at ease. It had been sent from the demon realm for a purpose, and I doubted it was to play fetch at the park. I added the incident to my long list of things to stress out over, switched the radio station to mindless music, and continued on home.

# Chapter 3

Arcane protections rippled over me as I drove up the winding driveway toward my house, and the familiar pine woods soon blocked all view of the gate, road, and outside world. A not-unpleasant background tingle touched my senses from the arcane valve by my pond like a subtle welcome home. It was one outlet of the complex relief valve system between the demon realm and earth, except instead of water or gas the system regulated arcane power.

My spirits lifted more as my lovely blue, single-story Acadian came into sight. My grandparents had built the house, situating it over a confluence of Earth potency flows and atop a low hill. The elevation made it possible to have a basement—a rarity in south Louisiana due to the high water table, yet perfect for a demon summoning chamber. My grandmother had also been a summoner, which meant it had likely been intended as such from the beginning.

To my surprise, I spotted Ryan's Crown Victoria in its usual place in the driveway as though he hadn't been incommunicado since my return. After parking, I hurried up the steps and into the house, more than ready for long overdue answers. No sign of him in the living room or kitchen, but as I turned to check the basement I caught sight of Jill through the kitchen window. She stood in the backyard, arms akimbo and facing away from me while several yards beyond her, Ryan paced, head lowered.

The screen door creaked as I stepped out onto the porch,

and the very pregnant Jill glanced my way. "I was about to call you," she said. "He showed up a couple of minutes ago and went straight there."

*There* was a circular concrete slab that I'd paid several nice rednecks to pour for me last week. More importantly, it was the mini-nexus. In the years since my grandparents built the house, the confluence had drifted from beneath the basement to my backyard—similar to the movement of tectonic plates. Several weeks ago, Mzatal and I spent the better part of a day refining and enhancing it to create an arcane focal point much like the nexus in each demonic lord's realm. Without othersight or arcane talent, it looked like smooth concrete and nothing more. But to those who could *see* or *feel*, it pulsed as a broad circle of pale blue luminescence and radiated potency like heat from asphalt in July. It amped up any arcane rituals, patterns, or processes conducted upon it, and Mzatal had used it as a "potency recharging station" to counter the draining effects of being on Earth. Eilahn took advantage of that feature of our nexus as well, which was how she could remain here without Rhyzkahl's support. She'd created a nest of pine boughs and leaves on the far side of the nexus, on the grass but flush against the concrete.

At the very center of the slab, stood Ryan. No, *Szerain*. The demonic lord had spent over fifteen years on Earth as Ryan, during which time he'd learned how to diminish his aura of potency and hide in the guise of a human. But he wasn't fooling me. I had no doubt it was one hundred percent demonic lord Szerain in control out there.

A quick survey of the area revealed Eilahn on the roof of the house, along with Steeev, Jill's bodyguard. Both were syraza in human form, watching the situation unfold and ready to intervene with demon speed at the first indication of danger. Eilahn crouched atop the chimney, her gaze riveted on Szerain. Steeev stood on the crest of the roof beside her, dark skinned, beautiful, and utterly motionless.

Szerain knelt and placed his palms flat on the slab. A wave of potency rolled over me, stinging like wind driven sand and setting the grass a foot around the concrete eerily vertical and vividly chartreuse.

Jill took a step back from the unnerving display as I moved up beside her. In the next instant the grass flattened toward the center, and I felt a tugging tickle as potency flowed toward Szerain. On my torso the eleven sigil scars left by Rhyzkahl prickled and itched while the twelfth—the sigil Szerain had altered and ignited—began to pulse at the small of my back.

Holding back a shudder, I sought a clue of Szerain's purpose as I concentrated on the feel of the potency flow and the reaction of my scars. "He say what he's doing?"

"Not a word," Jill said. "I might as well be a recording of 'Where have you been?' and 'What are you doing?'"

I had no answer to the "where" part, but I knew the "what"—at least vaguely, which was more than I would have had a year ago. Mzatal's training, along with all the intense practical experience of the past year, allowed me to discern that Szerain drew a delicate web of potency toward him, like a fisherman hauling in a net. But what was he trying to catch?

A pins-and-needles sensation prickled over me as I stepped to within a few inches of the outer edge of the nexus. "Ryan—*Szerain*—what are you looking for?"

"Not now," he growled.

Annoyed, I bit back a tart response. "I don't exactly know what he's doing," I said to Jill, "but disrupting it might not be the best plan since possible worst case scenarios could include the end of the world as we know it."

"Oh, is that all?" She folded her arms over her belly and narrowed her eyes at me. "How do you know he's not *trying* to end the world as we know it?"

Her remark hit too close to the truth for my comfort. Centuries ago, Szerain had triggered a cataclysm in the demon realm—changing that world drastically if not actually ending it. Moreover, for the past fifteen years he'd been imprisoned and exiled to Earth for an offense I had no information about. He'd only been free a short time and surely wasn't embroiled in anything that intense. Yet. I was *almost* positive. Gah.

I kept my expression confident. "I'm forming a judgment based on what I can sense," I gestured toward Szerain, "along with the fact that he hasn't screwed us over yet," *that we know of*, I silently added, "and my hope that I'm not being an idiot."

That final one was the kicker. My history with Szerain left me with more questions than answers. The last time I'd seen him on the nexus was shortly after the plantation conflict, when the Mraztur's "virus" threatened to strip my identity and transform me into Rhyzkahl's thrall, Rowan. Through drastic actions, Szerain removed the viral imprint in time to save me. However, the process not only allowed him to activate the twelfth sigil on my torso, but also let him reclaim his essence blade, Vsuhl. With the arcane support of the blade, he freed himself from his submersion and imprisonment as Ryan, rendering him fully able to speak and act as Szerain. Since then, to my enormous frustration, he'd given me no answers about the significance of the activated twelfth sigil or what he intended to do now that he was free.

The three essence blades were the wild cards in all of this. Millennia ago, Mzatal created Khatur for himself, Xhan for Rhyzkahl, and Vsuhl for Szerain. I knew they were far more than mere knives. I'd possessed Vsuhl for a short time and *felt* its sentience, and only later realized the subtle influence it had exerted over my thoughts and feelings. Perhaps the lords weren't as susceptible to the effect as a mere human was, but they most certainly weren't immune.

Uneasy, I watched as Szerain wound in the last strands of the net. Potency like blood-red lightning and shadow arced from his fingertips to the slab then spread over the circle like crimson fire.

*Rakkuhr.*

Nausea slammed through me. I clamped my forearm across my belly and fought to keep my knees from buckling. My mind swam with hideous memories of the same vile potency flickering on the blade in Rhyzkahl's grasp. Steeev screeched and made an inhuman leap from the roof to the ground, with Eilahn hot on his heels. The sigil at the small of my back writhed like a living thing, and I pressed my free hand over it in a useless attempt to still it. "Szerain! Stop!"

Eilahn bristled beside me, teeth bared. "*Kiraknikahl*," she said. The word cut through the air like a weapon. *Oath-breaker*. Growling, Steeev pulled Jill back from the nexus. She'd gone pale and had both hands clasped on her belly. The twelfth sigil flared like branding heat, and I sucked in a hissing breath. Jill let out a sharp cry of pain, and Steeev swept her into his arms and carried her away.

"Szerain! Stop it!" I screamed, fury rising as he continued to ignore me. How dare he use *rakkuhr* on Earth, on *my* nexus, and right next to a pregnant woman? Screw this. Maybe his intentions were all rainbows and butterflies, but how was I to know since he refused to tell me? All I had were my instincts, which told me this was *wrong* and I needed to stop it.

With Eilahn following me like a lithe shadow, I stalked the perimeter of crimson flame in search of a weak point I could use to disrupt Szerain's process. I stopped to assess each ripple in the pattern, frustration rising as I reviewed and discarded ideas.

Without thinking, I stepped over a small dip in the grass, then paused. I'd known the shallow depression was there because it was in *my* backyard. I'd lived here most of my life and remembered the tree that fell to make the dip—even knew which hurricane brought it down. And the nexus was mine as well. I'd played a major role in creating this hot spot. My confidence flowed back in, drowning the frustration. Maybe, just maybe, the nexus would listen to its mama.

Going still, I mentally extended—not to the *rakkuhr* or Szerain, but far below, to the lightning-forged heart of the convergence. I called to it, elated as I felt a sluggish response. "That's it," I murmured, weirdly reminded of connecting with the groves in the demon realm. "C'mon, sweetheart. I don't need much."

It didn't give me much, but it was enough. The ground shuddered, and the arcane light of Szerain's pattern flickered and dimmed.

Szerain spun to face me, desperation radiating from him as he fought to maintain the integrity of his patterns. Locking my eyes on his, I once again called to the nexus. The air crackled with our combined intensity, but a moment later Szerain let out a strangled cry of frustration and jerked his arms down to his sides. With the abrupt motion, his arcane structures shredded, dissipating both *rakkuhr* and normal potency with a shrieking hiss. The air around it went as well, and I staggered as the brief vacuum sucked my breath away.

An instant later the sigil at the small of my back went cold and quiet. Szerain strode away from the nexus without a glance my way. Off-balance both physically and mentally, I dragged in fresh air then scrambled to follow as he headed around the house.

"Hey!" I hurried to catch up to him, Eilahn in my wake. "Damn it, Szerain. Stop and talk to me!"

"I can't stop." He turned brusquely toward me, though he continued to walk backward. For the first time since arriving home I got a good look at his face. Ryan's ruggedly handsome features, but far more intense and with dark circles under keen, haunted eyes. "Especially not here," he went on, jaw tight. "Trashing my nexus grid was like sending up a flare."

I bristled at his arrogance. "You come here without so much as a phone call, flaunt dangerous-as-shit potency like it's nothing, and expect me to stand by and twiddle my thumbs?"

"*Rakkuhr* saved your life not so long ago." He pivoted sharply and continued toward the driveway.

"Trust me, I remember! And you haven't answered any of my questions about that." I broke into a jog to keep up with his long strides. "What's the purpose of the twelfth sigil? Why is it active?"

"Not here. Not now," he said without slowing.

"Why not here? Who or what are you searching for?"

"It doesn't matter now." He glanced back, and I saw a flicker of fear in his eyes. "This is bigger than you. Bigger than me."

Alarm shot through me. "The Mraztur?" Rhyzkahl, Amkir, Jesral, and Kadir—demonic lords who wanted unrestricted access to this world and didn't care who got fucked over in the process. "Is one of them on Earth?"

Szerain barked out a laugh, short and humorless. "I'm not afraid of those assholes." He reached his car and pulled the door open. "Stay low, Kara. Stay off the radar."

"Gee, that's so helpful," I said with a sneer, but his alarm had me unsettled. "Give me a hint of what to watch out for?"

He dropped into the seat and shoved keys into the ignition. "I wish I could." Before I managed to snap back at that lame response, his entire body jerked as if he'd seized a live wire. Fear spasmed across his face again. "I *must* go," he gasped, then slammed the door and cranked the engine.

"Are you *kidding* me?" I yelled over the revving of the motor. "Goddammit, Szerain, I need to talk to you!"

But apparently he didn't need to talk to me. Without another glance my way, he threw the car into reverse, sending gravel flying as he backed up, and forcing me to retreat or get nailed by the rocks. I extended my thumb and pinky in a mocking *call me* gesture as he turned and sped down the driveway, then I scooped up the biggest chunk of gravel within reach and hurled it at his cloud of dust. "You *suck!*"

Jill waddled out the front door and onto the porch. "You okay?"

"No!" I took a breath and mentally traced the *pygah* sigil to help me calm and center. "Yes," I said with far less rageface than before, "other than dealing with more demonic lord bullshit and having a billion unanswered questions." I quickly thanked Eilahn for her help and ordered her back to her nest to recharge, then joined Jill on the porch. Her color was back, I noted with relief. "How about you? Everything all right?"

"I think so." She rested one hand on her belly. "The bean went crazy when the grass went flat, then crazier after you yelled at Ryan to stop. Hurt like hell."

When he ignited the *rakkuhr*. It wasn't easy, but I managed to keep the frown off my face. "Different than normal?" I asked with polite interest and nothing more.

"More kicking and squirming than ever before, that's for sure," she said, nose wrinkling. "But since Zack's been away recovering from the plantation stuff, there've been times when it's felt as if she's nothing but bony elbows and heels."

"No need to worry," I said with as straight a face as possible. "It's just the wings and claws."

"Don't you dare tease me like that! I have ultrasounds that prove she's free of wings or any other weird appendages." Her smile eased into a frown. "Ryan was a dick, huh?"

"A-number-one," I said with a scowl. "I got nothing from him except attitude and a vague generic warning to stay low. Whatever that means."

"Maybe you need to stake out his office."

"It might come to that if this crap goes on much longer." I blew out a gusty breath. "I'm summoning Mzatal in a few days. If nothing shakes loose by then, I'll see if he has any bright ideas."

"If you two even bother with talking," she said with a mischievous grin.

I forced a laugh. "We'll manage to get a few words of conversation in between episodes of wild monkey sex." Except that there probably wouldn't be any wild monkey sex, not given his calculated emotional withdrawal. But no point in being mopey or making Jill feel bad for bringing it up.

Jill hooked her arm through mine. "If you're really nice I'll let you go to birthing class with me day after tomorrow."

"*Let* me, huh?" I smiled. "I'm not so sure about this deal." I'd go with her, of course. Though she hadn't said so, I knew she was asking me because Zack wasn't around.

"You'll love it!" she said as we headed inside. "Multimedia and everything."

"I don't want to see *everything*." Eilahn's cat Fuzzykins curled around her litter of kittens at one end of the sofa, but I managed to get Jill settled on the other end with only a single warning hiss from the aggravating feline. "I want to see the bean when she arrives. *After* she's all cleaned up and free of weird baby goo."

"Pretty sure babies are never free of weird goo," she said

then sighed. "I wish we'd moved beyond 'the bean' as a name before Zack . . ." Her shoulders slumped.

Damn it, this was a sucky time for him to be an absentee dad. Despite Jill's prodding, Zack had flat out refused to even toy with names, saying only that it was too soon to name her. We knew it was a "her" at least, but neither of us could get more than that out of Zack.

"We'll show him," I said. "By the time he gets home, we'll have her name picked out. Juliana Sidney Faciane."

Jill quirked a smile. "Yeah. Hannah Nicole Faciane."

"Tabitha Angelina."

"Athena Woodstock."

I held up my hand. "We'd better stop before we end up scarring Parsley Green Faciane for life," I said, grinning. "How much longer until we have a baby?"

Jill chucked a sofa pillow at me. "Three weeks. I'm ready for her to be *out*."

"When do you plan to stop working?" Jill was a crime scene tech for the Beaulac Police Department, though she was currently relegated to non-field duties until after she had the baby.

"I'm not planning on it," she said with a firm lift of her chin. "I'll take time after she's born."

"I knew you'd be stubborn like that," I said with a smile. "What does Steeev think about that?"

"He's overprotective and proud of it." Jill laughed. "I'm sure he'd prefer I hang out here all day and knit. Zack would too for that matter."

"You've talked to him recently?"

Her face fell, and I immediately regretted asking. "Early this morning. He sounded better though. Told me not to worry." She snorted. "Like that's going to happen."

"I can take pictures of you at the birthing class," I said in a valiant effort to deflect the conversation away from Zack's true state. "He'd love to see those." My phone rang with Pellini's name on the caller ID. "Sorry, I need to take this call. I won't be long."

Jill pushed awkwardly up from the sofa. "It's cool. I need to be going anyway. Steeev's mixing up an herbal concoction he says will be good for you-know-who." She pointed at her belly. "Better not be vile or he'll be wearing it. I'll catch you later."

I gave her a thumbs up and answered the phone. "Hey, Pellini."

"Thought you weren't going to answer," he said in an oh-so-Pellini abrasive tone. "Wouldn't be the first fucking time."

"I almost didn't," I said, "but then I realized I'd miss your friendly banter." I added "asshole" under my breath and didn't really give a crap whether or not he heard it. Obviously a full day of Pellini being civil was too much for the universe to handle.

A sensation like static electricity on steroids crackled from my feet through my head followed an instant later by a wave of dizziness. *The valve!* "Shit. Gotta go. I'll talk to you later." I dropped the phone onto the coffee table and ran for the back door.

# Chapter 4

Heart pounding, I burst out the back door and leaped off the porch. The valve's normal tingly feel spiked to a nasty visceral buzz, signaling destabilization as clearly as a smoke alarm signaled my bad cooking. I pelted toward the woods and barely avoided an ugly sprawl when another wave of dizziness washed over me. Through bouts of vertigo, I staggered forward, hit the trail that led to the pond and wove through the trees as fast as I dared. A destabilized valve meant a potential overload of potency. Though my understanding of the valve system was superficial, I knew I had to repair that valve or risk an explosion.

A sudden eerie silence engulfed the woods as though the birds, insects, squirrels, and the trees themselves felt a premonition of doom. Sick uncertainty gripped me as I raced down the trail. My only experience with valve repair came from when I'd barricaded the valve node at the plantation—and I only knew how to do that because Kadir implanted knowledge of the required methods. But I needed to repair, not secure, this valve. My only hope was that I'd figure out a way to adapt Kadir's info. Terrific. Our salvation depended on one of the Mraztur. My day was getting better and better.

I bolted into the clearing, then stumbled to an awkward stop and gaped in utter disbelief at the scene before me. The valve was on the far side of the pond, a rough circle of arcane energy approximately three feet in diameter. Jill stood in the center of it, surrounded by a twenty-foot high column of rippling arcane fire.

No. This couldn't be real. Even with a thirty-second head start, no way could Jill have waddled out here faster than I'd run. I took a step forward, and another, but the scene stubbornly remained the same.

It was real. Sheer terror for my friend slammed in and spurred me into motion. "Jill!" I screamed as I raced around the pond toward her. "What are you doing? Get off the valve!"

Ignoring me, Jill spread her arms wide, opened her hands and tilted her head back. Around her feet the normal blue-green shimmer of the valve undulated in fiery orange like molten steel. None of this made any sense, yet I knew I had to get her off the valve. I charged her with the intent of doing a flying tackle but two strides from the valve, vertigo struck like a fist. Reeling, I dropped to my knees and clutched at the grass as the world tipped. Within a few seconds the vertigo passed only to be replaced by a crushing sensation as though gravity had increased tenfold. The power coursed around Jill, and the ground trembled as the valve emitted a whine like a cloud of pissed-off mosquitoes. Potency crackled over me like static electricity.

Hands gripped my shoulders and yanked me free of the valve. I landed in an unceremonious sprawl several feet away and immediately, Eilahn straddled me, intense and ferocious. "You must retreat."

"No! I won't leave Jill!" Agonized, I scrutinized the valve for a miracle that could save Jill. The constraining energy strands that should have been tightly twisted around its edge pulsed outward, frayed and perilously close to giving way. My gut turned to ice. If they failed, the valve would release the back pressure in an explosive burst—taking Jill with it.

Seemingly oblivious to her peril, she had yet to shift from her pose of head tipped back and arms outstretched. I struggled upright, but Eilahn seized my arm in an iron grip.

Jill gasped and stiffened. An instant later dozens of luminescent blue-green potency strands snaked from her waist to her feet and then outward to the edge of the valve. While I stared in astonishment, they moved like living things and interwove with the failing border to reinforce it. Within seconds the fiery orange around the valve changed to a less-ominous yellow-green, and the column of energy dissipated in a shimmer of purple.

Jill took two steps forward and off the valve, then swayed. Eilahn released me, and I sprang up to wrap my arm around Jill's middle "You okay?" I asked, heart pounding as I anxiously searched her face.

She leaned against me and extended her hand toward the valve. "Made Zakaar's valve better," she said in a strangely lilting voice. "Not finished. You'll have to do it." She dropped her hand and lifted her face to mine, smiled. "Rhyzkahl cries for you, but don't worry, I didn't say hello."

The fuck? "Um. Yeah, that's good," I said, totally weirded out. This particular valve was one Zack had created off the arcane trunk that originated in Rhyzkahl's realm—which I knew only because Zack told me so. Maybe standing on the valve had allowed Jill to pick up impressions of that information? But that still didn't explain why or how she was out here in the first place. "Jill, what did you do?"

She sagged against me, eyes fluttering. "Kara?"

"The one and only." I carefully eased her to the ground then glanced toward Eilahn. "Where the hell is Steeev?" I hissed.

"Here," he said, standing demon-still only a few paces behind me. Had he been there the whole time? If so, why hadn't he intervened?

Jill sat up straighter. "How did I get out here?"

"That's what inquiring minds want to know," I said. "I was hoping you could tell me."

The whine of the valve deepened to a thrum, and the ground shuddered—a not-so-subtle reminder that there was work yet to be done. Steeev crouched beside us, scooped Jill into his arms and stood smoothly. "I will care for her," he said.

My questions clamored for answers, but this wasn't the

time. Jill's eyes drifted closed, and her head lolled against
Steeev's shoulder as he turned and strode toward the path.
I watched until they disappeared between the trees, then
dropped to my knees beside the unstable valve and got to
work.

Even with Eilahn's help, it took over an hour to get the
damaged border back to smooth coils and a blue-green
glow. Mostly. An occasional flicker of orange remained, but
I'd exceeded the limits of my knowledge, skills, and stamina.
It didn't help that odd percussion waves distracted me while
I worked, as someone else tampered with the valve system
either on Earth or in the demon realm. I had no way to tell
if they were stabilizing a valve or cocking it up. One thing
was clear: I was out of my depth when it came to valve repair.

Weary beyond measure, I dissipated my support sigils
then went stock still. Rhyzkahl. His aura swept over me—so
eerily strong that I had to look around, pulse hammering
even as my eyes confirmed he wasn't there with me. In the
next breath the feel of his aura faded, leaving me wondering
if I'd imagined it. Still, another dozen seconds passed before
my heartbeat returned to normal.

Jill's words whispered back to me. *Rhyzkahl cries for
you.* Had she felt the same thing?

Pushing the weirdness from my mind, I closed down my
work then collapsed, sweaty and exhausted, beside the
valve. Sometime later Eilahn prodded me up, and as we
walked back to the house she gave me a status update on
the now-sleeping Jill. The last thing Jill remembered before
she "woke up" at the pond was walking out the front door
after my phone rang. Moreover, Steeev reported that he'd
sensed nothing of Jill leaving the porch and going to the
woods—which was, according to Eilahn, impossible. Wonderful.

Eilahn saw me to the back porch then headed to her
nest. I flopped on the chaise lounge and considered the incident with the valve. As with any complex network, screwing around with one part affected everything else as well.

When the four Mraztur came through the valve node at the Farouche Plantation, it fucked everything up. No way was mine the only valve at risk of destabilization. Clearly, I needed to check the known valves and add preemptive reinforcement. The gigantic hitch in that plan was the pesky fact that working on one little valve had kicked my ass—and at least half of what I'd done was guesswork. Not to mention, I doubted I'd be efficient since didn't know enough about valves and how they worked.

But I knew someone who did.

Idris Palatino. An undeniably brilliant summoner, a friend, and—unbeknownst to him—my cousin. He'd spent the last several months as a captive of the Mraztur, forced to work closely with my nemesis, Isumo Katashi, toward the Mraztur's ultimate goal of establishing a permanent gateway between Earth and the demon realm. Our rescue of Idris had set our opponents back, but I wasn't foolish enough to believe they'd given up. Maybe Idris had recovered enough for Mzatal to send him here? That would be ideal.

I closed my eyes and listened to the familiar sound of the breeze through the pine needles, the croak of frogs, and the chirp of sparrows. Mzatal. He had his hands full in the demon realm with the disastrous arcane disruptions triggered by the plantation explosion, and I'd planned to delay summoning him for a few more days in the hopes that he'd be less slammed. Unfortunately, the valve issue and Jill's escapade required immediate attention.

I mentally reached for Mzatal. We shared a profound etheric connection beyond anything comparable on Earth—like a merging of essence beyond time, thought, and space. We still had plenty of disagreements, but we were good for each other.

Were. A familiar blanket of sadness settled over me as I reached for him and sensed only a wispy touch. He'd withdrawn mentally and emotionally in order to forestall another catastrophic flare of fury like the one that had occurred during the plantation raid. Only a tiny chink remained in his self-made walls, enough for a precious thread of lifeline between us. As I touched it, I sent the impression that I was ever here for him followed by the more practical message that I intended to summon him tonight. I doubted anything beyond a faint sense of my presence got through, but I tossed in, *We need Idris on Earth*, just in case. Couldn't hurt to try.

An angry hiss beside my head startled me out of my relaxed state, and it took a second for my brain to catch up with the fight-or-flight pounding of my heart. Fuzzykins. She stood on the porch railing by my head with her back arched and fur on end and gave me another heartfelt hiss.

"Really?" I said after a quick scan to see if there was anything wrong besides my presence. "You came out here just to hiss at me?"

The stupid cat sat and groomed her tail as though I didn't exist.

Muttering something about worthless, ungrateful beasts, I stood and stretched until my joints popped. Unless I wanted to trash the summoning of Mzatal tonight, I needed a nap.

I stumbled into the house but paused by the open door of the laundry room. A nest of soft blankets held a pile of sleeping kittens—and Mama Fuzzykins was still on the back porch. Smiling, I gently extracted Fillion from his siblings and snuggled him to my cheek. The kitten wasn't old enough to know it was supposed to hate all summoners.

Fillion and I snuggled into my bed, and the next thing I knew the dubious harmony of ringing phone and mewing kitten hauled me out of a deep sleep. I fumbled for the phone, squinted at the too bright screen before hitting the answer button. "Hey, Pellini." I croaked.

"It's only seven thirty," he said gruffly. "I didn't think you'd be asleep yet."

"Life of leisure and all that." I sat up and put the kitten on my lap.

"How about one p.m. for the plantation?"

"How about you tell me why you need me to go out there with you?"

"I don't need you," he said, "but with the kidnapping,

murder, and rape charges on Farouche's people, I think there might be a connection to the Palatino-Gavin murder case."

Idris's sister. The body in the semi-trailer. Damn. Pellini was actually sniffing down the right trail—one that led straight to my doorstep. I needed to keep a sharp eye on that. "And since my task force is attached to both cases, you want my input."

"I figure it's worth checking out."

"I can rearrange my schedule to make that work." Might as well let him think I was doing him a big favor. The truth was, after the near-disaster with my valve, I needed to get out to the plantation ASAP to make sure the valve node there remained secured and relatively stable.

"Meet me at the police station," he said. "I'll drive."

"Works for me. See you then." I started to disconnect, but hesitated when I didn't hear the expected "bye" or "see ya" from Pellini. "Is there something else?"

"Uh," he said then cleared his throat awkwardly. *Oh, crapsticks,* I thought in sudden desperation. *Please don't let him ask me out for a beer again!*

"Did you, uh, hear about the dog?" he said instead, as if we were making small talk over coffee at Grounds for Arrest. "The one animal control shot today?"

The kitten crawled off my lap to investigate a cozy spot beside my leg. "I heard a little on the radio," I said, doing my best to keep my voice casual. "What about it?" And why on earth was Pellini bringing it up to me?

"The, uh, dog showed up outside the station and scared the shit out of a clerk, then ran when a couple of officers came out," Pellini said. "I couldn't get outside quick enough to do anything. Animal control tracked him all the way to Leelan Park and tried to tranq him, but it didn't work." His voice carried a definite edge of distress and none of the confrontational air of the beginning of the conversation. "They shot him."

Him, I noted. Not it. Pellini sounded as if the incident affected him on a personal level. Was he a total softy when it came to animals?

"I know they wouldn't have killed it if there'd been any other way to stop it," I said as I filtered everything he'd told me. Given that the kzak first showed up at the police station, I had a sneaking suspicion it had arrived through the valve in the parking lot there. I stuck the PD at the top of my mental list of valves to check. It wasn't a long list, but it was a start.

Perhaps the kzak had been trying to escape through another valve? If so, it might have disappeared because it succeeded rather than because it died.

"They didn't find its body," I said in an attempt to reassure him. "Maybe they missed, and he got away."

"Yeah, I guess," he said, still sounding oddly distraught.

What did he expect me to say? You see, Pellini, it was actually a demon, not a doggie. So don't worry. There's a good chance it's safe at home in the demon realm now.

It turned out I didn't have to formulate a response. Pellini gave me a curt "See you at one o'clock tomorrow" and disconnected. I scowled at the phone. Obviously, he saved all his warm fuzzy niceness for animals.

Fillion mewed up at me pitifully. "Yes, I'm quite sure he'd like you," I told him. "How could he not?" The kitten clambered over my leg and let out another mew. "I hear you. I'm hungry too. Let's go take care of that."

The door swung open before I could move. With a menacing growl, Fuzzykins leaped onto the bed, hissed at me, snatched Fillion by the scruff of the neck, jumped down, and stalked out.

Didn't matter. I got snuggle time in before she took him back. Grinning in triumph, I pushed back the covers only to find the surprise darling Fillion had left for me. I pursed my lips and regarded the damp spot on my comforter, then shrugged, yanked it off the bed, and trooped to the laundry room.

How could I be mad? I got to sleep with a kitten.

# Chapter 5

Two hours later I chalked the final sigil of my diagram onto the concrete of the basement floor. Until I mastered all eleven levels of the *shikvihr* ritual, I was limited to using chalk on Earth rather than floating sigils. Not only did it take far longer with chalk to ready a diagram, but chalk tended to be less forgiving since it couldn't be easily altered during a summoning. Harder to clean up, too.

I stood to better scrutinize each mark and examine the pattern as a whole. No room for errors, not when summoning a demonic lord. Even a willing one. It would suck to get ripped apart by the portal because I forgot a squiggle here or a swoop there.

Satisfied with the diagram, I moved to the heavy oak table and dropped the chalk into the large wooden cigar box that held my summoning implements. On impulse, I leaned close to the box and inhaled. The aroma of incense and candle wax triggered memories of the first time I summoned a demon, here in this basement, with my aunt guiding, encouraging, and supporting. I'd been completely terrified, hands shaking and voice little more than a squeak, yet the triumph when the demon appeared within my circle had been the greatest I'd ever felt in my life. In that moment I knew *this* was my calling. I was special, gifted, and destined to be more.

I chuckled softly at the naïve certainty of my younger self. Oh, I'd been destined for more, all right, though not the "more" I expected. Yet even though I'd been through unimaginable hell, I couldn't regret becoming a summoner. My life before summoning had, frankly, sucked ass. Orphaned, acting out, and doing a variety of self-destructive stupid shit. Summoning had literally given me a new life.

The wooden box held a few other items as well. Two tiny bottles of oil—sandalwood and neroli—which I used with chalk and blood for the central sigils. A shallow blood collection bowl that hadn't seen use in years. Though I now had far more skill in making a cut in the midst of ritual, I couldn't bear the thought of tossing out the bowl. And, finally, my ritual knife. Nothing fancy—a simple buck knife with a wooden handle and a five inch single-edged blade in a plain leather sheath. But Aunt Tessa had given me that knife before my first summoning, and I'd never used any other for an Earthside ritual.

I picked up the knife, suddenly wistful. If I ever mastered the shikvihr I'd have no more need to shed blood for basic summonings, and the knife would become as obsolete as the bowl. I squared my shoulders. No, not "if." *When* I mastered the shikvihr. So what if I had no idea when I'd be able to return to the demon realm for more training—or if Mzatal would be available to train me. I'd already achieved the seventh ring, and I damn well intended to get the rest.

The scent of cured tobacco mingled with the other aromas, and I smiled as older memories rose. My grandfather, Mike Pazhel, sitting on the front steps of this house with a cigar between two fingers, grinning and opening his arms to me as I ran to him after my first day of kindergarten. Walks through the woods with my hand in his as he pointed out wildlife and spun fantastic stories of the secret lives of the squirrels and birds and raccoons. He'd built this house with my grandmother, Gracie, who'd died a year before I was born. The cover story blamed a freak water heater explosion, but in fact Rhyzkahl had killed her along with four other summoners during a botched summoning of Szerain.

After her death the family fell apart. My grandfather tried to drown his sorrows in whiskey, my mom ran off and married my dad, who she'd been dating for two years, and

Tessa left for Japan to study under Katashi. Mom got pregnant with me only a few months later and, due to financial circumstances, she and my dad ended up moving back into this house. My grandfather quit drinking, and for eight years I had the advantage of growing up with a loving family. Then my mother died of ovarian cancer, and less then two months later a heart attack claimed my beloved grandfather. Three years after that, a drunk driver killed my father, which indirectly started me on the path to becoming a summoner.

I unsheathed the knife and closed the box. Time to get down to business.

After one last inspection of the circle of chalked sigils on the floor, I took my place at the perimeter and concentrated on Mzatal and our bond. I'd hoped that doing so would help clear the pathways for the summoning, yet instead it rekindled a deep and distracting ache. I drew a breath and released it slowly, pushed aside the ache. There was hope for us, but not yet.

I gathered potency and sent out the preliminary "knocking" call that would let Mzatal know I wished to summon him. Continuing to hold the strands, I counted to one hundred then made a precise cut on my forearm and dripped blood onto the diagram. I sank into the rhythm of my chanting, and soon the summoning portal opened like a vortex of lightning-threaded, purple clouds. Unusual but not detrimental. Wind whipped around me as I set the knife down and lifted my arms. The binding strands jerked wildly in my grasp, but I adjusted expertly, held firm, and called out his name.

"Mzatal!"

My heart leaped as I felt him answer the call, but an instant later the portal lurched in a way I'd never experienced before, nearly causing me to lose my hold. Sweat dripping, I wrestled the potency flows, yet everything I did seemed to have the opposite effect of what I intended.

"Fuck you, you piece of shit portal!" I yelled into the vortex. "That's the way you want to play? You think this is my first rodeo?" Pausing, I watched the mad flailing of the flows then yanked hard to damp the resonance. "Yeah, that's right, bitch. You can just calm your ass down." I continued to make careful corrections and finally constrained the vortex enough to pull Mzatal through. The swirling wind whined then dropped to nothing, leaving the smell of sulfur in its wake.

Breathing hard, I anchored the flows and sank to my knees as my muscles refused to hold me up any longer. Mzatal's aura engulfed me like heat off lava, and I dragged my eyes up to him. He stood in the center of the diagram, silhouetted against the lightning flashes of the closing portal, with his feet shoulder width apart and hands in fists at his sides. Blood dripped from his nose to skitter and hiss across the arcane pattern on the floor like water on a hot griddle.

The portal closed behind him with a sharp crack, plunging us into semidarkness. "Kara Gillian," he said in a voice rich, deep, and hard. "The timing is inopportune."

Loss and dismay shot through my heart. "Lord Mzatal," I said, doing my best to keep my own voice strong and steady. He'd closed the chink in his walls to a pinprick. "You have withdrawn more."

Lifting his hand, he traced a pattern high in the air. Scintillating golden light followed the path of his fingers and settled into a slowly spinning sigil that cast a soft amber glow over us. "I do what I must," he said through clenched teeth. With a swipe of his hand, he burned away the blood that flowed from his nose, though it remained as dark blotches on the burgundy of his shirt. Black hair threaded with strands of gold hung in a thick tightly woven braid over his right shoulder.

Searching his face, I stood. "We are stronger together."

A muscle in his jaw twitched, but his face remained otherwise inscrutable. Only his eyes—flint grey, ancient, and beautiful—hinted at the turmoil within. "The potency flows of my world have degraded more. You felt the effects during the summoning. Why have you interrupted my work?"

I mentally reached through the pinprick in his wall, caressed him. "The valves are unstable, and I can't maintain them on my own." I lifted my chin. "We need Idris here. Has he recovered enough?"

"Sufficiently to work with me," Mzatal said. "He is needed in my realm." He moved toward me, and I took in his familiar scent like a sea breeze laced with musky spice.

"And what happens to *your* world if the valves collapse?" I narrowed my eyes. "Katashi is still here and continues with the Mraztur's plans." Mzatal could read my thoughts, so there was no need to offer lengthy explanations. "Only this morning a kzak was pushed through. What if that was a precursor for another incursion by Jesral or Amkir?"

Mzatal touched my bloody forearm and sent healing warmth into it, then lifted his hand and ran his fingers through my hair in a tender gesture. An instant later his hand tightened to grip my hair close to my scalp at the back of my head, holding me fast. The pinprick widened to a crack. "Without the valves my world would die. Yet it shakes itself apart now with anomalies and disruptions in the flows."

"Then send Idris to me," I said, pulse thrumming. "You have the other lords there." I basked in the glimmer of our connection and yearned for its fullness. "I have no resources other than Eilahn. Zack is out. Szerain is a loose cannon. Bryce and Paul are in the demon realm. I only know the basics about the valves, and Katashi and his crew are out there somewhere. I need—" I leaned closer, pulling against his hold on my hair. "I *need* . . . Idris."

His grip tightened as he drew my face close to his. "What you need is what I need," he growled, breath hot on my cheek, and his lips almost brushing mine. The crack widened a fraction more. I could *feel* him on the verge of shattering the walls to open to me. In the resurgence of connection I silently urged him on. Together we could rise above anything.

We stood thus for several pulse-pounding seconds, then he released me and took a step back, narrowed the crack to the width of a hair. "But we must both be denied," he said.

I dragged in a breath as he withdrew. "Why, Boss? *Why?*"

My head knew the answer, but I had to ask for the sake of my heart.

"Because I do what I must." The intensity of his voice drove the words through me. "I can remain no longer. Matters are dire in the demon realm, and I abandoned Seretis and Amkir in the midst of the repair of an anomaly." He backed to the center of my summoning diagram. "Idris is best equipped to engage the valve issues here, but I will not be without a summoner. Contact Rasha Hassan Jalal al-Khouri. Tell her to be in her summoning chamber at dawn."

"I'll ask her." No way would I *order* the elderly summoner to go to the demon realm. She might leap at the opportunity, or she might prefer tea and solitude.

Mzatal inclined his head. He understood that I intended to allow Rasha to choose whether to go or not. "Prepare to receive Bryce in the third hour after sunrise tomorrow," he told me. "*If* I have acquired Rasha, I will send Idris as well."

Dread flooded through me at Bryce's name. He'd been Paul's bodyguard and handler ever since the young computer genius had been kidnapped to work for Farouche. Over time Bryce had come to care for Paul as deeply as if they were the closest of brothers, and his role as bodyguard had transformed from a duty to a labor of love. No way would he leave Paul behind. "Is Paul . . . dead?"

"No, Kadir took him five days ago," he said to my combined relief and horror. The creepy and unsettling Kadir had been instrumental in saving Paul's life, but for Paul to go *live* with him was a different matter. Yet I couldn't imagine that Mzatal would let Paul go with the psychopathic Kadir unless it was *only* possible option. "Bryce currently abides with Seretis," he continued, "but he requires distraction from his worry for Paul and can be of use to you. Third hour after sunrise. Summon from our nexus, *zharkat*." And with that he vanished in a flash of light.

I shielded my eyes, feeling his caress as the word whispered to my essence. Whether he was open or closed, I knew I would always be zharkat—beloved—to him. *Dear one.* That's what Rhyzkahl used to call me. The difference between my connection with Mzatal and my so-called relationship with Rhyzkahl was as stark as the difference between moldy bargain-shelf white bread and gourmet New York cheesecake. I'd never fully trusted Rhyzkahl, even though I'd been needy and gullible enough to fall victim to his ploys. Not so with Mzatal. Our union had stripped away all pretense and guile. I knew without a whisper of doubt that he would never betray me with intent.

Wearily, I gazed with pride at my diagram and my summoning chamber. I lived a life that mattered, and right now that was more than enough. Had my grandmother felt the same way? She must have, otherwise why do it?

I wiped down the knife and sheathed it, placed it in the cigar box and put it away. I needed Idris, and the only way for that to happen was for Rasha to go to the demon realm. Weighing the various aspects, I climbed the stairs and emerged from the basement to a silent house. Jill was probably already asleep in her mobile home, with Steeev not far from her side. Eilahn was most likely on the nexus. I headed to the living room and plopped onto the sofa. Without Idris to manage valve repair, we'd lose ground to Katashi—with potentially catastrophic results. It had to be Rasha's choice to go to the demon realm, but I sure as hell needed to get my sales pitch in order before I called her so she'd make the *right* choice.

As it turned out, I needed the preparation. Relocation from Austin to the demon realm was a brand-new concept for her, and she was firmly settled in her ways and her home. A twinge of guilt twisted my gut when I presented the end-of-the-world-as-we-know-it argument, but by the time I got to the part about how her arthritis would be cured and she'd be summoning again, I was in the flow of the debate. After some sweat on my part and tears on hers, she got on board, and an edge of excitement came into her voice. My guilt slid away, and I couldn't help but smile as I listened to her list of what needed to be done and what mementos she wished to take with her. I made sure she understood what time she needed to be in her summoning chamber, then made my goodbyes and disconnected.

I reclined and gazed up at the ceiling, exhausted but pleased with the outcome. In a minute I'd get up and go to bed. Yep, any minute now.

Screw it. The sofa was comfortable enough.

# Chapter 6

Sleep didn't come immediately, and I drifted in a state of don't-want-to-move. Thoughts tumbled sluggishly. *What if the Rasha-Idris deal goes wrong, and Mzatal doesn't send Idris? No. It can't. She'll come through. Bryce and Idris need a vehicle. Jill has an old car that she rarely uses. I'll ask her if I can borrow it. Sheets and towels. They'll need those. Clean ones. Bryce in the guestroom, and Idris in the basement. That'll work. If Ryan comes home and wants the basement back, he can suck eggs.*

*What does that even mean?* An image rose of Ryan tapping a hole in one end of an egg and slurping out the contents. *That doesn't seem all that dire.*

*It's probably something filthy. Dirty eggs.*

*Chickens are messy.*

*And who put a stupid nightlight sigil on the ceiling?*

A voice brushed me, like a whisper of breath on my cheek. Familiar and unwelcome. I twitched physically and mentally, awake enough to ward off the encroaching nightmare.

"Kara?" Again. Clearer. Seeking.

Heart pounding, I jerked fully awake and sat up. *Rhyzkahl.* That was Rhyzkahl's voice. *What the fuck?*

I looked around me. My living room. My sofa. The afghan in a heap on the floor. Fuzzykins perched on the recliner. The song-rasp of crickets. The whirr of the air conditioner cycling on. *Normal.*

I was definitely awake. I'd experienced enough dream visits from the treacherous Rhyzkahl to know the difference. I drew the afghan up and hugged it to my chest. My pulse slowed as the familiarity of my home embraced me. Fuzzykins hissed, her eyes round and locked onto me. She flattened her ears, hissed again. Yep. Normal.

Or not.

A dim amber sigil glowed on the ceiling. Not my sigil. Not my *ceiling*. A mosaic dome with its apex and sigil just below my tongue-and-groove paneling. Transparent, like an overlay.

"Kara?" Thin. Weak. "Are you . . . here?" In front of me.

My gaze snapped down. Superimposed over my fireplace was a ghostly image of *Rhyzkahl* upon a bed, naked except for a twisted sheet draped over his hip.

"What's going on?" I demanded, breathing shallowly. "What the fuck are you doing?" Panic clawed within my chest as I recoiled on all levels.

The vision faded to little more than a shadow. "I . . . am here." Distant. Desperate. "Stay. Kara."

Stay? I hadn't moved. The shadow brightened and clarified into the vision of Rhyzkahl in his bed over the backdrop of my living room.

"You still have a fucking link to me?" My voice shook with anger and visceral terror. "You worthless son of a bitch." I should have known he'd find a way. Had he made this link as part of the *rakkuhr* virus? I squeezed my eyes closed in an attempt to shake the connection. Though I no longer saw the physical aspects of the living room, potency strands and my protective wards shimmered in othersight as expected. Yet the vision of Rhyzkahl intensified—vibrant and textured and *real*.

My eyes flew open, and I sucked in a breath as my living room returned with only a ghost of Rhyzkahl. *I'm seeing him with othersight?* That was different. In other dream sendings, I'd been fully asleep while he manipulated my experience to feel like reality.

"Kara!" He lifted a shaking hand toward me.

Heart hammering, I closed my eyes again. Slipped out of

othersight. My wards dimmed. Rhyzkahl solidified more. A reyza bellowed in the distance. The heady fragrance of flowers mingled with an acrid tang of sweat and pain.

The cushions of the sofa pressed against my back, yet at the same time I stood beneath a domed ceiling with Rhyzkahl before me. *This is beyond weird.* His usual dream projections were *nothing* like this.

Opening my eyes, I withdrew to the living room. Then twice more. With each shift, my control of how much I saw and felt increased.

*Weird . . . and cool.* Concentrating, I called forth Rhyzkahl's shadowed chamber. Heavy drapes hung over the windows with only the faintest hint of daylight at the edges. The sigil in the ceiling cast a sluggish illumination onto the bed and little more.

I stood near the bed with my chin up and my gut churning. His silky white-blond hair had been cropped to finger length, and he currently had a serious case of bed head. The faas had probably cut it since several feet of hair would be a stone bitch to keep tidy on a bed-bound patient. His beautiful face was haggard and drawn, and he looked as if he'd lost a solid thirty pounds since the plantation battle.

Breathing unsteadily, he fought to sit upright but could only manage to prop on an elbow. "What is it . . . you want?" he croaked.

Delicious shock coursed through my veins. *He* wasn't controlling this. His reactions were too natural—unmeasured and unscripted. I was in *his* dreamspace, not the other way around. And that meant that what I saw here was his reality—the weight loss, the cropped hair, the shadowed room.

This had the potential to be very *interesting*. I finished my perusal of the chamber before answering. "Want? From you?" I snorted and raked my gaze over him. "Seeing you like this is a damn good start." My tormenter helpless and in pain. A decent and noble person would have at least a whisper of sympathy for Rhyzkahl. Not me. The asshole had willfully duped, used, and tortured me, had been party to submerging Szerain in his horrific imprisonment as Ryan, and had sponsored human trafficking. And that was only what I knew of.

Frowning, I sauntered to the side of the bed. He followed my movement warily, trembling as though in pain. I paused to test the dual awareness, saw my living room, felt the afghan. It really did seem too good to be true, which meant I needed to stay on my toes. I wouldn't put it past one of the Mraztur to set an elaborate trap using Rhyzkahl as bait.

"What are you playing at now?" I asked him, wary. Testing. "Why did you call me to your dreamspace?" Experimenting, I pictured butterflies erupting from the cushion beside him. To my surprise and delight, dozens streamed forth in an iridescent flutter to circle and float in the dome. Verrrrrrrry interesting. "That's what this is, isn't it? *Your* dreamspace?"

Disbelief widened his eyes as he stared at the spectacle. "No . . . no!" He swallowed noisily and turned his head toward the door. "Rega," he called out in little more than a hoarse whisper. "Rega!"

I laughed as the door stayed firmly closed. "The faas can't save you from yourself, Rhyzkahl," I told him. "No one is going to answer your call."

His gaze skittered around the room in wild panic. "This cannot be," he rasped in distress. His fingers plucked feebly at the sheet. "No. It cannot."

His dream sendings to me had felt utterly real. Was that how he perceived this? "What cannot be?" I asked with a tilt of my head. "That I'm in your crib? That you can't read me?" I sidled closer and regarded him. "Damn, you look like shit."

Breathing raggedly, Rhyzkahl again tried to sit up only to sag into the cushions. "You *are* here." A wild and desperate look came into his eyes. "You are here. I feel you. *Here*."

"Would you stop fucking saying that?" I snapped. "Yeah, I think we've established that I'm heeeeere." I slung my hands out wide to encompass the whole dreamspace then dropped them to my hips. "And now I get an early Christmas present." Pursing my lips, I gave him an obvious once-over. "Are you hurting?" Not that I really needed to ask. He was devious, sneaky, underhanded, and deceitful, but even he couldn't fake all the signs of pain. Cautious breathing, muscle tremors, sunken cheeks, and the misery that colored his aura. Still, I wanted to hear it from him.

"Yes." His throat worked, and a deeper agony lit his eyes. "Zakaar."

"What about him?" I asked, voice hard as obsidian. "Don't you dare try and tell me you give a flying fuck about his condition."

Desolate despair etched more lines into his face. "I cannot . . . *cannot* exist . . . without Zakaar."

Yep, as I suspected, his "concern" went no further than how Zack's condition affected his own. Rhyzkahl was a hot mess because of the broken ptarl bond, but Zack suffered far more—locked in human form and unable to touch the other demahnk. I leaned close and bared my teeth. "Zakaar *warned* you. He gave you every chance to stop being a fucking asshole."

"Cannot fault Zakaar," he rasped. "He will . . . return." He lifted a shaking hand to touch my forearm. "He will."

I jerked away and stepped back, ignoring his low moan as I pulled my arm from his touch. "I wouldn't hold my breath on that, if I were you," I said. "I don't see him returning to kiss your boo-boos and make them better any time soon." I paused to savor the moment. "*Or ever.*"

He made a desperate reach toward me. "No, no . . . stay close," he pleaded then withdrew his hand as if realizing it might be a deterrent. "Stay close. *Please.*"

Suspicious, I considered him. "Why?" I edged a bit closer, watching him carefully. He closed his eyes, and a small amount of the tension eased out of his face and body.

"Hurts less." He swallowed. "I can think more clearly . . . when you are near."

Perhaps my presence grounded him since he no longer had Zakaar to give him balance? But why me? Somehow I doubted that any random human had the same effect. Maybe it was my affinity with the demon realm groves that made me a walking Vicodin for the fucker? Or perhaps it had to do with Elinor—the summoner who'd inadvertently triggered a cataclysm in the demon realm hundreds of years ago. A fragment of her essence lingered on mine, which was a large part of why Rhyzkahl had oh-so-nicely picked me for his torturous sigil scar ritual. For that matter, maybe it was those fucking scars. Whatever the reason, it meant I now had serious leverage over the son of a bitch.

I poked him hard in the shoulder with a knuckle. "How's that?" I asked with false brightness. "Does that help?"

To my shock my little jab might as well have been a tiny charge of power. A look akin to orgasmic relief bathed his features, and the anguished feel of his aura eased a smidge. "Yes," he replied, deathly serious as he met my gaze.

Mouth pursed, I nodded, then punched him in the face as hard as I could.

"Fuck You!" I shouted as he let out a wheezing cry of pain. I danced back from the bed and shot him the bird with both hands.

Heedless of the blood pouring from his nose, he struggled off the bed and to his feet as I continued to withdraw. "Kara, no," he gasped. "Do not . . . leave me." He collapsed to the floor, hand extended and face panicked. "No, Kara . . . do not leave me. *Please*."

"Buh-bye, *dear one*." I blew him a mocking kiss. "Now, *wake up*."

With no more effort than it took to breathe, I withdrew from the dreamscape into the full presence of my living room. Not a trace of Rhyzkahl in sight or arcane sense. Awake, super-charged with adrenaline, and feeling insanely *alive,* I shoved the afghan aside and leaped to my feet. Humming with elation, I flipped on the light. Everything dripped with color and vibrancy, and my blood thrummed through my body.

"Rot in hell, motherfucker," I sang then proceeded to dance badly around the room with only Fuzzykins to judge me.

It didn't take long for my overall fatigue to catch up and tell me to cut out the dancing crap. I yanked my summoning journal from the bottom of the pile of papers and notes on the coffee table, settled in the recliner and flipped to a blank page. Though I was craptastic about keeping up with day to day journaling, I was trying hard to keep a record of important occurrences. This dream-thing most certainly ranked right up there in importance, especially since I didn't know how it happened. Could it possibly be connected to the incident with Jill on the valve? She'd said Rhyzkahl cried for me. Yeah, well, he could keep crying for all I cared.

I dutifully recorded the event—along with some choice expletives. I intended to share this incident with Zack and Mzatal and absolutely no one else, which meant I needed to safeguard my notes. Though the journal itself was warded, I traced three intricate aversions on the page, then added a fourth for good measure. A far cry from the pink diary I had as a kid with its lock that could be picked with a bobby pin.

Riding the tide of my wild and crazy journaling frenzy, I also made notes on the pond valve weirdness with Jill, then dragged my notebook from my purse and transcribed Zack's sleep-talking into the journal.

*Jill. Rhyzkahl. Szerain. Ekiri akar. Sovilas mir nah shey. Xharbek. Ashava.*

Next, I flipped back to find Marco Knight's strange warning.

*Twelve. The twelfth is a radical game changer. Spawned of fierce cunning. Beauty and power exemplified. Beware the twelfth.*

All sunshine and lollipops. That sucker belonged with the info from when Szerain altered and activated the twelfth sigil on me. I backtracked to that entry in my journal. The words Szerain spoke when he called *rakkuhr* to consummate the sigil loomed in the middle of the page.

*Vdat koh akiri qaztehl.*

Qaztahl was the demon word for a demonic lord. I'd asked Eilahn about the phrase, and she had explained that the shift from the "a" sound to "e" in qaztehl simply designated uber power. It roughly translated to *Infinite resources to the all-powerful demonic lord unfettered.*

Unsettling enough on its own and, paired with Knight's

ominous words and Szerain's unknown motivations, enough to give a girl nightmares. I tucked the journal back under the papers, returned my notebook to my purse, then toddled my ass off to bed. Nightmares or not, I intended to sleep like the dead.

# Chapter 7

No nightmares, eight hours of sleep, and a fresh pot of coffee had me feeling like a new woman. Voices in conversation reached me as I poured a cup. Coffee in hand, I stepped out onto the front porch and waved to Jill and Steeev as they crossed the yard. "Are you sure you feel okay to go to work?" I asked her after I descended the steps.

Steeev opened the passenger door of her car, then stepped aside and waited. Jill frowned up at me with one of her *Of course I'm fine* looks. "Steeev told me what happened, but I don't remember any of it," she said with a shrug. "Then again, I got fourteen hours of sleep last night, so I can't complain too much." She grinned at my discomfiture. "Don't worry, I won't make that my routine sleep aid."

"Damn right you won't," I said as I approached and looked her over. She seemed fine, but it bugged me that we still had no clue how she'd gone from the house to the pond in a split second. "Anything funky with the bean after all that?"

"Nothing other than being quiet and letting me sleep all night. I'm usually up a dozen times to go pee."

"Almost forgot to tell you, there's been a change of plans," I said. "I summoned Mzatal last night, and he's sending Bryce and hopefully Idris through this morning. We'll have a full house again."

She eased herself into the passenger seat. "*You'll* have a

full house. I have my mobile home to add one layer of separation from the chaos."

I waited for her to lower the window after Steeev closed her door. "Speaking of chaos, do you mind if they borrow your other car?"

"That old thing needs a lot of love," she replied with a snort, "but they're free to use it if they're mechanically inclined. It's parked by the crime lab because that's where it last broke down. Keys are in it."

"Guess we'll see if Bryce knows engines," I said, grinning. "If he can't get it working, I'll rent something."

"You might want to get your credit card ready."

"Call me if anything weird happens, okay?"

She rolled her eyes. "Yes, mom."

I forced a smile. She hadn't seen herself all lit up with power on the valve. Yeah, I was going to worry a teensy bit. Fortunately for my peace of mind, she had a demon bodyguard watching her every move. "See you tonight," I said, then climbed back up the steps and watched them drive off. Weird life. *My* life.

After finishing my coffee, I headed out to the nexus. I wouldn't be *summoning* humans from the demon realm this morning. Instead, with Mzatal and another qaztahl "pushing" from the other side, my role would be more like catching a ball than reeling in a fish. Though I knew the theory, confidence warred with nerves. I enjoyed the challenge of new undertakings, and I had faith in my skills and training but, on the flip side, it *was* new. If I fucked up, the ones to pay the price would be the guys being sent to Earth.

No pressure, right?

Eilahn lay curled in her makeshift nest, and had probably been there all night absorbing energy. She lifted her head as I approached, then stood in a single fluid motion, bounded to the tree by the porch, and was up and onto the roof in a heartbeat.

Slowly pacing around the perimeter of the nexus, I searched for any residuals from Szerain's escapade yesterday, relieved when all appeared normal. I moved to the center of the platform and reviewed my plan. Under ordinary circumstances, I wouldn't need to do a thing to help bring the guys to Earth. After all, only a few weeks earlier Mzatal and Kadir had pushed me through without any help from this end. But with the arcane flows so discombobulated now, it would be harder for the lords to judge the trajectory and force of their push—like not knowing if a slide was greased.

In other words, I needed to make a big ol' pillow—or a catcher's mitt—with the shikvihr as the stuffing. The shikvihr was the advanced ritual foundation for arcane work, and thus far I'd mastered seven rings. Though its floating sigils wouldn't coalesce for me on Earth until I acquired the eleventh ring, it still boosted my capabilities overall—like having an extra battery. I didn't have to use a separate storage diagram anymore to stockpile potency for rituals.

I set the knife by my feet and chalked Mzatal's sigil eleven times in a circle around me, then twice I mentally traced the simple flowing lines of the pygah sigil. Calm settled in, and I felt a click of connection with the nexus. I stood and began to dance the circles of the shikvihr, visualizing each sigil as I traced it in the air. Seven rings of eleven sigils each. As I completed and sealed the last circle, a tingle began in my feet and inched upwards. Laughing, I pumped my fist in triumph then hurriedly checked my watch. Five minutes until go time.

The potency flowed like wispy streams beyond the nexus. I extended my arcane senses into it, gathered strands to me then waited. A few minutes later the strands vibrated, signaling the beginning of the push. Focusing down into the nexus, I channeled potency and wound the strands through and around the shikvihr. The vibration increased, and without warning an arcane gale-force wind rose vertically from the ground, nearly ripping apart my magic catcher's-mitt-pillow-thing. Heart hammering, I pulled more strands from beneath the nexus, reinforcing the entire structure. Seconds later a vortex, twenty feet across, opened below me, and I balanced on a tiny island above a roaring, lightning-shot chaos maelstrom.

*Holy fucking shit!* Gulping down panic, I regrouped and

struggled to keep my mitt-pillow as stable and secure as possible. The resonance in the strands fluctuated, and the roar of the vortex refined to a low pure tone. An instant later, specks from far below grew and resolved into Idris and Bryce hurtling upward. *Wait. Crap!* I was above them. How the hell was I supposed to catch them without my mitt-pillow blocking their ascent?

Thinking quickly, I choked off the potency, like crimping a water hose, enough to alter the consistency of my mitt-pillow into a squishy-cloud. Bryce and Idris rose on the wind, tumbling and flailing to ground level and past. They slowed as they hit the squishy-cloud, yet the propelling force from the demon realm drove them through it and upward.

Grabbing strands, I slammed the vortex shut, but to my horror the two men were already at least fifteen feet above the ground. The arcane wind dropped to nothing, and they let out shouts of alarm as they stopped rising and tumbled down. I released the crimp in the potency hose and shoved power into the squishy-cloud-mitt-pillow even as both hit it. They slowed abruptly, then landed with a *thunk* on the concrete.

"Are you guys okay?" I called out as I anchored the wild flows.

Idris lay with his arms and legs splayed, staring up at the sky, his chest heaving. Bryce sat up and rubbed his shoulder. "Jesus fucking Christ!"

"I'm so sorry!" With sharp movements, I dispelled the shikvihr. "That didn't exactly go as I'd expected."

Idris rolled to his side, spat out blood, then shifted to sit crosslegged. "What a ride! I've never seen a portal like *that* before. And cool work with the impact cushion."

I let out a weak laugh and plopped to sit. If it was new and different, Idris was all over it. At only twenty years old, he possessed an insanely keen knack for the arcane. He'd cropped his halo of blond curls down to a short and tidy style since I'd last seen him, and a selfish, wistful pang went through me at the sight. Not the sweet, innocent boy anymore. He looked years older now, features stronger. Coupled with his tall muscular build, he gave off a distinct "man to be taken seriously" vibe. Which he was, especially with Rhyzkahl for a daddy. Not that either of them knew.

I turned to Bryce. "You okay?"

Bryce stretched his arms out, nodded. "I'm good. The rough landing was more of a surprise than anything." He stood up then grinned as I gaped in shock. "You think it'll do?"

"Uh, yeah," I said, still staring. Idris had cut his hair, but Bryce . . . I knew it was Bryce only because he'd come through the vortex. His previously brown hair was now jet black, and there were subtle changes to his facial structure as well. Higher, broader cheekbones. A cleft in his chin. An aquiline nose. Even his overall skin tone was somewhat darker.

"That's *incredible!*" I said in astonishment. "And, hot damn, this sure solves a problem that's been bouncing around in my brain."

Bryce chuckled. Voice was slightly different too, I noted. "You mean that whole 'wanted by the law' detail?"

"That's the one," I replied with a smile. Though Paul had stripped electronic records of himself, Bryce, and Sonny from Farouche's files before he sent them to the Feds, there were plenty of incriminating paper records remaining. "Who did the work?"

"Elofir and Seretis," he said as he gave Idris a hand up. "Neither had ever done anything like this before, so I'm glad I ended up with something resembling a face."

His smile widened and his voice held a fascinating warmth when he spoke Seretis's name. Interesting. According to Mzatal, Bryce had spent the last week in Seretis's realm. Great friends, or more? Though Seretis was bisexual, I'd been under the distinct impression Bryce was as heterosexual as they came. Whatever the situation, Bryce looked more relaxed than I'd ever seen him, despite having been shoved through a wormhole between universes . . . and despite being separated from Paul.

"Do you have a new name to go with your new face?" I asked.

"New last name only. Taggart."

I gave him a teasing smile. "Afraid you'd forget to answer to Ignatius or Wally?"

"I'd refuse, not forget," he shot back.

"What about fingerprints?" I said more seriously. "All it would take is an overachieving Fed to hear the name and wonder about a Bryce hanging out with me."

He waggled his fingers. "The lords took care of that too." Then he laughed. "As long as the lords didn't accidentally match them to a suspect on the most wanted list, I'm good."

"You sure seem to be," I said. "The only way to nail you would be with a DNA comparison, and if you're not already in a database that's even better." I gave him a questioning look, relieved when he shook his head. "No scars either," I noted as I peered more closely. "Zero evidence of plastic surgery. You're golden."

I looked over at Idris and found that he'd efficiently tidied up the residual potency while I admired Bryce's new look. "Thanks, dude," I said with a smile, then picked up his duffel and slung the strap over my shoulder. "Least I can do is be your pack mule after dropping you like that. Let's get y'all settled, and then we'll catch up on news.

"I figured I'd let you have the basement," I continued. "My summoning chamber takes up half of it, and Ryan turned the rest into a little man cave."

Idris nodded, expression stony, then surprised me by taking his duffel back. "Katashi. Jerry Steiner. Aaron Asher." His grey eyes darkened as he named the three men who had ritually raped, tortured, and murdered his sister Amber. Anger radiated from him like heat from a furnace, reminding me unpleasantly of a demonic lord's aura though nowhere near as strong. "Do you know where any of them are?"

Yes, he was definitely one to take seriously. "The Feds and local authorities are looking for Jerry," I told him, calm and clinical. "Last sighting was at a local hospital the day after the plantation raid, and then he dropped out of sight. I've heard nothing on Katashi, but I'm narrowing down possibilities for where he might be based in this area. No news on Asher either, and I suspect he might yet be in the demon realm."

He closed his eyes and went still for several seconds. When he opened them again I saw cold focus in place of the anger. "Basement?" he asked.

"Middle doorway on the right side of the hall," I said with a gesture toward the back door. "Let me know if you need anything." I watched him stride off, then turned to Bryce. "Intense much?"

"You should've seen him a week ago," he said grimly. "He's out for blood. I understand why, but I hope it doesn't get in the way of what needs to be done here."

"You and me both," I said with a sigh. "C'mon, you can take the guest room, and once y'all settle in we can sit down and make a plan."

We headed inside, and Bryce detoured to the guest room to drop his satchel. He and Paul had stayed at the house before, which meant I didn't have to show him around. After a few minutes he returned to the kitchen.

"Coffee?" I asked him as I shoveled cream and sugar into my own cup.

He dropped into a chair. "Actually, I'd love juice, if you have any."

"Sure do. You have a choice between orange and orange."

He chuckled. "I'll take the orange, please."

Smiling, I poured a glass and passed it to him. "How's Paul?" I asked as I settled in the chair across from him. "Mzatal said Kadir took him."

Bryce hesitated only an instant before replying. "He's doing okay now," he said, all humor gone. "Seretis, Elofir, and Mzatal did everything they could, but . . ." He took a sip of juice as if needing the strength to get through the painful memory. "Paul wasn't getting better," he went on. "He kept fading away, and finally Mzatal called for Kadir's help."

In other words, Mzatal had exhausted all other options. "Why did Kadir take Paul away? He wouldn't agree to help him in Mzatal's realm?"

"He *couldn't*," Bryce said. "From what I understand, Kadir and his realm are 'out of phase' with the rest of the world, like a piano key out of tune." Grief shadowed his face. "And, ever since the plantation, apparently so is Paul."

I fought down a shudder. I could barely tolerate Kadir's presence for a few minutes. What kind of hell would it be to *live* with him? "Psychopath" didn't come close to describing Kadir. Neither did "creepy, brilliant, tormented, sadistic, and unpredictable." Not long after Mzatal's flare of rage accidentally burned Paul, I'd worked side by side with Kadir to mitigate the damage. In the process, I unwittingly activated Kadir's sigil scar on my side and merged with his consciousness. That link had lasted only seconds, but I gained uninvited and unwanted insight into the mental chaos the lord endured.

But surely Mzatal had forged an ironclad agreement that would keep Paul safe from the horrors of Kadir-style torment. Otherwise, why bother saving his life? "I'm glad he's doing okay," I said and tried hard not to let any of my apprehension show. "He's a good guy."

"Yeah." Bryce met my eyes. He saw my worry and echoed it back tenfold, but neither of us voiced it. That would make it too real.

"What about Rhyzkahl?" I asked in a sharp change of subject. "Anything new with him?" Not that I gave two shits about the treacherous lord's health, but curiosity drove me to compare reality to the dream visit.

Bryce seemed grateful for the shift in topic. "The demonic rumor mill says he hasn't left his quarters since his return from the plantation and that he's dependent on megadoses of pain concoctions." He snorted. "I don't know what Zack did to him, but it knocked him out of action."

"Gee, that's too bad," I said with a syrupy smile. Fuck Rhyzkahl.

Bryce grinned. "I had a feeling you'd be real torn up by the news."

The basement door opened, and Idris stepped out, messenger bag slung over one shoulder. I gave him a smile as he strode our way, but to my surprise he continued through the kitchen and toward the back door.

"Idris, wait," I called after him. "I need to get you caught up on a few things."

"I have to do something first," he said tersely as he stalked out.

Bryce spread his hands and shrugged. Groaning under my breath, I moved to the sink and peered out the window. Idris crouched in the center of the nexus, then placed an oddly shaped object swathed in red cloth on the concrete and carefully unwrapped it.

I squinted to be sure I really was seeing a human forearm and hand there on the cloth. A second later, Idris dispelled my doubts by lifting the thing and holding it up like an offering to an unseen god of the sky.

"Are you shitting me?" I blurted.

"What's wrong?" Bryce asked.

I pushed away from the sink. "Apparently I cut summoner class the day they taught Ritual Use of Body Parts for Fun and Profit," I said, then ran out the back door and across the yard.

At the edge of the platform I paused to make certain Idris hadn't activated the nexus. He held the severed arm aloft, his head tipped back and gaze locked onto it. Sweat glistened on his face, though I didn't know if it was from whatever he was doing or the midday Louisiana summer sun. I eased closer then stopped a few feet away and waited. The arm had been severed below the elbow and cauterized, but more disturbing was how fresh it appeared, as though it had been attached to its rightful owner only minutes before. A thin-skinned and wrinkled owner.

A shimmer on the inner arm caught my eye.

*No freaking way.* Shock and disgust roiled through me as I stared at the arcane symbol that glinted like a fine tattoo of delicate golden light. Mzatal's mark—which meant this was *Katashi's* arm. A vicious smile tugged at my mouth. About six months prior, Katashi betrayed Mzatal and tried to capture me for the Mraztur. In what I considered a perfectly appropriate response, Mzatal sliced off Katashi's arm right before his allies teleported him away. The Mraztur had since regenerated the missing limb for Katashi, but apparently this original arm—which bore Mzatal's mark—had been arcanely preserved to keep it from rotting.

Idris remained in that position for several minutes, then lowered the arm and set it on the cloth. "Goddammit. Nothing."

"What did you expect it to do?" I asked tartly. "Fly to Katashi like a homing appendage?"

Idris frowned at me. "I know it sounds crazy, but I'm sure I can use it to track him." He scrubbed a hand over his face. "Obviously it's going to take more work than I'd hoped."

I crouched beside him. "You're serious."

"Dead serious," he said. "Mzatal didn't strip the mark which means Katashi carries the resonance." He ran his finger over the parchment-thin skin and its intricate sigil. "Feel it."

"Ew." I made a face. "No thank you."

He rolled his eyes. "Seriously?" He didn't actually say *You're a total weenie* but he might as well have.

"Ugh. Fine." I brushed the mark with my fingers and caught my breath when a tingle shimmied up my arm. More Mzatal than Katashi in its feel. Emboldened, I laid my palm over it, smiling at the vivid sense of Mzatal's presence. Yet beyond it a background vibration thrummed. Katashi. "That's cool. And creepy." I pulled my hand away, then wiped it on Idris's shirt in the guise of patting him on the shoulder.

"I'll find a way to use it." Idris wrapped the arm in the silk and tucked the bundle into his messenger bag. "But first I need to assess the local valves."

"Speaking of valves, there's new info we all need to discuss."

"I'm sorry I was so rude earlier," he said quietly.

"It's cool. Let's go see if Jill left any cookies in the house."

Jill had, indeed, left cookies in the house—white chocolate chip with macadamia nuts. The three of us sat at the kitchen table and munched cookies while I brought the guys up to speed on the latest Earthside events, including the blurry photo, Zack's condition, Szerain's antics, the pond valve instability, and Jill's inexplicable actions on said valve.

Bryce's eyes narrowed with worry as I related the last item. "She's all right?"

I gave him a reassuring smile. "Right as rain, and the bean is still kicking up a storm." Then I sobered. "I don't know what happened out there, but I do know that if we hadn't stabilized the valve, it could have been really bad. It's why I asked Mzatal for help." I snatched another cookie off the plate, grimaced. "The thing is, I have only a vague idea of how the valve system works. I know where a handful of valves are, and a little about stabilizing. I get that the Mraztur want to use the valve system as their personal highway to Earth, but that's pretty much it."

Idris jerked his shoulders up in a dismissive shrug. "All you need to know are the basics, and I can brief you on those," he said. "You—I mean summoners in general—don't have the skills to alter the valves."

It wasn't *quite* an insult, especially since I suspected he was correct. "But Katashi does," I said. "And *you* do."

"I don't have a tenth of his knowledge, but I understand what he's doing."

"All right, I'll leave the tricky bits to you," I said then gave him a cheeky smile. "So, what does lowly little me need to know?"

Bryce snorted, but Idris merely frowned a *My sense of humor is temporarily out of order* frown. "The problems started when Rhyzkahl came through the plantation node before it was ready," he said, leaning forward. "Like a man trying to cross a suspension bridge that only has five cables attached out of twenty."

"Oh, I get it!" I said. "Those five cables aren't enough to handle the stress, so crap starts breaking and swaying, which makes more things break, and so on."

"Exactly. It damaged the node, and instability cascaded throughout all the valves, particularly in this area." He snagged a cookie and began to break pieces off.

Bryce frowned. "But why have a valve system in the first place if it's so damn touchy?"

Idris looked as shocked as if he'd suggested doing away

with all the pesky wet stuff on the surface of the Earth. "Because the demon realm would destroy itself without it!"

"How?" I asked. "Why?"

"I don't know details, but it's as if the demon realm—the planet—has a generator at its core, and without an outlet it'll overload and tear itself to pieces." Idris crumbled the remaining cookie in his hand for emphasis. "The whole valve system bleeds excess potency off the demon realm and dumps it on Earth."

"Is that what causes the valve node emissions that you and Katashi were tracking in Colorado and Texas?" I asked.

"Those are part of it, yes," he said. "There's a steady flow of potency to Earth along with occasional bigger bursts. Node emissions normally follow a regular pattern, whereas unpredictable emergency overloads surge through the whole system and disperse via both nodes and valves." He scowled at the crumbs before him and swept them into a pile with sharp movements. "The problem is that instability screws up the distribution. Instead of an even spread, one valve gets an overload for the duration of the burst. Too much for too long, and it creates a situation like you had at the pond with the potential for a lot of damage."

"How is a node different from a valve?" I asked. "Apart from size, I mean."

"There's not much difference on the Earth side," he said. "Nodes are more robust than valves, like a branch compared to a twig. Functionally though, they're the interdimensional conduits between the demon realm and Earth, which is how the potency actually gets from there to here."

"Like an oil pipeline," Bryce put in.

"Close," Idris said with an approving nod. "Combine that with the bridge analogy and you have it. The nodes are big tunnel-bridges that carry the potency from the demon realm to here. When the potency gets to the end of the tunnel-bridge it empties into the pipelines—the valve network."

"The node is in both worlds, but the valves are fully on Earth?" I asked.

He nodded. "Twelve trunks on the demon side—one in

each lord's realm and one with the Council. Each trunk splits into two valve nodes to create the bridges. The Earth end of each node branches into two valves, and each valve splits into a bunch of micro-valves."

"To disperse the outflow," Bryce said with a slow nod. "Without the valves and micro-valves the potency pollution could dump all in one place—"

"—and cause damage or disruptive changes," Idris finished for him.

"Do you know the locations of all the local valves?" I asked.

From the side pouch of his messenger bag, Idris pulled a battered map that had been folded to isolate eastern Louisiana. Numbered red circles marked close to a dozen locations. "These are the sites Katashi shared when I was with him, but you might have some that I don't."

"Hang on." I hurried to the computer room and returned a few seconds later with a map almost as battered as his and a single sheet of paper. "On this map are the valves I found when Tracy Gordon was trying to make a gate, along with locations that Rhyzkahl searched for on my computer." I handed it over, then smiled and held the paper up. "But I also have Tracy's journals—with map coordinates plus dates and times for the valve node emissions y'all were chasing. And, because I'm super awesome, I'm giving you this summary page so you don't have to decipher the journals." I placed it on the table with a flourish.

Idris offered a genuine smile. "Cool. That'll be really helpful," It took him less than a minute to compare both maps. "You have a few that I don't," he said as he marked them on his copy. "This area has the highest concentration of valves in the world." He pushed his map to the center of the table so we could see. "Five nodes and ten valves within a hundred miles of here."

"That explains why this place is so fucking weird," I muttered.

Bryce let out a bark of laughter. "What I don't get is, if they could build a valve system to cross dimensions, why couldn't they make it vent to space or onto an unpopulated planet?"

"I have no freaking idea," Idris said with a helpless shrug. "I asked Katashi the same question, but if he knew he didn't want to tell me."

"Speaking of that steaming piece of shit," I said, "how do we fix what he's screwed up?"

"I'll know more once I check out a few valves," Idris said. "In theory, the ones he worked with directly are most likely to destabilize, so for now the plan is to assess the valves and stabilize as needed."

Bryce cleared his throat. "Why can't we put an end to this shit by closing off the valves before Katashi gets to them? Like Kara did at the plantation."

Idris gave me a startled look. "Close off valves? How?"

Oh, right. He hadn't seen what I did to the plantation valve node because he'd already left with Mzatal by the time I sealed it. "Hate to rain on your parade," I said, "but it's not that simple. The barricade seal is a last resort. Think of it as a storm grate. It lets potency flow through while keeping lords out. It also does a decent job of stabilizing. The problem is that it blocks about thirty percent of the potency flow."

Idris winced. "So it's a good emergency measure, but too many valves and nodes blocked like that would create back pressure in the system."

"Yep," I said. "Kablooey."

"All right, we'll stick to the plan. Assess and stabilize." His voice went hard and cold. "*Then* we take down Katashi."

"I know the area pretty well," Bryce told Idris. "I can take you where you need to go."

"And I have a lead on a half-dozen properties where Katashi and his crew might be based," I said. "Since I can't see them holing up in a motel, my hunch is that they're renting a big house in the area. Maybe you two can scope out the addresses while you're out checking valves."

"Yeah, that'll work," Idris said and tucked the map back into his bag.

"Excellent," I said. At least I hoped so. There was probably nothing to worry about. After all, how much trouble could an ex-hitman and an angry, obsessed, summoner child of a demonic lord get into?

Whatever happened, at least we had cookies.

# Chapter 8

Shortly after noon, I delivered Idris and Bryce to the crime lab and Jill's olive green 1974 Chevy Malibu. With them was a big box of tools Bryce had found in my shed.

What began as a casual query about what tools I owned soon morphed into *Indiana Bryce and the Holy Shit, Check This Out!* after I opened the shed and told him to help himself. Apparently my dad and grandfather had amassed an enviable collection of tools, hardware, gadgets, and I had no idea what else. While Idris and I looked on, Bryce conducted an archaeological dig punctuated by exclamations such as "Oh my god, I wonder if this still works!" and "My grandpa had one of these!" and "Christ on a crutch, is that a jack for a Model T?!"

If not for the annoying detail that the fate of the world was at stake, Bryce would have delved for the rest of the day. Or longer. That said, he also knew how to use the tools, and after forty minutes and plenty of colorful language the Malibu sputtered to life. I made sure the boys had spending money and cell phones, then left them to their own mission and drove the two blocks to the PD and my meeting with Pellini.

The Beaulac PD detectives' parking lot had been restriped with fresh and perky white paint, and smooth asphalt now filled the hole where lightning had struck and revealed a valve. Fortunately, a physical barrier had no effect on my ability to sense the valve. Damn good, since it allowed me to see the flickers of orange within the normal blue-green hues of the valve. Crouching, I pretended to search for something I dropped while I made a closer assessment. Now that I had a better idea what to look for, I had no trouble discerning the fraying border. Idris would need to put this one near the top of his list.

"Gillian?"

I looked up to see Cory Crawford standing a few feet away, his expression one of pleased surprise. Cory was my former sergeant in Investigations, and one of the few non-arcane people who had any knowledge of my not-so-normal abilities. He hadn't changed one bit in the six months since I'd seen him last. Hair and mustache dyed the same dull-brown of his eyes. Tan dress shirt, brown slacks, and a tie with an eye-gouging design of purple and green swirls. Until this moment, I hadn't realized how much I'd missed him.

I straightened with a smile. "Hey, Sarge. Long time no see!"

"Too long," he said then gave me an openly appreciative once-over. "You look great. I almost didn't recognize you."

"Thanks," I said, smile widening. "I kinda got in shape." My time in the demon realm had included quite a bit of physical training, and I couldn't help but be pleased with the results. I'd actually *gained* weight, but none of it was flab.

Well, maybe a pound or two. The faas loved to cook, and one of Jekki's souvenirs from his time on Earth was an Italian cookbook titled, *I'm Gonna Make You a Ravioli You Can't Refuse.*

"Pellini told me you'd be stopping by," Cory said. "Gotta say, I never thought I'd see you two work together without the threat of a court order."

I laughed. "Yeah, it must be a full moon."

A wince flashed across Cory's face. Though he knew I dabbled in "extranormal activities," he didn't enjoy reminders. He busied himself with pulling a cigarette out of a pack. "Have you been officially called in on the plantation investigation?"

"Not officially." I did my best to make it sound as if it was only a matter of time before that happened. "However, I'd like to get an idea of what occurred and determine whether it was an isolated event." *I also* need *to check the valve node out there*, I added silently. It wasn't that I didn't trust Szerain to keep the node stable, secure, and intact, but . . . I didn't trust Szerain. With anything. Not at the moment.

"Whatever happened out there was fucked up, that's for sure." He lit the cigarette, shifted to stand where the smoke wouldn't blow in my face. "There's been a lot of that lately," he added, unease in his voice. "Agent Kristoff filled me in on a few things after you disappeared last year, but I have a feeling that was only the tip of the iceberg."

"How much do you want to know?" I asked. He hated the weird, but he was also a damn good cop.

He flicked off ash and met my eyes. "Enough to get out of the way of a shit boulder before it flattens me or someone else. Right now I have no idea what to watch out for."

"I think we'll be seeing a lot of shit boulders in the coming weeks," I said with a wince. "As far as what to watch out for, off the top of my head I'd say earth tremors, weird creatures, or anything that feels off where you can't put your finger on why. And don't hesitate to call me, even if you're not sure it's part of my particular 'specialty.' I need to know about that sort of thing. Also, I wouldn't park in the middle of this lot if I were you." I angled my head toward the repaired hole.

He dropped a startled glance to the fresh asphalt and visibly fought the impulse to step away from it. "Should I find a reason to cordon it off?" he asked.

"Might be best. Several feet around it as well."

"I'll think of something."

"Thanks. And I'll do my best to keep you in the loop."

"Great," he said with the tone of a man who really didn't want to be in the loop at all but knew the need for it.

I left him to finish his smoke and headed inside. Pellini was on the phone when I reached his open office door. "I didn't ask whether or not you could do it," he was saying, voice gruff. "Just get it done. We're heading out that way now." He hung up.

"Everything cool?" I asked.

"Ran into a snag getting authorization to visit the plantation," he grumbled. "Kristoff pulled some crap this morning, and now the feds have it locked down tight."

My desire to check on the valve node ratcheted up several notches. "What did he do?" I asked casually.

"I don't know any specifics." Pellini stood and tugged his pants up a bit higher. "There was a strange event that apparently no one can fully remember or explain. Next thing anyone knows, Kristoff has command authority over the entire scene, and access is way more restricted."

I turned to glance at the clippings pinned to his wall while I fought to hide a face-contorting frown. Easy to get that command authority when you were a demonic lord with the ability to manipulate people's thoughts and memories.

"You're on his team. Surely you can get us in." Pellini's voice held an odd edge, but I couldn't tell if it was uneasiness, desperation, or simple curiosity about my role on the task force.

"I can try," I said as I scanned the clippings. Several were news reports of arrests he'd made or cases he'd worked, but one stood out from the others. "I have my task force ID with me and might be able to bluff my way through," I continued. Worst case scenario would be that I'd take a long drive with Pellini for nothing. Weirdly, that wasn't as horrifying as it once was. Especially now that I was looking at a picture of Pellini and Boudreaux dressed up as—according to the caption—a Dark Angel and the Crystal Incubus. Boudreaux wore all white sewn with a billion crystals, an intricate mask, and cool-as-all-hell shimmering wings. Pellini, face shadowed in a deep hood, stood half a foot taller than normal in a flowing black robe. Huge feathered wings crested well over his head and folded behind him.

"Go ahead and laugh," he said with a snort. I glanced at him, and he gestured toward the clipping. "Everyone else did."

It spoke volumes that he had the picture up in his office at all, knowing how much ribbing he'd get. "You made these costumes?" I asked, incredulous.

"Yeah, and got into a shootout during the contest." He shrugged. "No point trying to keep my hobby quiet after that."

It sounded as if there were previous costumes and contests that he'd kept secret with far more success. I quickly skimmed the article. He and Boudreaux had broken up a drug and human trafficking ring, and took down the head bad guy in a firefight, during which Pellini got shot. All while in awesome—though unwieldy—costumes. "Dude, that's seriously cool," I said with genuine awe. "How'd you learn to make costumes like that?"

He grabbed his keys and notebook and exited the office, leaving me no choice but to hurry after or be left behind. "My parents." he said over his shoulder after I closed his door and caught up with him. "Dad was a tailor, and mom was a seamstress and costumer. She worked on Mardi Gras costumes pretty much all year, every year I can remember." A smile of pride touched his mouth as we exited the building. "She was always in high demand 'cause of how good her stuff was."

"You ever do that as a side job?" I asked. "Or does that take the fun out of it?"

He unlocked his car and waited until we were both in before answering. "I tried my freshman year at Northwestern State but didn't have the time for it. Too much going on with football and classes, and I didn't want to lose my scholarship."

"You had a football scholarship?" I asked, impressed yet again.

"A small one," he said as he started the car. "Barely covered the cost of books, but I liked playing. I had an academic scholarship that paid for most of the rest."

He pulled out of the parking lot while I fought to hide my surprise—along with my shame for jumping to conclusions. Clearly he hadn't always been a slacker. *So what happened to him?* My fingers itched to dig for my smart phone and look up anything I could find on him but I managed to resist. For now.

"I can't see football and costuming going together very well," I said.

"About as well as costuming and being a cop," he replied with a wince. "Boudreaux caught it harder being Sparkle Pants, though. At least I was a menacing Dark Angel."

"He gets plenty of shit already," I said, thinking back to any number of interactions between Boudreaux and other members of the department. Cops tended to be macho assholes, and short, scrawny Boudreaux was an easy target.

"He's tough," Pellini said. "Can't survive as a runt around here if you're any other way."

"Yeah, I guess so." *Runt. Scrawny.* We all participated in the casual abuse without thought. Sure, Boudreaux survived, but that didn't mean he remained undamaged.

Pellini turned onto the highway, accelerated, and set the cruise control for ten miles over the speed limit. "He's catching grief now because of Angus McDunn being his stepdad. So far it's indirect, but it's still bullshit."

"He can't take a leave of absence?" But even as I said it I realized Boudreaux wouldn't. That would be admitting defeat.

"He took one day off to see to his mom," Pellini replied. "I tried to get him to take a week but he refused." He flicked the radio on to play classic rock at low volume, and I didn't protest—both of us content to let the conversation die.

I pulled my wandering thoughts back to the here and now when Pellini shut the cruise control off. Half a minute later he made the turn onto the long gravel driveway that led to the Farouche Plantation gate.

Though I'd been here before, this was my first time actually *seeing* where I was going. On the previous trip I'd been in the back seat of a Lexus SUV with my wrists zip-tied and a bag over my head while I pretended to be kidnapping victim Amaryllis Castlebrook.

Old, perfectly trimmed oak trees lined the drive, shading

us from the midday sun. In the distance, the mansion stood—tall and stately on the left, and jagged, collapsed, and burned on the right. The gate was closed, with a grey Crown Victoria bearing government plates parked to one side of it. As we neared, a clean cut man wearing tactical pants and a black FBI t-shirt stepped out of the car and glowered at us.

I quickly dug my FBI special consultant ID out of my bag. "Let's hope this works," I said, and Pellini gave a mutter of agreement.

My fantasy of gaining entry to the plantation with the power of my ID crumbled swiftly. The agent barely glanced at it before handing it back with a shake of his head.

"Restricted access," he stated, setting his oh-so-square jaw.

"I'm on Agent Kristoff's team," I told him. "Is he here?"

"No, ma'am. He left a few hours ago."

"There are a few things I really need to check on," I insisted. "Could you please call him and get his clearance for us to go in?" At this point I had nothing to lose by trying.

The agent's expression turned more forbidding, but he tugged his phone out of the holder on his belt. "Who's your partner?" he asked with a lift of his chin toward Pellini.

"Vincent Pellini, detective with the Beaulac PD."

The agent stepped away from the car and dialed a number on his phone. A few seconds later I heard low conversation. Great, so Ryan answered this guy's calls and not mine? Jerk.

My annoyance melted to relief as the agent returned with the sign-in log. "You're both cleared. Don't enter the mansion itself or the Ops building without an escort."

I thanked him profusely, and while he opened the gate we signed the log. A faint prickle of the arcane washed over me as the car passed through the entrance. I noted that much of the warding that had previously graced the gate was gone. Szerain's work, I figured. Would be tough for the FBI to conduct any sort of investigation if its agents kept getting turned away by aversion wards and other arcane protections.

"What a mess," I breathed as I took in the sight of the

damaged mansion. Once again, I didn't have to pretend to be seeing it for the first time. The mansion had been ablaze last time I was here, courtesy of Mzatal and lightning, and before that I'd only seen the side that faced the lawn and the pond. Was it even a pond anymore? Most of the water had boiled away when Mzatal grounded his power. It would probably take several months of Louisiana rainstorms to fully restore it.

Pellini parked in the visitors lot and killed the engine. A weird quiet enveloped us as we exited the car, and the closing of the doors echoed like gunshots. The valve thrummed in my arcane senses, low and insistent, like music with a heavy bass playing several blocks away.

I meandered in the vague direction of the back of the mansion, and Pellini followed a few seconds later. The once luscious lawn with its copious flowers and ornamental trees lay in ruin—plants trampled, crushed, and strewn with rubble. Yellow crime scene tape bounded large swaths, and an odd, fresh ozone scent lingered over a more earthy foundation of mud and charred wood. Potency arced like violet lightning between chunks of debris. Steam rose from the pond basin, and the mud boiled in slow bubbles near the center. Several agents moved among the outbuildings but none gave us more than a passing glance.

"Anything jumping out?" Pellini asked, cutting into my musings. I glanced his way to see him watching me. *Oh, right, I'm supposed to be helping him find a link between what happened here and his murder victim.* In fact, there were plenty of links, but none I'd be stumbling over on the lawn, nor any I chose to share with him.

"It's not like I get weird vibrations or anything, y'know," I lied with what I hoped was the right combination of sincerity and tartness. Pellini didn't need to know about my arcane skills. I started to add that I wasn't a clairvoyant like Marco Knight but clamped down on it. I had no idea whether Marco's talent was simple clairvoyance or an ability far more complex.

I continued to wander in aimless fashion while Pellini dogged me several steps behind. Ahead of us lay the shattered remains of the gazebo—with the valve node at its center. Broken columns rose from the edge of the raised stone platform. A pillar of potency flashed in the center, oscillating from brilliant peacock to deepest midnight blue.

"Looks like a bomb went off there," I remarked as I headed toward it. In othersight, residual potency drifted like fragile luminescent tumbleweeds.

"The reports agree that there was an explosion centered at the gazebo," Pellini said.

His eyes remained on me as I cautiously stepped through the residue and to the center. *He won't have any idea what I'm doing.* To anyone without the ability to see the arcane it would appear as if I was idly flexing my hands. Keeping my back to him, I went to one knee and pretended to peer at the cracked and crazed marble at the center of the gazebo floor. To my immense relief there was no sign of instability or fraying within the node. Damn good thing since it would be nightmarishly difficult to get Idris out here to fix it. For security, I retraced the barricade seal, and Kadir's implanted training rose to guide my movements. The intricate barricade comprised of Kadir-style sigils prevented the node from being used by the demonic lords as a passageway to Earth.

Energy flared as I completed the final sigil, and I jerked aside to avoid the burst. I shot a look behind me only to see it head straight toward Pellini like a flickering golden basketball. A warning shout rose in my throat, but I swallowed it back. The arcane burst wouldn't *hurt* him. At most he might experience a few seconds of discomfort, like a stabbing headache or a sudden deep chill.

Yet, as the flare reached him, Pellini casually brushed it aside with one hand as if waving away a fly.

*He just moved that potency!* I mentally screeched. No, surely I'd misinterpreted a coincidental movement, or my eyes were playing tricks on me. No way had Pellini—*Pellini* of all people—swished arcane power aside. Physically manipulate errant potency? I sure couldn't do that. I had to rely on tracings and sigils to guide and shape power into the needed form.

What the hell was I supposed to do with Pellini now?

Confront him? *Yo, dude, I happened to notice you got you some arcane skillz there. Wassup wit dat?* I'd worked with the guy for years and never seen any hint that he was anything but mundane. Then again, I'd managed to hide my own weirdness for a long time.

No, confronting him wasn't the right move. Not yet at least. Pellini didn't know I'd seen him flick the potency away, which meant I had time to come up with a brilliant idea for how to handle the situation. It seemed outrageous, but I had to consider the possibility that Pellini was working for Katashi and his crew. Had he seen me reinforcing the node barricade? I'd blocked his view as much as possible, but he still might have seen me tracing sigils.

Maybe Pellini wasn't aware of what he'd done? But how was he able to do it at all? Most people with any sort of arcane talent developed it during or immediately after puberty. How could a guy in his mid-forties suddenly come up with those kind of skills? Then again, maybe the not-long-after-puberty rule was yet another of my many erroneous beliefs.

"What did you find?" he asked.

Standing, I dusted off my hands and gave a super-casual shrug. "Nothing of interest. Stone's cracked all the way through, that's all." *And you batted potency away!* I turned a circle in pretense of investigating. "There's nothing out here. Maybe the house has something that might connect to your case?" Anything to divert his attention from the node.

An unsuccessful effort, as it turned out. Pellini's gaze remained heavy on me, mouth pursed in an expression I'd seen him use on suspects who were feeding him a line of bullshit. "Maybe," he finally said. He looked toward the center of the gazebo. "But I have a feeling there's more to be found here."

Crap. Good guy or bad guy, I didn't want him anywhere near the node. No way would I have brought him this close if I'd known about his potential talent.

His phone *dinged* with a text message, and I silently thanked the universe for the brief reprieve. Pellini read the text then scowled in either frustration or disappointment. "Boudreaux's at the gate and needs to see me now."

"No problem," I replied, being very understanding and accommodating of whatever would get us the fuck away from this spot.

Pellini remained silent as we returned up the long driveway. When we neared the gate I could see Boudreaux pacing in front of his car and smoking a cigarette with sharp, quick motions.

After exiting the gate, Pellini parked next to the agent's Crown Vic, then signed out on the crime scene log before heading over to his partner. Boudreaux's gaze snapped to me as I got out of the car. His face flushed red, and his hand tightened on a paper he clutched. I offered him a light smile then pointedly looked away and walked over to the agent. I refused to get worked up over Boudreaux's open hostility, especially considering that he'd never been remotely friendly with me in the past.

"You must be bored out of your mind with this," I said to Agent Square Jaw as I took the scene log.

His stern expression melted into a friendly smile. "Gives me plenty of time to study," he said and waved a hand toward a stack of textbooks on the front seat of his vehicle with titles like *Mock Trial Case Files and Problems* and *Question and Answers: Torts*. His phone buzzed, and he murmured an apology before turning to answer it.

Clipboard in hand, I signed out, then paused at the sight of Ryan's name near the top of the page—signing in this morning at 1003 hours and out at 1034.

After a glance to make sure the agent was still on his phone, I flipped through the old pages. Agent Ryan Kristoff had been at the plantation every day since the investigation began and, with the exception of today, for anywhere from three to eight hours.

Which, of course, signified absolutely nothing. After all, there was a shitload to go through on a very large plantation. I handed the clipboard to Agent Square-Jawed Law Student and strolled back to Pellini's car, glancing at him and Boudreaux in time to see the latter again glare daggers at me. I returned a bland look.

Boudreaux shoved the piece of paper at Pellini. "Why is

she here?" he snarled, gesturing my way with a sharp slash of his hand. Without waiting for an answer, he reached through his car window to grab a folder then stormed toward me, teeth bared.

I instinctively shifted into a defensive stance. This was way more than his usual Kara-you-suck attitude.

"What the fuck did you have to do with all of this?" he demanded and swept his arm up to indicate the plantation. "What did you *do?*"

*Son of a bitch.* "Back off, asshole," I shot back. "I don't know what the fuck you're talking about."

Boudreaux flipped open the folder to reveal an enlarged copy of the photo Pellini had shown me in the restaurant. "That!" He jabbed a finger at blurry me behind McDunn. "You were *here,* not three feet from Mr. Farouche."

I scoffed. "Seriously? That's not me dude." Admit nothing, deny everything. "Don't know who it is, but just because I'm kinda female-shaped doesn't mean I'm every female."

His expression hardened as he pulled a sheet from beneath the photo and slapped it on top. "Fuck. You."

*Fuck me is right.* It was a computer-aided police artist sketch of a woman who looked an awful lot like one Kara Gillian. I fought to channel my shock and dismay into a wrongfully accused and pissed reaction.

Boudreaux shook the folder at me. "That's a little more clear than 'kinda female shaped.'" Anger sharpened his tone. "*Tell me!*"

I pygahed then lowered my voice. "Boudreaux, it's not me," I said, calm and insistent. "I don't know what's going on here."

The fury in his eyes faded into desperation. "Gillian . . . just tell me what happened." His words resonated with pain and confusion. His need for information had nothing to do with making an arrest and everything to do with finding closure for his own grief.

Farouche had been responsible for a host of evil acts, but he'd clearly been very important to Boudreaux. An ache of sympathy bloomed in my chest. If I came clean to him right now there was every chance he wouldn't pursue it any further. Unfortunately, I couldn't leave it to chance. Too many other lives were at stake.

"Boudreaux, I can't."

His eyes went flat as he slapped the folder shut. He knew I was holding back. "You're done," he said through clenched teeth, then strode back to his car and drove off.

Pellini ambled my way. "What's up with that?" His tone stayed mild, but he watched my every reaction.

I let annoyance creep into my voice. "What's up with what? A sketch of a woman who he's decided is me?" I shook my head. "He's never liked me, and I'm an easy target for his anger."

Pellini regarded me in silence. "Yeah. That must be it," he finally said, sounding utterly unconvinced. "I've had enough of this place. Nothing here for me. You ready to roll?"

"Gladly."

Pellini kept the radio on for the drive back which once again saved us from awkward silence. It remained plenty awkward as we sat there not talking, but Pink Floyd was singing about being comfortably numb which at least saved us from the silence part. I wasn't bored, though. I spent the majority of the drive going over options regarding Pellini and the shocking way he'd batted that potency aside.

I'd worked with Pellini for years and hardly knew the guy. What I needed was a chance to determine whether or not he possessed any sort of arcane skill. It still seemed ludicrous—after all, this was *Pellini*—but it would be the height of stupidity to not check everything out.

My thoughts continued to churn in a messy useless sludge, and when we pulled into the PD parking lot I was no closer to a defined course of action.

Pellini cleared his throat as he parked. "I, uh, know the plantation was a bust, but maybe we could get together for a beer later today, and I could pick your brain about other possible connections to my case?"

And, like that, a solution emerged. "I'll do you one better," I said brightly. "You can come over to my house to-night. Say around seven? A couple of friends are staying with me for a few days, and we're going to grill up hamburgers and ribs. You're welcome to join us, and after we eat you and I can discuss the case."

Tension melted away from him, and he smiled. Not a nasty smile, either. "Seven. Yeah. I can totally do that. I'll bring the beer."

*And I'll bring the demon.*

# Chapter 9

As soon as I had the AC going in my car I called Idris and Bryce and gave them a quick recap of what happened with Pellini. Idris made a few interesting strangled noises when I described how Pellini batted potency away but agreed that my barbecue idea was a good one since further assessment was clearly needed.

"How's the Malibu running?" I asked.

Idris made a rude sound. "Like a one-legged gazelle. Bryce says he'll work on it more this afternoon."

"Good," I said. "He needs a hobby."

I hung up with them, and my phone immediately dinged with a text from Tessa: <Back home!>

I smiled. Short, sweet, and to the point—just like my aunt. Well, mostly like her. The sweet part was debatable.

<Yay! Will call when I get home> I replied.

<Got a minute to swing by? Picked up some turquoise that I think you'd like. And fudge!>

Yep, she knew how to get my attention. Presents *and* sweets.

<On my way!>

A crew of orange-vested city workers had part of Tessa's street torn up, though I couldn't tell if it was for a drainage project or road repair. Either way, it obviously required a bunch of sweaty men to stand around and peer thoughtfully into one of several six-foot-wide holes in the street. At long last I navigated the slalom course of orange cones to Tessa's house, trotted up the steps and knocked on the door.

My aunt opened it a few seconds later, smiling brightly. "Kara!"

"Welcome back!" I said as I pulled her into a hug. Petite, bordering on tiny, she made up for her lack of height with an iron will and a wild fashion sense. Her current outfit was a symphony of pink and black—light pink sandals, black miniskirt, dark pink belt, medium-pink blouse over a black tank top. Even her frizzy blond hair bore a pink streak on one side.

She gave me a squeeze before releasing me. "Not for long!" she said with a laugh then pulled me in and closed the door. "We're heading out again as soon as I get a call back from Melanie about staffing at the store."

"Carl can get that much time off?" I asked.

Tessa blinked, shook her head. "Carl? Goodness, no." She headed down the hall toward the kitchen. "I'd never be able to drag him away for this long."

An unpleasant feeling crept in, as if I was seeing a math error where I'd made a mistake in the first step. I followed my aunt as pieces of information coalesced into a new picture. *Old man.* She'd said she was going to Aspen with the old man. She'd never actually said she was going with Carl. I'd simply made that assumption since he was her boyfriend.

"Who are you going with?" I asked. A chill snaked through me as the answer took shape.

"Isumo," Tessa said in a *Who else would it be?* tone as she stepped into the kitchen.

Isumo Katashi. He was there, sitting at the counter in the kitchen with a steaming cup of tea before him. He regarded me with keen eyes then inclined his head and offered me a thin smile.

I stopped dead in my tracks. "You son of a bitch."

Tessa whirled to face me. "Kara Gillian! Master Katashi is a guest under my roof. I know you have your differences, but I will not tolerate such rudeness."

"Differences?" My hands clenched. "He *murdered* Idr . . . a friend's sister!"

Tessa lifted her chin. "There's a lot going on right now, and facts get skewed easily. I don't expect you to agree, but I do expect you both to remain civil while in this house."

"I did not murder her," Katashi said, voice even and mild. He lifted his cup and took a careful sip.

"You fucking well were a part of it," I snarled. "Aunt Tessa, I know what this man is capable of." My chest tightened. "I love you, and you can't expect me to *not* be concerned for your safety and well-being when you're with him."

To my dismay, Tessa moved to stand beside Katashi. "Kara," she said, voice abruptly gentle. "Sweetling. This is one of the reasons I asked you to come over. With all the craziness of the past couple of years, there've been a lot of misunderstandings, and I haven't always set things straight when I should have." She placed a hand on Katashi's shoulder. "The fact is, I've been with Isumo for over thirty years," she continued as my stomach knotted tighter. "He's my mentor and my friend. He's not going to hurt me, and I refuse to stop associating with him because of your own prejudices."

Outrage flared. *Prejudices?!* No, my hatred of Katashi was based on cold hard facts. I drew breath to argue, but stopped at the faint smile on the man's face. He watched me, calm, cool, and so very fucking confident.

Over thirty years. The weight of it settled onto me. She'd started training with Katashi before I was even born. Lived with him in Japan for almost ten years. *She's been his student a year longer than I've been alive.* That's what I was up against—a loyalty so deep it was beyond her comprehension that her beloved teacher and friend could be guilty of heinous acts. And I suddenly knew that if I tried to force her to see the truth I might lose her forever.

*If I ever had her.* Certainly not in the way I'd always assumed.

Katashi spoke to my aunt in Japanese. She replied, also in Japanese, and with an ease and speed that marked her as fluent. Anger and dismay spiked through me at the deliberately secret conversation. Tessa had never once spoken a word to me in Japanese. Their brief exchange was a combination slap in the face and indisputable evidence of her connection to Katashi.

To my surprise she gave his shoulder a light squeeze of affection then left the room. Ordered to, or requested? New hatred for him unfolded within me, like a fresh petal on a great big ugly hate-flower.

"I don't care how old you are, or who you have as allies, or how powerful you think you are," I said, not bothering to try and keep my voice steady or calm or any shit like that. "If you hurt her in any way, I will hunt you to the ends of the universe and make you suffer." I smiled thinly. "And I know a thing or two about suffering."

Porcelain clinked against polished granite as Katashi set his cup down. "She is safer with me than if she remains here."

"From what?" I shot back. "Certainly not you."

"From all else."

There was plenty else out there, I knew all too well. He probably harbored a certain amount of affection for Tessa and intended to protect her from the more dangerous elements in play. But right now Tessa was hostage and pawn, even if she refused to admit it.

"Don't underestimate me," I warned him.

Katashi met my eyes. "I never have."

A chill walked up my back. Thirty years was a long time to build up loyalty. And obedience. Had it been her idea to call me over here or his? What better way to lead me into a trap. Sweat pricked beneath my arms, and my pulse quickened. More of his people might be in the house or on the way at this moment.

I shot Katashi a glare full of pure venom then strode out of the kitchen and toward the door. Tessa stepped out of the sitting room and gave me a questioning look.

"You can't leave so soon," she said. "I haven't given you the turquoise and fudge!"

"Forgot an appointment," I blurted then pulled her into an embrace. "I love you. Please stay safe."

"No other way to be," she replied, tone bright as she returned the hug. "I love you too, sweetling. You keep yourself safe as well, okay?"

Nodding, I released her then hurried past and out the door. My aunt remained behind—a loyal associate and friend of one of my greatest enemies.

# Chapter 10

The instant I made it into my car I hit the speed dial on my phone for Bryce, then backed out of the driveway as it rang. The sheer number of emotions tumbling through me could have filled the Superdome, but the two front runners were confusion and disbelief with anger a close third.

"Taggart here."

"Put it on speaker." Stress clipped my words. "Idris needs to hear this."

"Done. Go ahead."

I kept an eye on Tessa's house in my rearview mirror as I drove down the street. "Tessa texted me to come over because she was back in town, and when I got there Katashi was drinking a fucking cup of tea in her kitchen. He's there now."

Idris let out an explosive curse. "We're over half an hour away. Out by the parish line. Can you stick close and stake it out?"

"Already on it." I whipped a U-turn less than a block away and tucked my car behind a parked minivan where I had a good line of sight on the house. And none too soon. Tessa and Katashi stepped out as a bullet-grey sedan glided into the driveway. "Shit. Shit. Shit. A car just pulled up. They're leaving." A man I didn't recognize jumped out of the driver's seat and hurried to open the back door for them.

"You have to follow!" Idris shouted.

"Only if you think it's safe," Bryce cautioned. "For you *and* for your aunt."

"I'm pretty sure my aunt's in no danger," I said bitterly. Or was she? Katashi wouldn't let affection stop him from using her as a hostage if he felt the need. I seethed, watching helplessly as she and Katashi settled into the back of the sedan. The driver hopped in then pulled out and headed away from where I was parked.

"All right, I'm following," I said. "Eilahn's behind me. The driver must've been waiting right around the corner." I gritted my teeth as I navigated the construction zone and barely avoided losing them in the crush.

"Be careful," Bryce said. "I'm sure I don't need to tell you to stay out of sight, but stay out of sight."

"Yeah, thanks for the advice." The instant the words left my mouth one of the cars between mine and the grey sedan changed lanes, forcing me to drop back and do the same or risk ending up too close. "Looks like they're heading out of town. With any luck I can tail them long enough to narrow down where Katashi is based."

"We're on our way back to Beaulac," Bryce said. "If they try to force a confrontation, get the hell out of there. Got it?"

"I will, I promise." I was pissed and worried, but I wasn't stupid. Or at least not *that* stupid. I continued to give terse updates as I maintained the pursuit, though my worry changed to bafflement after the sedan made a turn that took it through a residential area. "Not heading out of town after all," I said. "I can't figure out where the hell they're going. They're not trying to shake me, that's for sure." I hung back as the sedan stopped at a corner before turning. "They seem to be driving around randomly. Could they be tracking some sort of arcane signature?" *Or, they know I'm following them,* I thought with a wince.

"It's possible," Idris said uncertainly though no less tense. "Try to keep track of your route so we can see if there's a pattern."

My phone beeped with an incoming call and *Cory Crawford* on the caller ID. "Hang tight, my former sergeant is calling. I should take this." I stuck them on hold without waiting for an answer and accepted Cory's call. "Whatcha need, Sarge?"

"Hey, Kara, I got two people dressed as surveyors over here," he said. "They have the equipment, but they're not using it. They're camped out on that asphalt patch in the parking lot. I'm sending you a pic."

"Shit!" I took a hard right into a driveway and slammed to a stop then pulled up the picture. "The red-haired woman goes by Gina Hallsworth, though no guarantee that's her real name. I don't recognize the man with her, but I'm willing to bet he's armed. Gina might be too, for all I know." Katashi and Tessa weren't driving around to track arcane crap. They were leading me on a wild goose chase to keep me fucking *distracted*.

"Son of a bitch," he breathed. "You want them off the parking lot, I take it?"

"Not if you risk getting hurt."

He let out a disparaging grunt. "Gimme a fucking break. I'm a cop, remember?"

"I vaguely remember that," I said, smiling despite everything.

"I think I miss your sweet charm the most," he said. "Anyway, I'm on it. I'll let you know what happens."

I switched back over to the boys and filled them in.

"We'll meet you there," Bryce said, then hung up.

When I arrived at the PD, there was no sign of surveyors, fake or otherwise, though I saw that orange cones and caution tape now cordoned off the valve. On the far side of the lot Cory leaned against his personal vehicle, an old but lovely Chevy Nova with a giant antenna on the trunk. I parked and did a quick in-passing assessment of the valve as I headed his way.

He lifted his chin toward the cones. "I asked them why they hadn't posted an SG-243 placard by the work site," he told me. "They said they'd go get it and skedaddled."

"I doubt they wanted to get into a confrontation in a police station parking lot," I said. "And what on earth is an SG-243 placard?"

Cory shrugged. "Some shit I made up. You don't make sergeant without serious bullshitting chops."

"Niiiice." I grinned. "I also like how you've found the farthest possible place away from that asphalt patch, short of leaving the lot."

"You think I didn't consider doing just that?" he said. "I'm heading out of town right after work and didn't want to risk that Bertha might get sucked into a black hole or eaten by a dragon or whatever the fuck else might happen."

I gave him a blank look. "Who's Bertha?"

He patted the trunk of the car. "This is Bertha. 1976 Chevy Nova. V-8 engine. Sucks enough gas to make a tree-hugger cry, but I've had her since college."

"Uh huh. Why do you have 'kasoxe' on the license plate?"

Cory grinned. "K-A-5-O-X-E. I'm a ham radio operator. That's my call sign."

That explained the big horking antenna, and the arrival of Bryce and Idris cut short any further discussion. I introduced Bryce and Cory, but Idris veered straight to the valve, dropped into a crouch, and unslung his messenger bag from his shoulder.

*Oh, fucking shit*, I thought in sudden panic, *please don't pull Katashi's arm out in the middle of the PD parking lot!* To my undying relief Idris simply removed a notepad and pen, and proceeded to scribble notes while he muttered under his breath.

"He'll be like that for a while," I told Cory with a wince of apology.

Cory let out a resigned sigh. "I'll tell people he's an asphalt inspector."

Sure beat the hell out of the truth.

# Chapter 11

As soon as we made it home, Eilahn set to work adjusting the warding to respond to Tessa as an enemy. Ugh. I grabbed my laptop, flopped onto the sofa, and pulled up all the photos I had of Katashi and his people. After reviewing them for anything odd—such as a demon in the background—I emailed them to Cory as persons of interest along with a request to notify me if any of them showed up on his radar.

My phone buzzed beside me right after I hit send, with Sonny's name on the display. *Please let this be good news about Zack*, I prayed as I picked it up. *And if not that, I'll settle for boring requests like a sudden need for toothpaste or toilet paper.* "Hey, Sonny."

"Got trouble," he said in a strained whisper against raised voices in the background. "Ryan is here arguing with Zack. I think he's trying to take him away."

I shoved the laptop aside and shot to my feet. "Arguing about what? Where does he want to take him?"

"I don't know!" he said. "They're not speaking English."

"Crap. I'm on my way. Do whatever you can to stall them!"

Szerain's voice. Closer. Commanding. "Sonny. Put down the phone."

"Let me talk to Ryan!" I shouted. The phone clunked. "Ryan! Szerain! Dammit. Talk to me!"

Son of a bitch. Szerain was doing a top-notch job of

maintaining his position as Gigantic Fucking Loose Cannon. Holding my breath, I listened. Scuffling and a heavy thump. Szerain speaking in demon. Zack replying in kind. The rustle of the phone being picked up. Szerain speaking again in the background, my name followed by more demon. More jostling of the phone.

"Kara." It was Zack, voice hoarse and stressed.

"Zack? Are you okay? What's going on?"

He drew a shaky breath. "Leaving for a while."

"Where to?" I jammed a hand through my hair in frustration. "For how long?"

"I don't know. I'm sorry. I'm really sorry." He paused as Szerain spoke, clipped and urgent. "Out of time," Zack continued. "I have to go. He's taking Sonny as well. I'm sorry."

"No no no, Zack!" I paced frantically in the living room while I tried to think of a way to intervene. "Don't let him do this to you. He's too unpredictable right now. Please, think of Jill. Think of the baby."

"He is." Szerain's voice on the line now, clear and uncompromising. I stopped pacing, hand tight on my phone. "Keep your focus on Katashi," he continued. "Do *not* seek us." His voice held a lord's strength, but behind it I felt the fear—a visceral terror I recognized from when he faced re-submersion in his nightmarish prison. Loose cannon? No, he was a loose high-yield nuke who would go to any length to remain free.

"If you hurt Zack," I said, voice shaking, "I swear, demonic lord or not, I'll—" The connection went dead. I let out a scream of frustration then derailed the urge to smash the phone against the wall by hurling a sofa pillow instead. Breathing hard, I struggled to find a glimmer of hope in the madness. Zack had saved Szerain from insanity during his imprisonment. That had to count for something, right?

Sure, with humans. But I wasn't dealing with humans. Zack and Sonny were gone, and there wasn't a damn thing I could do about it. On top of that, Pellini was coming over in a few hours. How on earth was I supposed to pretend to be sociable, with Tessa off with Katashi, and Zack and Ryan who knew where?

I threw the pillow against the wall a few more times, then dropped down in front of the TV and hauled out the game controller. Half an hour of blowing aliens to green bits improved my mood somewhat. As I put the game away the gate panel chimed, signaling the arrival of Bryce and Idris.

A couple of minutes later the guys came in, both heavily laden with grocery bags. "We hit the store for barbecue supplies after we left the PD," Bryce said as the two dropped the bags onto the kitchen table.

I joined them in the kitchen. "Damn glad you did," I replied, wincing. "This has been such a crazy day I totally forgot. So, is the PD valve all right?"

"It's stable except for a few minor irregularities," Idris said as he stuck packages of ribs, hamburger meat, and hot dogs into the refrigerator. "Hallsworth was most likely evaluating a recent emission. I'll recheck that valve right before its next emission in five days."

I sorted out immediate barbecue needs from general groceries. "Nice to have a little breathing room. Did you make it to any of the other valves before I called you?"

"A couple," he said. He tossed a head of lettuce to Bryce who caught it one-handed and set it on the counter. "No problem with the swamp valve out by the Alligator Museum," Idris continued. "Stable and quiet. But the valve node in the river was wonky as hell. I'll have to go back and do another round on it."

"*In* the river?" I asked then rescued a bag of tomatoes from the game of catch. "How'd you manage to deal with it?"

Bryce snorted. "It wasn't easy," he said. "I had him dangling by a rope from the bridge. We were lucky no cops drove by."

The mental image had me grinning. "That would've been fun to explain," I said. "Wouldn't a boat have been smarter—I mean, easier?"

"Both." Bryce chuckled. "Time constraints. When we go out there again, we'll rent one."

"Smart man," I said. "Which river?"

"Kreeger."

"The bridge out by the parish line?"

"That's the one."

I let out a low whistle. "I never knew that was a node. But it saved my ass." At Bryce's blank look, I continued. "Last year a perp ran my car off that bridge and into the river. I'd have drowned if I hadn't tapped in to some wild nature potency and busted out of the car." I shook my head. "I'd never felt anything like that before. I wonder if bleed-through grove potency made it possible?"

Idris glanced back at me. "That's actually a sound theory. The groves are the trunk focal point of the valve system in each realm."

"Now that's damn cool information." I shoved veggies into the fridge and closed the door. "On a less cheery note, Sonny called half an hour ago. Szerain showed up at the house and pretty much kidnapped him and Zack." I filled them in on the rest of the sketchy information. "No idea where they went."

Idris muttered a long string of expletives. Bryce leaned against the counter and folded his arms across his chest. "He'd better not screw with Sonny."

"I'm with you on that," I said. "Maybe Sonny's talent for keeping people calm will work on Szerain."

"It grew stronger over the years," Bryce said. "I wouldn't be surprised if it worked on a demonic lord. Farouche had a lot of faults, but his talent for enhancing skills wasn't one of them."

"No," Idris said. "That wasn't Farouche's talent. Angus McDunn's the enhancer."

I stared, as dumbfounded as if he'd said guns fire sausages instead of bullets. Idris had spent time with Farouche's people, so I had no reason to doubt him. "Wonderful. That's just what we need—Katashi and all his asshole minions getting a talent upgrade."

Bryce pushed off the counter. "Too late to stop it now. I'll get the marinade going."

Right. Time to deal with issues we could handle. "Do

that," I said. "Then we can discuss our strategy for this evening."

After a short meeting with the boys to hammer out a plan for how to assess Pellini, I headed to the basement to prepare a summoning. Of the twelve varieties of "summonable" demons, I only knew of two—*kehza* and *nyssor*—that could detect innate summoner ability in a human. Kehza were man-sized and winged, with a plethora of claws and teeth and a head that resembled a Chinese dragon's. Nyssor resembled angelic human children except for their too-large eyes with slitted pupils and a mouth bristling with pointed teeth. Either would do a bang-up job of telling us what we needed to know. However, the nyssor creeped me the hell out, which meant I'd be summoning a kehza, thank-you-very-much.

Of course, the other option was to throw Fuzzykins at Pellini since she didn't like summoners one bit. Unfortunately, that method—while entertaining—wasn't fully proven, and we needed to be sure. Then again, if Pellini did anything to annoy me, I could throw the cat at him anyway.

I retrieved my box of implements, set it on the table and removed my chalk and knife. My phone buzzed the moment I unsheathed the knife. Sighing, I peered at the number. I didn't recognize it, but that didn't always spell bad news. Right? A total stranger might call to tell me I'd won the lottery or inherited money from a heretofore unknown relative.

Yeah, because I was oh-so-lucky like that. Ha.

I set the knife down and scooped up the phone, then yelped as excruciating pain shot through my hand. Hissing curses, I peered at the source of the agony: a splinter the size of a telephone pole lodged beneath the nail of my middle finger.

The stupid phone continued to buzz, not giving a shit about my dire straits. I thumbed the answer button. "Kara Gillian."

"Ms. Gillian, this is Detective Rob O'Connor with the St.

Long Sheriff's Office." His voice sounded light, congenial. Didn't matter. I recognized the threat. The splinter receded in importance. "I was wondering if you might be able to spare some time tomorrow morning to come to my office?" he went on. "Or, if it's more convenient, I can meet with you at your residence."

I forced my face into a smile. It didn't matter that he couldn't see me. Smiling helped me *sound* friendly. I knew O'Connor used the same trick. "I'm sorry, can you tell me what this is in reference to? If it's one of my previous cases I'll need time to get my files."

"It's not related to the any of your cases, ma'am," he said. "It has to do with the events at the Farouche Plantation."

*Shit. Fuck. Damn.* My heart thudded as adrenaline dumped into my system. Didn't matter that I'd known this was coming. "You mean the fire?" I asked in my best innocent and bewildered voice. "I'm not sure how I can be of any help. I'm not part of the FBI's investigation."

"Ma'am, this isn't in reference to your role as a consultant." It sounded as if his forced smile was starting to hurt his face. "I'm simply trying to clear up a bit of confusion. A couple of witnesses reported seeing a woman matching your description at the plantation during the time in question. If you'd come down to the station and give a statement concerning your whereabouts and activities for that day, we can get this whole mess settled."

"Is that so?" I kept my voice calm. I wasn't smiling anymore. No need to make *my* face ache. "All you want to do is talk to me? Clear up any confusion and get this silly mess sorted out before it gets ugly?" Right. Get me to come in and give a statement, answer a few questions—with no need for an attorney since it was all so friendly and casual-like. And hope I'd cough up conflicting or incriminating information they could later use to pressure me.

"Yes, ma'am," he replied. "I know you want nothing more than to put all this behind you."

My finger throbbed around the splinter, and I used the pain to focus my thoughts. I rolled my neck on my shoulders, felt a few vertebrae crack. "Well, Detective O'Connor. Since you're asking me to come in as opposed to showing up at my doorstep with a warrant, I'm going to assume you don't have anything resembling probable cause. That means you're a thorough investigator who's trying to shake something loose, and I respect that." With my uninjured hand I gripped the hilt of the knife, gouged its point into the cracked wood of the tabletop and twisted. "However, I think I can save us both a lot of time and trouble," I continued. "If I come down there tomorrow, I'm going to drink your terrible coffee and engage in stupid small talk. After that, I won't say a single word in reference to anything that may or may not be related to the Farouche Plantation incident. I won't give me a statement, and I won't answer any questions. Not one. And before you try and give me the saw about 'if you have nothing to hide,' please remember that I'm former law enforcement, and I know how this all works." I wrenched the knife, and a sliver of wood gave way with a sharp crack. "I don't care if I'm accused of stealing a gumdrop or of killing the president with a velociraptor, I'm going to invoke my right to remain silent because that *is* my right. I'm also going to invoke my right to not waste my time and my gas coming to your office for no good reason."

I heard him sigh. Poor guy. I'd frustrated him.

"Yes, ma'am, that is indeed your right," he said, nice and calm. "Sorry to have troubled you."

"No hard feelings," I said. "I know you'd do the same if our roles were reversed."

"Yes, ma'am. You have a good evening."

"You too, detective."

Exhaling, I disconnected. The simmering worry over the blurry photograph congealed into a thick dread that settled deep within my chest. Everything had consequences. I knew that. But damn, the timing of this one sure sucked ass.

I dropped the phone onto the table then used the tip of the knife to pry the splinter from beneath my fingernail. New pain lanced through my hand, but it soon faded to a dull ache. Too bad I couldn't excise my worry with equal ease.

Surgery accomplished, I set the knife down and scowled at the table, even though I knew it didn't deserve my ire. I'd been meaning to sand it down for ages and hadn't. Consequences.

At least I could still flip people off with that hand. Sometimes you simply had to focus on what was most important.

# Chapter 12

Despite hellacious disruptions of the flows, I managed to bring the kehza Juke through without injury. This particular demon adored pistachios, and I tossed it a five-pound bag the instant we sealed our agreement. Juke let out a screech of unmistakable delight, then expertly split shells with its claws and munched on the nuts while I explained the plan. That done, Eilahn escorted it to the woods to wait until I gave the signal. I helped get food ready and pretended this was nothing more than an ordinary backyard cookout with friends. Because, y'know, I did that sort of thing *so* often.

At five minutes before seven the security panel dinged. Bryce checked the camera. "He's at the gate. We're on."

"Excellent." I grabbed a towel to wipe my hands. "Buzz him in, please. Y'all remember to play nice, y'hear?"

Smile gone, Idris muttered something under his breath about *No Promises* and stalked out the back door. Bryce snorted.

I rolled my eyes and headed out to the front porch in time to see Pellini pull up in a silver Chevy pickup to park beside the Malibu. He climbed out then fished a twelve-pack of beer off the front seat.

"Glad you could make it," I said with a smile.

He nodded and cast his gaze around, taking in the surrounding woods as well as the mobile home situated fifty yards to the east of the house. If he saw any of the arcane protections, he didn't react to them.

"Nice place," he said, starting up the steps. "Not what I expected."

"Thanks," I said brightly, determined not to rise to any sort of bait during his visit. "It's been in the family a long time. Come on inside. I'll introduce you to a couple of friends of mine."

He followed me in and to the kitchen where I introduced him to Bryce and Idris. Bryce greeted him with a friendly smile and nice-to-meet-you, and Pellini responded in kind. Idris's greeting was only a hair shy of surly, and to everyone's relief he excused himself after the minimum length of time required to be sociable.

"Jill will be over in a few minutes," I told Pellini then grabbed a bowl of chips and pushed it into his hands. "Can you take these out to the table on the back porch? It's a nice evening. We might as well enjoy it."

He seemed glad for something to do, and I followed him out with a vegetable tray, plates and napkins. I gestured toward the tree line. "Zack and Ryan built a kickass obstacle course through the woods a few months back. Feel free to indulge in ludicrous exercise if the mood strikes."

"Ain't happenin'," Pellini said with a snort. "But on the off chance I head that way, feel free to knock some sense into me."

Jill wandered over with Steeev, and Pellini relaxed more with the presence of another familiar face. After Jill introduced him to Steeev she started a light chat about a silly case they'd both recently worked. With devious finesse a dirty politician would envy, she skillfully dodged any opportunity for Pellini to pose questions about Steeev. Curiosity flickered in his eyes, but he remained polite and on topic.

Bryce handed Pellini a beer then excused himself to go tend the grill. Idris stalked farther out into the backyard and onto the nexus. Even though the entire event was a setup to evaluate Pellini, everyone appeared to be having a good time. Apart from Idris, of course. If Pellini suspected anything, he didn't show it. A wave of guilt struck me at the subterfuge, but we were in too deep for second thoughts. A few minutes later Bryce returned to the table with a platter of grilled sausage, chicken, hamburgers, corn, potatoes and, apparently, anything else grillable he'd found in the kitchen.

I piled sausage, chicken, and corn onto my plate, while Pellini built a hamburger. Halfway through my chicken I felt power stir on the nexus—a buzzing vibration in my gut and head. I shot a quick glance toward Idris to confirm him as the source. Pellini put his hamburger down, a frown tugging at his mouth. He definitely sensed it. I was right about that much at least. Steeev touched Jill's arm in a prearranged "time to skedaddle" signal. Jill heaved up from her chair and gave everyone a bright smile as she patted her tummy.

"Sorry to bail, y'all, but the bean says she's had enough," Jill announced to my relief. Best she wasn't around if things got *interesting*.

A chorus of "goodnight" arose, and Steeev escorted her back to the mobile home. The instant the door closed behind her the nexus flared. I held my breath as a filament of sapphire energy shot toward Pellini's feet with the speed of a coachwhip snake. Pellini jolted out of his chair with a choked cry of alarm. He stumbled back a step as it struck him then, plain as day, he kick-pushed the potency away.

"What the hell's going on?" he demanded, breathing hard. Idris withdrew the filament, but stood tense and watchful, still assessing. Bryce continued to calmly eat his mashed potatoes but monitored, ready for damn near anything.

"I'm sorry," I said as I got to my feet. "I had to be sure of what I saw at the plantation."

Confusion clouded Pellini's face. "What? What did you see?"

I narrowed my eyes. "You physically manipulated potency."

"I did?" He paused, frowned. "You mean by the gazebo?"

"Yes! You deflected it. And again just now. How the hell do you know how to do that?"

To my surprise his ears turned red with embarrassment. "It's, um, part of what I've wanted to talk to you about for the past few weeks."

Few weeks? *Shit.* Amber Palatino Gavin's body had been found a few weeks ago. "The murder scene at the eighteen wheeler. You asked me out for a beer."

"Yeah." He nodded once, stiff and uncomfortable. "That scene was bad."

"Yes, it was." I sat and hoped he would as well. "I never pegged you for someone who could see the arcane." Idris stepped onto the porch and took up a position behind Pellini, glowering and with his arms folded over his chest.

Pellini glanced at Idris then sat heavily. "The arcane," he said, as though trying out a new word. "Whatever it is, I don't want to see it twenty-four-seven."

"How long have you been able to see the arcane?" I asked. Casual. Friendly.

He shrugged. "As long as I can remember. Used to be I could choose to see it, but not anymore. It's always there."

Perpetual othersight, like in the demon realm. On Earth I had to consciously switch to othersight. Or did I? Was that *true* anymore? I'd spent so much time in the demon realm I felt blind without othersight, so always had it engaged. Experimenting, I tried to *not* see the potency flows around us. And tried again. Though the flows appeared faded without othersight, they were still easily perceptible.

"So, why did you want to talk to me?" I asked, puzzled.

"Because I can't shut it out anymore," he said, desperation thickening his voice. "Not for the past couple of years. And then that murder . . . I *needed* to shut it out, but I couldn't."

I shook my head. "I still don't get why you thought I'd be of any help."

One side of his mouth twitched. "It was all the little marks you left on your door or your desk," he said. "I realized you could sense it, too."

Little marks. Wards. Aversions to deter coworkers from raiding my chocolate drawer. An alarm on the door to warn me if anyone went into my office. In a million billion years, I never would've imagined that Pellini, of all people, could see them.

"Why is everything stronger now?" he asked. "Why can't I shut it out?"

"A lot of shit is happening," I said remaining vague for the moment. "How long have you been able to move potency?"

Pellini exhaled. "Since my senior year in high school."

"What happened then? Did someone start teaching you?"

He cleared his throat. "Never talked to anyone about this stuff before," he confessed, then added, "I mean, no *people*."

Idris and I both tensed. "What non-people have you talked to about this?" I asked, doing my best to remain outwardly composed.

Pellini licked his lips before speaking. "Shit. I had an imaginary friend when I was little." A flush darkened his face. "I called him . . ." He hesitated then took a deep breath and plunged on. "I called him Mr. Sparkly because that's what he looked like. For as long as I can remember, until I was in second grade, he'd find me when I was in the sandpit in my backyard and take me away."

"Wait. Away?" I asked. "Where to?" Maybe Mr. Sparkly was just an ordinary creeper?

He chewed his lower lip. "The place I saw him wasn't like Earth," he said. "It was like that." To my shock he gestured toward the nexus. "Energy and colors and light."

So much for my Ordinary Creeper theory. Idris remained perfectly still, but the intensity of his gaze could have drilled a hole through Pellini's head.

"And it was always in your backyard?" I asked, suspicion forming as he nodded. I was willing to bet Fuzzykins' non-existent tail that Pellini's sandpit had contained a valve. "Can you describe this Mr. Sparkly?"

Pellini's eyes went distant in memory. "Like a man made out of a billion pieces of crystal. Long hair. Purple eyes."

Shit. Fuck. Son of a bitch. Purple eyes. *Violet* eyes. Kadir fit the description of Mr. Sparkly right down to the Creepy part. Hostility rolled off Idris. Holy shit, was I ever glad I had the kehza standing by as physical backup in case the situation went tits up. Not that I was sure it could get much more screwy after Pellini's revelation of a lifelong association with the shrewdest of the Mraztur.

I took a few seconds to keep my composure intact. "What happened to Mr. Sparkly?"

Pellini shrugged. "He stopped showing up to take me away the summer after I turned seven. The last few times didn't last very long, and everything was more, um, transparent, I guess." He frowned. "He said it was harder for him to reach me, but I didn't understand why. He didn't come back for ages."

I itched to ask Pellini *when* Kadir returned and to where, but first we needed to get him assessed so that we knew what we were up against. "And you're hoping I can do what?" I asked. Under the table I sent a quick text asking Eilahn to bring the kehza out. "Explain all this? Partner up with you? Teach you more?"

"Partner up? No. No!" He shook his head. "I don't understand what's happening. Why can't I stop *seeing* and *feeling*?" He gave me a look full of pleading. "I just want everything to get back to normal where I can shut it off."

A rustling of leaves was the only warning before the kehza bounded across the lawn toward Pellini with great sweeps of its wings.

"Shit!" He jerked to his feet, eyes locked on the creature headed straight for him. The kehza's claws dug furrows in the grass as it stopped at the base of the steps. Growl-hissing, it leaped to the porch, broad nostrils flaring as it took in Pellini's scent.

Pellini stood motionless, eyes wide as dinner plates. He didn't appear scared though.

"It needs to touch you," I told him. "That's all."

The kehza moved closer, but to my shock Pellini stepped forward to rub the edge of its wing—the equivalent of scratching a dog behind the ears.

"*Chu,*" he murmured, doubling my shock. "Chu" was a *demon* greeting.

"Needs to touch me?" Pellini said without taking his eyes from the kehza. "Why?"

I stared at the kehza and then at Pellini. A kid meeting up with Kadir in interdimensional space was one thing. Familiarity with physical demons took it to a new level. And this was *Pellini!* Asshole. Rude and obnoxious. Ordinary. "How the hell do you know how to interact with demons?"

"Demons?" He glanced at me with a frown even as the demon placed its clawed hand on his forearm. "You mean—" He nodded toward the kehza.

"Yes, creatures like this one," I began, but Idris had reached his limit. He took a step forward, hands clenched at his sides.

"Step away from the kehza and sit down," he ordered, voice harsh.

Pellini pivoted to face Idris, shoulders tensing at the overt hostility. Though Idris didn't appear to be armed, Pellini no doubt sensed he had the potential to be dangerous. He lifted his hand from the kehza and took a slow step back. I signaled to the demon, and it moved away from Pellini to crouch by my side.

"*Dahnk*," it said to me, settling its wings close on its back.

I murmured acknowledgment, weirdly relieved. "Dahnk" meant "not" in demon. In other words, Pellini was *not* a summoner, and Idris's glower confirmed he'd heard the verdict. I pulled a hunk of sausage off the platter and offered it to the kehza with a murmur of thanks. It growled and bounded to the porch rail with its prize.

"Maybe I should go," Pellini said, wary.

"I'm sorry about the sudden hostility," I said and wished Idris would crank it down a few fucking notches. "But you come out of the blue and do—" I waggled my hands in an over-the-top copy of how he'd batted the potency away. "I've been training a decade and can't do anything like that. You've raised a whole lot of questions that we *need* answers to."

For all his faults, Pellini wasn't stupid. He rubbed at his brow in apparent frustration but sat down. "I bet I have way more questions than y'all do," he said. "But as to how the hell I know about demons, Mr. Sparkly came back when I was seventeen, and right after that a few demons began to visit regularly. Kuktok and Sehkeril mostly, but there were a couple of others, too."

Sehkeril. One of Kadir's reyza. That clinched it. "Whose side are you on?"

For the first time, Pellini looked truly flummoxed. "Side?"

"Your Mr. Sparkly is—" I was reluctant to say "enemy" because I didn't think that was a correct definition of Kadir's role in all of this crap, "—not an ally of ours. And there are other arcane practitioners who will do, and have done, horrific things to further their cause. The murder victim in the eighteen wheeler? That's the level of stakes we're dealing with."

"I don't know anything about 'sides,'" he said. "There's nothing going on with me and the demons and Mr. Sparkly now. He cut me off twenty years ago." Anger flashed across his face combined with a shimmer of loss. "Nothing," he repeated, voice strained.

"Why did he cut you off?" I asked. "What happened?"

Pellini spread his hands. "Dunno," he said. "After he returned, every third full moon he'd take me to the between-space. This went on for seven years, but that last day he was late, and when he showed up I could hardly see him. He didn't explain, just reached out and—" He swallowed and rubbed the center of his chest. "I don't know what he did, but it felt as if he ripped my heart out." His voice dropped, turned hollow. "He said, 'hide,' then vanished. After that, everything fell apart."

Idris marched off the porch and back onto the nexus. I didn't know what he was up to now, but at least he wasn't glaring holes through Pellini anymore. I suspected Kadir had extracted an arcane implant from Pellini when he told him to hide. Whatever the purpose of the implant, I could only suppose that it would have drawn unwanted attention to Pellini.

"Who were you hiding from?" I asked.

"No idea," he said. "He never told me about enemies."

My brow furrowed. "And you haven't seen him for twenty years?"

"That's right. I kept to myself. He told me to hide, and who the hell would I talk to about that shit anyway?" He paused. "Then you came along with your little marks."

"Why didn't you say anything?"

He took a deep breath. "I didn't know what I was hiding from. Or who." He picked at a pulled thread on his trousers. "But then shit got intense and, well, here I am."

I remained silent while I considered everything. Why hide? What happened with Kadir twenty years ago? "You never asked Mr. Sparkly for his real name?"

"Of course I did," Pellini replied. "He told me names have power and it was dangerous for me to know it." He shrugged. "I was a kid. Not knowing his real name made the whole thing even cooler."

I sat back and regarded him. It was, of course, possible this was all an elaborate scheme to plant him as a mole. But, if that was the case, it made no sense to freak us out by mentioning Kadir. Besides, I'd known Pellini for years. If he was a mole, he'd been put in place long before I finished my training as a summoner. Kadir had been grooming Pellini for a reason, but what? Regardless, Katashi and company would be more than happy to scoop him up and use him against us.

Pellini grabbed his beer and took a long swig. "Who the hell *are* y'all? And what kind of fucked up business ends up with a ritual rape and murder?"

"Idris and I are both summoners," I said. "What that means is that we have the ability to open a portal between this world and the one where the demons and Mr. Sparkly and others like him reside." My gaze went to Idris, and I lowered my voice. "His last name is Palatino."

Comprehension dawned on Pellini's face. "I'm not usually so slow on the uptake," he muttered. "There aren't that many guys named Idris hanging around. The murder victim was his sister, and you were looking for him because he'd gone missing." He eyed me. "What was the deal with that?"

"He's talented and powerful, and the faction we're trying to stop kidnapped him because of that." I took a deep breath. "The ritual murder of his sister was to enforce his cooperation and set an arcane trap for me."

"Fuck," Pellini breathed. "And he thinks I might be an enemy. No wonder he looks like he wants to skin me."

"Even if you're not an enemy," I said, choosing my words with care, "you're a potential threat. You have unusual skills, and you don't know what the hell's going on."

Pellini threw his hands up in frustration. "I can't *do* shit. Sure, you can't move the energy the same way, but so what? Fat lot of good it does me. And maybe it's best I don't know who's who in whatever this war is. I didn't ask for any of it."

"I stand corrected," I snapped. "You're a potential threat *and* a danger to yourself and others because you're un-trained, and you have no fucking clue. This *war* is heating up and isn't going away."

Anger flashed across his face, but before he could retort he jerked back in his chair as if grabbed by an unseen hand. His eyes went wide, and his face blanched paper-white.

*He's having a coronary!* I barely had time to form the thought before the same force grabbed me and pressed me down in my seat like a lump of iron above a giant magnet. *An attack?* On the other side of the table Bryce gripped the arms of his chair, breath hissing through his teeth. Idris stood on the nexus, unaffected.

Fury burned away my shock. *Idris* was doing this to us. It had to be an unplanned assessment of Pellini. I seethed as I forced myself to breathe through the pressure. He could've at least given Bryce and me some goddamn warning. Or, better yet, found a means that didn't *suck* quite so hard. As arduous as it was for me, it was exponentially worse for Pellini since the ritual targeted him. Guilt swam through me as panic and agony contorted his face. No matter the intent for inviting him to my house, he was a guest. This was *so not* how we did shit in the south. And what if this gave him a heart attack for real? *Oh, so sorry we KILLED you.*

The pressure eased, only to be replaced by the unnerving sensation of being naked while fully clothed. Comprehension clicked into place. The naked sensation was the complete lack of the arcane. Idris had pulled it all away from Pellini in order to make a true evaluation of him. Bryce and I had the crappy luck to be caught in the area of effect. Didn't change my level of pissed-off, but at least I knew what was happening.

It stopped as quickly as it had begun. Like a stretched rubber band returning to normal, the arcane snapped back into place. From the roof Eilahn let out a shriek of rage, dropped to land in a crouch by the porch then bounded to me, concern twisting her features.

"I'm okay," I told her as soon as I caught my breath, then turned to where Pellini gasped like a stranded fish. "I'm sorry," I said with deep chagrin. "I swear I didn't know that was going to happen. Are you all right?"

He lifted a trembling hand to wipe sweat from his face, mouth pressed tight as if about to vomit. I subtly scooched my chair back a few inches. Just in case.

From the nexus, Idris cursed as he closed down his ritual, obviously not at all happy with whatever he'd learned. I forced down my residual anger at his methods. One way or another, we needed to know what Pellini's deal was. The stakes were way too high to have an unknown player on the field, even if he insisted he wasn't playing the game.

Bryce staggered to his feet and peered at Pellini with concern. "Breeeeathe," he told him, resting a hand on his shoulder. Pellini inhaled noisily then blew out hard, but his next breath was more controlled. The grey cast left his face, and a hint of normal color crept in.

After a moment he lifted his head with obvious effort. "God damn," he croaked.

"I'm sorry," I repeated. "I didn't know he was going to do that."

Pellini managed to straighten. "Why . . . ?"

Idris bounded up the stairs. "Bryce, watch him," he ordered with a jerk of his head toward Pellini. "Kara, with me." He beckoned imperiously and moved to the far end of the porch.

Pellini scowled and tried to stand, but Bryce touched his

arm and gave a slight head shake. "Probably best if you sit until you get your color back," he said, tone mild. Pellini's scowl deepened, but he settled back in the chair. Though he'd been around Bryce for less than an hour, he had enough cop-sense to recognize him as a man of action with skills honed by ugly experience.

I was dying to tell Idris what he could do with his imperious beckoning but since I really did want to know what he'd discovered I went ahead and followed him.

"I hope that stunt was worth it," I said with a black scowl, though I kept my voice low.

"He's marked by Kadir," Idris replied matching my scowl and volume. "Head to foot. Inside and outside. Even with all potency stripped, he reeks of Kadir's resonance." Suspicion darkened his eyes. "I don't know *what* he is, but I know he absolutely can't be trusted."

The declaration put my back up. "I agree that we don't know what he is, arcanely," I said, "But the not trusting him part doesn't necessarily follow. He said 'Mr. Sparkly' came to him in his backyard, which leads me to believe it contains a valve."

"And I intend to check that out," Idris said. "However, right now this dude needs to be locked down."

I counted to five in my head. "Yes, he's a loose cannon and a *potential* threat," I said. "He can stay here until we know more or can train him."

Outrage flashed across Idris's face. "*Train him?* That's like loading a gun and passing it to the enemy!" He flicked his hand out as if brushing my comment aside. "You don't know that he's untrained." He sneered. "You're taking his *word* for it."

My hand itched to smack the sneer off his face. "I've known the guy for a long time," I countered hotly. "If he's a mole he's a damn good one. But, hey," I continued, loading my voice with sarcasm, "maybe we should kill him to be on the safe side."

"I didn't say anything about killing him," he shot back. "But I *do* say lock him down in the demon realm until he's cleared. Neither of us knows what Kadir could pull off through him—even if he's as innocent as he claims to be."

"Right, because locking a potential threat down in the

demon realm worked out so damn well when you and Mzatal did that to *me.*" Or had he forgotten that they had, in fact, fucking kidnapped me? *And* that it nearly ended in disaster when I escaped? "Sure, send him to the demon realm where he can be closer to Kadir. Great idea!"

A vein pulsed near his temple. "Yes, closer to Kadir, but away from people and places on Earth!" Tension held his shoulders stiff as he took a step toward me. "You don't seem to get it. Kadir set him up to use him *here.*"

Lifting my chin, I held my ground and matched his anger with my own. "And Rhyzkahl set me up to use *me,*" I replied in a snarl. "You remember how close Mzatal came to killing me because of that?"

"I remember," he said. "I also remember that, against all odds, he rescued you after he spared your life and you ran to Rhyzkahl." His eyes went stone cold. "If he hadn't pulled you from that ritual, the Mraztur would have turned you into Rowan, and everything would be fucked."

I could only stare at him, gut punched by shock. "You . . . you think it would've been wiser for him to *kill* me?" I managed to reply, literally trembling. "You who were under the influence of the Mraztur for *months?*"

"I've been cleared," he snapped. "And I didn't say he should've killed you. I just want you to get what we're dealing with and the potential damage that could come from the wrong decision."

"I do get it, Idris," and I managed to not add *you condescending fuck* to that. "Trust me, every time I look in the mirror and see the scars, I get it. But even so, I think it's really shortsighted to lock up everyone we don't understand or who might pose a threat. If you want to make more enemies, that's the way to do it!"

"This is *not* simply someone we don't understand!" He flung his arm in a harsh gesture toward Pellini. "Kadir has imprinted him. *Kadir.* One of the goddamn Mraztur."

My eyes felt hot and gritty. "Your solution is to lock him down indefinitely all because he played in the wrong goddamn patch of sand when he was a kid."

"Until he's cleared," Idris corrected, but I saw in his eyes that he knew it might not be possible to clear Kadir's influence from Pellini—and wasn't swayed by it. "And *if* his sandbox story is true," he went on, "then no, it's not his fault, and that sucks, but we can't let a time bomb loose out of pity."

"It's not pity, it's compassion," I snapped. *Learn it*, asshole, I added silently. "*Maybe* we can gain an ally instead of guaranteeing we end up with an enemy."

Bryce stalked over and pierced us both with a glare. "Pellini has more fucking sense than both of you put together," he said, voice scathing.

"Excuse me?" I asked then realized with chagrin that Idris and I hadn't kept our voices low. *Crap. Pellini heard all of that.*

"He gets that he's between a rock and a hard place." Bryce's glare didn't let up one bit. "He also gets that the entire situation is dangerous and *he's* a danger." He snorted. "He was smart enough to figure we weren't going to let him leave. All he's worried about is his dog alone at his house. You two hot shots need to come to a compromise between damnation and 'Fly! Be free!'"

Fuck. It was a sad day when Pellini was the reasonable one. Idris looked similarly chastened by the dressing down.

"Maybe . . . locked down here, unless he's with one of us?" I offered.

Idris visibly fought down his resistance to the elimination of the demon realm option, and I was pretty sure he pygahed. Twice. Maybe three times. "Locked down here?" he finally said. "How?"

"He moves in here," I suggested and prayed that Idris's receptive mood would continue. "If possible he takes a leave of absence from work, and we would reassess as needed."

What followed then were negotiations that rivaled the Louisiana Purchase. With Bryce's not-always-gentle guidance we managed to reach a compromise that kept Pellini from being summarily deported to the demon realm while also keeping him from roaming free. Idris wasn't happy with it, and I hated screwing Pellini over like this, but it was the best possible compromise in a horrible situation.

"I'm sorry it has to be this way," I said to Pellini after everything was decided. "Is there anything you need right now?"

"Another hamburger," Pellini grumbled. "The demon ate mine."

# Chapter 13

After Pellini ate a replacement hamburger, Bryce accompanied him to his house to pick up his dog and a few days worth of clothing and sundries. An hour later they returned with Sammy, a goofy chocolate labrador retriever with a dangerously exuberant tail. Though uncertain at first with all the new smells, it only took a few minutes for Sammy to decide that having the run of ten acres—full of wildlife to bark at—was the absolute Best Thing Ever.

Fuzzykins was less keen about the presence of a DOG in her demesne, and wasted no time establishing the pecking order. The silly dog wanted nothing more than to be best buddies with the cat and made many enthusiastic overtures of unconditional friendship. It took a muzzle covered in bloody scratches for him to accept the futility of his efforts. Poor guy.

Bryce relinquished the guestroom to Pellini and took over the sofa, more to monitor Pellini's movements than to be nice. Pellini had the run of the property, but surveillance cameras, the perimeter fence, and Bryce's eagle-eyes kept him under polite house arrest. I gave Pellini the basic tour, set out fresh towels for him, then finally fell into bed long after midnight. At least I didn't need to set an alarm for the morning.

Once asleep, I drifted in and out of a weird dream involving giant mosquitoes with human faces auditioning for a talent show. The bizarre scene faded, only to sharpen into a vivid and strange landscape of shifting color and light. Fine threads of lightning coruscated through clouds of energy accompanied by a soft, pleasant crackle. I floated among the clouds, passing through and between them, delighted when I found myself able to choose my direction at will.

"Kara Gillian."

My name slid through me—felt, not heard—and lured me to its source. I reached up to touch my ears but, where my arm should have been, there was nothing but a swirl in the clouds. *Gah! Where's my body?* Even as the panic began, I coalesced into a semitransparent shimmery form as though I'd willed it all into existence. I turned my hands over, flexed my glittering fingers. *Too cool.*

"Kara Gillian." The call came again. Closer this time and familiar. I spun toward it and saw Kadir. *Sparkly* Kadir, composed of a billion twinkling crystals like perfect grains of sand, colorless except for the striking violet of his eyes. Behind his left shoulder drifted a man, semitransparent and shimmery like me, and an equally shimmery Paul knelt close to Kadir's right leg.

This was some dream.

"Wow, Paul," I said. "You look really good."

Kadir laid his hand on Paul's head. "Kara Gillian."

The resonance of my name drew me more into myself. "Yo, Kadir. 'Sup?" I laughed and threw a mock gang sign. "Weird having you in my dream."

Kadir drifted closer. "*Wake up.*"

The command echoed through every fiber of my being. The surreal landscape leaped into greater clarity. In shock, I recognized the shimmery man behind Kadir as a much more trim Pellini. Everything felt utterly real—not like a lucid dream anymore. Sonofabitch. Kadir had called me into Pellini's out-of-body wonderland.

Pellini gestured toward Kadir. "Mr. Sparkly."

"I see that," I said, cautious and alert now. *How much time has Pellini already spent with Kadir tonight?* "What's going on?"

"Chaos," Kadir said, and lightning flickered through the colored energy clouds around us. "My world disintegrates."

"So I've heard," I said. "We're doing what we can on the Earth end, but your friend Katashi is hell-bent on screwing things up."

"I am friend to none," he said. "Isumo Katashi is a necessary component, though he neglects symmetry for the sake of haste. This must be corrected." He opened his hand and set a mass of wriggling potency strands spinning in the space between us like a glob of entangled worms. A discordant buzz rattled my teeth as if I'd had twenty cups of coffee and was poised to vibrate apart. Kadir passed his hand over the strands, transformed the raw potency into a radiant electric blue sigil. It spun in perfect balance and the buzz lifted to a clear tone. With another pass of his hand Kadir warped it, and it lurched around its axis.

"Still functional," he said, "but asymmetry engenders instability." Kadir blew on it, and the sigil shattered with a sound like a hundred fingernails screeching across a blackboard. His violet eyes met mine. "Asymmetry engenders instability. It must be corrected."

Instability. *Valves.*

"Let me get this straight," I said, eyes narrowing. "You don't have a problem with what Katashi's doing with the valves, only with *how* he's doing it. He's in too much of a hurry to do it your way." I gave him a sour look. "In other words, you want *me* to help *you* by improving on Katashi's method."

"Yes," he said. "By symmetrizing the valves."

I laughed outright. "Why the hell would I do that?"

"Because each symmetrized valve impedes his progress and stabilizes the system." He paused and lowered his head, eyes on me. "This is a desirable outcome for you."

Slowing down Katashi might buy us time to find a way to stop him for good. *If* Kadir was telling the truth. I glanced to shimmery Pellini to check his reaction to all of this, but he offered me a helpless shrug. He probably didn't know enough about the dynamics to contribute to either side.

Kadir continued as I mulled it over. "If you do no more than patch valves as they destabilize, Isumo Katashi *will* succeed—at enormous peril of catastrophic implosions on Earth."

Fuck.

I hated to agree with anything that had the potential to advance the Mraztur's cause. But Kadir had unparalleled skill with potency flows and the valves, and had an obsessive interest in stability. What he proposed made sense in a mutually beneficial way, though the benefit for us was short term.

Kadir's gaze intensified. "He will risk catastrophe with no qualms. Will you?"

"You already know the answer to that," I said with a scowl.

"I do," he said. "In this, you are not foolish." He stroked Paul's head as though he were a dog at his side, a gesture that left me chilled and unsettled.

"Paul," I said, "are you all right?"

He lifted his gaze to Kadir. "You may speak," the lord told him.

*Ugh!*

Paul leaned against Kadir's leg and brought his eyes to mine. "I'm good," he said. "Not dying anymore."

My concern spiked higher at the submissive move. "Not dying is good, unless the alternative is worse." I drifted closer. "Paul, you need to give me some kind of reassurance."

"No," Kadir said and stroked Paul's head again. "He does not. All that is required is that you learn to symmetrize a valve."

Paul rested his head against Kadir's thigh and gave me a smile, but didn't speak again.

Impotent rage settled into my gut. Kadir had saved Paul's life, but at what cost? I didn't want to think of what he'd done to Paul to force such subservience. "Paul, is there anything you want me to tell Bryce?"

Kadir sparkled brighter then began to disintegrate, even as Paul grew fully transparent. "You may tell Bryce Taggart that this one thrives."

"Wait!" I called out. "How am I supposed to learn to symmetrize a valve?" Kadir worked potency in a disturbing way, unlike any other lord or arcane practitioner I'd ever encountered. No way could I figure it out on my own.

Pellini, still shimmery, spoke up. "It's too late. He won't stop now."

An instant later I slammed into my body as if I'd dropped from a height. Heart pounding, I sucked in a breath. My limbs felt heavy and awkward, but the sensation passed before I could panic. *I need to go find Pellini!* No sooner had the thought formed than sleep overtook me again.

I woke to an urgent knock on my door and weak sunlight filtering through my curtains.

"Kara," Bryce called from the hallway. "We have a situation."

I rolled out of bed and yanked open the door. "What's wrong?"

"Pellini got past me while I was in the bathroom," he said. "He's on the nexus, and Idris just went out to confront him." With that, he strode off toward the back of the house. I started to follow then double-checked what I was wearing. A tank top and undies. No bra. I grabbed a pair of running shorts and tugged them on as I hurried after Bryce, but I couldn't shake the feeling I'd forgotten something important. Not the bra. Something else.

No time to stop and rack my brain. With Pellini on the nexus and an already suspicious Idris on the way there, bloodshed would soon follow. I flew out the back door, across the porch and down the steps to see Pellini at the center of the nexus, his back to the house. Idris prowled around the edge of the concrete slab like a predator seeking a way to reach its prey.

"Pellini!" Idris yelled. "Come out of there now!"

"What happened?" I asked as I slid to a stop on the dewy grass beside Idris. Déjà vu. I'd stood in this same spot a few days ago when Szerain commandeered the nexus. "What did he do?"

Idris spun toward me, face flushed in anger. "This!" He thrust his hand toward Pellini and struck a veil of transparent potency. Iridescent waves rippled away from the point of impact. "I can't get through. I've never seen anything like it."

I suppressed a groan. "Pellini, what are you doing?" I called out.

Pellini ignored us and turned in a slow circle at the center. Bryce descended the steps, gun in hand, and watched everything carefully.

Idris glared at me. "Happy now?" Once again he tried to penetrate the obstructing veil, this time with a punch so hard and fast I wondered if he'd backed it with potency. Pretty incredible feat if he had. The veil shimmered dark purple and green, but remained intact. He made an inarticulate sound deep in his throat. "We should've locked him down!"

"I don't need an I-told-you-so right now, okay?" I hated that he might have been right. "Give it a minute. He hasn't hurt anything."

Pellini continued to turn, waving his hands in front of him as if playing invisible bongo drums in slow motion. Where his hands passed, tangled strands of glowing chartreuse potency coalesced in the air. A moment later a ring of the weird-yet-familiar potency floated around him.

Idris let out a strangled cry of frustration. "What is *that?*"

"I've seen it before," I said. "When I helped stabilize Paul in the demon realm." No way was I going to mention Kadir to the already livid Idris. Not yet. My gaze lingered on the strands of potency. I'd seen it elsewhere too, hadn't I? Once again, the feeling I'd forgotten something important passed through me.

Pellini cupped a section of the ring between his hands, then withdrew them to reveal a strange floating sigil.

Idris went still, face a portrait of shock. "No way."

I stared at Pellini, mouth open. "He . . . created a floater." Neither Idris nor I could trace floaters on Earth. That required mastery of all eleven rings of the shikvihr. Moreover, Pellini hadn't traced the sigil—he'd created it all at once. Before either of us could process that bit of information, Pellini transformed the ring into eleven vibrant chartreuse and violet sigils.

"*Kadir*," Idris said through clenched teeth. He might not

have recognized the chaotic raw potency, but there was no mistaking the unique Kadir-style sigils. "Bryce, can you shoot him?"

"Hey!" I said. "No one's shooting anyone!"

Idris leveled a glower at me. "So, the dude imprinted by Kadir—the one who claims to know nothing of the arcane—is out on your nexus, fulfilling Kadir's agenda. And you're okay with that?"

"Will you please stop being an asshole for a few god-damn minutes?" I gestured toward Pellini and the ring of sigils he'd set spinning around him. "I have a way to stop him if I have to. It worked on Szerain, it'll work on Pellini." As the words left my mouth, the important thing I'd forgot-ten slammed into me with crystalline clarity. *Kadir and Pel-lini in interdimensional space.* I sucked in a breath. "I know what he created. It's a way to teach us how to symmetrize the valves."

"How do you know?" Idris asked with outright disbelief. "And why for chrissake would we want to do that?"

"I saw Kadir last night," I said with measured calm. "He drew me into a non-physical place between worlds, like Pel-lini described." I forged on despite the increasing *What the fuck?* on Idris's face. "He said the demon realm is in chaos, and Katashi moves too fast with the work he does, and that we needed to learn how to symmetrize the valves."

Idris eyed me warily. "You get that your explanation doesn't put me at ease, right?"

I rubbed my eyes. "I can't believe I'm trying to do this without coffee."

"Okay," Pellini said. He scrutinized the ring of sigils and gave a satisfied nod. "Okay." He stepped carefully between two sigils and made his way toward us. Bryce holstered his gun but didn't relax one bit.

"When did you learn how to do that?" I asked Pellini, pointing at the circle of sigils.

He stepped off the nexus and glanced back. "Just now, I guess."

"I don't understand," I said with gross understatement. "How did you know what to do?"

"Mister, um, I mean, Kadir said I'd know." He shrugged. "It's for you and Idris."

Without warning, Idris grabbed the front of Pellini's shirt with both hands to yank him away from the nexus. My gut clenched as potency shimmered on Idris, but I'd underestimated Pellini. The surly detective was overweight and out of shape, but he knew his training. In quick, reflexive movements, Pellini trapped Idris's hands against his chest, twisted, swept his leg, and shoved him facedown on the grass with his right arm up and held in a wrist lock.

"Fucking snot-nosed know-it-all punk," Pellini growled. "Do *not* lay hands on me unless it's a Heimlich or CPR." He released Idris and stepped back.

Idris rolled away and sat up, features twisted in anger and humiliation. "Won't happen. I wouldn't be able to get my arms around you to do the Heimlich."

Hurt flashed across Pellini's face before he buried it under a scowl. "That shit won't last long." He jerked his head toward the sigils. "Make the most of it." With that, he stomped away toward the woods. "Sammy!"

Bryce offered Idris a hand up. "I hope you know you brought that on yourself," he said to Idris—to my enormous relief because that meant *I* didn't have to say it.

Idris took Bryce's hand and stood. He muttered a couple of words that could have been either fuck you or thank you, then marched toward the ring of glowing sigils. Off to my right, Pellini disappeared down the trail that led to the start of the obstacle course, his dog cavorting around him.

Bryce pursed his lips. "Need me to follow him?"

"No, it's cool. He just needs some space," I said. "Can you hold down the fort? I need to take care of this nexus thing."

"I'm on it."

I turned to the nexus in time to see Idris attempt to disrupt the circle of sigils. "Hey!" I called out. "Hold on. Who put you in command here?"

The ring remained unaltered despite his efforts. He cursed and dropped his hands. "*Someone* has to deal with this crap."

"Not by destroying it before we check it out!" I moved forward and examined the slowly spinning ring of sigils. Though most of the sigils weren't familiar, to my delight I understood the whole of it. "It's a simulator," I said. "It's what we can use to learn how to symmetrize a valve without screwing up a real valve or blowing ourselves up."

"And you know this because *Kadir* told you." Idris made no attempt to hide the scorn in his voice.

I scowled. "Kadir said I need to learn how to symmetrize a valve, Pellini said this was for us, and that sigil," I pointed to three interlocked triangles, "is like one Mzatal always includes in his training patterns, only Kadir-style."

Idris folded his arms, face set in a frown. "Maybe it is a simulator, but what else? I don't intend to get influenced by Kadir."

"It's simple then," I said. "Don't use it." Part of me knew he had a point, but I did, too, and I was completely *over* his bullshit.

Without another word, I stepped through the gap between two sigils and onto the center of the nexus. At least that's where I thought I'd stepped. My heart pounded as the world faded to endless, silent grey. If it had been like this for Pellini, it was no wonder he hadn't answered us. Shivering, I gulped down my unease. The ominous feeling that Kadir stood right behind me was so strong I glanced over my shoulder to confirm he wasn't there. Marginally reassured, I watched in fascination as a replica of a standard valve, much like the one by my pond, appeared at my feet.

An ice-cold electric charge ran up and down my back, and understanding of the Earthside structure of a valve poured into my mind. Potency twisted along the valve boundary. Aspects that appeared flawless to my untrained senses resolved into subtle irregularities, like hair escaping a braid.

"Asymmetry," I murmured, ridiculously pleased that I could see it. I followed my Kadir-enhanced intuition to smooth out the flaws and, after what felt like half an hour of work, the valve emitted a flash of arcane blue light then settled into pulsing shimmery blue-green.

I did a fist pump and examined my work. Whereas Kadir's barricade seal inhibited the effectiveness of a valve or node, his symmetrization technique enhanced it, like clearing roots from a drain.

Damn, I had a cool job. *Now if only it could pay the bills.* But hey, couldn't have everything.

The grey, the valve, and all traces of Pellini's circle of sigils vanished, and I stood in morning sunlight on the nexus.

Idris stared at me. "How did you unravel it so fast? I couldn't touch it, but you did it in two seconds."

Well, *that* was interesting. However Kadir had rigged the training, it seemed to be outside the parameters of Earth time. "I learned what there was to learn," I said with a shrug. "I know how to symmetrize a valve now, and I'm not tainted by Kadir either." I hoped. Ignoring Idris's black look, I headed toward the house. "I'll put on the coffee," I called over my shoulder. "You can cook the bacon and eggs while I take care of the pond valve." I wasn't going to hold my breath for breakfast, but it felt good to say it.

Bryce angled my way and met me on the porch. "That didn't take long."

"Yeah, Kadir is slick." I looked sharply at him. "Almost forgot to tell you. I saw Paul last night."

His eyes widened in surprise. "How? Where?"

I briefed him on the circumstances. "He looked good," I said, leaving out the whole weird kneeling thing. "Paul said he's good and not dying anymore. Kadir said to tell you that Paul is thriving."

Bryce exhaled in relief as we entered the kitchen. "It's more information than I had before. Thanks." But then he peered at me. "What aren't you saying?"

I scowled. "You know, there are times it sucks how perceptive you are." I busied myself with the coffeemaker in an attempt to come up with a tame way to say it. No luck. "Paul was kneeling at Kadir's side while Kadir petted his head like a dog. And he gave Paul *permission* to speak." I winced. "Paul didn't seem to object."

A muscle in Bryce's jaw twitched. "Goddammit," he said,

and I knew he had at least as many horrible scenarios playing out in his mind as I did. "I need to see him."

"We'll find a way for that to happen," I said. "Either in that weird between-the-worlds zone or face-to-face." A glance out the window revealed Idris still in the center of the nexus. "I need to check on Pellini and the valve. You mind keeping an eye on our problem child for a few?"

"Do what you need to do," he said. "I'll be here."

# Chapter 14

I headed down the obstacle course trail and found Pellini sitting on one of the balance logs. Sammy lay at his feet blissfully chomping on a pinecone. "Sorry about the shit with Idris," I said. "Nice takedown though."

"The kid's wound way too tight," he said with a shake of his head. "He's going to get himself or someone else killed."

I sat on another log. "He's been through hell. I swear this isn't the real Idris. He's nice and friendly and sweet and," I sighed, "innocent. He'll get through this and back to himself." I hoped.

"Hell changes people," Pellini said. A hollow sadness swept across his face. Regret? "Idris will never be the same, but he's the only one who can choose how he looks on the other side of that kind of hell."

A squirrel leaped from the branches of one tree to another. Sammy lifted his head then resumed dismembering the far more catchable pinecone. "Sounds like you're speaking from experience," I said quietly.

Pellini shot me a sidelong look, then slid into his familiar glower. "I know hell," he said in a gruff throw-away tone. "Raised my fair share back in the day. Put some perps through hell, too." He picked up a pinecone and flung it with vicious force down the trail. Sammy leaped up and dashed after it. "I have plenty of experience."

"I bet you do," I said. Raising hell was a roiling smoke-screen, and he'd slapped on his asshole mask like armor.

What sensitive spot was he protecting? I stomped down the urge to pry more. For now.

Sammy galumphed back with the fresh pinecone, dropped it at Pellini's feet then shoved his head into Pellini's face to deliver a slobbery lick. "You stupid fucking mutt," Pellini muttered with a scowl, but he wrapped his arms around the dog and scratched his back while Sammy continued to apply enthusiastic doggy kisses. Pellini finally pushed the dog away and wiped his face. "You saw it all last night, didn't you."

"Kadir's playground? Yeah, I was there." I kicked another pinecone toward Sammy, who glommed onto it with enthusiasm. Pellini's shoulders relaxed, and I understood his relief. He'd lived a long time with a secret others would call a crazy fantasy. "What happened before I got there?"

"The 'devil dog' that animal control shot was Kuktok, a kzak I've known since I was a kid." He said it matter-of-factly, as though having a cozy rapport with a vicious demon species was no more unusual than a rain shower in Louisiana. "Kadir told me Kuktok was shot before he made it to a valve at Leelan Park . . . but hasn't arrived back home yet."

I exhaled. "I'm so sorry." I had no idea what would happen if a demon—or human—died in the valve system, between the two worlds.

Pellini shrugged it off, picked up a stick, broke it. Broke it again. "Are you going to tell me what the fuck's going on?" he asked. "I got a glimpse of Kadir's perspective, but I know there's more to it all."

"Can we do it over coffee?" I wasn't trying to stall him, but Pellini set his mouth in a stubborn line.

"I need to know."

Damn. *Note to self: Don't step outside the house without caffeine ever again.* "Let's take a walk to the valve by my pond," I said. "I'll tell you on the way."

We proceeded to stroll through the woods while I inundated him with a crash course in the arcane and its bizarre politics: the Mraztur, demonic lords, Katashi, the demon realm, valves, and summoning. I told him about my history with Rhyzkahl and how he'd betrayed me, and even showed him the sigil scars that the lord had carved into my flesh with his essence blade. I stopped short of telling him about anything to do with Farouche and the plantation raid. Pellini didn't need to know about that to understand the rest. Despite everything else, he was a cop—and the murder and mayhem at the plantation were crimes.

He seemed to take everything I told him in stride. When we reached the pond, I worked to symmetrize the valve while he filled me in on his experiences with Kadir. As I'd suspected, he'd received a "download" from the demonic lord, which imbued him with the knowledge of what to do on the nexus.

I finished smoothing out the irregularities and straightened with a pleased smile. My valve shimmered blue-green—quiet and stable. This symmetrization stuff rocked. Even if it helped Katashi and the Mraztur in the long game, we needed the short game fix.

Pellini scrutinized the valve. "You got it right first time out."

"You don't sound surprised."

"Nah, Kadir said you'd ace it," he said. "Makes sense, considering he created the simulator for you."

A hint of uncertainty in his voice caught my attention. I stood and faced him. "Pellini, what's up?"

"Not sure," he said. A frown curved his mouth. "I wasn't born to be a practitioner. Kadir said he created me."

I couldn't hide my surprise at that. An arcane implant or simulator was one thing, but to genetically engineer a practitioner through arcane means? The notion unsettled me, though I had trouble pinpointing why. It was more than unease over the concept of Pellini being a created practitioner.

"No use worrying too much right now," I said to reassure him. "I'm sure we'll find out more—" I froze.

*Created.* Kadir created Pellini.

Szerain's words echoed back to me.

*Slew Elinor. Created you.*

A chill swept through my body. He'd said that after I

confronted him about stabbing Elinor, but now I had a horrifying context for his words. Created *me*.

A flash of anger swept away the chill. What had he done?
And when? Mzatal once told me the Elinor memories and
influence clung to me like an afterthought, though they
were also integral to my being. Szerain had held Elinor's
essence captive in his blade, Vsuhl, for centuries. Had he
used that blade to alter me? If so, it would have been before
his exile—without Vsuhl—to Earth, which was at least fifteen years ago. And with Szerain who the hell knew where
right now, I had no way to find out.

"Kara," Pellini said, and I realized it wasn't the first time
he'd called my name. "You okay?"

I put on a big smile. "I'm cool. Need coffee, that's all.
Everything will be right with the world then."

What a lie.

Pellini followed me back to the house, but I got as far as dump-
ing out the stale coffee before my phone rang. I glanced at the
number then set the coffeepot in the sink and ran water into it.

"Who the hell's calling you at eight in the morning on a
Saturday?" Pellini asked.

"It's Detective O'Connor from the Sheriff's office," I
said as my phone continued to ring. I didn't have to answer
it, did I? Whether I talked to him or not wouldn't make a
difference in the long run. It wasn't as if there was anything
he could say that would change my mind about giving him
a statement.

Then again the same reasoning supported taking the
call. After all, what did I have to lose? Maybe it wouldn't be
as bad as I expected. Y'know, like a root canal.

Pellini had questions in his eyes that I didn't want to answer. I mumbled a "'scuse me" then snatched up my phone
and headed toward the living room as I answered. "Kara
Gillian."

"Ms. Gillian, it's Detective O'Connor." No fake smile in
his voice this time. Instead I heard a timbre of confidence
that didn't leave me feeling happy-go-lucky.

"Good morning, Detective." I continued through the living room and out to the porch, closing the front door behind me. "A bit early for a social call, which leads me to believe you have a more official agenda in mind?"

"You might say that, ma'am," he replied, cool and calm. I had no trouble picturing him in his office, kicked back in his chair with his feet up on his desk. "Ms. Gillian, if you'd be kind enough to spare me a few minutes, I'd like to tell you a little story."

Shit. I settled in one of the rocking chairs but didn't rock. "Be my guest."

"It's the story of a woman who got in over her head," he began. "It might have started when she was working a case. After all, investigations and undercover assignments can get pretty tricky, and lines get crossed. But however it came about, she made a big mistake and stood by while a man was shot twice in the head."

"Go on," I said in lieu of any number of smartass remarks that came to mind.

"The problem is that even though this woman isn't a bad person, now she's looking at being charged as a principal to murder." He paused. "She used to be a police officer, which means she knows it doesn't matter who pulled the trigger. Any principal to the crime gets the same sentence as the shooter."

"Yes, I've heard that." Anyone who aided and abetted in the commission of a crime was considered a principal. In other words, a guy who robbed a bank at gunpoint would be charged with armed robbery—as would the getaway driver and the third party who planned it, even if neither participated in the actual holdup.

But how did he think he could charge me as a principal? Even if they'd found my fingerprints and DNA at the scene, that was circumstantial evidence, at best.

O'Connor was clearly warming to his story. "The woman thought no one knew she was there when this terrible thing happened. And the detective thought he had no chance of ever finding the real shooter and solving this crime because, after all, she had no reason to risk herself by giving testimony. Or so she thought. But then . . ." He trailed off.

I was tempted to let the silence hang until he gave up and went on, but I decided being mean was pointless. "But then?"

"But then a witness appeared," he said, triumph dripping from his voice. "A dutiful citizen who came forward and placed the woman at that scene."

"There were a lot of people at that scene, from what I hear," I said, pulse hammering. "Do all of them get charged as principals?"

He rewarded me with a dry chuckle. "Well, you see, this witness saw her leave with the shooter. And that changes everything."

*The driver of the getaway car.* I tightened my hand on the phone to keep from shaking. With great effort, I forced myself to let go of arguments about the technicalities that separated Principal from Accessory After the Fact from Uninvolved. None of that mattered. But there was one point I couldn't hold back. "Pretty darn lucky for you that a witness decided to step forward after a couple of weeks of silence."

"Nothing to do with luck. Injuries sustained in the fire prevented the witness from giving a statement before now," he said, all trace of lightness gone from his voice. "But despite that, this person came forward and did the right thing. I want the shooter, Ms. Gillian. You also need to do the right thing, or you're going to find yourself wearing an orange jumpsuit. And ex-cops and prison don't always go well together."

The dread within my chest shifted, expanded. "Thank you for that advice, Detective," I said. "Enjoy your weekend." I hung up without waiting for a reply then set the chair slowly rocking. I remained there until my pulse slowed and my palms stopped sweating, then pygahed and rocked some more.

After at least ten minutes of doing and thinking as little as possible, I got up and returned inside. Pellini sat at the table, while Bryce busied himself at the stove.

"Was about to come get you," Pellini said. "Coffee's ready, and Bryce is making bacon and eggs."

I plastered a smile onto my face and pitched in to help Bryce. "Coffee and breakfast with friends. What more could a girl ask for?"

# Chapter 15

For being an enforced guest, Pellini wasn't a bad housemate at all. I had no idea if he was sucking up or naturally neat and helpful, but as soon as we finished eating he pitched right in with cleanup without batting an eyelash. Bryce got a pass on dishwashing since he'd cooked, and he marched out to do battle with the Malibu engine. Pellini impressed me even more by knowing how to load the dishwasher—wedging light items against heavier things so we didn't end up with cups full of dirty water.

Idris slammed up from the basement as I scrubbed cookware that couldn't go into the dishwasher. "There's bacon if you're hungry," I told him. "Or, if you want eggs or toast, that's no trouble."

I expected him to head straight through the kitchen and out the back again, but apparently his need for sustenance overpowered his dislike of Pellini's presence.

"Yeah. Thanks," he muttered. "Bacon sounds good."

"The plate's on the stove," I said. I rinsed the frying pan and handed it to Pellini for drying. Idris stuck bread into the toaster and did his best to pretend Pellini didn't exist. Pellini slid a look toward him, mustache twitching as though he held back a comment with effort.

This shit needed to stop here and now. I'd allowed a similar veiled antipathy between Ryan and Eilahn to fester for too long before I put my foot down. Learned my lesson. I was sorely tempted to let my snark-monster out and say,

"Now, boys, play nice and shake hands," but decided that might be counterproductive.

"We're living and working in the same house," I said instead. "*My* house, though I like to think of it as *our* house. You two are going to indulge me with a civil conversation if it kills you." I nailed both with a steely glare. *Common ground, here we come.*

Idris frowned as he settled at the table with bacon, toast, and juice. I ignored the frown and turned to Pellini. "I've been thinking over what you told me," I said and passed him another pan to dry. "I can't imagine how hard it was for you to see the arcane and not have *anyone* you could share it with. I mean, I had my aunt from the very beginning to tell me what the deal was."

Pellini hesitated, face bunching into a scowl as he decided whether or not he'd play my game. "It sucked. Not going to lie." He dried the pan with harsh swipes of the towel.

"Have you ever told *anyone?*"

"No humans. Not once." He glanced at Idris then to me. "It was cool at first, y'know? Like being accepted to Hogwarts. I was *special.*" He snorted. "But imagine going to Hogwarts and being the only student there. Oh, and you still have to go to regular school but can't tell a soul about this other cooler shit."

Idris kept his eyes on his food, but I didn't miss that he had yet to take a bite from the bacon in his hand.

"Idris, you learned from a neighbor, didn't you?" I asked.

He blinked, dropped the piece of bacon back onto his plate. "Um. Yeah."

I waited to see if he had more to say, but he remained silent. He wasn't going to make this easy, but at least he hadn't stormed out. "You were what, fourteen?" I asked. "Fifteen?"

"Fourteen," he said with obvious reluctance then blew out a breath as if accepting my refusal to give up. "I'd been with the Palatinos three months when this dude moved in across the street. A week or so later I started seeing strange glimmers around his house. He noticed me gawking." Idris jerked his shoulders up in a shrug. "Started training as a summoner not long after that."

Did Pellini know Idris was adopted? Probably so, I decided. He would have researched everything he could find on anyone related to the Amber Palatino Gavin case. Idris had been adopted twice, once as a baby, and then by the Palatinos when he was fourteen after the first couple died in an automobile accident.

Pellini tugged at his mustache. "I swear to god I'm not trying to stir shit," he said, "but doesn't it strike you as awfully convenient that a summoner moved in across the street right when you started seeing all the woowoo crap?"

For an instant I thought Idris would respond with a snarl, but instead he picked up his fork and jammed it into his bacon. "Yeah," he said, jaw tight. "My *convenient* neighbor and mentor for the first year was Anton Beck—one of Katashi's inner circle summoners."

A chill shuddered through me. "That explains how you ended up training under Katashi so young," I murmured. Truths I'd avoided up to this point clarified into a lump of ice in my gut. "If my dad hadn't *conveniently* been killed by a drunk driver, Tessa wouldn't have raised me, and I wouldn't have become a summoner."

"It sounds premeditated," Pellini said with dark suspicion. "Who orchestrated it and *why?*"

Idris shoved a mangled piece of bacon into his mouth. I rubbed the back of my neck, rankled that I didn't have a satisfactory answer for Pellini. "We've each been molded and exploited to suit the goals of others," I said. "And none of us know why, though at least Idris and I had context for most of it."

Idris glanced at Pellini then dropped his gaze to his plate. Good. Harder for him to paint Pellini as the devil incarnate when he had something in common with him.

"I'm going to take a walk with Sammy," Pellini announced before heading outside to cope with the shit in his own manner. I dried my hands, refreshed my coffee then took a seat at the table. My horrific exploitation pissed me right the fuck off but, until I scraped up more info, further brooding was a waste of time and energy. Besides, my focus needed to remain on my current goal—a cease fire in the Pellini-Idris war.

"Don't say it," Idris said as he slathered jelly on toast.

"Don't say what?" I asked.

"Don't say whatever you're planning to say about how awful it must have been for him never being able to tell anyone."

I shrugged and took a sip of my coffee. "Okay, I won't say it."

He gave me a withering look and took a savage bite of toast and jelly.

"What?" I asked innocently. "You told me not to say it, so I didn't say it."

"You might as well have. You do that thing with your eyes." He licked jelly off his fingers.

"*What* thing with my eyes?"

"You do this sort of narrow-eyed smug disapproval thing," he said.

"You're insane."

"And now you're doing it again."

I threw my hands up in defeat. Bryce unwisely chose that moment to step through the back door. "Bryce, Idris says I do a weird narrow-eyed smug disapproval thing with my eyes," I said. "Tell him he's imagining it."

Bryce stopped, frowned, looked from me to Idris and then back to me. "Sorry. No can do." He continued to the sink to wash grime from his hands.

"Afraid Idris will turn you into a newt?" I asked with a lift of my eyebrow.

Bryce shook his head. "No can do, because he's right."

"Traitor," I growled.

He dried his hands, challenge glinting in his eyes. "You want to get Pellini's take on it?"

I started to say yes, that was exactly what I wanted, but stopped before the words left my mouth. "No. He'll agree with you both."

A sound that might have been a chuckle came from Idris, but he took another bite of toast before I could be sure.

Bryce gave me a wink then headed down the hall to the computer room. I masked a smile. Bryce was a damn good addition to the team.

"For what it's worth," I said to Idris after a moment, "apart from being victims of the overall machinations, you and Pellini have at least one common goal."

Idris shoved up from the table, took his plate over to the trash can and scraped his crusts into it. "Fine, I'll bite. What's our common goal?"

"He's hell-bent on nailing the perps in his latest case— your sister's murder."

He went still, fork poised above his plate. "Okay," he finally said then took plate and fork to the sink. "Will you tell Bryce I'll be ready to go in fifteen minutes?" It might have been wishful thinking on my part, but I detected less of the jagged edge in his voice than before.

"Sure thing."

He met my eyes and nodded once then went down to the basement. When the door closed I blew out a breath. It was a truce of sorts. I hoped.

I headed to the computer room—formerly a junk room that I'd pretended was a home office. The majority of the equipment was Paul's from when he was briefly our resident computer supergenius. Unease whispered through me. Paul was with Kadir. But for how long? He was "out of phase" and would die if he left the matching out-of-phase-ness of Kadir's realm. Would he ever be able to return to Earth or was he damned to spend his entire life kneeling at Kadir's feet?

I pushed the unsettling questions aside. The answers would be worse than not knowing.

Bryce sat at the desk, fast-forwarding through surveillance video from my driveway gate and fence-line cameras.

"Idris will be ready in fifteen," I said then lifted my chin toward the screen. "Anything good?"

"Family of raccoons on the northwest side. Nothing else of interest."

"Baby raccoons?"

"Three of 'em. I took a screen shot." He pulled it up so

that I could make the obligatory *awwwww* noise. He snorted. "Adorable rabies factories."

"I'll gush over them from a distance," I said as I settled in the chair beside his.

"Agreed. That's why I'm not . . ." He trailed off, eyelids fluttering as he stared off into space.

Seizure? Worried, I grabbed his arm and shook him. "Hey, Bryce! You still with me?"

"Yeah, sorry," he said to my relief then smiled wryly. "Seretis. Checking in, so to speak."

Releasing him, I replayed his words in my mind, but they made no more sense the second time around. Why would a demonic lord be checking in with Bryce? And how? "Huh?" I asked oh-so-brilliantly.

Bryce *beamed* then swiveled his chair to face me. "The connection you have with Mzatal?" he said, leaning forward. "I, uh, kinda have that with Seretis. It's not like we *talk* with words, but we can sense and understand each other."

I stared at him, stunned. I'd have been right on board if he'd told me Seretis had placed a sigil on him or given him an artifact. But comparing it to my unique and *intimate* essence connection with Mzatal? A number of possible explanations ran through my mind, though none seemed to fit the scenario. Seretis and Lord Rayst were partners, but that meant little since the demonic lords weren't much into the whole jealousy thing. After a few thousand years of existence, those sort of insecurities went out the window—if they'd ever had them in the first place. However, Seretis was bisexual and, as far as I knew, Bryce was firmly heterosexual. Not that it had ever come up. More than possible that I'd jumped to conclusions.

"Oh, okay," I said as I readjusted my assumptions. "You and he are . . . lovers?"

Bryce laughed. "No," he said, sitting back. "There's no sex. But we hit it off from the start—like that childhood friend you wanted to do everything with and couldn't imagine living without, only as adults."

"Gotcha. A major bromance."

"I guess," he said reluctantly, "though I wish there was a more, er, macho description."

"A sweaty bromance?"

"That's worse."

"A machomance?"

"Oh god, please stop," he said with a laugh. "Anyway, now we have an essence bond. A conscious one." He shook his head. "I realize now I should've told you earlier, but I'm still getting used to the concept, and things have been crazy since I got here."

"Nah, it's cool," I said as I tried to shuffle pieces of info into a picture that made sense. Mzatal had what he called an essence bond with the reyza Gestamar, and Turek, an ancient savik, was essence-bound to Szerain. Maybe my bond with Mzatal was the same as that? Except, y'know, with sex.

The rest of Bryce's words filtered into my brain. "You said that your bond is 'a conscious one.' What do you mean?"

"That's kind of an odd story," he said. "It didn't start out conscious." He ran a hand over his hair, blew out his breath. "After Paul went to Kadir, Mzatal sent me to Seretis's realm. Considering all the shit I'd gone through with the plantation, Farouche, and everything else, I needed the mental health break and a change of scenery. For most of the first day everyone left me alone, and I wandered around or sat out on the beach. But that evening Seretis came out to talk to me and, well, we clicked." A smile lit Bryce's face. "We were damn near inseparable after that—like we'd known each other forever."

I couldn't help but echo his smile as his joy in the friendship resonated through his words. And holy shit, did he ever deserve it. Bryce had spent the last fifteen years as a reluctant hitman and muscle for Farouche—a tough and terrible life that had ripped at his essence. Though he'd committed terrible crimes while in Farouche's service, Bryce was one of the most compassionate and empathetic people I knew. Farouche had turned a kind and caring man—who'd been training to be a veterinarian, for fuck's sake—into his personal monster. For that alone, I was glad Farouche was dead.

"On the fourth day we were on his veranda," Bryce continued, "and Seretis initiated a bond—and not in a figure of speech way. Spontaneous. Instinctual. It felt like a linking of minds at that stage. I didn't understand what was happening, but I didn't want to stop it either." He grew serious. "Right in the middle of the process, a chunk of masonry the size of a Volkswagen fell onto the veranda not even a dozen feet behind us."

I straightened. "To stop you from bonding?"

"That's what I believe." Anger and worry darkened his eyes. "Seretis didn't think it was an accident either, and got pretty shook up." The worry deepened. "But when he tried to figure out who might want to stop it—and why—he got a killer headache. It wouldn't go away until he let go of thinking about it."

"Shit," I breathed. "When I introduced Mzatal to Jill, he connected with the baby and immediately got slammed with that same kind of headache. He told me it had happened many times before." I already knew the demonic lords were manipulated to block awareness of their maternal human origins. Clearly there were other secrets they weren't allowed to know. My mouth twisted as I met Bryce's eyes. "It's as if someone doesn't want the lords to think about certain things."

A muscle in his jaw twitched. "Yeah, well, I didn't bring up who might've shoved a couple of tons of masonry off the wall."

"Can't imagine why," I said with a disingenuous bat of my eyelashes. "By the way, on a *totally* unrelated subject, what's the name of Seretis's ptarl? I don't know all of the demahnk yet."

Bryce snorted and folded his arms over his chest. "That would be Lannist."

Yeah, he and I were on the same page. A big strong demahnk like Lannist would have no trouble pushing giant chunks of masonry around. And the Demahnk Council—or some faction of it—were my number one suspects as the source of the headaches.

"How did you end up with an essence bond if it was so rudely interrupted?" I asked.

The smile returned to his face. "Helori," he said, referring to the demahnk who'd confirmed other sensitive info for me. "The next day he took us out to an Ekiri pavilion in the jungle. He told Seretis everything would be clearer for him there."

*That* was interesting. The Ekiri race had taught the demons how to use the arcane. Though they'd abandoned the demon realm millennia ago, their stone pavilions continued to radiate potent arcane energy. Perhaps that energy mitigated the effects of the manipulation on the lords or served as a source of information? I filed that tidbit away for future reference.

"Being in the pavilion was like being in low gravity while time stood still," Bryce continued as his gaze went distant. "I *understood* the bond—the commitment, and what it all meant. Seretis asked me if I wished to continue." His smile softened. "It felt *right*, so I said yes." He blinked as if coming back to himself. "I can't begin to describe it, but I think you know what I mean."

"I do, and I'm insanely happy for you," I said fervently. Bryce deserved a break, and he looked more at peace than I'd ever seen him.

Idris leaned in, messenger bag slung across his chest. "You almost ready to go?" he asked Bryce.

"One minute," Bryce said and tossed a set of keys that Idris caught easily. "You can get the AC going if you want."

Idris departed. Bryce pushed back from the desk and grabbed a knapsack from beside his chair.

"Thanks, Kara," he said. "Oh, and you don't really get a weird look in your eyes."

"Now you're lying to me."

He laughed. "Yeah, I am." And with that he strode out.

I headed out to the nexus, thoughts whirling. Even when Mzatal was open, we never had the depth of communication between the two worlds that Bryce had with Seretis.

Ours was a vague sense of presence—certainly not to the point of "checking in."

Yet I found myself more perplexed than envious. As far as I knew Mzatal hadn't "consciously" formed our bond. Was it not as complete because he'd acted through instinct? If so, what did that mean about our relationship? Bryce had entered into an essence bond without it being a partnership or sexual relationship. And, if it was the same kind of bond, how and why did Mzatal and I get away with it, yet an attempt was made to stop Seretis and Bryce?

Helori had intervened to help those two. Maybe the same had been done for us, through indirect means.

Too many questions and unknowns. The few answers I had left me all the more unsettled. Fortunately for my state of mind, maintenance of the nexus was overdue and required full concentration. I settled on the concrete and threw myself into the work, eager to immerse for a few hours and bury the overwhelming sense that I was no more than a pawn in someone else's game.

# Chapter 16

I didn't intend to be one of those people who freaked out over the gory realities revealed in childbirth classes. But damn, the class with Jill was *way* more educational than I wanted.

It didn't help that I'd missed the previous sessions. From what I gathered, the first sessions eased people into the bizarre concept of squirting a living being out of one's nethers. But Jill had only a few more weeks to go before her due date, which meant I got thrown into the deep end—breathing and pushing and relaxing and blood and fluid and poop and holy shit was it ever a good thing I loved Jill.

Jill listened and took notes with the determination of a lawyer preparing to go before the Supreme Court. Steeev leaned forward in his chair, so fixated on the instructor's every word that more than once she grew flustered by his intense regard and lost track of what she was saying. Though I couldn't match his zeal I did my best to pay close attention. All the while I hoped and prayed to whoever might be listening that Zack would miraculously recover in time for the birth and let me off the hook.

At long last the class finished, freeing me from videos of devoted husbands counting breaths for panting wives. Jill and I headed out while Steeev hung back to collect one of every single guide and pamphlet the instructor had available.

"You want me to be in your face counting like the guys

in the videos?" I asked her with a grin as we started across the parking lot.

"You'd get to 'one' before I punched you," she said with a sweet smile.

I laughed. "Note to self: Stay out of punching range."

"And whose idea was it to park in the last row because walking would be good for me?" she said in a tone perilously close to a whine.

"Steeev's, along with everyone who parked in all the closer spaces," I replied. "Though, if I was a meaner person, I'd say it was great payback for those times you forced me to go running with you."

"At least I don't complain as much as you did," she said, passing between two cars.

I fell back to walk behind her in the narrow space which meant she couldn't see me roll my eyes. "Suuuure you don't."

"Are you rolling your eyes?" Jill asked, passing between another line of cars. "I can hear you rolling your eyes."

"Hey, you're not a mom yet," I pointed out. "I'm pretty sure you don't get 'hear rolling eyes' superpowers until the kid can walk and talk."

Jill stopped to let a van pass and glanced back at me with a smirk. "I have 'I know Kara Gillian' superpowers," she said then frowned and opened her purse. "Crap. What did I do with the breast pump coupon they gave me?" She asked. "Do you have it?"

The van took its sweet time making its way down the row of cars. "Yeah, I stuck it in my bag," I said as the van slowed more. Maybe they were stopping to ask us directions?

The side door slid open, and in the next instant Steeev shoved me hard against the car to my right as he bounded past with demon speed. Pamphlets rained down around me as his next leap took him onto the trunk of the car with Jill in his arms. A man in a ski mask reached from the van's door to grab the empty air where she'd been a split second before.

"Fuck!" The man jerked back. "Get out of here!" he snapped to the driver.

The man behind the wheel slammed on the gas, leaving the stench of burning rubber in the air as the van tore off. I scrambled to recover my balance and staggered out from between the cars in time to get the license plate number. Not that it mattered since I had a feeling it would come back as stolen. The man at the door of the van had only said five words, but I recognized that harsh edge. *Jerry Steiner.* One of the vilest of Farouche's henchmen. And the driver had been a big, stocky, broad-shouldered man. Angus Mc-Dunn, Boudreaux's stepdad. I knew it in my bones.

Pulse still racing, I pivoted back toward Jill where she sat sprawled on the trunk of the sedan, one hand on her belly. Steeev stood over her on high alert like the protective ba-dass demon he was.

"Are you all right?" I demanded.

"No!" she snapped back, eyes wide in shock. "What the fuck was that?"

I didn't see any injuries on Jill—not even a scraped knee—which upped Steeev's awesome factor by several notches. He continued to scan the parking lot, but I knew that if Jill or the baby were hurt in the slightest he'd have whisked them to the ER.

"I'm pretty sure those two men used to work for Farouche." I helped her down from the trunk. "They've likely hooked up with Katashi," I added, grim. "With Farouche out of the picture, they have little reason to be operating solo."

"And I got in the way of them trying to grab you," she said with a scowl. "You can thank me later. With ice cream."

I hesitated before replying and looked up at Steeev. He leaped from the trunk to land with light grace beside us. I pretended not to notice the dent he left behind and instead picked up his scattered pamphlets.

"Kara Gillian was not the intended target," Steeev told Jill, confirming my blossoming suspicion. "You were."

She gaped in astonishment. "The hell?"

"Hey! You guys okay?"

We whirled to see the birthing class instructor hurrying our way, face twisted in concern.

"What happened?" she panted. "Was anyone hurt?"

"Some asshole racing through the parking lot almost hit Jill," I said, and it didn't take much effort for me to put on a glower for the instructor's benefit. "Good thing Steve pulled her back in time."

"Good thing indeed!" she said, turning a look of approval onto Steeev as he stood there radiating Badass Manly Man. "Did anyone get the tag number? I can call hospital security and let them know, unless you want to report it to the police?"

"I got the license plate," I said and rattled it off. "If you could pass it on to the appropriate authorities, that would be great."

She went off to make the call, and Steeev herded Jill to our car and stuffed her into the passenger side while I climbed into the back.

"One of you better explain why you think they were trying to kidnap me," Jill said as soon as Steeev pulled out of the parking lot.

"Because Zack outed himself at the Farouche plantation," I said, mentally kicking myself for not having thought of this earlier. "He named himself as Zakaar when he confronted Rhyzkahl, and word must have reached Katashi." Though the Mraztur knew of Szerain and Zack, the demons and lords had been oathbound to not speak of it which explained why the baby had only now become a target for Katashi.

"But why come after me—" Jill stopped. Blinked. "Oh. Now they know . . ."

"Now they know you're carrying the child of a demahnk," I finished for her.

Jill's expression went flat and cold. "They're not getting my baby," she said with fierce certainty. "Steeev, drive to my house." *Her* house, where Zack was staying. *Was.*

Shiiiiiit. She was going to *flail* me. "Zack's not there," I said. "He's gone. He left with Ryan and Sonny yesterday."

The seat belt and her belly kept her from pivoting, but she flipped down the visor and snapped the mirror open to scour me with an angry gaze in the reflection. "Gone *where?*"

"I don't know," I groaned then related the phone

conversation—what there was of it. "I swear I wasn't intentionally keeping it from you," I continued. "But the Sheriff's Office called me right after that, and then you were gone this morning . . . I'm so sorry. It completely slipped my mind. I promise."

Jill flipped the visor back up, but not before I caught a glimpse of the hurt that slashed across her face. I knew it wasn't because of me, but that didn't make me feel any better. From her viewpoint Zack had ditched her right before she needed him the most.

*Damn it.* "Jill," I said, "I can't imagine any scenario where he'd distance himself from you and the bean unless it was to keep you safe." But what did I know? He was a demahnk playing at being human.

She remained silent for several seconds, and when she finally spoke her voice was soft and sad, echoing my thoughts. "He's not human."

The weight of those three words hung in the air. She hadn't said them to describe Zack but to affirm her recognition of his "not human-ness" and all it entailed. She was *accepting*—though she hated to do so—that she couldn't expect him to act as a human would. And, whether any of us liked it or not, she couldn't depend on him in the same way she could a human.

She let out a soft sigh and stroked her hand over her belly. "I don't think I can do this anymore."

I knew she didn't mean the baby, but I had to clear the somber mood. "That's cool, I'll do it for you. C'mon, shove that belly up against mine and we'll squeeze her through the belly buttons. I'm in good shape. I can carry her for a while."

She let out a weak laugh. "Yeah. We could get it on video and be an internet sensation." She rolled her neck on her shoulders and lifted her chin. "No matter what happens, I'm getting an awesome baby out of all of this." The good ol' fierce Jill strength returned to her posture. "No way am I giving her up. To *anyone.*"

"Damn straight," I said, and even Steeev gave a firm nod of agreement.

We turned right at an intersection where we should have turned left to get to my house. "Where are we going?" I looked behind us in sudden worry. "Is someone following us? Are you trying to lose a tail?"

Steeev shook his head. "No, but it is imperative that you both consume ice cream."

I laughed. "I knew you were the perfect syraza for this job."

# Chapter 17

While Steeev navigated orange and white-striped barriers around road construction, I called Bryce and filled him in on the recent excitement. He listened in silence until I finished then said, "Put her on, please."

"Hey," Jill said into the phone after I passed it forward. Then, "Yeah, I'm good." A pause. "Thanks. That means a lot." She hung up and handed it back to me without another word.

I put my phone away and kept my questions to myself.

Ruthie's Smoothies and Other Frozen Goodies deserved its fame as the best frozen concoction establishment within fifty miles of downtown Beaulac. Even at well after sundown, half a dozen cars occupied the parking spaces in front of its rainbow-colored storefront. It was *the* place for the teen crowd to hang out and be seen, however, Ruthie maintained a zero-tolerance policy for any of the typical high-schooler shenanigans that might put off adult customers. More than once I'd watched her kick a patron out for disruptive behavior or poor manners. Adults were subject to the same standards of behavior, and rumor had it that a long-time city councilman was counting the days until the end of his one year banishment for an unknown offense.

Steeev parked well away from other cars, but when he

climbed out Jill stayed put except to undo her seatbelt. I
sent a questioning glance her way as I opened my door.
"You change your mind about ice cream?"

"As if! No, I'm not allowed to get out until he's made
sure it's safe." She seemed more bemused than annoyed.
"He glowers, and boy does he ever have a stubborn streak.
I swear to god. You should see it."

"I believe you," I said with a grin. "Syraza-stubborn. It's
how we ended up with Fuzzykins. I'll see if I can hurry him
along."

Steeev was already on the other side of the parking lot
when I headed his way. He stood motionless, attention riveted on a man leaning against a car not twenty feet from
him. Yet Steeev didn't appear to be in potential-threat
mode. It seemed instead to be a wary curiosity, like a dog
encountering a raccoon for the first time.

Steeev's reaction made far more sense as I moved closer
and recognized the man. Arms folded casually across his
chest, Marco Knight regarded Steeev with mild amusement
coupled with nonchalance.

"Hey, Marco," I said with a smile. "He's cool, Steeev. I'll
meet you and Jill inside in a few."

Steeev relaxed, apparently satisfied with my assessment,
and turned away to retrieve Jill.

Marco gave me a smile. "Hey, Kara. Nice night."

"And only going to get nicer once I get chocolate and lots
of calories in my tummy," I replied. "You here for ice cream?"

"No, I think I'm here because of you," he said. Apparently, whatever sixth sense he possessed had drawn him to
be here, and it was up to him to figure out the meaning behind it.

"From anyone else that'd be creepy as hell," I said with
a small laugh. "From you it's only the ordinary amount of
creepy."

He let out a dry chuckle. "I'm not sure how I should take
that."

"Best not to analyze it too much," I said. "Can I buy you
an ice cream?"

His eyes went to the door, and a faint wince crossed his face. "I'm not allowed inside at the moment."

"Oh." I wasn't going to ask why. Most likely an incident related to his talent. "I'm pretty sure I'm allowed to bring it out for you." At least I hoped so. Either way, I was willing to risk Ruthie's wrath for Knight's sake. "What would you like?"

He inclined his head in thanks. "One scoop of Razzy Snazzy Very Berry in a cup, if you don't mind."

"I'm on it." I headed inside to see Jill and Steeev at a table against the far wall and already digging into their ice cream. I gave them an "everything's okay" thumbs up then went to the counter to order Marco's ice cream and a scoop of Double Trouble Fudgy Rubble for myself.

Ruthie took the order with her usual pizazz and cheery banter. Thirty-something, she exuded a freedom of spirit with her spiky blond hair and full sleeve tattoos of vibrant exotic flowers. She flicked a glance out the front windows toward where Marco leaned against his car. Considering Marco's exile, I expected her to show anger or unease at the sight of him. But to my surprise her expression softened into a look of regret and sympathy, and she let out an almost soundless sigh. A heartbeat later she recovered and schooled her features to her normal perky-yet-tough persona. With practiced efficiency she scooped up both orders and handed the cups over with a bright "Enjoy!"

My curiosity rose at her reaction to Knight, but I tamped it down. Whatever the story was, I doubted it pertained to me, which meant any nosiness on my part would be tough to justify. I returned outside and handed Marco his cup, leaned against his car beside him, and for the next few minutes we ate ice cream in silence.

"I need to ask you a question," I said after my spoon scraped the bottom of the cup. "And if I'm intruding on a subject that's none of my business that's totally cool. I'll back off."

Marco licked red and white swirls from his spoon. "You know better than I do why I'm here."

I wasn't so sure of that but was willing to run with it for

now, especially since it justified this particular nosiness. "Why did you need to see Pellini the other day?"

"Urgent wild goose chase. Happens now and then."

"What do you mean?"

He ate another spoonful of ice cream before answering. "I connected him to a place. We got there, and there was nothing." He shrugged. "I mean *nothing* of interest."

"What was the place?"

Knight swept his arm in a broad gesture that included the line of shops and parking lot. "Right here. This area. Connecting you to it now." He frowned. "You weren't before."

"*Here?*" I slowly turned a full circle, seeking any hint of arcane activity that Knight and Pellini might have missed. Nada. Not a blip. Ruthie's, a dry cleaners, a dollar store, and a martial arts studio. All familiar and benign. "Nothing clicked for Pellini?"

"Came up completely empty," he said. "I didn't get anything more once we were here either." He scooped up the last bit of ice cream then took my spoon and empty cup and tossed the trash in a nearby receptacle. "I doubt he'll be calling me again for anything."

That took me aback. "Wait. Pellini called *you?*"

"When he couldn't get you," Marco said with a faint smile. "I guess he was desperate."

*The missed calls while I was in the demon realm.* "You came all the way from New Orleans to bring him here? That must have been a pretty strong feeling."

"Yep, it is," he said, and I noted his use of present tense. "I decided to take a little time off and go fishing while I was over here."

For a guy who *felt* or *knew* things about the people around him, fishing seemed the perfect hobby. A different form of peace and quiet than most people sought. "This is a great area for fishing," I said. "Or so I hear. I think I was nine when I last went fishing."

"It's not for everyone."

I smiled. "I'm willing to give it another try when things settle down." That was me stubbornly clinging to the belief that things *would* settle down. Eventually. "Pellini's going to be staying at my place for a while."

"It's for the best," he said as if he knew everything about the situation.

"Hope so. We left him with two associates of mine tonight. I'm one of Jill's birthing coaches now since Zack's . . . unavailable."

Marco looked away and remained silent.

My chest tightened into a knot of unease at his reaction. "She's going to have her baby soon," I said, watching his shoulders tense.

His voice was low and thick when he spoke. "I'm sorry."

The knot dropped, taking my stomach with it and leaving a cold fear in its place. Instinct told me to bail, to find an excuse to leave this man's presence, because no good could come from staying. But I didn't want to do that. I knew without a doubt people bailed on Marco all the time because of scenarios like this.

"My head tells me I shouldn't ask *why* you're sorry," I said after a moment. "But Jill's the best friend I have in this world, and I sure hope she and the baby will be fine and healthy and whole and all the other good stuff."

He shifted his gaze to a swarm of insects around a streetlight. "Some things aren't easy in the best of circumstances." With each word the air grew a little heavier. The insects faltered in flight. Distant chatter dropped away.

"What kind of fish do you hope to get in this lake?" I gasped out the question. *Change the subject. Stop whatever's happening.*

Marco smiled, and the air cleared. Insects buzzed, and conversation resumed. "Whatever takes the bait."

"Do you eat what you catch?" I asked. Keep the subject changed. That's it.

He shook his head. "Nope. Can't do it."

"Must be nice for you out in the boat." *Away from people who make you feel their terrible fates,* I added silently.

His smile relaxed a bit more. "Especially at night."

The dangerous moment was past. "I'd better go join Jill and Steeev," I said. "Thanks for talking to me."

"Call me."

"I will," I promised. And I would. I understood a little of how achingly lonely his life must be. His "gift" of clairvoyance—that sometimes expressed of its own volition—likely kept his pool of friends pretty shallow. With a parting smile I headed toward the entrance. In the glass of the door I watched Marco's reflection as he dropped his head, shoulders bowing under unfathomable weight.

A group of giggling teen girls pushed the door open, dispelling the image. I glanced back but all I saw was Marco climbing into his car. A few seconds later the engine revved, and he pulled out of the parking lot and disappeared down the street.

# Chapter 18

No one said much for most of the drive back to the house apart from conversational gems such as "Oh, look, they're building a new Save-Mart," from Jill, and "Is it supposed to rain tomorrow? I think it's supposed to rain tomorrow," from me, and even "Squirrels do not seem to like me," from Steeev.

But not a word in reference to the attempted kidnapping from any of us. Evidently, Steeev and I both adhered to the well-known adage *Don't upset the preggers chick while in a moving vehicle.* If Jill didn't bring it up, we weren't going to. For her part, she was either avoiding the topic or too deep in her own thoughts to talk. I decided it was probably the latter since, though she knew Marco Knight, she didn't ask about my little meeting with him. Or maybe she didn't ask *because* she knew him and his reputation. Instead, she toyed with her phone or gazed out at the exciting scenery of pine trees at night. Steeev remained on high alert as he drove, suspicious of any car that came near us. I sat in the back and tried not to fret.

Despite my best efforts, my thoughts kept circling back to Knight's reaction when I mentioned Jill's baby. *Some things aren't easy even in the best of circumstances.* I knew it was pointless to try and analyze his statement, but I also knew that too much sugar was bad for me yet I continued to load my coffee with it. Did Knight know about Zack? Maybe Zack was gone for good, and Jill was fated to be a single mom. That would certainly count as "not easy." Or, perhaps Jill would go into early labor, and Steeev and I would have to deliver her baby on the kitchen table.

I suppressed a shudder. Those labor and delivery videos remained vivid and gruesome in my mind. If Jill popped the bean out on my table, I'd be visiting the furniture store the next day.

My thoughts wandered into darker "not easy" territory, and I yanked them back. I didn't want to imagine what the worst possible scenarios might be. Not for Jill. Not for my best friend and her baby.

"Ruthie added new ice cream flavors since I was last there," I said, contributing to our scintillating conversation as I fought to distract myself.

Steeev glanced at me in the rearview mirror. "I quite enjoyed the Hazelnut Scuttlebutt," he replied with an overly bright smile — by human standards, at least. As a syraza, it was possible he truly found hazelnut-coffee ice cream deserving of enthusiasm. "Should we return," he continued, "I would be most pleased for the opportunity to sample the Beachy Peachy Luau Wow."

"That one's pretty good," I agreed. "Be sure to ask for the caramel syrup. Brings out the flavor of the macadamia nuts"

"I will do that," he said with a serious nod.

Jill let out a soft sigh. "Ice cream didn't help much."

With that sentence the mood in the car plummeted. A taut silence descended upon us as Jill alluded to the taboo subject. A dozen different responses leaped to mind, any of which had the potential to upset Jill or start an argument — even ones intended as comfort. Yet a glance out the window told me we weren't far from my driveway. I only needed to hold back another minute or two, and we'd be home.

Steeev hit the remote for the gate as he slowed to pull into the driveway. Concentrating with inhuman intensity, he assessed the gate's movement and adjusted the speed of the car to avoid the need to stop. Whether an intentional tactic or simply a game, there was no mistaking the gleam of satisfaction in his eyes when he made it through without a pause. The gate closed behind us, and gravel crunched as we continued up the driveway. A few more seconds and we'd be at the house. I didn't *really* need to raise an already sore subject with Jill, did I?

*Screw it.* "I think you need to start your maternity leave right now," I blurted then tensed for an acid response.

"I texted my captain when we were at Ruthie's," she said with the same ordinary, matter-of-fact tone that she would use to point out that pine trees had needles.

"Oh?" I replied, cautiously relieved. Very cautiously. She might have simply texted her captain about one of her cases. The woman was tricky like that. Steeev pulled up to the house and killed the engine but didn't get out of the car. It was obvious he desired absolute clarity on the matter as well.

She glanced at the two of us, amusement glimmering in her eyes at his hesitation and my wary tone. "I need to take a file to the lab in the morning, sign off on three cases, brief my replacement tech, and then I'm finished."

"Yay!" I snapped off my seatbelt and lunged forward to throw my arms around her and her seat. "Maybe Steeev will stop having that pained expression on his face all the time."

Jill let out an actual giggle. The syraza muttered under his breath in demon as he exited the car then executed a perfect backflip—his own brand of commentary on the matter. He bounded up the steps, and we climbed out and followed at a more sedate pace, smiling at his antics.

Jill paused on the porch to catch her breath as Steeev disappeared into the house. "Before you get any silly ideas," she warned me, "I'll be off work, but don't expect me to take over your chores."

"Are you kidding?" I let out a deep sigh of mock disappointment. "You got winded going up three steps. You're useless—ow!" I grinned and rubbed my arm where she'd punched. "Okay, not useless. Still a badass. I'll let you take the hold-down-the-sofa chore."

She smiled sweetly. "That's more like it."

"If you promise not to punch me again, I might even come over and clean your bathroom." I opened the door for her to enter, then followed. "I'm just glad those two ass-holes didn't—" I choked back the rest of my sentence at the sight of Pellini down the hall at the kitchen table. "—get . . . their ice cream," I said, blundering to a finish. Pellini didn't know any details of our interactions with Farouche and his men. It needed to stay that way, and not because I didn't trust him. Pellini was an active duty police officer. Though I knew he had suspicions, as long as they weren't confirmed, he couldn't get into trouble for associating with us.

Jill shot me a perplexed look, then followed my gaze. Fortunately, she caught on and gave an earnest nod. "Right! Wow. Ruthie was ruthless. Sucks for them because that place is *great*." Okay, maybe a bit too earnest.

To my relief Pellini didn't seem to notice Jill's terrible improv skills, and continued to read his newspaper. I rolled my eyes at her in exasperation, but she grinned and contin-ued toward the kitchen. "I'm stealing your butter," she in-formed me. "I want to make cookies and—" She stopped as we drew even with the open bathroom door. Steeev leaned close to the mirror above the sink and peered intently at his reflection. "Um, Steeev? What gives, dude?"

He turned to her, forehead wrinkled and mouth pursed. "Kara Gillian observed that I have a pained expression on my face at all times. I wish to rectify this, yet I do not per-ceive this appearance of agony."

Jill pressed her lips together to control her laugh. "C'mon, big guy," she said, tucking her arm through his. "You can help me make cookies, and I'll explain Kara's *unique* brand of humor."

After Jill left with the butter, I grabbed a carton of orange juice from the fridge and poured a glass.

Pellini looked up from the newspaper, brows drawn to-gether and face serious. "You changed gears midsentence with Jill as soon as you saw me."

*Crap. Busted.* I stuck the juice carton back in the door and closed the fridge. "Trying to preserve your plausible deniability," I said. "You know the deal. Once you know, you *know*."

The furrows between his brows deepened. "But I *need* to know, don't I. Even if it associates me."

"I won't lie. It would help if you could, ah, participate fully." I took a sip of my juice then sank into a chair at the table. "However, I don't want to associate you without your clear consent and understanding."

He leaned back in his chair and regarded me. "This is serious shit," he said after a moment. "Gimme a few to think it over." He dropped the paper onto the table, called for Sammy and headed to the back door. Sammy galloped through the kitchen in his eagerness to get outside.

Serious shit indeed. Once Pellini came on board and learned the full story—including all the pesky illegal parts—he'd be duty bound as a law enforcement officer to report all law-breaking activities to the appropriate authorities. Failure to do so would be . . . what was the term? Oh, yeah: Malfeasance in Office. Otherwise known as Dirty Cop. We could bleat all day that our cause was right and just and worth a few bent laws here and there, but at the end of the day it had to be Pellini's decision to wade into our particular flavor of dirt. No way would I yank him in against his will.

After finishing my juice, I pulled out my phone and sent a quick text to Bryce.

<FYI might be filling Pellini in re BM crap> I couldn't help but smile after I hit send. Paul used to call Farouche "Big Mack" or BM for short, and now it served as a useful code phrase on the off chance our calls or texts were being monitored.

His response came in less than a minute. <Gotcha. I trust your judgment>

I snorted. <Appreciate that. But not gonna out you w/o permission> It was one thing to tell Pellini about our role in the events at the Farouche Plantation. It was another to tell him Bryce was the one who put two bullets in BM's head.

This reply took longer.

<Trust you. And thanks. Yes, you have permission to out me>

I exhaled in relief. Would've been tough to skirt that

whole issue, but I'd been prepared to figure out a way. <Cuz you're fabulous>

<You know it. ETA thirty minutes>

I put my phone away then snuck a peek out the kitchen window. No sign of Pellini. Restless, I pulled the newspaper to me and flipped through it, then stopped and stared at a photo on the third page. Amaryllis Castlebrook. I knew that face all too well because a few weeks ago I'd impersonated her. She'd been targeted for abduction by Farouche, but my posse intervened.

Yet sick horror filled me at the sight of the headline. *Beaulac Woman Missing Since Thursday*. I skimmed the article, frustrated by the lack of details. She'd been last seen as she left work. No suspects at this time. Anyone with information was asked to contact the sheriff's office.

"Son of a bitch," I muttered. My gut told me it was no coincidence that she went missing after being previously targeted. Had someone picked up the human trafficking right where Farouche left off?

Before I could retrieve the laptop to check for updates on the case, Sammy bounded in and collapsed into a tongue-lolling heap on the rug by the kitchen sink. Pellini followed at a more sedate pace and dropped into the chair opposite me.

I set the paper down and did my best not to appear impatient for his decision. While I very much hoped he'd choose to hear me out regarding my posse's dicey history, I wouldn't blame him if he dodged the whole guilt-by-association bullet.

Pellini flicked his hand toward the Amaryllis article. "Tim Daniels is the hero on that one. He got the vic back alive *and* almost caught the perp."

"That's damn good," I said with undisguised relief. Tim was the all-around good guy and decent cop who I'd once sent on a wild goose chase to search for a nonexistent cat — which was how Eilahn ended up with Fuzzykins. "She's okay then?"

Pellini's expression darkened. "Got the dogsnot beat out

of her and was raped several times." He paused. "She'll recover, though. Physically, at least."

*And a lifetime of recovery for the rest.* I dropped my
hands to my lap and clenched them together. This attack on
Amaryllis was no coincidence. "Is there a description of the
perp?"

"Hold on." Pellini pulled out his phone and flipped
through items. "I was following the reports because it reminded me of the Amber Gavin murder." He stopped
scrolling and clicked a link. "Got it. Inch or two taller than
six feet. Brown hair. Possibly a black van. That's from Tim.
Not much from the victim yet." He turned the phone
around to show me a computer sketch. It was a pretty
crummy representation—not surprising if Tim didn't get a
solid look at him—but it was good enough for me.

Jerry Fucking Steiner. "Who has the case?" I asked.

"Boudreaux and Wetzer," he said. "Why? What's up?"

I leaned back and studied him. "I'd like to tell you one
bit of info that will fill in a few gaps without putting you in
an untenable position."

Pellini gave me a slow, considered nod.

"We had intel that Idris was being held at the Farouche
Plantation," I said. "We also learned that Farouche was having people kidnapped to be sent with Rhyzkahl to the demon realm. We found out the identity of the next target,
and I took her place as a means to infiltrate the security at
the plantation. The name of that target was Amaryllis Castlebrook."

His eyes widened in surprise before narrowing.
"Fuuuuuuuck."

"It's not too late to remain uninformed," I said.

A shimmer of uncertainty lingered on his face. "I don't
know the details of what went down at the plantation that
night," he said. "But I can guess the grand finale, whether
you fill in the gaps or not."

"True," I said then shrugged. "However, you know as
well as I do that guessing and knowing are two different
things."

His hand tightened into a fist on the table, and he seemed

poised to get up and leave the room. But then he blew out a heavy breath. "It's too late to dick around with semantics," he said with no trace of doubt. "There are no laws that cover this shit, and I have a feeling you know what happened to this Castlebrook woman."

"Pretty sure I do," I said then, with a wry smile, added, "Welcome to the madhouse." With that, I launched into the story, doing my best to hit the high points and the pertinent details. Idris's captivity with the Mraztur and his transfer to Earth with Katashi. My first encounter with Bryce and Paul at the warehouse that held a valve node. Bryce taking a bullet for Paul, and Mzatal saving his life. Farouche's ability to make people do his bidding through implanted fear or adoration. His involvement with Katashi, the Mraztur, and Rhyzkahl. Human trafficking.

And, finally, the big fight at the plantation, where I stood by and watched while Bryce Thatcher executed James Macklin Farouche.

Pellini listened with quiet reserve. When I finished, he tipped his head back to examine a spot high on the wall behind me. "If you'd turned Farouche over to the legal system," he said after a moment, "he would've used that fear-love ability of his to get all the charges dropped and walk free." He dropped his eyes to mine again. "The only other option would've been to take him captive. That wasn't feasible from a logistics standpoint or with the risk of Farouche influencing you in the process."

"You nailed it," I said. "Bryce made a choice—the right one, in my opinion—and executed Farouche. Soon after that, Bryce Thatcher disappeared forever." Pellini opened his mouth to speak, but I forged ahead. "He had a brief stay in the demon realm that included facial reconstruction and new fingerprints," I paused for dramatic effect, "and returned yesterday as Bryce Taggart."

To my surprise Pellini let out a harsh, humorless laugh. "That's fucking hysterical."

Not exactly the reaction I'd expected. "Um. Why?"

He shoved out of the chair with a grunt and retreated to the counter. "Bryce isn't really a common name, and after I met him the night of the barbeque, I got suspicious. Witnesses had him at the plantation that night, *and* Boudreaux had that police sketch of you. I put two and two together, y'know? So I did a quick check on my phone of police photos of Bryce Thatcher." He snorted. "Didn't look a fucking thing like the man who gave me a hamburger, and I let it go."

"You have good instincts," I said, honestly impressed that he'd made the connection and followed up on it.

"I have my moments," he said then shook his head. "Hitman hamburgers. Damn."

"You needed to know about Bryce and his past if you're going to be part of this team." I sighed. "I know what it means to come to terms with being a cop and rubbing elbows with a hitman." It was one thing for him to accept that Bryce killed a man who needed killing. But coming to terms with Bryce's background was a different story, and I didn't know what to do if Pellini couldn't handle it. "Is this going to be a problem for you?"

"Nah, it's fine," he said without conviction. His jaw and mouth worked as he tried to choose his words, but then he shook his head and slashed the air in a stop-everything gesture. "No. Shit. I need more time to get my head around it."

While not an ideal response, it wasn't rejection either. I also understood why he couldn't come right out and say, *Yeah, I'm cool.* "Take a day or two to think things over," I said. "All I ask is that you not act on the information in that time."

"I can do that," he said. He gestured to the newspaper. "How does everything you've told me tie in with the victim?"

"Jerry Steiner was the driver when I was kidnapped in place of the real Amaryllis Castlebrook. He was also a key assailant in Amber Gavin's murder and rape, and I'm fucking positive he's the perp in this."

A teeth-baring smile curved Pellini's mouth. "I would fucking love to see him nailed to the goddamn wall."

"You and me both," I said in vehement agreement. "Maybe you can tell Boudreaux the sketch reminds you of Steiner. He could do a photo lineup with that asshole's picture in it for Tim and the victim. See what pops."

He snorted. "You almost sound like a detective."

"Really?" I tilted my head and offered him a mock-puzzled look. "You know how detectives operate?"

"Nah, I just watch cop shows." But then he sobered. "What about your part in all this? The Sheriff's Office considers you a person of interest in the Farouche murder, and you ducked out pretty damn quick when O'Connor called earlier. You getting pressured?"

I grimaced. "I wasn't too worried when all he had was a crappy police sketch to tie me to the scene," I said. Fortunately the one photo of me was too blurry to be used as evidence. "But it seems O'Connor now has a witness who saw me leaving the scene with Bryce after the shooting. He's threatening to arrest me for Principal to Murder unless I spill my guts."

His mouth twisted. "Interesting that a witness decided to come forward at this point," he said. "Especially with information that directly incriminates you."

"Isn't it though?" I scowled. "I *know* Katashi and his people are behind it. Getting me arrested is a damn good way to fuck with us."

"And there's not much you can do," he said.

"This is usually when I resort to chocolate."

"Makes as much sense as anything else."

# Chapter 19

The only chocolate in the house was chocolate milk mix, but that was better than nothing. I stirred up a double-strong glassful, then proceeded to the dining room with my chocolate milk, my guns, and my cleaning kit. Pellini entered a few minutes later with his own guns. I spread an old blanket over the table, and we settled in for a nice homey gun-cleaning party.

By the time Idris and Bryce arrived, Pellini and I had our handguns stripped down to component parts and were going to town with solvent and bore brushes. Bryce joined us with his backup piece—a compact Glock 26 9mm—along with a Sig Sauer P227 Zack had left at the house. Bryce's former primary weapon was a Glock 27 that currently rested at the bottom of Bayou Deschamps—stripped, filed, and dumped after he killed Farouche with it. I'd offered him use of the Sig since he needed a second gun, and I knew damn well Zack wasn't the type to mind.

Idris stepped into the dining room. His gaze traveled over the variety of lethal hardware spread out on the table, then he plopped into a chair and retrieved a whetstone from his messenger bag. As I glanced over with interest, he pulled a folding knife from his belt and opened it one-handed. It was a sleek tactical knife with a black handle and a beveled blade, lovely and deadly in a perfect melding of form and function. It probably served as his ritual knife as well as other necessary uses, I decided as I watched him sharpen the steel's edge. After several precise strokes of the whetstone, he tested the blade on a piece of paper. It parted with a whisper, like silk against a razor.

Oh yeah, I wanted one of those. That shit was going on my Christmas list.

As I ran a cloth through the barrel of my gun, I gave everyone a quick rundown of the abduction attempt on Jill as well as what happened to Amaryllis Castlebrook. "I'm positive Jerry Steiner is the perp in the Amaryllis case, and now we know that he and Angus McDunn are actively working against us—almost certainly with Katashi."

"Leo Carter is also with them," Bryce said. "Farouche's head of security. You saw him at the plantation." Then a smile split his face. "Our good news is that Idris and I found the Katashi base this afternoon."

"You did?!" I straightened abruptly and knocked the bottle of gun oil off the table. I snatched it up before more than a drop spilled then pierced Bryce with a look. "Tell!"

"It's the twenty-acre property from the list of possibles you gave us," he said. "Idris detected wards when we did a drive-by. We couldn't see the house from the road, but we set up not far away with a pair of binoculars and saw Carter and a female passenger drive out the gate."

Elated, I performed a brief and silly chair dance. "I *knew* they wouldn't hole up in a shitty motel. How heavily warded is the place? Any chance we can infiltrate?"

Idris spoke up. "We checked the fence line. Warded out the wazoo. Not *quite* as heavily as this place, but close." He dragged the red bundle out of his messenger bag and placed it on the table. "But here's the upside. Katashi has a way of camouflaging wards from othersight. It's sneaky because even if you *know* a ward is there, you can't sense it, which means you can't deal with it."

"Erm," I said, "am I missing something? That doesn't sound like much of an upside."

"Yeah, the hidden ward part sucks. But it turns out we have a detector, so to speak." He pulled the silk back to expose the Katashi forearm with its Mark.

"Jesus fuck!" Pellini blurted. "Is that an *arm?*"

Oops. Forgot he didn't know about Mr. Handy. "Katashi's," I told him. "Long story, but he totally deserved to have it chopped off. Promise."

Pellini muttered under his breath, but he didn't leave the room. I gave Idris a *Go on* nod.

"Here's the cool part," Idris said, and his eyes lit up. "This baby *twitches* when it's near a Katashi Special. Plus, if I manage to pinpoint and touch the sigil with the hand, BAM, the camouflage drops."

Its fingers jerked.

I recoiled in shock, but Pellini shot out of his chair and stumbled back, reflexively aiming his barrel-free gun grip at the arm. "Are you *shitting* me?"

Idris stroked the arm as though soothing an animal. "It's cool. It does that every now and then."

Heart thumping, I watched the thing warily. "Does that mean there's a Katashi ward nearby?" Pellini eased back into his chair, eyes never leaving the arm.

"No, the twitching for a ward is different. Regular. Frantic." Idris flicked his fingers open and closed several times to demonstrate the difference. "I haven't connected these occasional jerks to anything specific."

"That has to be the creepiest thing I've ever seen," I said and couldn't hold back the shudder, "but it does sound useful." I surveyed the table, then had to laugh. "Guns-a-plenty, and a magic arm. We're set."

"That arm looks fresh," Pellini said with dark suspicion. "Did it just get cut off?"

"Nah, it's been zombified for over six months," I said. "Mzatal put a demonic lord whammy on it to keep it from rotting."

Idris gave me a pained look. "A putrescence counter-cascade ritual," he corrected then re-wrapped the thing and tucked it away in his messenger bag. Pellini had a glazed look about him but resumed his gun cleaning once the arm was out of sight.

"We're pretty thin in the manpower area," Bryce said, disassembling the Sig as easily as breathing. "I can't see any way to infiltrate the Katashi household that won't end in disaster."

"Fair enough," I said. I wasn't going to argue the point. Bryce knew tactics better than anyone else in the room. "We've been stabilizing the valves, but we need to come up with a plan of action beyond that. Katashi has a clear goal and a strategy to achieve it." My mouth twisted. "I don't like feeling as if we have to wait for disaster to strike before we can act."

"Sounds like Katashi is the kingpin," Pellini said. "Take him out of commission and the whole shebang comes to a screeching halt."

Idris nailed Pellini with a *We don't need your input* look. "Really? Wow! Wish I'd thought of that."

Pellini tensed, and I spoke quickly to forestall violence. "We've *all* thought it, but now it's time to consider specifics. Idris, you've spent a lot of time with Katashi. What are we up against if we decide to take him out?"

His belligerence retreated. "Katashi is one of a kind," Idris said. "He's been a full-fledged summoner for over *ninety years*, and conducted the first summoning of modern times. He not only managed it without a mentor or *any* formal training, but he summoned the reyza Gestamar—hands down the hardest demon to summon." Unabashed awe flashed across Idris's face. Despite his hatred of Katashi, he respected the skill. "I don't know any other summoner who could pull that off," he continued, serious again. "He has techniques he doesn't teach anyone, and even his inner circle isn't privy to his methods and plans for the valves." He pinned us each with a dark look as he spoke. "Don't let his old man act fool you. Mzatal, Jesral, and possibly other lords trained him. The bastard is sharp and strong."

In other words, Katashi was an enemy to be reckoned with. I masked a grimace. I, too, was guilty of thinking of him as just another summoner—one who happened to be iconic. I'd certainly never thought of him as a mastermind. Once again, I'd underestimated him. Stupid and dangerous.

"His stamp is on everything that has anything to do with

summoning," I said, pulse thudding as the implications sunk in. "All modern summoners—*every single one of us*—has either been a direct student of Katashi, or a student of one of his students." *Like my Aunt Tessa*, I thought as a lump tightened my throat. Katashi had kept her on the sidelines for years before calling her into service. And though I didn't believe for a minute that she was complicit in any of the nastiness, she dropped everything and went to him the instant he snapped his fingers.

"That's right," Idris said, leaning forward. "And it means Katashi has neutral-to-favorable connections with every summoner in the *world*." He stabbed a finger toward me. "Except you," he jerked his thumb at himself, "and me."

Conversation died as the weight of what we faced settled over us. The sharp tang of gun oil wound through the room as we bent over our weapons and attended to issues that were easily dealt with. A spot of corrosion. A buildup of carbon.

Pellini reassembled and wiped down his gun, then rubbed a hand over the stubble on his chin, brows knitted in a frown. "There might be an advantage in this for us," he said. "Katashi's been the unopposed head honcho for all these years. If everyone has always been on his side, then he's not used to being a target. He might not be at the top of the game when it comes to defense."

Idris gave a reluctant nod. "He's near untouchable when he knows trouble is imminent but, yeah, constant vigilance isn't his specialty."

Bryce slipped the pieces of the Sig back together, loaded it, chambered a round and holstered it. "If McDunn and Carter have a say in his security, he'll be less vulnerable than before."

Pellini shifted, uneasy. "Are we talking capturing or killing here?"

"Killing," Idris said, even as I said, "Capturing."

Idris leveled a defiant look at me. "Killing is a helluva lot less risky. There's no advantage to capturing him."

"Less risky?" I scoffed. "Maybe in the short term, but

killing packs a mighty punch when it comes to consequences." And didn't I know it. "Look, Katashi is the eyes,
ears, and hands of the Mraztur on Earth. I doubt any of
them have a clue about his day-to-day operation." Idris
looked poised to interrupt, but I kept going. "You said that
his people don't know his plans and methods. If we kill him,
and his flunkies don't know what to do next with the valves,
the Mraztur are screwed." I narrowed my eyes. "But so are
we, since we don't know what he's put in motion with the
valve project."

"Capture him, and nothing changes other than the risk,"
Idris shot back. "He's not going to volunteer the info, and
the lords can't read him."

I shook my head. "Mzatal believes that three lords working together can read Katashi." Sighing, I tugged a hand
through my hair. "And, if they can't, then *they* can take care
of him as they see fit."

Idris folded his arms and slouched back. "Okay. Fine." It
wasn't a ringing endorsement, but I'd take it.

Bryce cleared his throat. "With capture on the agenda, I
propose surveillance as a first step. Get a feel for their
movement. We don't have the manpower for a stakeout, but
we can monitor the gate with a camera."

"It's a solid starting point," I agreed.

"Idris and I can buy one of those weatherproof mini
video cameras," Bryce said. "We'll get that set up tonight."

Idris stood and yanked the messenger bag across his
chest. "I'll be by the car," he growled and stalked out.

Bryce watched him go, exhaled. "I'll deal with him. He
wants Katashi's blood, but he sees the bigger picture."

"Thanks, Bryce," I said. "You rock."

"Yes, I believe I do."

"You need to leave before your head is too big to fit
through the door."

Bryce laughed. "It'll be wee hours before we get back.
Don't wait up."

I stretched and felt things pop and creak in my spine. "I
don't think I could if I wanted to." I said. "Be careful."

"The epitome of caution," he said and exited.

Pellini rubbed his face with both hands. "What have I gotten myself into?"

"Deep shit." I gave him a wry smile. "But we won't let you drown."

# Chapter 20

In a spontaneous act of self-motivation, I donned workout gear immediately upon waking the next morning, determined to tackle the obstacle course for the first time since my return.

Humidity smacked me in the face the instant I stepped out the back door, a reminder of why I'd decided fitness could take a brief holiday. *Ugh. Right. Summer in south Louisiana.* I sighed and stepped off the porch. It would be the height of wimpiness to bail out, now that I was dressed, ready, and outside. So what if it felt as if I sucked air through a towel from the floor of a sauna. I was tough. I was fierce. I was already sweating my ass off and hadn't even started to run yet.

Armed with that attitude, I managed to shamble through the damn thing, though I suspected that the guys had increased the height on the walls and made the entire course at least half again as long as it used to be. With no grace whatsoever, I clambered over the final wall then staggered into deep shade by the edge of the woods. Drenched in sweat, I flopped onto my back and tried to remember how to breathe like a human.

A few minutes later Idris stepped out the back door then took off for the start of the course at a brisk jog. I could only see parts of the circuit from my vantage, but every glimpse of him revealed driven determination as he assaulted the obstacles. Muddy and sweat-soaked, he finished in half the time I'd taken, yet instead of flopping on the grass like a sensible person, he immediately began the movements of the shikvihr. I watched in fascination—and a mad helping of awe—as he executed the shikvihr in a manner akin to an insanely complex martial arts kata, his face drawn tight as he concentrated. Like me, he couldn't actualize the sigils on Earth, but his crisp, fluid motions left no doubt which sigil he traced at any given time.

My respect for him ratcheted up several degrees. He'd have the full shikvihr in no time at all. He'd do it in Mzatal's realm on top of the basalt column with the terrifying abyss through its core—and he wouldn't bat an eye. He'd already looked into a different kind of hell when he witnessed the brutal murder of his sister.

Idris finished the ninth ring, raked a hand through his hair, and flicked sweat away. To my amazement, he ran to the beginning of the course to start again. I rolled over and pushed to my feet. For an outrageous moment, I considered following Idris's example and doing the course one more time. Fortunately, reason prevailed and reminded me that killing myself by heatstroke would be counterproductive. With that decided, I headed to the house—sweaty, muddy, and generally gross.

For everyone's sake, I went straight to the bathroom and took a nice hot shower. Dressed and clean, I came back out to the kitchen to find Bryce at the table with the laptop and Pellini pouring a cup of coffee. Mouth-watering smells wafted from the oven.

"You made the coffee?" I asked Pellini.

He nodded. "You drink coffee with chicory," he said. "I love that stuff." He slid a glance to me. "Not sure you could've convinced me to stay here if y'all didn't have decent coffee."

"It's the food of the gods," I said then peeked into the oven, thrilled to see biscuits baking. "Did you make those from scratch?" I asked.

Pellini leaned back against the counter. "Are you kidding? No, there was one of those biscuit dough-in-a-tube things in the back of your fridge."

I had zero memory of buying anything like that, but that didn't mean squat anymore in this household. I poured myself a cup of coffee and added my usual near-lethal amounts of cream and sugar. Once settled at the table, I idly watched Bryce skim through local news reports.

When the oven timer dinged, Pellini removed the biscuits and slid them onto a plate. He set them in the middle of the table along with butter and jam, and not ten seconds later Jill and Steeev entered through the back door.

"I need sustenance for my very last day at work," she announced as she dropped a file onto the table. She purloined two biscuits before snagging an empty chair next to Bryce, and damn if his face didn't light up every time she walked into the room. I clung to my faith in him that told me he would never press for more friendship than she was comfortable with, but I didn't miss the very warm smile he offered her. I also didn't miss that Steeev swiped two biscuits for himself.

"Last day, though not a full day," Steeev told her with a hint of the glare Jill had mentioned at the ice cream shop.

She grinned around a mouthful of biscuit and jam. "Wah owah ah mof."

His glare eased. "Yes, one hour at most," he said, impressing me with his ability to translate biscuit-speak.

"You got any plans for what to do while you wait to pop out that kid?" Pellini asked. He split a biscuit down the middle and slathered jam on each side.

Jill chewed and swallowed. "Oh, yes," she said with a smile. "I have plans. I have years of TV to catch up on or rewatch. I'm going to make our Internet connection scream for mercy with all the quality entertainment I intend to stream."

Pellini let out a low chuckle. "That's an enviable goal."

Jill got to her feet and glanced at the clock. "Unless I have to waste time hunting down my captain, I expect to start my movie marathon by ten a.m." She picked up the file, then she and Steeev headed out the front door.

Bryce turned the laptop so Pellini and I could see the screen. "Check it out."

A police sketch of Jerry Steiner glowered at me from a local news website. Right next to it was a driver's license photo of the man himself. I made a face and flipped him off.

"With the Farouche investigation, he's one face among many," Bryce said. "But doing that shit to Amaryllis put him in the spotlight for all the good ol' boys. He'd better keep his head down."

Pellini peered at the images. "Too bad he's so common looking. Hardass, but nothing makes him stand out."

Bryce pulled the computer back to face him. "One of his greatest assets. He could blend in, and his mark wouldn't notice him until it was too late."

All three of us jerked our heads up at a sharp *crack* from the direction of the highway.

"That was a high-powered rifle," Bryce said, alarm rising in his eyes. "It's not hunting season, is it?"

"Only for wild hogs," Pellini said, brows drawing together. "Open season on them because of overpopulation." But doubt threaded through his voice.

Bryce pushed back from the table and ran for the computer room with me on his heels. We'd only heard one shot. Maybe it hadn't been a gunshot at all. Sure. Three people in the room with firearms experience, and all of us wrong?

Bryce didn't bother sitting, simply wiggled the mouse and pulled up the security camera playback for the front of the property. The view of the highway and gate popped up on the screen, and Bryce rewound the image until we saw Jill's car pass through the gate as it opened then pause at the end of the driveway. A few seconds later a woman breezed by on a motorcycle, and Jill's car moved forward in a right turn onto the highway.

The instant the front tires touched the asphalt, the car lurched hard to the right then veered off the highway and beyond camera range. Bryce let out a curse and raced from the room. On the edge of the screen a black van came into view, but I only caught a glimpse before I sprinted after Bryce.

He burst out the front door and leaped from porch to ground without a break in stride. I snagged my gun and holster from the table by the door then ran down the steps as Bryce dove behind the wheel of the Malibu. I barely managed to get into the passenger side before he gunned it down the driveway, and I braced myself as he screamed around the curves.

He hit the remote to open the gate when we were fifty yards away then slammed on the brakes. He knew better than to drive right smack into a potentially bad scene. I already had my door open and jumped out before the car stopped moving. Bryce threw it into park and bailed out on his side. Together we approached the end of the driveway in a low run and with guns at the ready.

Jill's car remained cocked at an angle with its front fender against a tree. No sign of the black van I'd seen on the video or anyone else. My pulse thudded loud in my ears, and I took deep and slow breaths to control my reaction to the gallons of adrenaline in my system.

"See anything?" I asked, staying low. I didn't bother to keep my voice down. If anyone was out here, they'd see us.

Bryce hadn't stopped scanning for threats. "Clear so far," he finally said, expression intense. Together we moved forward until we could see inside the car. Glass fragments glittered on the dash and interior. Jill's purse and the case file lay on the floor on the passenger side. No sign of Steeev or Jill. An icy fist clutched at my gut.

"She's not here," I said, unable to keep my voice steady. I yanked the driver's side door open, and my heart dropped as the distinct odor of sulfur and ozone poured out. "They killed Steeev." Killed him on Earth, at least. As soon as he'd died here his body had discorporeated, but it remained to be seen whether he made it back home to the demon realm. My hand tightened on the butt of my gun. "And they have Jill. They got Jill."

Bryce remained silent, demeanor dark and scary. He scrutinized the hole in the windshield and the cracks that radiated from it, then leaned close to peer at the hole in the driver's seat.

"High-powered rifle," he said, voice so cold it could freeze lava. "Round went through the windshield, through

Steeev, and into the backseat." He pulled the back door open, snapped a knife out, and slashed the cushion. After a couple of seconds of digging, he held up a deformed copper projectile that looked more like a flower than a bullet.

"Three-oh-eight," Bryce said, tightening his hand around it. "I'll bet anything it came from a Bergara tactical rifle with a Schmidt and Bender scope." He swept an expert gaze at the surrounding woods. "Leo Carter. He has extensive sniper training. That's the rifle he uses, and this was no amateur shot." Bryce gestured toward a stand of trees by the curve in the road. "He most likely set up there. Clear view, and five hundred yards would be easy for Carter."

I didn't fucking care what kind of round or gun he'd used to kill Steeev. I wanted to scream that, but I knew focusing on these details was how Bryce kept himself from breaking apart. Throat tight, I gave him a nod. "We'll check it out," I said. "We'll check everything out. Good work."

My phone buzzed in my pocket, and my heart leaped when I yanked it out and saw Jill's name. Yet in the next instant it crashed again. It meant they had her and were going to make their demands. Rage burned through me as I jammed the answer button. "You goddamn motherfucking pieces of shit fuckstains," I yelled into the phone. "If you touch one hair on her head I'll—"

"Kara! Shut up!"

Jill. That was Jill's voice. She sounded upset, which was understandable. "Jill, don't be afraid!" I frantically beckoned Bryce over. "Those assholes won't dare hurt you, and I won't stop until I find you!"

"Yeah, finding me would be nice," she said. "I'm in the middle of the woods. What happened?"

I didn't want to tell her about Steeev, not over the phone. "They took you, but we're going to get you back. Can you describe anything around you?" Weird that they were letting her talk so freely. Maybe they didn't realize she had her phone?

"Took me? What are you talking about? Oh! I think I'm on your property. I see the high wall for the obstacle course. And I hear Sammy barking. At least I think it's Sammy."

It took me a stupid moment to comprehend, then I started jumping up and down like a third grader who'd won a trip to Disney. "She's here!" I screeched to Bryce, but he was already fishing the keys from his pocket.

"Go," he said, his voice thick with worry. "Send Pellini out here when you get to the house."

I snatched the keys from his hand and sprinted to the Malibu. Pellini was on the porch as I pulled up, a shotgun in his hands. Idris jogged from the backyard toward me.

"They shot Steeev," I shouted to them as I jumped out. "Jill's okay and in the woods. Pellini, go help Bryce. Idris, help me find Jill."

Neither questioned my orders. Pellini hopped in his truck and raced up front. With the help of Sammy, Idris and I soon located a very perplexed Jill. Idris helped me get her back to the house then joined the other two at the gate.

I settled Jill on the sofa then sat close by and peered at her with worry. She appeared completely unharmed other than a thin streak of blood on her cheek, likely from flying glass.

"Would you please stop looking at me like I'm some kind of alien," she snapped.

I winced. "Sorry. I'm trying to figure out what happened." As much as I tried to come up with other possibilities, I kept returning to the same conclusion. She'd been in the car one moment and in the woods the next. A few days earlier, she'd been on the porch then traveled instantaneously to the pond valve.

As if in response to my growing suspicion, she put her hand on her belly and shifted in discomfort. "The bean is wiggling hard. All elbows again."

"She knows you're upset," I said absently. The demahnk could teleport, so maybe the child of one could as well? It boggled my mind that an unborn baby could have enough awareness of the world outside its cozy swimming pool to consciously *teleport* and bring mommy with her.

Survival reflex? That was a little easier to handle. I snorted to myself. Right. I was fine with the concept of a teleporting demon baby but not with how *aware* it might be? I'd been dealing with this weird shit for FAR too long.

I dismissed all thoughts of instantaneous-hyper-aware-fetus transport. "What do you remember?" I asked.

Her brow creased. "Steeev was driving, and we headed out the gate. I told him he had biscuit crumbs on his shirt. He smiled and—" She stopped, blinked.

"And what?"

Jill stroked a hand over her belly, frowning. "Something hit the windshield," she said slowly. "Steeev jerked the wheel . . . and then I was standing in the middle of the woods." She turned to me. "Kara, where is Steeev?" Her voice stayed calm, but distress rose in her eyes. She wasn't dumb. She'd heard how upset I was when I answered the phone. More significantly, Steeev wasn't with her right now, caring for her.

I told her, then hugged her when she cried. "He's not *dead*," I reminded her and hoped I was right. Jill knew how that whole thing worked from the time I died in the demon realm and from when Eilahn was shot to death here on Earth last year. Chances were good that he'd pass through the void and survive, but there were no guarantees. It could be weeks before we knew for sure.

"I know." She sniffled against my shoulder. "But it's awful for Steeev, and I felt *safe* with him around. With Zack gone I really needed that."

I sighed. "Yeah, you did."

Footsteps on the porch reached us seconds before Bryce entered, followed by Pellini. Bryce's gaze went straight to Jill, and stark relief swam through his eyes at the sight of her safe and unharmed.

"You okay?"

She straightened and managed a wan smile as she wiped her eyes. "Yeah. Though now I'm all puffy and red-nosed."

"I hadn't noticed," he said with a fond smile and sat beside her.

Yeah, he'd have been a godawful mess if she'd been hurt. "Did you find anything?" I asked him.

"We found where Carter set up for his shot." He tugged a scrap of paper from his pocket and held it out to me. "And this, tromped into the mud."

Although stained from its time in the mud, most of the details remained visible on the ripped corner of paper. The top held part of a green logo of a stylized running horse superimposed on a star, and below that was a sketch of arcane glyphs with a section torn off. I examined it then shrugged, puzzled. "Not much here. Three partial sigils."

Bryce tapped the logo. "I don't know about the sigils, but this might be of interest. It's Emerald Star Thoroughbreds. Belonged to Farouche, and Angus McDunn's house is there."

That perked me right up. "You think he's been back there? I'm sure the feds have been all over the place."

"I'm thinking about his wife," Bryce said. "They had something special. We used to see McDunn with her every now and then. Always seemed like cognitive dissonance to see an ice-cold murderer like McDunn playing the loving husband and father. Happy." He shook his head as if still unable to believe it. "As far as I know, he kept his business completely separate from his home life. Anyway, if he contacted anyone, it would be her."

I processed that tidbit while I also wrestled their son Boudreaux into the picture. "We're looking for different information than the feds," I said. "Might be a dead end but worth checking out." I glanced at Pellini. "Are you up for a field trip to the stud farm?"

"Stud farm?" He lifted his chin. "I'll blend right in."

I rolled my eyes and held back a laugh. "In your dreams."

"What about Jill?" Pellini asked.

"I've got her," Bryce said. "Idris is here as well."

"I'm in the room, you know," Jill said with asperity then sighed. "Thanks, Bryce. I know I'm safe with you on the watch. And, before anyone starts lecturing me, I'm calling in immediate leave. The department can send a tech out to pick up the files. And, yes, I'll move into the house. I know that makes security much simpler."

"You can have the guestroom," Pellini said. "I'll take the futon in the computer room."

I huffed out a dramatic sigh. "Darn it! I had my compelling and heart-wrenching speech all ready, and Jill had to spoil it by being sensible."

"Save it for when you run for office," she said. "I'm not budging until after this kid is born. Except *maybe* to go to the hospital."

If my guess was correct about a headstrong teleporting baby in her tummy, I doubted she'd have a choice in the matter.

# Chapter 21

The windshield wipers beat in a furious *thwap-thwap* against the deluge of a summer squall. Pellini flipped on the headlights and settled into a speed sensible for the rural highway. "It's Sunday," he said after a moment. "Boudreaux might be home."

"Maybe he won't know we're there."

He shrugged. "No idea what the layout of the property is."

"He lives with his mom and McDunn?"

"Nah, he's on his own. Has a little house. That's all I know. He's never invited me out."

I eyed him. "I thought you two were pretty close."

"At work, yeah," Pellini said. "But he keeps his private life private. We go out for the occasional beer or watch football at my house." He shrugged. "This last year he helped with the costuming for the contest, but that's pretty much it."

I watched the rain sheet across the road. "Do you think he knew what his stepdad was into?"

His mouth twisted beneath his mustache. "Every now and then he'd crow about McDunn and how the Child Find League recovered or closed cases on twenty kids last year or whatever. Never a bad word." A wince flashed across his face. "Could be he knew about the ugly side and his talk was just a smokescreen."

"You don't believe that."

Lightning speared across the sky. "I've been wrong about people before," Pellini said. "And ninety-nine point nine percent of the world was wrong about Mr. Benevolent Saint Farouche. The press grabbed the story that most of the murders Farouche ordered were vigilante justice against child molesters and abusers, and now there are people singing his praises." He paused as thunder rolled over the truck. "Even considering what happened to his kid, who knows how much of that vigilante story is true?"

Almost twenty years ago, Farouche's five-year-old daughter Madeleine had been kidnapped and never found. Not long after that, Farouche formed the Child Find League and a number of other charities devoted to the welfare of juveniles—all of which had a stellar record for child advocacy. McDunn was Farouche's right hand man for all of it. How did such a noble mission go so far off the rails?

"Bryce would know how much is true," I said quietly. "He never talks about specific hits he made for Farouche, but he did tell me that Farouche had Jerry Steiner kill Paul's dad for brutalizing him. Given Farouche's personal history, the vigilante aspect makes a sick kind of sense."

Pellini scowled and scrubbed at his mustache. "And Steeev got snipered by a dead man's flunky." He made a turn onto a blacktop road that ran through a mixed pine forest. "What are Steeev's chances for, uh, surviving?"

"I told Jill they were high," I said without pulling my gaze from the monotonous scenery of pines. "But to be honest, I don't know." Sighing, I rubbed my eyes. "Theoretically, chances are decent the first time through the void. Not so much for a second death. He's never died on Earth before, so that helps his odds."

The rain stopped as suddenly as it had begun. Pellini clicked off the wipers, and within a quarter of a mile sunlight blazed down onto a bone dry road. Louisiana weather. Gotta love it.

Pellini smacked the steering wheel. "Shit!"

I jerked, startled. "What?!"

"You! You died over there! In the demon realm!" His mouth widened into a pleased smile. "That's why you appeared out of nowhere without a stitch on."

I couldn't answer for several seconds. "You saw me naked?"

His smile exploded into a grin.

Groaning, I dropped my head back against the seat. "Yeah. It was after I found out the Symbol Man was Chief Morse. I started the whole dying process here on Earth, but Rhyzkahl brought me to the demon realm to finish dying so that I had a chance of surviving it."

His grin evaporated. "Fuck me. I went out on that scene. Arcane garbage all over the place. And the chief . . ." He didn't finish the sentence, and I didn't blame him. Rhyzkahl had torn the chief's head clean off. It hadn't been a pleasant sight. Pellini cleared his throat. "So, did Morse shoot you? Is that why you were dying?"

I gave him a long look. "No. A reyza who was working with Morse eviscerated me." I paused, unsure if I should name names since the reyza in question was one of the demons Pellini said he knew. Then again, Pellini was bound to find out sooner or later. "It was Sehkeril."

"Shit." Pellini winced and shifted in his seat. "I feel like I should apologize."

"Not your fault," I said with a firm shake of my head. "I still don't know why he was helping Morse."

He chewed his bottom lip. "If Sehkeril was helping him, that means Kadir condoned what Morse was doing, right?"

"It means that Kadir condoned at least one facet that served his agenda," I said. "I don't know if it was the murders, the summoning and binding of Rhyzkahl, or an aspect I haven't discovered." *An aspect I haven't discovered.* The phrase reverberated in my mind. Kadir was beyond clever, and his extended and subtle grooming of Pellini demonstrated his patience. What kind of long game was the creepy lord playing? More importantly, what else had resulted from the Symbol Man's murder spree and summoning attempt?

"We're here." Pellini's voice broke through my thoughts. I sat up and paid attention. He turned off the road and passed through open wrought iron gates with "Emerald

Star Thoroughbreds" worked into a bronze arch above. A driveway lined with bright white fences crossed pastures toward a distant cluster of buildings. When the driveway forked, Pellini veered right toward two long barns and a tidy Acadian house with a small barn behind it. A large house and several other buildings hunkered a quarter mile down the other fork.

Pellini parked in a gravel lot that held a handful of other cars. I stepped out and slipped my sunglasses on. A light breeze carried the scent of newly mown grass, and a bay mare as pregnant as Jill nickered to us from a paddock.

We strolled to a pasture fence and watched the antics of a chestnut foal as he cavorted around his grazing mom. Less than a minute later the sound of boots on gravel had us turning to see a lanky black man with grey at his temples sauntering toward us.

"Morning, folks." His tone was friendly and open, but the wary flick of his eyes betrayed his suspicion. "What can I do for you?"

His caution didn't surprise me one bit considering that investigators had surely crawled all over the property and questioned everyone. I gave him what I hoped was a disarming smile. My mood was shit, but if I let it show I wouldn't get any of the information I wanted. "Hi, we're looking for Catherine McDunn." I jerked my thumb toward Pellini. "Tall dark and silent here is her son's partner at the PD."

The suspicion dropped away to be replaced by a broad grin. "Vince Pellini, 'bout time you made it out this way!" He extended a hand to Pellini. "Lenny Brewster. Barn manager."

"Nice to meet you, sir," Pellini said gruffly, shaking the offered hand.

"Ain't no sir," he said with a snort. "Just Lenny." He offered his hand to me next. "You also work with Boo?"

"Used to," I said. He had a strong grip and the rough calluses of a man who got things done. "I'm Kara Gillian."

"Ms. Gillian." He gave a knowing nod. "I've heard a lot about you."

Crap. That could span anything from the size of my tits to my role as a murder suspect in Farouche's death. I did my best to act unfazed. "I bet you have," I replied and faked a chuckle. "Though I'm sure I don't need to tell you that not all rumors are based in fact."

"Boo always said you were a sharp cookie," Lenny said with a friendly wink. "Never told me you were modest, too."

The hell? Boudreaux talked *nice* about me? That was a new one. "I have my moments," I said. Apparently Lenny didn't know about my alleged connection to Farouche's murder. "And please, call me Kara. Is Boudreaux around?"

Lenny waved a hand toward the woods and fields beyond one of the large barns. "He's out on the trails with Psycho right now."

*Whew.* With luck we'd be long gone before he returned.

"Psycho?" Pellini asked. "Is that a horse or a woman?"

Lenny laughed, from the belly and unashamed of it. "I gotta tell Boo that one! Nah, Psycho's a horse—top of the line stud. Miss Catherine's out by the track. Here, I'll walk you down."

With that he led the way along a path toward the breezeway of the small barn. Over the entrance "Copper to Gold" stood out in crisp white lettering, but above the name someone had painted "Psycho" in broad and deliberately crude crimson letters and allowed the paint to drip like blood.

"That's Boo's house there," Lenny said with a nod toward the white Acadian with green shutters. "Mr. Farouche had it built for him after the accident so he could be close to Psycho."

*Accident?* I started to ask what he meant, but my question fled my mind as we passed into the barn. Photos of a gorgeous chestnut horse lined the wall—in races, in winner's circles, and as a foal. I didn't know much about thoroughbreds, but I had to admire the fierce beauty of this horse.

I stopped dead in my tracks to stare at a large photo of Psycho. The jockey on his back had his helmet and goggles off, and a proud smile lit his face—

"Boudreaux was a *jockey?*" I blurted. Once again I had

to adjust everything I thought I knew about him. I felt like the GPS in my car every time I ignored its instructions and it began to bleat, *Recalculating . . . recalculating . . .*

"Yes, ma'am," Lenny said. "A damn fine one, too." He peered over my shoulder at the picture. "Boo always had a way with that horse like no one else." Pride softened his voice.

"You mentioned an accident," I said. "Is that why he isn't still a jockey?"

Lenny's smile dropped away. "Near thirteen years ago now. Bad race spill with Psycho that ended both their careers. Boo's femur got broke in three places. Psycho got a cannon bone fracture. Boo's leg healed, and he could still exercise ride, but couldn't hold up for racing." He exhaled. "Another jockey died, and Boo got blamed. And with Copper to Gold," he tapped the picture, "being an undefeated grade one stakes champion, the media took it and ran with it." Anger deepened the lines around his eyes. "Didn't matter that Boo got cleared of fault. Folks like having someone to blame."

"People suck," I said, more bitterly than I intended. Boudreaux's smile in the pictures was one of pure joy. He loved riding and racing, and had lost it all in one tragic moment. It didn't excuse his becoming a bitter, obnoxious asshole, but I valued the insight. "How'd he go from this," I said, gesturing toward the photos, "to being a cop?"

Lenny tapped the picture. "Losing this lifestyle just about killed him," he continued in a somber voice. "But Mr. Farouche never gave up on him. Not for a single minute. Stood by him through the accusations. Tried to keep him full time with the horses—training and exercise riding—but Boo shut it down. Had a bad spell with alcohol until Mr. Angus and Mr. Farouche shook him out of it. Boo took up policework thinking he could help protect kids."

*Protect kids.* "Because of Farouche's daughter," I murmured.

"Boo was only twelve when Miss Madeleine went missing," Lenny said, face long. "It hit him hard. He loved that kid. She used to follow him all over the farm, and he'd watch her like a hawk. I still remember him stapling flyers up all over town." He wiped his eyes on his sleeve without shame. "His dad started working for Mr. Farouche right after, and those two men made it their mission to do everything possible to keep kids safe. If Boo couldn't race ride, he wanted to follow in their footsteps." Lenny gave Pellini a sidelong glance. "I don't think becoming a cop worked out like he'd expected."

Pellini winced, nodded. Boudreaux's romantic notions of policework had probably died after a few weeks of dealing with drunks and responding to loud music complaints. I had a feeling the closest he'd come to protecting kids was directing traffic in a school zone. As long as I'd been a cop I couldn't remember a time when he hadn't been the target of department bullies and innocent jokesters.

*Recalculating . . . recalculating . . .*

Lenny continued through the breezeway and onto a pathway of spongy interlocking emerald green tiles. A dirt practice track lay a hundred yards ahead.

"Did you know any of this?" I asked Pellini under my breath.

"I looked him up right after we got put together as partners," he replied, voice low. "Saw the news stories and knew about the accident, but he never talked about it. Not once. Didn't feel right to push the issue." His gaze swept over the fields and track and barns.

Made perfect sense to me. If the guys at the station ever got wind of his former profession, the teasing would be merciless.

*A secret life*, I mused. I knew all about that sort of thing. As did Pellini, with his Kadir connection and, on a smaller scale, his costuming sideline.

Two horses and riders rounded the turn on the track and thundered down the straight, neck and neck. Lenny went up to the rail, leaned on it and put a foot on a battered crate that seemed to be placed for that very purpose. "Miss Catherine will be clear in a minute." He gestured to our right at a dark-haired woman in jeans, boots, and a blue t-shirt, who leaned against the rail in a similar pose by the gate about a hundred yards away. She divided her attention between a stopwatch in her hand and the two horses as they galloped by.

"How long has she worked here?" I asked.

"She grew up here just like Boo," he said. "Pops, her dad, used to be head trainer. She worked her way up and has been head now for close to ten years."

I caught Pellini's eye. "We should go introduce ourselves," I said to Lenny. "Would you excuse us for a few minutes?"

A flicker of worry passed over his face, but he simply gave a nod and went back to watching the horses.

Pellini and I strolled down the rail. "Boudreaux's family has been here for *generations*," I said. "No wonder he's so messed up about Farouche's death."

He nodded, grim.

We waited for the horses to slow before approaching. "Mrs. McDunn?" I said when she looked over. "I'm Kara Gillian. I used to work with your son. This is Vince Pellini, his partner."

"What do you want?" she asked, sounding more tired than defensive.

"I'm sorry, I know this is hard on you," I said. "I'm sure various investigators have already spoken to you, but I was hoping you'd answer a few questions about your husband, Angus."

To my relief, she gave me a firm nod. "I'll tell you anything you want to know," she said, mouth tightening in undisguised anger as she slid the stopwatch into the front pocket of her jeans. "I can't believe that man lied to me for all these years. All those terrible things he did! I hope they track him down and put him away for the rest of his life."

"You believe the accusations?" Pellini asked.

"Every one of them," she said with conviction. "The bastard called me the day after the plantation fire wanting help. He didn't deny any of it."

Pellini and I exchanged a quick glance. It was clear we shared the same thought. "Did the cops happen to get a recording of that conversation?" I asked.

"Not that one," she said. "But after that I gave them free rein to tap the phones." She pressed a hand to her mouth. "They got one last night when Angus called to try to tell me he loved me and god knows what else. I didn't want to hear it." She dashed away a tear from the corner of her eye.

"I'm sorry you had to go through that, Mrs. McDunn," I said. "I take it you—"

She yanked her hand up. "Ms. Kinsley," she corrected sharply. "I'm filing for divorce and going back to my maiden name."

"Understandable," I said, though I wondered how Boudreaux felt about that. "What did Angus want when he called that first time?"

"Cash," she said, a mix of fury and hurt in her eyes. "Can you believe that? Not, 'I'm sorry I ruined your life.' No. Money to get him by until he met up with some other people—other criminals, no doubt." Her eyes followed the two horses coming off the track. "I need to go. Anything else?"

Pellini cleared his throat. "No, ma'am. Thank you for your time."

She forced a smile and headed toward the long barn in the wake of the horses.

"Can you get hold of that recording?" I asked Pellini as we walked back toward Lenny.

"Tricky," he said. "I may have to call in a favor or two, but I'll do what I can. We *have* to hear it." He nudged me with his elbow and pointed toward the far side of the track.

A big chestnut horse the color of a burnished copper penny walked onto the track. Copper to Gold, a.k.a. Psycho, with Boudreaux aboard. "Holy shit," I said under my breath, eyes riveted on the pair.

Looking perfectly at ease in the saddle, Boudreaux brought the horse to the head of the stretch then let him run. For a moment I forgot all about Angus McDunn and Katashi and valves, enthralled by the beauty of motion, power, and speed. They galloped past, and I felt as though they carried me with them as they ran for the pure joy of running. Boudreaux slowed Psycho to a canter, then a walk,

before circling and heading back our way. Boudreaux patted the horse's neck, a broad smile on his face.

"He looks happy," I said. "Even with all the shit going
on, he looks *happy*. I've never seen him like that." I shook
my head. "We need to get out of here before he spots us."

Too late. Boudreaux's gaze snapped to us, and his smile
melted into a scowl. He stopped Psycho about fifteen feet
away and vaulted to the ground with a grace I never expected. Lenny ducked under the rail and eased their way.
Psycho laid his ears back and lunged toward Lenny, but
Boudreaux let out a short whistle. The horse immediately
settled down and allowed Lenny to take hold of his bridle
and lead him toward the gap in the rail.

Boudreaux yanked loose the strap of his helmet and
stalked toward us. "What the fuck are you two doing here?"
he said then glared at Pellini and stabbed a finger in my
direction. "How could you bring *her* here?" He didn't add
*you traitorous piece of shit*, but he might as well have.

Pellini lowered his head and shifted his weight. "We
wanted to check out a few things. Didn't know you'd be
home."

Boudreaux stepped closer, jaw so tight the muscles on
the sides of his neck stood out. "What things? Nothing for
either of you here."

I lifted my hands. "Look, maybe we shouldn't have come
here, but we did. We'll go now."

"No!" Outrage mottled his face with red and white
patches. "You can't just invade my home and *la dee da* waltz
out again. You *owe* me."

I met his eyes steadily. "I know what you want, but I can't
give it to you."

He bared his teeth. "We'll see what you have to say
when—"

A horse neighed in the big barn, and he jerked his gaze
that way. Catherine stood by the entrance, one hand shading her eyes as she watched us. "My mom. Goddammit. You
talked to her." Worry covered his anger. He tore off his helmet to reveal hair plastered to his head from sweat. "What
did you say?" His voice shook. "Did you upset her? She

doesn't need any more shit." Without waiting for a response, he took off toward Catherine at a jog then turned, eyes on me. "Get the fuck out of here." He shot me the finger for emphasis before running toward his mom.

"Well." Pellini grimaced. "I'd say that's our cue to depart."

"Boo ain't happy, and I can't say I blame him." I struck out toward the parking lot with Pellini. "At least we didn't say anything upsetting to his mom."

"You hope."

I sighed. "Yeah, I hope." And I hoped the lead on the phone call would be worth antagonizing Boudreaux even more.

"Who do you know over at the Sheriff's Office?" I asked after we were on the road again. I was on a first name basis with quite a few of the detectives there, but at the moment that meant absolute zilch. Even if I wasn't currently a person of interest in a very high-profile active investigation, I was no longer a cop and therefore had no pull.

"I know a few guys over there," Pellini said. "I think I can get a copy of the recording without too many questions asked. I'll say it might pertain to the Amber Gavin case." He scowled. "Not that it matters, right? If I try to build a case against the shitholes who raped and murdered her, it'd draw too much attention to the arcane side of things."

I sighed. "Yeah, it would be risky. I'm sorry,"

He echoed my sigh. "It fucking sucks shit."

Led Zeppelin came on the radio, and I waited for them to finish singing about the land of ice and snow before I spoke again. "Probably doesn't help much, but Amber was murdered outside of Beaulac. Wouldn't be your jurisdiction anyway."

"Where?"

"Austin, Texas."

He made a disgruntled noise. "Yeah. I hate working with out-of-state cops."

We both knew it would never come to that, but I didn't press the point.

"What do you know about Rob O'Connor?" I asked after another few minutes. "He's the detective investigating me."

Pellini considered carefully. "He's a real straight arrow," he finally said. "The Farouche case is a huge deal to him for obvious reasons."

I understood that. This area didn't get many murders, especially not one this meaty—prominent local businessman gets murdered execution-style and turns out to be involved in who-the-hell knows what. Any detective worth a shit would love to sink their teeth into an investigation like that.

"He's a good detective," Pellini continued, frowning.

"But?"

Pellini shook his head. "There isn't a 'but.' Sorry." He offered me a sympathetic look. "O'Connor *really* wants to close this case and find the shooter."

In other words, the dude wasn't going to give up simply because I refused to talk to him. Wonderful.

"Guess I should put his number in my contacts."

Pellini snorted. "Not a bad idea."

# Chapter 22

Pellini paced near the tree line with his phone to his ear and Sammy trotting happily beside him. Back and forth. Back and forth. Every third round or so, he would pick up a stick and chuck it across the yard without a break in his conversation. Each time, the dog rocketed after the stick, brought it back to drop at Pellini's feet, and resumed trotting at his side.

Fuzzykins lay draped over the porch railing, regarding the dog with the utmost disdain. Me, I lazed on the back porch and watched the dog and his man, unable to keep from smiling at Sammy's antics. It was on Pellini to pull strings and get us a copy of the McDunn phone call recording, so all I could do was wait and see. And relax.

After several minutes Pellini clipped his phone to his belt and returned to me with Sammy gallivanting in circles around him. The triumphant smile on his face told me the outcome of his calls. "Man, I had to call in a lot of favors for this one," he said. "But the guy who has the case is emailing the recording to me right now."

"Sweet!" I stood and stretched then gave him a rueful smile. "I hate to admit it, but I wasn't sure you'd be able to pull it off."

Pellini twitched his shoulders in a shrug. "I have a few connections."

"As long as it gives us a lead, I don't care if you sold your soul to the devil."

He made a noise in the back of his throat. "Pretty sure I did that a *long* time ago."

"Dude, I hear you."

We proceeded inside to the dining room. Pellini retrieved his laptop, flipped it open, then drummed his fingers impatiently as he waited for his email to load. "There it is," he said. He clicked on the file and adjusted the volume. I pulled up a chair beside his and leaned close to the speaker.

A series of clicks.

*"Hello?"* Catherine McDunn's voice.

A pause. Silence.

*"Hello?"* Catherine again.

A man spoke. *"Catherine."*

Her sharp intake of breath. *"Angus."*

*"Oh god, I'm sorry. Sorry for everything."*

*"You're sorry? And that's supposed to fix it? How could you do this? To me. To Marcel."*

*"It wasn't supposed to be like this. I swear."*

*"But it is like this, Angus."* Pain threaded through her words.

*"Baby, please."* His breath shuddered. *"Please, just hear me out."*

*"Why? So you can ask me for money again or something else that puts me in danger?"*

*"No! God, no, I never wanted you to be in danger. Catherine, I love you."*

Her breath caught in a sob. *"I love you too, Angus, which makes all of this hurt so much more. We wouldn't be in this nightmare if you'd talked to me the first time Macklin asked you to . . . to . . ."*

*"It killed me not being able to tell you, baby. You have to believe me."*

*"I love you. I've been here for you. And . . . all those years of lies. How can I believe anything you say now?"*

*"Dammit. I was trying to protect you and Marcel. I couldn't tell you."*

*"Protect us? From what? It couldn't be worse than this."*

*"Look, baby. I can't go into that. Even now. All I'm asking is for you to trust that I—"*

Muffled voices in the background that didn't belong to Angus or Catherine, but too low to make out any words.

*"Hang on a sec."* Angus again, but sounding as if he spoke over his shoulder to another person.

*"Angus?"* Catherine, worried. *"What's going on?"*

*"It's cool, baby. I promise I'll—"* More background voices. A few words rose above the others: *Timetable. Critical. Master.* A voice that might have been Jerry's. A curse from Angus, then a rustling as if he'd put his hand over the phone. *"Number six."* Muffled but audible. Angus, taut and stressed, speaking to the other person. *"You and the boss are doing number six this afternoon. Now leave me the fuck alone for two goddamn minutes."*

More rustling. *"Catherine. I love you. That will never change."*

A ragged breath. *"Then do the right thing. Turn yourself in."*

*"I can't do that."*

*"Won't! You* won't *do it."* An angry sob. *"I don't know who you are anymore. Where's my hero?"*

*"I'm right here, baby. Listen to me—"*

*"No! I'm through listening. You had* years *to talk. Years, Angus."* Voice shaking. *"Don't . . . don't call me again."*

*"Catherine, baby. Don't cut me out of your life. Please."*

*"You cut me out of yours, you lying son of a bitch!"* Crying. *"You've left me no choice! I have to protect myself and my son. I . . . hate you. I* hate *you."*

*"Baby, no! Listen. I'm—"*

A click, then silence.

Pellini exhaled and rubbed a hand over his jaw. "That's all of it."

"Wow," I breathed and sat back. "Bryce wasn't lying about how those two were with each other."

"Yeah. They sounded like the real deal. And he trashed it."

An odd catch in his voice drew my attention, but before I could pry into the cause he shoved away from the table and stomped out of the room. Taken off guard, I stumbled up to follow.

"Pellini? You okay?" I made it to the hallway in time to see him stiff-arm the back door open, shoulders hunched and head down. Mystified, I continued after him. What in blazes had triggered this? Sammy ran up to him but, instead of frolicking as usual, he dropped his ears and pressed close to Pellini's leg as if sensing his human's mood.

Pellini stopped in the shade of a tall pecan tree then crouched and hugged the dog to him, not resisting when Sammy offered slobbery dog-kisses.

I cleared my throat softly. "Do you need anything?"

He blew out a breath and shifted to sit on the grass. Sammy draped himself over Pellini's lap, eyes on his human's face. "Sorry," Pellini said with a grimace. "Old ghosts."

I sat a few feet away. "Related to Angus and Catherine?"

"Nah, but they reminded me of some personal shit." He stroked his dog's ears. "Angus is a turd, and they're going through hell right now."

"And you know hell," I said, echoing his own words from the other day.

Pellini didn't bluster defensively this time. Instead he sighed. "We all do. Some more than others." He lifted his chin toward me. "Like you and your scars and what Rhyzkahl did to you. And Idris . . ." He scrubbed a hand over his face. "I can't imagine having to *watch* what happened to his sister. Makes my shit seem pretty insignificant in comparison."

"No," I said with force. "No, that's total hogwash. You can't compare your trauma or grief to anyone else's. Telling yourself that you have to smile through your pain because the guy next to you has it worse is as dumb as refusing to be happy because the other guy is having a better day." I stabbed a finger at him. "Don't invalidate your own feelings."

Pellini blinked at me. "Did you really just say 'hogwash'?"

I rolled my eyes. "Yes, and I can't believe that's all you got from that."

He let out a low snort, looked down at the blissful dog in his lap with a soft smile. "Nah. I heard you. Every now and then you make a little sense."

I held back a tart reply and waited. After a moment he

let out a long sigh. "Kadir was a huge part of my life for seven years, and then out of nowhere he abandoned me. Shook up my whole world." His lips pressed together. "Less than a week later my mom passed away."

"I'm so sorry," I murmured.

Old pain pulled at his face. "Just like that, two of the three most important people in my life were gone. I fucking fell apart."

"Who was the third?" I asked.

"My fiancée, Vicky Malone." His voice caught on her name. "She was the love of my life. Understood and supported me. Got my dumb sense of humor. Funny and smart." He exhaled a shuddering breath.

"Did . . . she die too?"

Pellini shook his head. "No, I drove her off. She'd try to console me about losing my mom, then I'd get *pissed* because she didn't understand that it wasn't just my mom. My whole world had collapsed, and I couldn't tell her." His gaze turned bleak and haunted. "I took it out on her. Jesus, I was the biggest fucking asshole to ever walk the earth. She stuck it out for three months then finally gave up." He tipped his head back to look up at the sunlight piercing the leaves. "For close to a year I told myself I hated her. By the time I figured out what a goddamn jackass I'd been and tracked her down, she was married to another guy, with a baby on the way."

"Shit." I didn't know what else to say, but apparently that was enough. He dropped his gaze to me, nodded in agreement.

"Anyway, listening to those two on that recording brought all that back. McDunn screwed up."

I winced. "Poor Boudreaux."

"Yeah." He paused. "Let's hope to god he *never* hears us say that about him."

A bark of laughter slipped out. "Oh, *hell* no!" The crunch of gravel in the driveway heralded the return of Bryce and Idris. I clambered to my feet. "Let's play the recording for the boys. I bet 'number six' is a valve and, if so, hopefully Idris will know which one it is."

\*　　\*　　\*

Number six was, indeed, a valve.

"Nature center," Idris said the first time he listened to the recording. Pellini played it twice more, volume turned all the way up as the entire posse clustered in the dining room. At the end of the table Bryce sat beside Jill as she took notes, both with matching grim expressions. Eilahn stood near the door, arms folded. Tension held Idris in a solid grip as he paced by the table.

"He's going to be there," he said after the third time through the recording. He raked a gaze around the room. "Katashi. He's going to be at the nature center valve this afternoon. There'll be an emission at 2:47." Anger boiled through the excitement in his words. "We can get him. This is our chance."

"You're *sure* he'll be there?" I asked.

His head jerked in a nod of assent. "Completely. Even if they changed the numbering system—which I doubt— there's no other valve that has an emission this afternoon. And the 'master' is Katashi. He'll be there for the burst. I *know* it!"

"All right," I said. "Our strike team will be me, you, Pellini, and Eilahn. That's it. Bryce stays here with Jill. Who else will be with Katashi?"

"He doesn't like a lot of people around him when he works," Idris said. "One security guy and one other summoner. Tsuneo, most likely. He knows the valves almost as well as I do." Idris wasn't bragging either. He was stating a fact.

"Does Tsuneo carry a weapon?" Jill asked.

Idris shook his head. "Arcane and some martial arts, but I've never seen him with a gun."

A charged excitement filled the room. "This could work," Pellini said, stroking his mustache. "We get there well in advance, stake out the valve, and take them down."

"Bryce?" I said. "You're our tactical advisor. Can you work up a plan for us in the next, oh, twenty minutes?"

"I can," he said.

I rubbed my hands together. Damn, it felt good to take action. "Then let's have us an ambush."

I pulled Eilahn aside before she could return to the backyard. "I think you need to remain here for this," I said, letting my worry show.

Her lips pursed as she regarded me. "Then there is great error in your thinking," she replied, enunciating each word to ensure I comprehended.

So much for my fantasy where she agreed without argument and toddled off to her nest. "I don't want you to get hurt," I insisted. "You've passed through the void once already, and . . ." I didn't want to finish the sentence.

"It is no different than the risk you take," she said with a pointed look.

Crap. She was using logic. I didn't like that she was right. "You're not at full strength."

She set her jaw stubbornly. "I am not weakened to the point of jeopardizing the excursion," she said. "The benefits far outweigh the risks."

I knew when I was beaten. Exhaling, I wrapped her in a hug. "Okay. Fine. But I'll be really pissed if you get hurt. Or worse." Nope, still couldn't say it.

She embraced me close. "Should you choose an irrational emotional response, it will not alter my opinion of you."

I snorted, smiled. "I love you, too. So there."

# Chapter 23

Pellini was nice enough to let us use his truck with the comfy seats and the extended cab and all the bells and whistles. Damn nice since our alternatives were my puny car and the Malibu, which continued to have occasional operational issues.

Pre-ambush jitters had my heart pumping. *I should be an old hand at this.* I'd been eviscerated, sliced, and stabbed during previous engagements, but the common factor in every incident was a demonic lord. No demonic lords today, so my chances of losing large quantities of blood were slim, right?

Pellini drove a few hundred yards past the entrance to the nature center and turned onto a narrow dirt road through the woods. We bounced over ruts for close to a quarter mile before he pulled over and climbed out of the truck. He gestured to a break in the underbrush. "That game trail leads to the picnic area."

The instant my feet touched the ground, I flinched. The arcane broadcast of the valve jarred through me—a *wrongness* like the *kathunk-kathunk* of a washing machine out of balance. Idris muttered a curse and took off down the trail.

"The valve's unstable," I said over my shoulder to Pellini as I started after Idris. "That's far more urgent. Ambush has to take a back seat until we can fix it."

Cypress trees draped with Spanish moss crowded close, and overhanging branches of willows and white oaks

choked the trail. Bullfrogs croaked off to the right, and cicadas rasped their harsh songs all around. Nearly two hundred yards in, Eilahn seized my arm and dragged me to a
stop. "Others are at the valve."

*Demon senses for the win.* I hissed a warning to Idris
then turned and motioned for Pellini to stop. "Someone's
already at the valve," I whispered.

"Bad guys?" Pellini asked, breathing hard from the run.

"Well, it probably ain't Girl Scouts."

He let out a mock sigh of relief. "Good thing. Those little
bitches are tough."

I stifled a laugh and continued onward with caution. The
valve instability rattled through me like a car shaking itself
apart at high speed, and increased with every step we took.
After another fifty feet, the trail opened up into a picnic
area with a few weather-beaten tables and concrete barbecue pits. On the far side of the clearing, red-orange potency
sprayed from the valve like water from a loose fire hose.
Katashi and Tsuneo flanked the valve, both scrambling to
stabilize it before it blew. Katashi worked the containment
with fluid, sweeping movements. On the opposite side of
the valve, Tsuneo sweated and worked the flows in more
conventional ways, his too-pretty face contorted from extreme effort.

Idris's lips pulled back from his teeth in a snarl. "Do you
have your gun?" he asked, gaze riveted on the two enemy
summoners.

"Of course," Pellini and I answered at the same time.

"Wound them," he ordered. "We'll have them, and we
can finish with the valve on our own."

"I suppose you'd like me to shoot them in the legs?" Pellini replied with derision while I winced at the ignorance of
Idris's demand. "And be such a good shot that I miss the
femur, pelvis, femoral artery, and anything else life-threatening?"

Idris sneered at Pellini. "I wasn't expecting *you* to do
anything. I was talking to Kara." He pointedly shifted his
attention to me in clear dismissal of Pellini. "Anything you
can do to take them out from here?"

Pellini's hands clenched into fists. Right now I wouldn't blame him one bit if he popped Idris. Hell, I was tempted to do so on Pellini's behalf.

"No," I said flatly, "for all the reasons Pellini gave." Katashi and Tsuneo weren't aware of us yet, but only because they were engrossed in their efforts to prevent disaster. "There's no way they'll get that valve under control in time on their own, and we sure as shit can't either." Trusting Pellini to watch my back, I strode out of our concealment, ignoring Idris's choked growl. "You need our help," I called out, tone as firm and confident as I could make it.

Tsuneo's head snapped up in surprise, but Katashi merely shifted to the far side of the valve.

"Agreed," he said. I closed the distance at a jog, assessing. To my surprise and relief Idris moved into position beside me. I had no doubt he crushed the urge to throttle Katashi then and there only because we'd all be dead if the valve blew. Priorities.

Idris gathered potency as it spewed from the damaged valve, shaped and passed it to Katashi and Tsuneo, obviously very familiar with working with the two. I copied his technique then paused, fixated on the valve. Between one heartbeat and the next the entire structure leaped into focus like one of those Magic Eye pictures that became three-dimensional if you knew how to view it. I sank my consciousness *through* the surface chaos and down to the valve foundation. Subtle asymmetry and imperfections became apparent exactly as they had in Kadir's simulator on the nexus and at the valve by my pond. I *understood* how the technique would augment the integrity of the valve and halt the cascade to disaster. Sure, Kadir was a complete nut job, but he was also fucking brilliant. Katashi's method was a Band-Aid where Kadir's was a cure.

With an unexpected rush of jubilation, I ignored the wild eruptions from the valve, concentrated on the foundation and shaped potency as I never had before. Imperfections stood out as clearly as ink blots on paper, and I filled, smoothed, and balanced as though second nature.

Katashi murmured to Tsuneo in Japanese, then passed

strands—and the lead—to me. I accepted potency from all three summoners and continued to sculpt and place it as needed.

"Kadir's influence," Katashi said after several minutes with an unmistakable undertone of annoyance.

Tense and composed, I continued to symmetrize while the others contained, collected and recycled the outflow from the valve. "Yeah, Kadir and I are tight, y'know," I snarked.

"No," Katashi said. "That is untrue of any."

Memory rose of Paul kneeling at Kadir's side. Though Katashi had interpreted my sarcastic comment literally, he was still wrong. I didn't understand the relationship between Paul and the demonic lord, but I knew in my gut they were, in fact, *tight*.

At long last the valve emitted harmonious tones, and the raging red-orange emanations settled into a gentle blue-green flow. Absurdly pleased, I worked the final strands to complete the process. Tsuneo released his hold on the flows, and Katashi strode to the far side of the picnic area.

An arcane shockwave jolted through me as dozens of floating sigils ignited around Katashi. In the next instant a familiar prickle swept over my skin like a million running ants. *A ritual, and I'm the target!*

I lurched up in an attempt to escape the epicenter. "Idris! Pellini! Run!" I choked out as an unseen weight crashed into me, plastering me to the ground as if I weighed a billion tons.

Sick horror clawed at me as I struggled in vain to free myself. This was like the arcane-draining ritual Idris used on Pellini—only Katashi's had to have been prepped and readied long before we arrived. *A trap. And we walked right into it—cocky and certain that we had the jump on them.*

Idris was beyond my line of sight, and I had no idea if he'd managed to get away. I saw Pellini bring his gun to bear on Katashi. At that point I had zero problem with Katashi getting shot in the leg, and so fucking what if it shattered his femur and he bled out.

I fought to reach my own gun, but the crushing pressure

held me almost immobile. The simple act of moving my hand felt as if I hauled a loaded pickup truck. *One millimeter, two.* Pellini got a shot off, and bark flew from a tree not far from Katashi, but the old summoner stood unfazed at the center of his ritual. Behind Katashi a black man I recognized from Farouche's plantation stepped out of the brush. Leo Carter. He fired at Pellini, but Eilahn tackled the detective to the ground with milliseconds to spare then leaped to her feet and bounded my way. Carter shifted his aim to her while I watched in rising dread.

"Do not kill the syraza!" Katashi ordered. *Because of Rhyzkahl,* I thought with relief. The syraza and the demonic lord remained connected, and if she died it would debilitate him even more.

Yet with Katashi's ritual in effect, she still wasn't safe. As she started toward me, I croaked out a warning for her to stay back, but her stubborn loyalty drove her onward despite the danger. Ten feet away, she dropped to her knees as the ritual sucked away her already scant arcane resources like a swarm of leeches. She went prone and extended her hand toward me, wriggled across the ground as determination glowed in her eyes. With every inch she paled more and her movements grew weaker. I struggled to scream at her to stop, to get out of the vicious ritual, but the words wouldn't form. *Go back,* I shrieked at her in my head. I'd never known her to read my thoughts, but it was all I had. *Stop hurting yourself!*

Pellini started to rise, and Carter fired in his direction with an insultingly casual air. Pellini dropped flat again, rolled to his side and squeezed off two quick shots. The air shimmered golden in front of Katashi, and none of the men so much as flinched.

"Fucking hell," Pellini shouted. "They have some kind of goddamn forcefield shit!"

A smile spread across Carter's face as he put a bullet into the tree behind Pellini, keeping him pinned down. A broad-shouldered man with red and grey hair stepped out from the brush behind Katashi and moved toward me. *Angus McDunn.*

I saw a flicker of sigils around him before Katashi's ritual drained the last bit of my arcane sense. Pushing against the unseen power, I forced my hand a few millimeters closer to my gun and touched the holster, muscles trembling. I managed to get my hand to the butt of my gun and wrap my fingers around it, then had nothing left to pull the gun free of the holster.

McDunn appeared unaffected by the overwhelming weight of the ritual as he approached. Frustration and anger coursed through me. The sigils protected him like arcane armor. Yet more evidence that Katashi had planned this in advance.

McDunn crouched at my side, unconcerned by my hand on my gun. He reached for my shoulder then hesitated, his mouth drawn down by indecision. My breath hissed through my teeth as I continued the futile attempt to draw my weapon. I knew it was hopeless since I'd be unable to bring the gun to bear and fire it, but no way was I going to lie there and take whatever it was these assholes intended to do to me.

*Angus enhances talents.* That's what Idris said. But it made no sense that he'd want to beef up my abilities.

McDunn regarded me with keen hazel eyes set in a craggy face but remained motionless, hand inches from my shoulder. His inaction freaked me out more than if he'd attacked me. What the hell would a cold-blooded killer be reluctant to do?

"McDunn!" Katashi spoke his name like a slap. "Do it *now!*"

"No," I tried to gasp, and when McDunn's eyes swung to mine I knew he'd heard me.

He closed his hand into a fist and withdrew it. A pale flicker of hope ignited within me. Was he having second thoughts? He shifted his weight to stand, but Katashi's voice cracked out again.

"Jesral."

McDunn flinched and drew a sharp breath. Regret lingered in his eyes, but his expression tightened with a determination that gutted my hope. Whatever threat the demonic lord Jesral held, McDunn was no match for it.

He gripped my shoulder, firm and heavy, and a wave of dizziness swept over me. Eilahn let out a shriek of rage even as a second, harsher wave crashed through me like the stab of a live wire. Blood roared in my ears, muffling all other sound. Yet another electroshock wave struck. And another. Color faded to shades of grey. In desperation I locked my eyes on McDunn's face and sought to anchor myself against his assault.

His hand tightened on my shoulder. Wave after wave pounded me, deadening my senses as if wrapped in smothering layers of wet cotton.

"St-stop . . . please." I forced the words out.

A droplet of sweat rolled down the side of his face. "I can't," he said, voice strained. He squeezed my shoulder again, plunged me deeper. A strangled cry escaped me as another vicious breaker scoured me, pulverized an essential aspect of my *self* to sand and washed it away. I scrabbled for it only to have it slip through my grasp.

"It's all I could do." McDunn's low, rough words cut through the surreal fog. He released my shoulder, stood and backed away several steps, then flinched at an abrupt flurry of gunshots. Pellini had given up on shooting directly at Katashi and company and instead emptied his mag into the branches high above them.

One large branch made an ominous *crack* as debris rained down, which was all the distraction Pellini needed. While the bad guys dodged pinecones and the falling branch, Pellini started toward me in an impressive low crawl that I'd have been hard pressed to match even at my best. McDunn reached for the gun at his hip, and for an instant my heart stopped, certain Pellini was going to get a bullet in his head. Yet instead McDunn inexplicably dropped his hand and jogged back to the others. Maybe because Pellini was his son's partner? More likely he didn't want the hassle of cleaning up after a murder.

Jaw set, Pellini waved his hands as he approached as if shoving trash out of his way. The crushing weight began to lift. *Pushing potency away and dispelling the shit affecting me*, I realized. I couldn't see the flows, but that had to be because the ritual had temporarily pulled the arcane away.

Katashi let out a harsh curse in Japanese and made a sharp gesture toward the woods. Carter, Tsuneo, and McDunn followed him to beat a hasty retreat into the trees. Pellini shifted up to his knees and continued the pushing motions. I drew a gasping breath as the vicious pressure eased more, then groaned as nausea rose in its place.

Idris let out a cry of rage and scrambled into view on hands and knees. He staggered up and toward where the men had disappeared into the brush only to collapse halfway there and heave his guts out. I held back my own puke, aware that Pellini's efforts had probably saved Idris from being taken prisoner again—a very real threat considering how gifted he was. Katashi and the Mraztur would pee themselves in excitement to have Idris working on the valves for them again.

Eilahn pressed up to sit. Face pale and eyes closed, she remained quiescent as Pellini stood and moved around us, continuing to wave his hands as if dispersing smoke. Most of the oppressive ritual weight faded within half a minute, but everything still felt *wrong*, and I couldn't stop shivering. I managed to push up to kneel then retched into the pine needles and dirt.

"Ah, shit." Pellini grimaced and made more pushing motions around me. The dizziness receded, but confusion replaced it. The ritual had been dispelled, so why couldn't I see the potency flows yet? I'd recovered immediately from Idris's arcane draining ritual at the barbecue.

I spat into the dirt to try and clear my mouth, wiped my face with a trembling hand. "S-something's wrong."

Pellini stepped around my puke splatter then pulled me to my feet. My legs refused to hold my weight, but Pellini slung me over his shoulders in a fireman's carry and hauled me the hell away from the ritual residuals. As soon as he reached the woods he lowered me to sit on the ground then peered down the trail to check on the others.

I did my best to remain upright as shivers wracked my

body. Nausea lurked at the back of my throat, and the wrongness took on a defined shape. "The . . . valve. I can't . . . I can't feel the valve."

Pellini frowned. "It's there. Steady and blue."

I closed and opened my hands in a useless attempt to get them to stop shaking. "C-can't feel it. Can't see it." I heard the distress in my voice. "I don't feel right."

His eyebrows drew together. "You don't *look* right."

Heart pounding, I struggled to my feet. "You . . . you don't either." I swayed.

Pellini wrapped an arm around my waist to steady me. I swung my gaze around in mounting desperation. "Everything's wrong," I told him, voice quavering. The trail and surrounding forest remained the picture of serenity, birds twittering as though nothing was amiss.

But it was like looking at a picture with one color missing.

True fear filled my gut. "Pellini, make a sigil."

"A what? Oh, one of those drifty things?" He carefully lowered me back down to sit then frowned in concentration, lifted his hands and moved them around. "How's that?"

The empty air between his hands mocked me. "I can't see it." I hugged my arms around myself. "Do another. Please."

Frown deepening, he flicked his fingers then held his hands a foot apart and waggled them again.

I knew better than to ask if he was screwing with me. Out of habit I tried to pygah. The loops of the calming sigil were so familiar as to be second nature, yet though I remembered what it looked like, I didn't know how to trace the pattern. It was like forgetting how to hold a pencil.

No, it was like forgetting what to use to draw a picture.

An eerie and fragile calm settled over me. I didn't want to speak or move because then it would shatter and the bad thing would be real. But the bad thing *was* real, and refusing to face it wouldn't change a thing.

"He took it," I said. The calm fractured into a billion pieces.

"Huh?"

"McDunn." I swallowed, concentrated on the mechanics of my simplest bodily functions. "He took the arcane from me. I can't sense it anymore. Nothing."

"Shit," Pellini murmured then shook his head. "It'll come back. That ritual thing you were in pulled all the arcane away, that's all."

"No!" Deep in my gut I knew he was wrong. "The effect of the ritual was temporary, like at the barbeque when Idris did it to you. Katashi isolated me from the arcane so McDunn could fuck me up." Crippling me was the intent from the start. In one well-planned stroke, Katashi had removed me from the game board.

"Right now we need to get the hell out of here." Pellini hauled me upright again, draped my arm over his shoulder to steady me as we made our way down the trail. "You're going to be okay. We'll figure this out. Eilahn and Idris are right behind us, and we'll get back to your house and fix it."

"I'm gonna throw up."

Pellini reacted like a man who had way too much experience with people about to blow chunks. In a split second he unslung my arm from his shoulders and lowered me to my knees. He scooped my hair back with one hand and steadied me with the other, all while keeping himself out of the line of fire. "Right into the grass there."

After I finished, I remained on my knees and attempted to trace a sigil. I formed the lines well enough, but when I tried to draw power to make it more than mere scratches in the dirt I might as well have wished for fairies to appear.

Footsteps approached. I straightened to see Idris jogging up the trail, face contorted with anger. He'd recovered quickly from being caught in the edge of the ritual. Eilahn wasn't far behind him, pale but no less determined.

"We need to keep moving," Idris said, tone harsh as he passed us without a second glance. Pellini helped me up, but Eilahn scooped me out of his grasp.

"Not much farther," she said. She hurried me up the trail after Idris, leaving Pellini behind.

I clung to her arm as I staggered along. "Where's Pellini? He helped. He stopped it."

"He follows."

I craned my head around, relieved to see him with his gun out and ready as he surveyed the woods in all directions, covering our retreat.

"My arcane senses will return?" I asked Eilahn, desperation making my voice crack. "What McDunn did to me will wear off, right?"

"You are a summoner," she replied, implacable.

I gulped. "Not if I can't touch or see the arcane."

"Precisely."

A brief flare of exasperation pushed aside my fear. "Yeah, and I *can't* touch or see the arcane."

"I know this," she said, speaking slowly and clearly. "You are a summoner. Summoners see and touch the arcane." She nodded as if certain it would all be clear to me now.

Dismayed, I gave up debating the point. Did she understand what I was experiencing? Not that I was sure *I* understood. But for the first time I wondered if there was a logical gap in her thinking. To her it was clear: summoners could see and touch the arcane. I was a summoner. Therefore, I could see and touch the arcane. Except that she couldn't seem to grasp that the reverse was also true: without the arcane a person *wasn't* a summoner. Maybe she couldn't comprehend such a radical change? Perhaps to her it was like a terrier saying it wasn't a dog anymore. I couldn't blame her. I didn't want to comprehend it either.

Idris stood a few feet back from the end of the trail, listening and sensing. He traced his fingers over the bark of a tree beside him, shaping an alarm sigil to notify him if people passed near—though I only knew what it was because I recognized the wrist-straining twist of his hand at the end. Eilahn stopped a short distance behind him and made a careful scan of the road and truck that waited beyond the edge of the woods. Her nostrils flared delicately as she scented the air and assessed for active or potential threats. After another tense moment she said, "I sense nothing amiss."

Pellini clicked open the locks with his remote. "Y'all get in," he said, still on guard. Eilahn helped me into the back and got me buckled, while Idris threw himself into the front passenger seat and slammed the door. Pellini climbed in and started the truck, then performed a quick three-point turn and got us on our way.

"Feeling any better?" he asked, looking at me in the rear view mirror.

*No, everything's wrong!* I wanted to yell, but I held it back and offered a shrug instead. "I don't feel like puking quite as much."

"They knew we were coming," Idris said, hands clenched into fists on his thighs. "The fracture of the valve threw them off, but they were waiting for us."

The truck jolted over a rough bump, and I gritted my teeth against the answering queasiness. "We were cocky and got caught," I said once I could speak. A shiver passed through me, and I rubbed the gooseflesh on my arms. No matter how hard I tried to see the arcane, the world remained dull and ordinary.

"We walked right into it!" Idris raged, face red. "Katashi was right there! We could've had him if we'd blasted him in the first place like I said!" He shot me an accusing glare.

My battered self-control disintegrated into pain and loss and fear in the face of his oh-so-righteous anger. "*I'm sorry*," I screamed at him. "I'm so fucking *sorry* I fucked your day up by getting caught in their trap!"

He swiveled to stare at me, annoyance drawing his mouth into a deep frown. "What the hell is wrong with you?"

My hands trembled. "While I was so *inconveniently* caught in that trap, McDunn . . . *did* something to me."

"What are you talking about?" His eyes narrowed. "He enhances talents and intimidates people. That's pretty much it."

Did he think I faked the puking and feeling like shit? "Who knows, maybe this was his first time," I said stiffly. "But what he did to me was the *opposite* of enhancement."

It took him only a second to grasp my meaning. "Damn. I didn't know that was possible." His mouth twisted in thought. "They wanted you neutralized, not dead." He exhaled. "Then again, with Rhyzkahl's and Szerain's influence on you along with *Kadir's*, it's safer for everyone now. Even you."

For a moment I couldn't breathe, shocked to my core as much by the casual delivery of the comment as the words themselves. Would he be this casual if they'd killed me? *Gee, that's too bad, but at least we're all safer.*

Pellini's hands spasmed tight on the steering wheel. "You'd best turn your ass around and keep your mouth shut for a little while, son," he ordered. Idris opened his mouth to respond, but I found my voice first.

"Did you just say . . ." My voice shook so much I had trouble getting the words out. I shoved to sit more upright and tried again. "Did you just say it's fine and cool that I've lost my arcane ability because it's *safer?*"

He scowled. "Sure. For now. You're not a player anymore." His tone was patronizing, as if I was an emotional idiot to be so worked up instead of seeing the bigger picture. "You won't be a target, and they can't use you. It buys us a little breathing room." He finished with a there-you-go shrug that sent my fury spiraling higher.

"You arrogant, unfeeling asshole!" I sputtered. "Would you say the same thing if I'd been blinded? Because that's what it feels like. That's what it *is!*"

"Blinded?" he said, incredulous. "Give me a break, Kara. It's not the same thing at all. I get that it sucks, but at least some good comes of it."

Gravel crunched under the tires as Pellini pulled the truck onto the shoulder and threw it into park, but I barely heard it over the hammering of my pulse. "And it's cool that you still have all your skills," I said through ragged, uneven breaths, "because you're so perfect and untouched and *uninfluenced?*"

"I never said I was perfect," Idris retorted, face flushed, "but I've been *cleared* by Mzatal *and* Elofir."

Agonizing rage tore at my essence. "Cleared?" I let out a harsh sound—more sob than laugh. Loss and betrayal goaded me on. "You're hauling around more influence than everyone in this truck put together considering Rhyzkahl's your *dad!*"

Idris gave me a withering look. "That's the best insult you can come back with?"

"Enough of this bullshit!" Pellini snapped. "I'm taking Kara home." He leveled a black glare at Idris. "You either shut up or get out and walk."

But my reply spewed out. "We're cousins," I snarled at Idris. "I have the DNA results to prove it. My aunt was manipulated to think her baby was stillborn. But he wasn't. He arrived after she spent time in the demon realm. With Rhyzkahl."

Silence descended. Idris glared at me, a heartbreaking range of emotions galloping through his eyes. After several tense seconds he flung open the door, climbed out and slammed it, then strode off down the highway shoulder.

Pellini muttered a stream of obscenities under his breath and killed the engine. "My goddamn truck better be here when I get back," he said then pulled himself out and started after Idris.

Two seconds later I opened my door and vomited onto the gravel, dry heaving when nothing more came up. After a moment the nausea faded, and my rage drained away with it, leaving me empty and cold. My cheeks were wet, but I didn't know when I'd started crying. *Nice going, Kara.*

Shaking, I pushed myself upright and closed the door. I made a tentative mental reach for Mzatal but pulled back when I felt nothing. I didn't have it in me to extend and try again. Not now. Couldn't face that possible loss yet.

I abruptly realized Eilahn had gone silent and unmoving, and a fresh wave of misery settled over me. Had she known about Rhyzkahl and Idris? I found it difficult to believe she had, not that it mattered at this point. I wouldn't blame her one bit for being furious at me for blurting that out. Even if she wasn't, I was angry and upset enough at myself for both of us. "Eilahn?" I said tentatively. "Are you okay?"

"I am well, Kara Gillian," she replied, voice steady and without the faintest hint of anger. She *was* disturbed,

though. I'd known her long enough to recognize how unease manifested in her human form. A faint crease between
her eyebrows. Her lower lip jutting out ever so slightly. No.
She hadn't known.

I lowered the window, suddenly desperate for air or a
breeze or maybe a tornado that could suck me up and away
from all of this. A few seconds later Eilahn lowered the window on her side, though her forehead remained creased.

A breeze drifted through, bringing an earthy aroma of
grass and moss and pine that clashed with the stench of hot
asphalt. The buzz of cicadas mingled with the *rat-tat-tat* of a
woodpecker, and in the distance a hawk screamed. I
dropped my head back against the seat and tried to chill,
but I couldn't stop reaching mentally for something that
wasn't there. I also couldn't stop trying to figure out where
we went wrong. How had Katashi been so certain we'd
show up? Yes, we'd followed clues, but none of them were
glaringly obvious. In fact, if we hadn't listened to that phone
call, we never would've . . .

*Shit.* We'd gobbled up their lures like hens on corn. Angus McDunn had worked with Bryce for fifteen years. He
knew how thorough Bryce was, and he'd been confident
Bryce would find the "dropped" piece of paper that led us
to the horse farm and Catherine McDunn.

My mouth tightened as I replayed the conversation in
my head. It had all been an act. If she hadn't dropped the
info about the calls from Angus, we wouldn't have heard
"number six" and known where and when to walk into the
trap. Yeah, she was good. I couldn't wait to have another
nice chat with her—as soon as I stopped feeling like
pounded shit.

*"That was fucked up how Kara dropped that on you."*
Pellini's voice, barely audible and only because the breeze
was right. I peered ahead and saw Idris sitting on the grass
ten or so yards in front of the truck, head in his hands and
elbows on his knees. Pellini sat crosslegged a half dozen feet
from him. I slumped down a little so I could still see, but not
be quite so obvious I was watching them. I was already an
asshole for using personal information about Idris as a

weapon. No need to add to it by flagrantly invading the privacy he needed right now.

"*It can't be true*," Idris said after a moment, voice unsteady.

"*Well, so what if it is?*" Pellini replied with a shrug. I knew I should close the window and stop being an intrusive jerk, but I didn't.

A motorcycle zoomed past, covering Idris's reply. "*Look*," Pellini said, "*one thing you do know is that you have a fuckload more potential than you ever imagined.*"

"*I guess so. If it's true.*" A pause, followed by an incredulous, "*The demonic lords have* children?"

I snuck a quick glance at Eilahn. I suspected she'd been surprised by that detail as well. *Note to self: don't ever let anyone entrust you with a really sensitive secret ever again. Dumbass.*

Pellini blew out a breath. "*I've known Kara a long time. She can be a stone cold bitch when pushed too far, but I've never seen her lie or throw out something that big without knowing for sure.*"

Wonderful. I was a bitch who knew her shit. This was a prime example of why eavesdropping was a Bad Idea. Yet I still didn't raise the window. Hell, I deserved to hear any and all criticism. Plus, I was nosy.

"*She's my cousin.*" A rustle of grass and gravel as Idris stood. "*Tessa is my birth mother . . . and Katashi has her.*" Even from this far away I heard the dread and horror in his voice. Katashi had brutalized his sister. Idris had no reason to believe Tessa couldn't be subject to the same fate even though Katashi treated her well now. "*I'm going to kill him,*" he said, rage in his voice once again. Gravel crunched as he strode toward the truck.

"*Idris. Stop.*"

To my surprise, he did.

Pellini clambered to his feet and caught up to Idris.

"You and I need to get something straight," Pellini said. The words carried clearly with them nearer. "I didn't ask for any of this shit, but since I'm in it neck deep the only thing I can do is make the best of it. Because of that, because I'm on this team or posse or whatever the hell you want to call it, I consider you a teammate. I'll go the distance for you and pound anyone who tries to fuck you over."

Silence as they faced each other.

"But?" Idris finally replied.

"It's not a 'but.' It's an 'and,'" Pellini said, voice hard and uncompromising. "*And* the same goes for Kara. She's my teammate, too. As wrong as she was to dump that crap about your parents on you, you were just as wrong to tell her it's no big deal that she lost a fundamental aspect of who she IS."

Damn it, my face was getting all wet again.

Pellini wasn't finished. "This arcane and demon-summoning shit is everything to her. She doesn't know it, but I've done a shitload of checking up on her. I'm pretty sure that becoming a summoner saved her life when she was younger."

Wait, what? He knew my history of acting out with drugs? Jeeeez.

"So if I hear one more fucking word from you about how it's better for everyone that she had the craft she loves ripped away from her," Pellini continued, tone harsh enough to melt stone, "I'll pound you flat, and I don't care who the fuck your daddy is. Y'got me?"

"Yeah," Idris replied, all belligerence gone. "Yeah, I do."

"Good," Pellini said, friendly again. "Let's get back to the house so we can regroup and figure out what to do next."

I stabbed the window button as they approached, relieved when Eilahn did the same. A few seconds later the guys climbed into the truck and closed the doors. Pellini pulled back onto the highway, and we rode in taut silence.

After several minutes Idris cleared his throat and gave me a sad and uncertain look. "Sorry I was a dick."

I nodded. "Sorry I dropped a bombshell like that on you."

He returned my nod, and I knew we were cool again.

"Katashi has my mother." His shoulders tensed.

"He's been her mentor for thirty years," I said, unable to

keep the stress from my words. "For what it's worth, I don't think she's in danger." I hated that. And I hated that I hated that. I didn't want her to be in danger. But I also didn't want her to be so close to Katashi.

"He's not soft."

"No," I said. "But he rewards loyalty."

He stared out the window. "Especially if it fits his plan."

# Chapter 24

Idris made a quick call to Bryce to tell him things didn't go as planned but everyone survived—in about as many words. Aside from that, the ride back to the house remained devoid of conversation.

The quiet gave me way too much time to obsessively review the entire incident. I ached for a nugget of information that would miraculously reverse what happened to me or give me a shred of hope that the effect was temporary. When that line of thinking grew too frustrating, I gave myself a headache by trying to sense the arcane, mentally "squinting" into a spectrum I could no longer see.

But at least I didn't feel the need to puke anymore. Woo.

Pellini pulled up to the gate and hit the button on the remote. I straightened. "Y'know, we should go to the store while we're out. We need laundry detergent."

Eilahn put a hand on my arm. "Enough detergent remains for forty-three normal loads. Your request is irrational." She opened her door as I scowled at her response. I really *really* wanted to go to the store. Why was that irrational? "Remain in the vehicle," she commanded, stepping down from the truck. "Vincent Pellini will drive behind us." With that, she closed the door and walked toward the gate.

My annoyance gave way to bafflement. "What the hell?"

Idris grimaced. "Aversion wards. They're attuned to you."

"Of course they are," I began, then my heart sank. I cast

a despairing look at Idris. "No. They *were*. They were attuned to the me who had an arcane signature. They don't recognize me as me." Because I wasn't "me" anymore.

Pellini winced and muttered a curse but kept watching Eilahn as she worked. Idris let out a heavy breath then climbed out to help her. I dropped my head back against the seat, gut aching as if I'd been sucker-punched. The urge to do random shopping eased as Eilahn and Idris reworked the wards, but left sick emptiness in its wake.

Pellini followed the pair to the house, parked and killed the engine. He looked at me with worry, but Eilahn bundled me out of the truck before he could speak. Idris set out toward the backyard without a word to anyone.

"You will take a long bath," Eilahn told me. "That always lifts your mood and helps you relax."

Pellini headed into the house. I paused at the bottom of the steps and struggled without success to *see* the warding, to *feel* the nexus.

Eilahn nudged me forward, and this time I didn't resist.

Pellini was already in the kitchen when I entered, and Jill and Bryce sat at the table.

"There's meatloaf on the stove," Jill said to Pellini. Her eyes rested on me, gaze filled with deep concern. She knew me too damn well to miss that I was a wreck.

I couldn't stomach the idea of rehashing the nightmare with the others. "You should go to the nexus," I murmured to Eilahn. "I'll take a bath." She offered no protest, a clear indicator of her exhaustion. After escorting me to the bathroom, she trudged down the hall and out the back door.

I closed and locked the bathroom door, started the water and shed my clothes. Scars still covered my torso, hideous remnants of sigils I could no longer sense. I twisted to look in the mirror at the small of my back. Szerain had activated the twelfth sigil there—the only one that wasn't a scar anymore. It should have glowed a gorgeous sapphire blue.

Nothing. Not a glimmer. Was it simply invisible to me, or had it been deactivated along with my arcane ability?

Straightening, I stared at my reflection. The sight of the scars destroyed the last thread of my stoic façade. *If I have to lose my abilities, why couldn't these terrible things go as well?*

Stupid question. *Because that's how shit goes for me.*

Lower lip trembling, I stepped into the tub and slid down. The water was only a few degrees shy of scalding, but I barely noticed the sting of it. Eyes closed, I steeled myself to test what I'd put off, dreading the answer. "Mzatal," I whispered. Even with him withdrawn, I'd always been able to sense his presence when I tried. I opened my eyes, called to him, mentally reached.

*Mzatal.*

Nothing.

*Mzatal.*

Tears blurred my vision. As a final, giant fuck you from the universe, I'd lost the remaining wisp of my connection with Mzatal. Katashi had severed me from the arcane *and* my lover—a lover who needed me as much as I needed him. My silent weeping turned into heaving sobs drowned out by the sound of running water.

When the water began to lap at the edge of the tub, I pulled myself together enough to shut off the faucet, then lay back again, wrung out and exhausted. I wasn't ready to get out and go to my bedroom. I didn't want to see or talk to anyone. Didn't want to face all the reminders of what I'd lost. I soaked in the heat and hoped it would fill the gaping void.

A light tap on the door was followed by, "Kara?" Jill's voice, heavy with concern. "You need anything?"

"No," I said then added, "thanks." I rested my head against the edge of the tub and gazed up at the ceiling. "I just need a little time."

"Okay," she said though she sounded no less worried. "If you get hungry, there's meatloaf out here. And ice cream."

"Thanks," I said again and left it at that. A few seconds later I heard her footsteps retreating down the hall. I closed my eyes, not worried about falling asleep in the tub. Not with my mind jabbering as I struggled to make sense of the loss and twisted injustice of it all. When the water cooled to where it was barely tolerable, I let some out and ran more hot water in.

*Eilahn was wrong*, I thought. The bath didn't help. It wasn't bringing my arcane senses back. It didn't change what happened to me one bit.

Well, maybe it helped a little. I didn't smell like vomit anymore. I slid down until my ears were beneath the surface, and sound became surreal, distorted, and muted. I pretended that the outside world didn't exist and that it didn't matter that I wasn't a summoner anymore or that I couldn't feel Mzatal. I stared at nothing and clung to my sliver of peace as hard as I could.

A knock on the door echoed oddly through the water in my ears. "Hey, Gillian." Pellini this time.

"What."

"About time to come out, don't you think?"

I had no idea how long I'd been in here. Nor did I care. I wanted to stay in the tub. Didn't want that ripped away from me too. "I'm *fine*."

"I didn't ask if you were fine or not."

I twitched in aggravation, lifted my head out of the water. "Leave me alone, okay?"

A pause. "For five more minutes. I'll be back."

"Don't bother," I said. Two minutes or five minutes, I'd have the same answer for him. I squeezed my eyes shut and slipped fully under the surface, and came up only when my lungs started to ache. All of my senses returned to normal except for the *other* which remained nonexistent.

Pellini's heavy knock rattled the door again. I had a feeling he'd given me more than five minutes, but it was still less than "as many minutes as I damn well wanted."

"Come on out," he ordered.

"Leave me alone," I ordered right back.

"I'm not going to do that."

I pressed the heels of my palms against my eyes. I knew he was worried I'd do Something Stupid, especially since I sounded nothing like my usual perky self. *But it's my house. My bathtub. My time. My skin that's wrinkled like a Shar-Pei. And I'm* fine.

All I wanted was to be left alone in my own fucking bathtub. How goddamn hard was that to comprehend? And who the hell did he think he was, anyway? My dad? Fuck that shit. I hadn't been able to fight back against Katashi and McDunn, but I could hold my ground against Pellini and this particular invasion. "Five more minutes," I lied.

He blew out a breath. "No more minutes. Get the fuck out of the tub."

"Go. Away."

"I'm counting to three, then I'm coming in for you," he said in an uncompromising tone. "Your choice whether to grab a towel or not. One . . . Two . . ."

"Leave me the fuck alone!" I yelled. Tears of frustration stung my eyes. Where were Bryce and Jill for all of this? Were they hanging back and watching Pellini be a jerk-ass control-freak buttinsky?

Apparently so, since the next sound to reach my ears was the *click* of the lock in the doorknob. Son of a bitch. Other than the door to the basement, all the locks inside the house were the cheap-ass kind with a center hole requiring only a nail or wire to unlock.

"Three." He entered and closed the door behind him, a flicker of triumph in his eyes.

Dismay washed over me. Not only was I stark naked, but no one had cared enough to rush to my defense while he invaded my space. With a sob-cry of rage I hurled a bottle of shampoo at him, but he ducked and deflected it with his forearm.

"Get out of the tub, Kara," he said with infuriating calm.

I no longer cared that I was naked. Hell, he'd already seen my *everything* after I died and came back to Earth in the PD squad room. "Why can't you leave me alone?" I demanded, voice cracking.

"Because I'm an asshole," he said. "Get out of the tub." He picked up a towel then had to duck again as I slung a bottle of conditioner at him.

I seized the body wash and cocked my arm back. A lot of different people had been living in this house, and there were at least a dozen bottles of hygiene products within my reach. I could keep this up all night, and would, if it meant winning this battle.

Pellini regarded me with narrowed eyes and pursed mouth. My arm trembled as I held eighteen fluid ounces of Silky Peach Blossom Skin-Nourishing Body Wash, but if I lowered it at this point in the standoff, it would be admitting defeat. I watched the thoughts tick through his head, and I wondered if he'd resort to dragging me bodily from the tub. I couldn't even hope for Eilahn to save me if he did. As drained as she'd been, it would be several hours before she budged from the nexus.

The shaking of my arm increased due to my own exhaustion combined with the hot water and lack of food. But before I could chuck the bottle at Pellini to avoid holding it any longer, he shrugged and began to unbutton his shirt.

"All right," he said. "If you won't come out, I'll have to come in."

I sputtered in shock and let the body wash drop into the tub. "No! Fucking hell, are you nuts?"

He stripped off his shirt and dropped it, then untucked the less than fresh white t-shirt beneath. Not that I had any room to judge freshness or lack thereof considering how gross I'd been before my bath. "Get out of the tub and stop me," he challenged as he wrestled the t-shirt off.

Did he really think I would cave that easily? I crossed my arms over my chest and glared at him in defiance. No way would he drop trou in front of me. He was bluffing. I was certain of it.

He unclipped his holstered gun from his waistband and set it on the counter, then reached under his belly for his belt buckle. I tensed but managed to hold back an outright flinch. He was bluffing. He *had* to be. I remained immobile while he unbuckled his belt and undid the button of his pants. Any second now he'd stop and switch to a less humiliating tactic. Right? Then again, he didn't look like a man on the verge of humiliation. He calmly tugged the zipper down, giving me a glimpse of red and black striped boxers, then took hold of pants and boxers at his hips and—

"Shit! Stop!" I grabbed for the towel. To my relief he took his hands from his waistband, though he waited until I pulled the plug before zipping and buttoning his pants again. Scowling, I yanked the towel around me and climbed out of the tub. As I pushed past him, I thought I saw a hint of relief in his eyes, but then again I'd been convinced he was bluffing, so how was I to know? I stomped down the hall and into my bedroom, slammed the door, then sat on the edge of the bed with the towel clutched around me. Part of me knew how irrational my thinking was, and the rest of me grudgingly admitted that Pellini's concern wasn't at all misplaced. Still, the sight of him calmly disrobing was one that would stick with me for a very long time.

Something touched my back. I startled and twisted to see what it was, then stared in surprise at the sight of Fuzzykins. She lifted her head and gave me a *Mrowr?*—perfectly normal and without a hint of hate or growling or hissing. She bumped her head against my arm, and the ache within me tripled. She hated summoners. But she clearly didn't hate me anymore because I wasn't a summoner.

I scratched the silly cat's head, and she rewarded me with a thunderous purr and more head butts, followed by full body rubs against me. Okay, I could *almost* see why Eilahn liked her so much. Exhaling, I continued to pet the damn cat, mostly because I didn't have a choice in the matter. She seemed to be making up for all those months of being so nasty to me. I tried to withdraw my hand, but she hooked it with her paw and pulled it back for more affection. Fine. Maybe she'd stop puking in my shoes.

I froze at a light knock at the door. "It's me," Jill said as the cat jammed her head against my hand again.

"*You* can come in," I said. No way in hell did I want anyone else in here with me.

Jill entered and closed the door behind her. "You're all wrinkly."

"And clean," I said. "Don't forget clean."

She let out a soft snort. "I have a feeling there wasn't a lot of scrubbing going on, but you were in there long enough to soak off pretty much anything." She came around the end of the bed and hiked herself up to sit beside me. Almost beside me. Between us, Fuzzykins was busy having a passion attack.

"The cat likes me now." My voice broke, and I looked up at Jill, feeling utterly bereft. I figured Pellini had filled her and Bryce in on everything that went down. The sympathy that swam in her eyes told me she understood the deeper and unwelcome symbolism of the cat's affection.

"Is there any way it can be fixed?" she asked gently.

Fuzzykins arched and purred as I stroked her furry belly. "I sure hope so. We don't need more kittens around here."

"Not the cat, you dork," Jill said with a weak chuckle and thwacked my arm.

I managed to hold a smile for a few seconds before it faded again. "I don't know. I'm trying not to rule anything out or give up hope." *Or hold onto unrealistic hope*, I added silently. My throat tightened. "I'm not a cop anymore, and now I'm not a summoner either. What am I supposed to *do* now that I'm . . ."

"Normal?" Jill finished for me, cocking her head. "I'm not sure you could ever be *normal*, darlin.'"

"Tell me again why I'm friends with you?"

She smiled and pulled me into a hug, ignoring the protests of the cat between us. "Because you're Kara Gillian."

I hugged her back, pushing down the uncertainty and doubt and grief that roiled through me. No matter what, Jill was precious to me. I didn't know *what* I was anymore, but for now my mission was to do whatever I could to make sure Jill and the bean stayed safe. And, I'd find a way to help the others track down that shitstain, Katashi. "Yeah, I'm Kara Gillian," I replied then released her. "At least that's what I put down the last time I did my taxes,"

"Ugh. Taxes." She shuddered. "Even I don't want to be *that* normal." She patted my leg and stood. "Get dressed and come eat. Meatloaf."

"What about the ice cream?" I whined.

She smiled serenely. "Meatloaf first."

"You already sound like a mom."

"Yeah? Cool. I've been practicing."

# Chapter 25

Raised voices from the driveway alerted me to trouble before I was halfway through the slice of Jill's awesome meatloaf. Dread rising, I dashed to the front porch only to see Pellini blocking the driver's door of the Malibu as he faced off against an angry Idris. Bryce stood on the bottom step, vigilant and poised to intervene.

Pellini folded his arms. "Now isn't the time for you to go off on your own," he said to Idris with implacable calm.

Idris lifted his fist, face flushed. "Who the fuck are you to tell me when the right time is?"

Bryce breathed a low curse and started forward, but Pellini didn't flinch at the threat. He seemed ready and willing to give Idris an outlet for his churning emotions by taking a punch, however I didn't want to see either one of them get hurt.

"Idris. *Idris*," I said as I moved down the steps and toward them. "You can leave if you want, but will you please talk to me first?"

Seething, he rounded on me, fist raised. I stood my ground, braced for him to tell me where I could shove my offer of conversation. Yet, after only a few tense breaths, he lowered his hand. "Sure." He sounded more exhausted and miserable than aggressive. "Yeah, I'll talk to you."

Sympathy squeezed my heart. "Why don't we go to the pond."

Without a word, Idris strode off and around the house,

which I decided to take as a "yes." I shot a grateful smile to Pellini and Bryce then hustled after Idris, but halfway down the trail through the woods, I slowed. Chest tight, I blinked back tears. This was where I should have been able to feel the valve, like tingling waves over my skin, but I sensed nothing of the arcane. *Nothing*.

I continued to the pond clearing and stopped a few feet from the water's edge. With single-minded determination, I tried to perceive anything beyond the standard five senses. *Nothing*.

Horror crept through me. Like a dream within a dream, memory of the *feel* of the arcane faded even as I sought to remember it. Would I eventually forget it altogether?

Idris stood near where I knew the valve to be, yet nothing distinguished the location from any other grassy patch by the pond. Not even the faintest shimmer. I found a dry spot on the leaves a few feet away and sat heavily. After a minute or two, Idris dropped to sit crosslegged in front of me.

"How is it?" I asked with a nod toward the valve, relieved that my voice remained steady.

"Stable enough for the moment." He paused, and a slight frown tugged at his mouth. "More than stable."

"You don't sound thrilled." I eyed him. "What's wrong with mega-stable?"

"Nothing." He glowered down at the leaves between us. "Believe me, I tried to find faults."

The reason for his annoyance clarified. "Kadir's method," I said. "I symmetrized the valve yesterday, and you don't want to admit that it worked. *Really* well."

Heaving a sigh, he flashed me a weak smile. "You're right, I don't," he said. "But I have no choice. The valve is stable and so clear I can feel Rhyzkahl's nexus through it."

*Feel Rhyzkahl's nexus through the valve?* How incredible that must be.

I shoved down the grief and battled to get it nicely tucked away again. The embodiment of Pellini's stone cold bitch. Under control.

Nope. Didn't work. "I can't feel *anything*," I managed to gasp. "Can't see *anything*." And then my gut caved in on itself, and a wave of sobs rose to choke me. *No no no!* I couldn't lose it now. I scrambled to get up. All I wanted was to run away and hide somewhere, anywhere.

Idris grabbed my arm and pulled me back down, called my name. I clawed at him, fought, screamed at him to leave me alone, to let me go. I couldn't see through my tears. I couldn't see. I couldn't *see*.

He wrapped his arms around me, pulled me close to his chest and refused to let me go no matter how much I thrashed and shrieked and cursed. He held me until I stopped fighting him, my throat raw and head aching. Worn out, tired of fighting, tired of *everything*, I finally buried my face against his shoulder and shook in big snotty wet sobs. Even then he didn't release me but gently changed his hold to an embrace.

Eventually I wound down to snuffly hiccups. I remained blind to the arcane, but I felt better, more clear. Drawing a shaky breath, I sat up straighter. This time Idris let me go— with caution, as if releasing an alligator back to the swamp. I wiped my face with the bottom of my shirt. "Thanks," I said and offered him an unsteady smile, then winced. Three scratches scored the side of his face along with several on each forearm. "Crap, Idris. I'm sorry. I didn't mean to—"

He cut me off with a lift of his hand and a ghost of a smile. "Don't worry about it," he said. "I have older sisters, remember?"

I didn't miss the haunted pain behind the sincere words. "Explains why you're such a sissy," I said as I gave his shoulder a light shove.

Idris chuckled, but it faded along with his smile. Shifting to face the pond, he gazed out over the water. "How long have you known?"

I rubbed my puffy eyes. "I've only known for sure since the day after the plantation raid," I said. "However, I suspected Tessa might be your mom back in Mzatal's realm, after you two rescued me from Rhyzkahl." I gave him a tentative smile. "Your hair and eyes and features. When I returned here I asked her if she'd ever had a baby, and she told me she had but that it was stillborn. And, well, I'm a sneaky bitch. I collected DNA samples from both of you and had them tested." I let out a long sigh. "I knew she'd been in the demon realm with Rhyzkahl not long before the baby—you—were born. Rhyzkahl was my prime suspect, and Zack confirmed it."

Idris dug a golf ball sized rock from beneath the leaves and threw it hard at the water. It struck with a heavy *sploosh*, sending up a spray of sparkling droplets. "Does Rhyzkahl know?"

"No," I said softly. "And neither does Tessa. Someone manipulated her to believe you'd been stillborn and that the dad was an American in Japan who loved her and left."

He frowned at me. "Who did the manipulation? Mzatal? Jesral?"

"I don't know," I said. "When I found out, I assumed the manipulation had been in place for twenty years." I pressed the heels of my hands to my temples. "But now I'm not so sure. She's off with Katashi—willingly. Maybe the manipulation is more recent."

He toyed with a twig on the ground in front of him. "When were you planning on telling me?"

Exhaling, I dropped my hands to my lap. "You've been kind of a mess, and I didn't want to screw you up more." I shook my head. "So, of course, I went ahead and did exactly that. Idris, I'm so sorry."

He went eerily still. "It's okay. It's out now, and I'm fine."

"Uh huh. As fine as I was a few minutes ago."

"I'm dealing with it," he said through gritted teeth. "I'm *fine*."

"Idris," I said with extreme gentleness, "you're not fine. You haven't been fine since you witnessed Amber's murder. It broke you."

In a mercurial moment, Idris shot to his feet. "You don't know," he said, breathing hard. "You don't know what it did to me! *I'm dealing with it*."

Remaining seated, I tipped my head back to regard him. "How?" My already hoarse voice cracked. "By staying angry and hostile all the time? By lashing out at the people around you at the slightest provocation?" I drew a deep breath and forged on. "You're pushing everyone away as hard as you can because, if no one's close to you, maybe a death won't hurt so much."

He flicked his hands dismissively. "I'm not doing that. I just have to get those fuckers. No bandwidth for social shit."

"Idris, you've barely smiled since you arrived," I said. "You go off on your own at every possible opportunity. And it's a miracle I still have a tongue considering how many times I've bitten it after you've made an asshole-ish comment." I kept my eyes steady upon him. "That's *not* the Idris I once knew. That Idris is broken, and he keeps kicking the pieces farther apart."

"Yeah? Well, shit has changed." Idris pivoted away and folded his arms across his chest. "When I've dealt with Katashi and Steiner and Asher, *then* you'll see me smile."

"That's what scares me."

"What the hell is that supposed to mean?"

"It scares me that revenge is the only way you'll find joy," I said. "With your lineage, you're pretty powerful. What'll happen after you kill or capture those men? Will you return to being the Idris who can sing silly songs with his family at Christmas? Or will you hunt down the next target?"

Idris glanced back at me, a deep scowl on his face. "Won't know 'til I get there, will I?" he said gruffly then shifted his weight from one foot to the other. "Nothing for you to be scared of, though."

"Until you decide it's better for everyone if I'm removed from the picture," I replied, keeping my tone even. "Why gamble that my arcane abilities could be restored?" I found my own rock and chucked it into the pond. "I'm defenseless against the arcane right now, and you scare the crap out of me."

He spun to face me again. "Bullshit!" he shouted. "I didn't take your abilities or try to have you locked down. Yeah, I said it was safer—*after* McDunn had already stripped you. I shouldn't have said it, but I do believe it's true for now." Anger settled on him more heavily. "But that doesn't give you any reason to believe I want to eliminate you."

My experience and intuition told me it would be foolish to push him more on the subject. He wasn't even all human. Who knew how he might react? Besides, my emotional reserves registered at nil. "Fair enough," I said as lightly as I could manage. Speedy extrication from the subject was in order. "I think we should go to Tessa's house. There's a valve in her library that should be checked and, well, I can't do it."

His features relaxed at the change of topic. "It's on the list to be assessed."

Relieved, I nodded. "My schedule is quite free at the moment if you want to head over there tonight."

Idris extended his hand to me. "C'mon. I need to grab some food, then we can go."

Taking his hand, I stood, but then he caught me off guard by pulling me into a hug. Before I could return it, he released me and headed for the trail. Sighing, I watched his retreating back. An instant longer holding that hug and he'd have broken down. Idris *needed* to break down—scream and sob and let out the grief that tore at him. Yet I also knew how much he needed that anger to keep him going. With me already out of the game, we couldn't afford to lose him on any level.

"Meatloaf," I muttered and trudged after him. "Everything's better with meatloaf."

# Chapter 26

Idris pulled into Tessa's driveway, shut off the headlights, and let the darkness surround us. The ache of loss settled in my chest as I climbed out and surveyed the well-maintained yard and house. All distressingly ordinary.

I dredged up the memory of how it used to appear in my othersight—arcane protections glowing on every surface like phosphorescent filigree. The effort of clinging to the recollection was like trying to remember a dozen phone numbers at once. After a few precious seconds, I let it slip away with a resigned sigh. "It looks and feels so different," I murmured.

"Yeah, I bet," Idris said, already absorbed in examining warding. He winced as he realized his gaffe. "Shit. I'm sorry."

Plastering on a smile, I squared my shoulders and moved to the walkway, then stopped and shook my head. "You know, I never got to finish my meatloaf. Let's go to Lake O' Butter and get waffles. We can do this tomorrow."

I started to walk away, but Idris grabbed my upper arm. "Aversions," he said. "Keep your eyes on the house. It's all about willpower."

The gloom hid my flush of embarrassment. Why hadn't I remembered the aversions? "Right." I swallowed. "Got it." Ruthlessly, I moved forward and drove down the craving for waffles. With lots of butter. And bacon.

Idris lingered behind. "Kara, wait," he said when I reached the steps. "I need to assess the protections."

Tense and jumpy from the aversions, I stopped. Wards were stupid inanimate things, I told myself, stomach knotting. So what if they didn't recognize me. I shouldn't let it bother me. I lifted my chin. *It doesn't bother me.* "Can you unweave them?" I asked over my shoulder.

Idris peered at the house through narrowed eyes. "There are a buttload of wards," he said with dismay. "Looks like a mix of demon and Katashi's work." He swore under his breath. "I'm not going to be able to get through them."

Well, that sucked ass. Too bad we didn't still have the arcane-dampening cuff that I'd used to keep Mzatal and Idris from summoning me. I could have plowed through the wards with that. I retreated from the house, noting without humor how the desire for waffles faded with each step away from the aversions.

"I think it's the same all the way around," I told him, "but you might as well check."

Idris began a slow perusal of the perimeter. I watched him until he disappeared around the corner of the house, then nearly startled out of my skin when the porch light flicked on and the front door creaked open. My hand flew to my gun, but I relaxed as Tessa's boyfriend stepped out. "Carl! You scared the shit out of me."

"Sorry about that, Kara." Lanky and soft-spoken, with short, near-colorless hair, Carl seemed an odd match for my petite and flamboyant aunt. Yet I'd always felt he understood her far more than most people—including me, at times.

I managed a weak smile. "It's cool. Your car wasn't out here, and I didn't see any lights on. Had no clue you were inside."

"Come on in," he said then looked toward the corner of the house where Idris disappeared. "Where'd your friend go?"

"Checking out protections," I said, remaining where I was. Carl had a talent of arcane immunity which allowed him to slip through wards as if they weren't there. Unfortunately, that didn't help me one bit. "I was hoping to get a few books from the library and check the valve at the same time, but I can't get through the protections." I proceeded to give him a quick and dirty update on my condition.

"That's rough," he said, expression barely twitching from its usual impassiveness. "You want me to get the books for you?"

After brief consideration, I shook my head. "Thanks, but I don't have specific ones in mind. Besides, the valve is the most important project." I faked a casual shrug. "We'll come up with a new plan."

Carl closed the door behind him and took a seat on the steps. "Seems as if quite a bit is going on," he said calmly. Not that I'd ever seen Carl anything *but* calm. Ever. As a morgue assistant for the coroner's office, he handled all manner of dead bodies and bizarre crime scenes with cool aplomb and a dry-as-the-desert sense of humor. "If you need any help, I have time on my hands."

"Because Tessa's out of town?"

"Because I retired last month." A whisper of a smile passed over his mouth.

"Nice," I said with what I hoped was the right amount of enthusiasm to cover my surprise. He couldn't be older than mid-forties and hadn't worked at the coroner's office *that* long. Then again, he might have added the time to a previous pension. "What on earth is Dr. Lanza going to do without you?"

"Curse a lot," he replied.

"I don't doubt it," I said with a brief laugh, but I quickly sobered. "Thing is, Tessa went off with her old teacher, and it has me pretty worried. Did you know about that?"

Carl shrugged, an almost imperceptible gesture. "Doesn't much matter one way or the other. We're not together anymore."

"Crap. I'm sorry. I didn't know." Tessa sure hadn't mentioned a breakup. Tilting my head, I peered at him. "Please don't take this the wrong way, but if y'all aren't together anymore, what are you doing here?"

"Like I said, I have time on my hands. I come by every few days and check on the place. Fix what needs fixing." One side of his mouth twitched. "What Tessa doesn't know won't hurt her."

I wasn't so sure. Intruding on Tessa's affairs was a dangerous game at the moment. I knew that all too well. "Be careful," I said. "All you need is one neighbor to call the cops, and you're hosed."

He remained silent for a moment. "I'll keep that in mind, and you keep me in mind if you need anything. I'm handy. Painting. Cleaning gutters." He paused. "*Other* tasks."

"I appreciate the offer," I said. With Steeev gone and me next to useless for arcane projects, we were at a severe disadvantage. I'd never thought of Carl as a resource, but we were desperate, especially for anything in the *other* category. "We could sure use the help."

Idris rounded the corner, frowning.

"What's wrong?" I asked after he reached me.

Idris flicked a questioning glance at Carl then gave me a head shake. "Nothing."

"Oh, sorry," I said. "Idris, this is Carl. He used to date Tessa, and I've known him for years. He's cool. He, ah, knows we mess with arcane stuff."

Idris lost a measure of his wariness and gave Carl a nod. "Warding is wicked all the way around the house," he told me.

"Figured," I said. "We'll find another way to get in to deal with that valve." Maybe Idris could summon a demon to take down the wards. "We have to get going," I said to Carl. "You need a ride?"

"I'll walk," he said. "Thanks anyway."

I let out a low whistle. "You must have titanium skin to be willing to brave miles in mosquito paradise after dark."

"The world is full of strange and curious things," he said with a straight face then climbed the steps to the porch. "Don't forget to call me."

*And one of those strange and curious things is you*, I thought with mild amusement. "No worries there," I said. "You'll probably regret volunteering soon enough, though."

I kept my tone light, but I had a feeling he didn't really know what he was getting himself into.

"Time will tell, Kara Gillian," he said as he opened the front door and entered the house. "Time will tell."

Jill and Pellini had gone off to their respective beds by the time Idris and I made it back to the house. The only light still on was the one over the stove in the kitchen, but the empty sofa indicated Bryce was awake. Though I didn't see him in any of the common areas, I felt no need to worry. I knew he wouldn't be far from Jill.

Idris headed straight for the basement to map out the valve repair plan for the next day. With Bryce taking over Jill-duty, Idris would be partnered with Pellini. That would be *interesting*, to say the least.

I slouched into the recliner, too wired and unsettled to go to bed. My routine for the past few weeks had been to check the nexus and survey the protection wards before turning in, but obviously that would need to come off my chore list. Along with a dozen other tasks that Idris would have to take over. *This sucks*, I thought in ginormous understatement.

Out of habit I reached for Mzatal, with as much result as if I'd reached for the moon. My breath shuddered out. The loss of the bond gnawed at me, and my overall uncertainty salted the wound. I wanted—*needed*—to talk to Mzatal, get his advice and opinion about what happened to me, as well as his comfort and support. The bond had been an intrinsic part of our relationship for six months, and I felt its absence now as keenly as if I'd lost my right hand. Did Mzatal feel the same way? What was six months against the thousands of years he'd lived without a bond? I didn't know if the relatively brief time would make it easier for him to handle the loss or if it made it all the more tragic.

My chest tightened as I ran my thumb over the curled prongs of my ring. If only I could *touch* him, I'd feel better. A whisper. That's all I needed—

"Stop it," I growled to myself and stomped down my self-pity. I was mooning and moping like a lovesick teenager, for fuck's sake. How was that going to solve my problems? Maybe I wasn't thousands and thousands of years old, but I'd managed perfectly fine for thirty years without any sort of quasi-telepathic connection. Sure, it hurt like walking barefoot over broken glass, but there were other ways to send word to Mzatal. Idris would need to summon a demon to deal with the wards on Tessa's house anyway, so it might as well be one of Mzatal's.

Cursing, I pushed up from the recliner and stalked to the kitchen, unable to keep my frustration at bay. Sending a message to Mzatal via demon was a lousy and not-always-reliable substitute for the conversation with him I truly craved. Hell, even if our bond was working at its best, a mental touch wouldn't give me any answers. I'd need an interdimensional connection like the one Bryce and Seretis had, with a true exchange of thoughts.

I stopped dead in the hallway. *Bryce and Seretis!* Maybe Bryce could get word to Seretis and ask him if my affliction could be reversed? Short of returning to the demon realm, I saw no other way to get the direct input of a demonic lord.

Excited by the possibility, I proceeded to hunt for Bryce. A *teensy* part of me wondered if he was in the guest room with Jill, considering his obvious-to-me deepening affection for her. I instead found him in a rocker on the back porch, a shadow in the shadows.

"Hey, Bryce," I said. "You okay?"

"Hey," he replied. Quiet. Subdued. "How'd it go at your aunt's house?"

I winced. "Not so great." I sat in the rocker next to his and filled him in on the salient points.

"Damn," he said when I finished.

"Yeah." I went quiet, listened to the chirp of crickets in the dark and the croak of frogs from the woods and pond. Not far above the trees, the moon waxed gibbous. *Four days until the full*, I thought idly. Easy to pinpoint the moon's phase after more than a decade of obsessing over it. A year and a half ago I'd have been chafing at having to wait four days to summon again.

I had one hell of a long wait in front of me now.

"My condition screws up the team," I said. "Idris is now the only one who can perform the necessary arcane maintenance. It helps that Pellini can see the arcane, but it's not enough. We need to find a solution as soon as possible." I looked over at him. "Do you think you could ask Seretis what he thinks?"

My eyes were adjusted to the gloom enough to see his grimace. "I already tried with no luck," he said, regret coloring his words. "I couldn't get the specifics across. I'm sorry."

"Oh. Yeah, okay," I said with the lightness of a bowling ball covered in concrete. "It was worth a shot. Thanks for trying." Back to square one—wherever that was. Stupid tears pricked my eyes, and I blinked furiously, grateful for the darkness.

His shadow shifted, and he put his hand over mine on the chair arm. "I'll connect with Seretis in the morning from the nexus. It's the best time of day, and the link is always stronger there. I think I'll be better able to get my point across to him then."

I turned my hand over, threaded my fingers through his, drew from his strength. "Thanks, Bryce." Any other words on the topic seemed unnecessary. I squeezed his hand. "What about you? What has you brooding in the dark with the mosquitos?"

He exhaled. "Security gets trickier when long-range weapons come into play."

"Good news is they don't seem to want Jill dead. They could have accomplished that today. They want the baby—alive."

He disengaged from my hand and stood, moved to lean on the porch rail and lifted his gaze to the moon. "I need to get you and Pellini up to speed on the camera security system," he said. "While you and Idris were gone, I made notes on everything I could think of regarding Jerry, McDunn, and Carter. The file is on Paul's system and the laptop."

Ice slid between my ribs. "You're *leaving*?" I barely got the words out then couldn't stop the torrent. "I understand. I really do. Better for you to be close to Paul. And Seretis. Mzatal shouldn't have sent you here in the first place. Did he even *ask* if you wanted to come? I know he can be presumptuous—"

"Kara! I'm non-essential."

"No! That's bullshit! We'd be up shit creek if you weren't—"

"Kara. So was Steeev."

The ice drove deeper as his meaning penetrated my thick skull. Non-essential to *Katashi*. "Oh. *Damn.*" I stood and joined him at the rail. "You think you're next."

"Knocking out security is a sound plan," he said. Clinical. Detached. "With Steeev, they didn't have a body to deal with. No need to worry about police involvement. I believe the only reason they haven't taken me out yet is because the right opportunity hasn't presented itself. It makes sense to give you everything I know while I'm still alive and kicking."

I placed my hand on his shoulder. "You could go to the demon realm."

He turned to face me. Moonlight lit his features in shades of grey like a charcoal drawing. "I'm staying."

The words rose on my tongue to argue, to tell him to go where he'd be safe. His eyes met mine, and I swallowed my words. He knew his business. He'd put his life on the line for assholes like Farouche and taken a bullet to the chest for Paul. He'd take one for Jill, or any of us.

"Damn glad to have you." To hell with Katashi and his crew. They didn't have half the heart of my posse.

# Chapter 27

Idris and Pellini were already gone by the time I woke up, but a note in Pellini's handwriting by the coffeemaker informed anyone who cared that the coffee had been made at 6:30 a.m. *I* certainly cared because, even though I was no kind of coffee snob, I disliked stale coffee as much as the next sane person. As it was barely 7:15, the coffee was still good and drinkable, and all was right with the world, at least for a few minutes.

Bryce came into the kitchen before I finished my first cup, poured one for himself then plopped into an empty chair. "I take it there've been no reports of them killing each other yet?"

"Yet," I said, sipping my coffee. "The day is young."

He chuckled. "They'll be all right. Idris would never admit it in a million years, but I have a feeling he has a lot of respect for Vince." At my disbelieving look he went on, "Yesterday was a turning point for them. Vince has a lot of issues, but he keeps his head in a crisis. I think deep down Idris appreciates that."

I had to nod in agreement. "I've worked in the same department with Pellini for years, but never worked *with* him on a case. This is the first time I've really seen him in action."

Bryce's mouth twitched. "And Idris really likes his silly dog. After you went to bed, he came out and threw the tennis ball for Sammy." He took a sip of coffee. "Not sure, but I *might* have heard him laugh."

"Now you're talking crazy. That dog can't laugh."

"I'm sure you're right," Bryce said with a smile. "It was late." He glanced at the clock. "Gimme ten minutes, and then I'll head out to the nexus and check in with Seretis."

"Enough time for another cup," I said and headed to the coffeemaker to get started on that.

Bryce sat crosslegged in the middle of the nexus, eyes closed and mouth tight in concentration as he reached between the worlds to Seretis. I sat in a similar pose a couple of feet away and watched him. Sammy lounged in the grass, his eyes on us as if to be sure he wouldn't miss it if one of us threw a stick for him. Eilahn lay curled in her nest like a cat, recharging. Fuzzykins slept draped over her hip, and I unobtrusively slipped my phone from my pocket and took a picture of them. They were too damn cute.

After several minutes Bryce's face relaxed, and a smile touched his mouth. "The connection is stronger."

I ignored the dull ache of my lost link to Mzatal. "That's awesome," I said, tone chipper. "Strong enough to talk to him?"

"Working on it," Bryce replied. "He knows I want to."

The concrete slab leeched the warmth from my butt, and I tried without success to keep from fidgeting. It felt like several minutes to my impatient internal clock before Bryce spoke again, though it was probably closer to thirty seconds. "He's in Rhyzkahl's realm."

"Why the hell is he *there?*" I asked in surprise.

Another few seconds of silence and then, "There was an anomaly. It's settled now."

"Oh, crap." I winced. "Yeah, Rhyzkahl can't fix those in his current condition." Anomalies were rifts in the dimensional fabric, remnants from the cataclysm that had nearly destroyed the demon realm. They couldn't be ignored since they caused a lot of damage and destabilization if not dealt with promptly.

"All the lords and demahnk were there," Bryce continued, frowning. "It was bad."

"Does that mean you're talking to Seretis?" I asked, leaning forward.

He gave a shrug and nod. "It's not like thinking *words* to each other, but yeah."

I knew what he meant from my own experience with Mzatal. It was an exchange of concepts and thoughts that made for a far deeper communication and understanding than mere words could manage. "Can he help me?" I asked.

His face abruptly scrunched, and he jerked his hands up to grip his head. "Shit," he gasped. Eilahn sat up, displacing the cat.

Worry spiked through me. "What is it?" I demanded. An attack? I swept my gaze around but saw nothing out of the ordinary. Then again, that didn't mean shit since I had no way to detect arcane use. "Bryce, tell me what's wrong!"

He dropped to his back. "Ver . . . tigo," he groaned, still gripping his head.

I crouched and put my hand on his shoulder, at a loss for how to help. "Eilahn? Do you sense anything?"

"I sense no attack," she said, but her eyes remained narrowed as she scanned around us. She staggered to her feet, swayed.

"Sit down," I ordered, surprised when she did so without protest, though her frustration with her weakened state showed in the droop of her shoulders.

Bryce cursed and slapped his hands onto the concrete as if to keep from sliding off a tilting earth. Sammy leaped up and began to bark, but I ignored the excitable dog and held onto Bryce's shoulder in the hopes of giving him a sense of stability. Sammy bounded toward the woods, barking with increased intensity.

"Shit shit," Bryce hissed through clenched teeth. "Valve."

My heart skipped a beat. "It's gone bad?" *Shit.* There was no one home to stabilize it. Sammy charged into the woods and down the trail toward the pond, continuing to bark his damn head off. "Oh, no," I breathed. If that stupid dog got himself hurt or killed by an unstable valve, Pellini would lose it.

"I'll be right back," I told Bryce then took off after the dog. "Sammy! Here boy!"

The dog paid me zero heed and raced on ahead without

a single break in the barking, quickly disappearing from sight. "Sammy!" I yelled, running as fast as I dared along the trail without risking smacking into a tree. "Stop! Heel! Sit, dammit!"

A pain-filled yelp cut off the barking, followed by an ominous silence. My gut turned to ice. "Sammy!"

An unearthly screech ripped through the woods, chilling me further. I didn't need arcane skills to know that was no hawk or owl. I slapped at my hip for a gun that wasn't there. *I'll see what I'm up against*, I told myself as I slowed. With a shred of luck maybe I'd be able to grab the dog and run the hell away.

Three more cautious steps brought the pond clearing into view. A horse-sized creature with claws and scales and too many legs flailed on the ground as white light streamed from a long rent along its torso. A *graa*—an eighth-level demon. A heartbeat later the light spiderwebbed over its body and flared. Before I had time to cringe, a sharp *crack* echoed through the clearing. I blinked spots away from my vision and saw the demon was gone, leaving behind nothing but trampled grass and the stench of rotting flowers and sulfur. Sammy lay sprawled half a dozen feet away, bleeding heavily from several ugly wounds.

"Oh, *no*." I ran forward, only now registering that someone else was there, crouched beside the injured dog.

"Seretis?" I blurted in shock. Tall and handsome, with brown hair that waved past his shoulders, and sculpted cheekbones. A flowing red poet-style shirt was paired with dark blue breeches and black boots with gold stitching. It was definitely him, though he looked more than a little worse for the wear. One sleeve bore a rip from shoulder to elbow, mud caked his left boot to the ankle, and blood oozed from a palm-sized abrasion on his cheek. He ran his hands lightly over Sammy and murmured in demon. I fumbled for words, torn between the desire to ask how the hell he was here and my worry for the dog. "Please, can you help him?" I asked as I dropped to my knees by Sammy. Other answers could wait.

"I seek to do so, Kara Gillian," he said. "The flows here

are odd and far weaker than I am accustomed to." His aura surrounded me like a soft summer breeze. Though muted without my arcane senses, it remained clearly palpable.

"Thank you. He's very dear to a friend and ally." The dog whimpered, and I stroked his head. "It's okay, boy," I said to him. "The nice man is going to help you."

Sammy shifted only enough to lick my hand as the demonic lord worked on him. The bleeding soon slowed to mere seeping, but the wounds remained open and ugly.

"A support diagram would serve well," Seretis said without lifting his eyes from the injured animal.

My stomach knotted. "I can't," I said, voice rough. "I don't have my skills anymore."

"Ah," he said simply. "That is unfortunate."

*Not quite the word I've been using*, I thought but kept it to myself. Damn it, Seretis *needed* support. Sweat beaded his face, and his skin had a pale cast to it. An unfocused look in his eyes told me he fought dizziness. He needed better access to potency, like a human at high-altitude in need of an oxygen tank.

I gave myself a mental head-slap. Duh. There was a big ol' tank of potency right in my backyard. "Can you stand?" I asked him. "There's a nexus right down that trail which should help you."

"I will manage," he replied then deftly traced a sigil I couldn't see which he placed on the dog. To ease pain, I figured. I'd been through that process a few times and knew the general motions.

Sammy's whining eased, which told me I was right. Seretis gathered the dog in his arms and stood. "I have told Bryce to remain where he is as he was afflicted by my transit through the valve."

Through the valve? That explained part of how he got here, though I still had plenty of questions. "Yeah, it knocked him for a loop," I said then took hold of Seretis's arm to steady him when he swayed. "C'mon, it's not far."

He cradled Sammy to him and allowed me to lead him down the trail. When the dog whimpered he spoke gently in demon to ease him. "How did you lose your touch to the arcane?" Seretis asked me in an equally gentle tone. "To tell me, you need only bring it to mind."

Relieved, I did so. I had no desire to tell the painful story again. After a moment he nodded. "I will assess your condition after tending to this Sammy."

At least he didn't say I was fucked. I could cling to hope a while longer.

Seretis steadied more as we left the trail and moved out into the open, no doubt already drawing the potency he so desperately needed. Bryce sat in the center of the nexus with a huge grin on his face, but his delight faded at the sight of the bloody dog.

"Shit," he breathed. "It'll kill Pellini if Sammy dies."

Seretis placed the dog on the slab then rested a hand briefly on Bryce's shoulder. "Give me but a moment, *ghastuk*," he said with a rich warmth in his voice. He placed both hands flat on the concrete, and though I couldn't see the power he drew into himself to "recharge," I had no trouble seeing the results. In less than a minute his color returned to normal, the abrasion on his face diminished then vanished, and his gaze sharpened.

He lifted his hands from the slab with obvious reluctance then placed them on Sammy. For a moment nothing happened, but then the wounds started to close like a cool and creepy special effect. Sammy's tail thumped as the nasty gashes thinned. By the time the injuries resolved to unblemished skin, he wagged his tail with enough exuberance to send up clouds of dust and dog hair. Pellini would shit a brick when he saw the hairless stripes, but I had a feeling Seretis didn't have enough mojo at the moment to re-fur the bare skin.

The goofy dog wiggled and climbed to his feet, *shooooook* as if shedding a lake full of water, then happily proceeded to lick and slobber all over the demonic lord's face. Seretis laughed and scratched Sammy behind his ears as he accepted the effusive affection, but after a moment he looked into the dog's eyes, expression serious. Bemused, I watched the dog go still and attentive as the two locked gazes. Perhaps Seretis was warning Sammy about tangling with anything that came out of the valve. Maybe he was instructing the dog to be on guard and let him know if anything strange happened—like giving a kid a Very Important Duty to make them feel special while keeping them out of more trouble.

Finally Seretis smiled and stood. The dog gamboled around him in delighted excitement then raced off, perhaps to begin whatever task the Nice Man had given him. Seretis gave Bryce a hand up, and the two embraced like friends who'd known each other their entire lives.

"Kara asked me to try to contact you," Bryce said, "but I have no idea what happened after that."

"After our initial contact, I departed through Rhyzkahl's grove to return to my realm," Seretis said then grimaced. "Normally a simple transit, one I have made countless times. Yet today the flows warped, and I became disoriented in the interspace. I could find no familiar markers, however I sensed you clearly and followed that flow."

Bryce whistled low. "Damn good thing I tried to reach you when I did."

"Indeed, it was, ghastuk," Seretis said. "With you as a beacon I reached a node and realized I was entrapped in the valve system." He paused as Sammy ran up. The dog proudly dropped what looked like the hindquarters of a long-dead rabbit at his feet then looked up eagerly. Seretis scratched the lab's ears and fell silent for a few seconds, no doubt clarifying his previous instructions. Sammy barked once and dashed off again. Amusement flashed in the lord's eyes but he sobered as he resumed his tale.

"With me in the node was a panicked graa," Seretis said. "Its attempts to free itself had shattered any usable flows, and I had no option but to clear the entanglements and push it onward or remain ensnared myself. I drove it before me, ever following your call. I passed through your valve at the moment the graa clawed Sammy." Distaste twisted his mouth. "Fekk. One of Jesral's."

"Jesral sent the graa through on purpose?" I asked with a frown.

"That is my suspicion," he said, expression dark. "I do

not know how long Fekk was entrapped, but a cross-current in the node led me to believe she was destined for another valve."

"Wonderful," I said sourly. "Only a matter of time before we have selfies with demons going viral online." I took a deeper breath and gave him a crooked smile. "Anyway, I'm glad you made it through in one piece. Was grove travel this messed up after the cataclysm?"

Old grief shadowed his eyes. "The groves retreated into the soil at the very start of the cataclysm," he said. "Most returned after fifty years, though were unusable for close to a hundred. Szerain's remained quiescent for a full century and a half."

"Oh. Right." Now I remembered hearing that from the reyza Safar at Szerain's palace. Felt like a lifetime ago. "Well, I'm going to take the fact that the groves haven't retreated as a good sign," I said brightly. "Maybe the demon realm *isn't* going to hell in a handbasket anytime soon."

Seretis chuckled. "You speak with good sense. I will maintain this conviction."

I bit my lip, shifted. "I didn't expect a house call," I said, "but now that you're here, what can you tell me about my condition? Is there any way it can be reversed?" A fountain of hope rose, and I made no effort to hold it back. Intervention by a demonic lord might very well be my best and last chance for a remedy.

Seretis lifted a hand toward my head then paused, waiting for my permission to fully connect telepathically. As soon as I gave him my nod he rested his hand against the side of my head while I did my best to remain still, both physically and mentally.

It was several minutes before he lowered his hand. "I do not have an answer, Kara Gillian."

The wave of hope crashed onto the rocks of Fuck You Beach, and it was several seconds before I could speak. "Hey, it was worth a shot, right?" I said, voice quavering only a little. "And you were here to save Sammy, so it's all good."

"A solution may well exist," he said. "I am not the qaz-

tahl most versed in such matters." But a frown lingered on
his face. "I sensed an echo of Kadir."

"Oh." I wrinkled my nose. "I used his technique to
symmetrize the valve at the pond and the nature center.
Probably left some Kadiriness behind, like bad cologne."

His frown deepened more, and his gaze went to where
Pellini had created his ring of sigils. "It is more than bad
cologne."

It took me a second to make the connection. "The simulator," I growled. "That son of a bitch used it to put his slime
on me." Idris had been right. Damn it. Despite everything,
a laugh escaped me, harsh and humorless. "Well isn't that
fucking great. I lose everything arcane except *that.*"

Seretis shook his head. "The resonance of Kadir is not
arcane," he told me. "It is of the essence. Integral. Yet apart
from Kadir's imprint, a seed of the arcane remains within
you."

I stared at him. "What does that *mean?*" I finally asked,
afraid to draw my own conclusions.

"It means that the one who stripped you did not take it
all, either by choice or because he was unable. But I know
not if it has meaning with regard to potential restoration."

McDunn's words came back to me. *"It's all I could do."*
That fit both possibilities. He hadn't wanted to take my abil-
ity from me—his hesitation had made that clear. Maybe
McDunn had left a seed as an act of subtle rebellion against
Katashi, on the chance that more could grow from it. Like
leaving one intact nerve in a spinal cord.

I restrained my hope to no more than a flicker. I didn't
know if this "seed" meant anything at all. Better to expect
nothing than be crushed by the pain of disappointment.

The glimmer of true sympathy in Seretis's eyes told me
how slim my chances of recovery were. Still, I remained
grateful for his sentiment, especially considering that it
came from a demonic lord. Most human worries would
surely seem insignificant to anyone who'd lived thousands
of years and seen countless numbers of humans live and die.
Seretis was a frontrunner among the lords as far as compassion and plain old empathy.

"You're a demonic lord!" I blurted. Bryce let out a soft laugh, but Seretis merely smiled.

"To my great consternation at times, yes."

I gave him a weak grin. "I know you jumped through the valve in search of a relaxing vacation with your best buddy here," I punched Bryce in the shoulder, "but it so happens we could use someone with a demonic lord's skill set. I really need the wards at my aunt's house undone so that I can get a few things out of her library while she's off with Katashi."

"That, I can accomplish," he said once he read the subtleties from me. "Though I do not have extended time here, unfortunately." He looked around with a wistful gaze. "My world demands my presence, and your world is unkind to my kind," he added in a light tone belied by the essence-deep weariness in his eyes.

Only Rhyzkahl, Szerain, and Mzatal had ever remained on Earth for an extended period. My gut told me it was no coincidence that they were the three who'd possessed the essence blades for millennia. "We could go to Tessa's house right now if you think you could last a few hours," I said with a glance to Bryce to see if he had any objections or concerns.

But Bryce appeared thrilled with the idea. "It'll give you a chance to see a bit more of the area," he told Seretis with undisguised eagerness. I fought down a laugh at the sudden image of those two hanging out and seeing the sights and hitting the bars. Talk about the ultimate bromance sitcom.

Seretis smiled broadly but in the next heartbeat he looked toward the front of the house. "Two have passed through your warding and approach," he said even as the crunch of gravel in the driveway reached me.

"That'll be Idris and Pellini," I said. "Perfect timing since I was going to call and have them meet us over at my aunt's house. Idris will need to deal with the valve there." A whisper of concern passed over Bryce's face, and I added, "I'm sure Pellini will have no problem staying here with Jill so Bryce can go with us." No way would Bryce want to remain behind while Seretis was here for such a short visit.

Bryce let out a self-conscious chuckle. "Thanks. Should've known you'd understand."

Conversation halted at the sound of running footsteps. An instant later Idris pelted around the house and toward the nexus in clear distress.

"Kara! The valve! The nexus—" His eyes widened as he registered the presence of Seretis, and he literally skidded to a halt, mouth open in an O. "Lord Seretis?! How? I don't . . ." He trailed off, and his gaze snapped to the pond trail. "You came through the valve." His distress deepened. "My lord, I mean no disrespect, but passing through the valve was foolish."

"It wasn't intentional," I told Idris. "He was fixing an anomaly in Rhyzkahl's realm." I quickly explained the circumstances. Idris exhaled, nodded.

"Forgive me for the hasty judgment, my lord," he said, though his brow remained creased with worry.

Seretis regarded Idris. "My lack of foolishness is no reassurance to you."

"It's not," Idris agreed. "The cross-current flow between nodes, plus Jesral's demon, *plus* the relative ease of your arrival means that Katashi has succeeded in anchoring a node. It's what he was close to doing with the plantation node." A muscle in his jaw twitched. "He doesn't care how much damage he causes as long as he's one step closer to a permanent gateway between the demon realm and Earth."

Pellini rounded the corner of the house in ground-eating strides with Sammy bouncing and barking at his side. *"What the fuck happened to my dog?"*

To my undying relief, Seretis stepped forward. "Sammy sustained grievous injury while defending this property against a vicious demon," he said smoothly. "His actions were heroic, and his selfless efforts not only protected me from harm but distracted the graa enough that I could dispatch it. I was able to heal Sammy's wounds, but my control of the potency flows in this realm is insufficient for me to stimulate the regrowth of hair. For that I offer my deepest apology."

Pellini stopped and looked down at his dog with an expression of heart-melting pride usually reserved for a parent whose child receives the Congressional Medal of Honor. "Nah, that's cool. Chicks dig heroes, right boy?" He ruffled the dog's ears while Sammy leaned against him and whacked Pellini's leg with his tail. "Thanks for saving him," he said, emotion thickening his voice, then he looked up at Seretis with a frown. "Who are you?"

I made quick introductions and was poised to explain how a demonic lord happened to be in my backyard when Pellini locked gazes with Seretis.

"Seretis," he murmured. "The dreamer by the sea."

I shot Pellini a baffled look. Where in blazes had he come up with that?

Seretis went lordly-still, and even without my arcane senses I felt his aura sweep over me like a grassfire driven by a desert wind. For a whisper of an instant I was almost grateful I wasn't subject to the full and staggering impact of the lord's reaction. Bryce paled, and Idris's gaze dropped to Seretis's clenched fist. Though I couldn't see the potency, I knew it gathered there.

Heart slamming, I stepped in front of Pellini. "What's going on?"

Seretis took a step closer. "What more has Kadir told you?" he demanded, gaze locked on Pellini over my head. Idris eased further away, but Bryce moved in and put a hand on Seretis's arm. Though his face remained pale, Bryce's eyes held equal measures of worry and support for his friend.

"We're aware of Kadir's influence," I said with a lift of my chin. "Pellini used to play on a valve node when he was a kid, and Kadir found him and . . . molded him." I planted my hands on my hips. "But he's our ally, and I trust him."

Pellini put his hands on my shoulders then gently but firmly shifted me aside. "Look, I am who I am," he said to Seretis. "Kadir told me the dreamer thing and more. If that's a problem, don't dick around. Lay it out."

Seretis lowered his head, eyes hard on Pellini as he no doubt read the "more" from him. "I do not trust Kadir outside of a formal agreement," he said. "You know why." A whisper of a flush touched his cheeks. Embarrassment over whatever Pellini knew?

Bryce cleared his throat. Seretis turned to him, and they stood face-to-face in silent communication. After a moment, Seretis opened his hand, releasing the gathered potency—or so I hoped. Bryce smiled, clearly relieved. Seretis shifted his gaze back to Pellini. "Your intentions are benign," he said. "But you cannot hope to know Kadir's."

Pellini gave a light shrug. "Yeah, and humans deal with that uncertainty every goddamn day," he said. "We know all about caution and suspicion because we've never had the advantage of telepathy. As a cop I know that everyone I deal with might be ready to stab me in the back." As if to illustrate his point he slugged me lightly in the shoulder. "But we keep our guard up," he continued, ignoring my exasperated look, "and we try to do the right thing."

"This time, the uncertainty lies within you, Vincent Pellini," Seretis said. "You carry the imprint of Kadir and must watch yourself with suspicion if you hope to prevail."

Pellini gestured to indicate Idris, Bryce, and me. "They have my back," he said. "I trust them to take me out if I, ah, lose perspective."

Seretis smiled, warm and genuine, and inclined his head to Pellini. "May that need never arise."

"Right there with you," Pellini replied.

# Chapter 28

Seretis sat in the front of Pellini's truck for the drive to Tessa's. Despite the scorching heat and auto fumes, he kept the window rolled down, at times leaning out with the same delight I imagined Sammy held for the activity. His demonic lord aura and Spanish-soap-opera good looks drew more than a few interested stares, but if any traffic accidents ensued because of the spectacle I was unaware of them.

Bryce drove right by the house without slowing, doubled back after another block, then once again continued past it before returning to pull into the driveway and kill the engine. Eilahn parked her motorcycle beside us, then leaped into the branches of an oak in order to act as lookout. After we exited the truck, Seretis made a slow turn to take in the neighborhood then looked over Tessa's house to assess the warding.

"Formidable," he said after a moment.

"Do you think you can undo it all?" I asked, fidgeting as my stomach rumbled.

One side of his mouth kicked up in a smile. "I can."

"Good, because right now I'm craving waffles."

He let out a low chuckle and moved closer to the house. "Here, I will unweave the aversions." He made a few subtle gestures with one hand. "Better?"

"No more desire for waffles!" I announced with a smile. "I mean, no more than usual." It was too bad Seretis had such a short time to spend on Earth. I very much wanted to see his reaction to the Lake O' Butter pancake house.

Seretis continued forward while Bryce trailed him by a few steps and kept watch for potential interference from unfriendlies. I remained several feet back to be certain I wouldn't get zapped, sort of like following someone clearing a minefield. Fortunately we had a kickass minesweeper, and it took less than a minute for us to reach the porch.

Seretis's lips twitched in amusement at the cheery *Welcome!* sign on her door. "Tessa most assuredly did not want visitors." He scrutinized the warding then made a single sweeping gesture with one hand, in a single second destroying defenses that took many hours to lay. "There are alarm sigils placed throughout the protections, but I am disabling those as we proceed." He opened the door, stepped in and took stock. "The only way Tessa Pazhel will know the warding has been stripped is by direct observation."

I nudged Bryce with my elbow. "Your friend comes in real handy."

"Yeah, he's all right," he said then gave an exaggerated sigh. "Now if I could just get him to stop dressing like a complete dork."

Idris shot Bryce a startled look, but Seretis laughed. "You envy my panache."

It took no time at all for Seretis to clear the hallway and continue on to the library. The door was ajar, but I knew it bristled with wards that rendered the physical lock little more than ornamental.

I snapped my attention toward a scrape of noise from the back of the house and drew my gun as Bryce did the same. I caught his eye and angled my head toward the sound in a *We'll check it together* motion. Yet before we were halfway down the hall, Carl stepped out of the kitchen with a wrench in his hand and a tool belt around his waist.

"Kara?" His eyes went to the people with me, especially Bryce who remained alert and ready with his gun trained on Carl.

I lowered my gun. "He's cool, Bryce." I leveled a wry

smile at Carl. "I've almost shot you in this house a few too many times. What are you doing here?"

"Fixing a plumbing leak," he said with a vague gesture toward the kitchen. "Noticed the dripping last night."

Bryce and I holstered guns, and I made quick introductions. Bryce and Idris were easy ones, but Seretis was a different matter. "Um, this is a friend from out of town. Larry," I said, seizing the first name that came to mind. "He's another arcane practitioner."

Carl wasn't looking in Bryce's direction, or he'd have seen the eye roll followed by the incredulous *Seriously?* expression Bryce gave me. Even Seretis flicked a quizzical glance my way, but fortunately Carl didn't notice. He offered a faint smile. "Welcome to Beaulac, Larry."

"Thanks for fixing the leak," I hurried to say before Carl could ask any questions to which I could give more dumb answers. "We're doing a little, um, arcane maintenance."

"Sure thing," he said. "Should I leave?"

I gave the others a questioning look, but everyone seemed content to follow my lead as far as whether to trust Carl. I wasn't sure if Seretis could read the arcane-immune Carl but, either way, the demonic lord didn't appear bothered by him. *Whew.* Felt good to have another potential ally in all this shit.

"We'll be working mainly in the library and attic," I told Carl. "I'm sure we can stay out of each other's way."

"Good deal," he said then returned to the kitchen.

Seretis made short work of shredding the wards protecting the library. We all filed in, and Idris went straight to work on the valve. Bryce let out a low whistle as he took in the horrific majesty of my aunt's library. Shelves covered every vertical surface, all crammed with books, scrolls and papers. Books lay in tumbled disarray on the floor and in precariously balanced stacks on the heavy oak table. A crystal chandelier fit for a ballroom hung in the center of the room.

"Dear god, is Satan her librarian?" Bryce asked in amazement.

I laughed. "It's insane, especially compared to the rest of her house which is always neat as a pin. I've never understood it."

Seretis inspected the contents of the shelves, while Bryce peered at the books and papers on the table. I sent a calculating look around the library, mouth pursed.

"I'd love to relocate as much of this to my house as possible," I said then sighed. "Except that it would piss off my aunt big-time."

Bryce let out a rude snort and gave me a sidelong look. "You've pissed people off before, once or twice."

"I have no idea what you're talking about," I said with an air of total innocence that earned me an even ruder snort. "That said, this *is* my aunt, and she's been a major part of my life for almost twenty years. The destruction of her wards will have her furious enough as it is. I'll restrain myself and only take a few books that might be useful." And what would those be? *Arcane Fun Without the Arcane*? *Ordinary People*?

Maybe I could write one. *No Skillz, No Prob: A Primer for the Arcanely Challenged.*

Seretis paused in the far corner by a collection of various outdated publications with stimulating titles such as *The Chemical Rubber Company's Handbook of Chemistry and Physics 37th edition* or *The Grand Tour Correspondence of Richard Pococke & Jeremiah Milles, Volume 3: Letters from the East (1737-41)* or, for extra thrills, *Ag and Food Statistics 1981: Charting the Essentials*. But instead of moving on like a sane person, he leaned closer, scrutinizing the books before glancing my way with a slight frown. "Have you ever used these volumes?"

I angled my head. "Logarithm tables, and the collected works of Leonid Brezhnev—in the original Russian? Gee, can't say that I have. Why?"

He straightened, expression serious. "This section is warded specifically against you."

A weird rush of cold filled my stomach. I swallowed. "I assume you can unward it?"

"Perhaps." His fingers moved in deft execution of wards I couldn't see. "I am not certain."

The cold increased. "Who could ward it that you wouldn't be certain?"

He exhaled. "Rhyzkahl."

My blood pounded in my ears. I'd never taken any interest in the books on that shelf. *Ever.* They'd been there for as long as I could remember. Boring. Unappealing. Even now the thought of reading one filled me with a sense of annoyance at myself that I'd waste my time on an activity so stupid and pointless. "Can you bring out whatever's in there? Please?"

Seretis considered for a moment. "I can. The protections on the individual volumes are not as dire as those on this area." He fell quiet, fingers moving in infinitesimal gestures. After several minutes, he gathered up a half dozen books and brought them to the table then made a second trip with another half dozen.

The books still had ordinary faded bindings and boring titles, but any curious kid would have pulled them out at least once. Unless, of course, powerful aversions countered that curiosity. I opened one after another, essence-deep chill increasing with each one. The faded bindings were fakes that hid other books—ones I would have pored over for hours on end. An ancient volume with hand-scribed information on the demonic lords. Histories of summoning. A ragged bestiary of non-summonable demons. A treatise on fundamental summoning, including the pygah sigil, which I'd never heard of until Mzatal taught me.

And, a journal filled with neat script on translucent vellum from the demon realm. Not Tessa's handwriting either. The front sheet bore a beautifully rendered mark of Szerain in gold ink. On the following page was an exquisite portrait sketch of a young woman, with "Graciella Therese Pazhel" written in a bold hand below it.

I traced the curve of her cheek with shaking fingers. Gracie Pazhel. My grandmother, killed by Rhyzkahl over thirty years ago. I'd seen pictures of her, but this sketch by Szerain captured far more of *her* than any mere photograph. Proud and confident, with a half-smile as if she held a delicious secret. One she'd died for? Why had Tessa hidden Gracie's legacy from me? And what else didn't I know? The foundation I'd relied on for most of my life now felt as sturdy as tissue paper in a rainstorm.

"Were these warded against my aunt as well?" I pushed the words past the bitter taste that filled my mouth. Though I knew the answer, I had to ask. Had to cling to the hope that we'd both been duped and used.

"No."

Emotions churned as I dropped my gaze to the journal. "She lied to me," I said, voice cracking.

"The qaztahl and their summoners are devious," Seretis said with a heavy touch of self-loathing.

"I finally get hold of stuff I've needed, and now I can't even use it." My fingers dug into a fake binding, and I slammed the book against the table. "Ain't that a piece of shit."

Bryce muttered a curse. "You still balking at taking what you want?"

"Not anymore." I lifted my chin. Hurt and anger and betrayal ricocheted within me. The last twenty years of my life—all a lie? "We're taking it. We'll rent a fucking moving van if we have to."

He pulled out his phone. "I'll get a rental. Don't want to risk anything flying out of the bed of Vince's truck. In fact I'll see if he can call it in for me." With that he stepped into the hall to make the arrangements.

Seretis gestured to an old photo of Tessa standing in front of her store for its grand opening. "This is the one you name Tessa Pazhel?"

"Yes, that's my aunt," I said. "After my dad died, she raised me and taught me how to be a summoner." I scowled. "Except for the part where she left a bunch of crap out on purpose and lied to my face."

"I remember her," he said.

My eyes narrowed. "What do you remember?"

"She was Rhyzkahl's shadow during the conclave twen-

ty-two years past." He studied the photo, stance rigid, eyes
reflecting an anguish I couldn't fathom. Because of Tessa?
After a moment Seretis drew a deeper breath and turned
away from the picture, face composed again. His regard settled upon me, and I knew he was reading my relationship
with Tessa and anything relevant and on my mind. I shot a
quick glance toward Idris, but he was so involved with the
valve I could have been tangoing naked with Bryce and he
wouldn't have noticed.

"Her summoning chamber is in the attic," I told Seretis.
"Would you mind checking it as well?"

"If there are other locations such as this one, I will find
them." He rested a hand on my shoulder for a heartbeat
then exited. Buoyed by the gesture, I busied myself pulling
out books that I thought might be of the most use to us. I
tucked my grandmother's journal into my bag. I didn't want
to share that with anyone until I'd read it.

Bryce left and returned half an hour later with a beat up
Y'all-Haul cargo van, attached trailer, and a billion boxes.
By then Idris had finished with the valve, and I related a
quick and dirty recap of the discovery for him. He let out a
low whistle as he took stock of the hidden books.

"You learned to summon without ever mastering anchor
lock sigils?" he asked, tone incredulous yet holding a dose
of admiration.

"Yeah, well, I guess I'm good at bullshitting my way
through life," I said wryly.

He snorted then sobered. "Did you find any indication
she knew about me?"

"Nothing yet," I said with quiet sympathy, "but there's a
lot more to go through."

He gave me a stiff nod then pitched in to help Bryce
pack books.

"Is everything all right, Kara?" Carl said from the doorway. His mellow gaze took in the activity.

"Yeah, everything's cool," I said. I'd forgotten he was in
the house. Not surprising considering how the discovery of
Tessa's perfidy had consumed my thoughts a teensy bit.
"Need to move the contents of the library to my house." I

didn't bother trying to blow smoke up his ass about how it would be safer there or anything like that.

"Ah," he said. "Yes, better to spend the dragon's hoard." Without another word he slid into the room and joined our work. I didn't try to make sense of his statement. This was Carl.

"Kara," Bryce said some time later. "Seretis needs you in the attic."

My mouth went dry. No way was that a good thing. I thanked him and headed upstairs.

The comfortable twenty by twenty foot space of the converted attic could have easily been used as an office or another bedroom, but served Tessa well as a summoning chamber. The high, peaked ceiling easily accommodated large demons, and the floor had been painted to create a good surface for chalking sigils. A recliner and a small side table were tucked against the wall to the left. No other furniture.

That was how I'd always seen it, at least. But now Seretis stood near the recliner, beside a wall-mounted shelf I had no memory of. A pile of books and other items rested on the seat of the chair.

"Very heavily warded. Against *you*," he said, voice low, "by both Isumo Katashi and Rhyzkahl." He lifted a hand toward the pile then dropped it as if the weight was more than he could bear. "*Tah sesekur di lahn.*"

*I hold sorrow for you.* That was the closest translation of the demon phrase. An expression of the deepest sympathy. I crossed to him and knelt by the items on the recliner. Two ancient volumes on summoning. A framed photo of a much younger Tessa smiling beside Katashi. Calligraphy mat, paper, brushes, ink. A dip pen. A ribbon-bound packet of air mail letters. A Japanese hand scroll. A stenographers pad. *Memorabilia*, I told myself. Nothing but relics from a time long gone. Except that one of the ink bottles appeared brand-new, and the date on the cover of the notepad was only three months past.

I snatched up the pad and flipped through it. Only the

first half bore writing, but there was more than enough to shake my world to the core. To-do lists such as *Call Tsuneo re Isumo's progress in Texas* and *Notify Gina of the revised schedule*. Plus notes for the creation of a ritual I didn't recognize, with sigils drawn and scratched out—several pages of a portion of a diagram, like drafts of a document with each successive rendition containing fewer corrections as she closed in on the solution.

Frustrated, I stared at the last page, certain I'd seen the order of those sigils before but unable to rely on my faulty memory of the arcane.

"Seretis? What would these sigils do?" I asked, extending the notepad to him.

His jaw tightened as he skimmed the page. "They would be part of a larger ritual," he said. "This section would serve to draw low-frequency potency to a point below the intended target. A segment like this for each frequency range would be quite effective to isolate the target from the arcane."

*Isolate from the arcane . . . She helped* design *the ritual that let Katashi hold me helpless while McDunn took my abilities.* How long had that plan been in the works? Long enough for the technique to have been perfected and Idris to have learned it from Katashi.

Reeling from the revelations, I sat heavily on the floor and struggled to make sense of it all. How could any of this be true? "I don't even know what to believe anymore," I said, voice quavering. "She was like a mother to me."

Seretis trailed his fingers over the empty shelf, rested his hand on its edge. "I am so weary of the machinations," he said, despair and fatigue in his eyes and in the set of his shoulders. His hand tightened on the shelf in a white-knuckled grip. "And Mzatal is on the verge of closing off again because of them." With a guttural snarl he ripped the shelf from the wall and flung it across the room. After a few seconds he drew a deeper breath, and a portion of the dark mood faded from his stance. Bryce, lending support from downstairs through their bond.

I stood and offered Seretis my hand. "Let's get everything packed up and ditch this party."

He took my hand, gave it a light squeeze that conveyed far more than mere words, and together we returned downstairs.

# Chapter 29

We proceeded to fill the ten billion boxes to the brim with the contents of the library. Before I had a chance to tremble in horror at the mountain of *stuff* that needed to be loaded up, Bryce rolled in with an industrial-strength hand truck.

"Rented this as well," he said. "Figured it might come in handy. Oh, also got a ramp for the front steps."

"You're the most brilliant man I know," I breathed.

Bryce struck a pose. "Call me 'Lazy Enough to Find An Easier Way Man!'"

With the help of physics and the invention of the wheel, we made short work of loading the van and trailer. The only snag came when a nosy neighbor wandered over on the pretense of walking her yappy dust mop of a dog, but Seretis deftly intervened. I didn't hear what he said to her, but she left with a silly grin on her face and a bounce in her step.

Idris joined me in the rental for the return home, while Bryce and Seretis took Pellini's truck, and Eilahn followed on the Ducati. As we got on our way, I couldn't help but snort. "The last time I rented a vehicle, it was a fourteen foot moving truck to transport Kehlirik from my house to Tessa's," I told Idris.

"Why?" he asked, bewildered.

"A little over a year ago, Tessa lost her essence in the Symbol Man's ritual and was in a coma," I said. "I needed Kehlirik to remove the wards in her house so I could search her library for a way to save her." I paused as I muscled the wheel through a turn then wrinkled my nose. "Funny thing, Kehlirik never said a word to me about the valve in there. And he sure as shit didn't remove the wards from the hidden books. Or tell me about them."

Idris sighed. "Rhyzkahl's reyza."

"Yup." I made a face. "I did plenty of whining back then about the library as a whole being warded against me, especially since I was her only known relative and her student. But she was in a fragile state when I confronted her." I made a rude noise. "Tessa told me she 'thought it was the right thing to do at the time,' and instead of getting a Clue and digging deeper, I let her get away with that lame excuse."

We fell silent for the remainder of the drive. After I pulled up in front of the house and killed the engine, I announced to everyone that we'd unload the van and trailer *later*. Amazingly, no one argued. Hell, my property was warded to the teeth. No one was going to steal the stuff.

Idris jogged inside to enlist Pellini's help in clearing space for when we finally got around to unloading the boxes. Too much energy, that one. Eilahn climbed off her motorcycle and trudged straight to her nest. Seretis stepped out of the pickup then grabbed at the door to steady himself.

Bryce rushed to his side. "Slow your roll, dammit," he said to the pale and shaking lord, voice gruff with affection.

"He's been here too long?" I asked with worry.

"He pushed it," Bryce said, "but he needs to recharge on the nexus before he goes back."

"Got it," I said. "Anomalies and grouchy lords on the other side of the valve."

Seretis straightened as he drew reserves from proximity to the nexus. "Grouchy *and* obstinate," he said, mouth twitching into a smile, "and unlikely to reform." He hooked one arm through Bryce's then slipped his other through mine. A casual, friendly gesture, but it was clear he needed the added support.

"How bad are things in the demon realm right now?" I asked as we made our way to the backyard.

He sobered. "The flows are in chaos and cause tremors in every realm. Anomalies grow more frequent and more bizarre." A shudder passed through him that I noticed only because of his arm against mine. "Fire rain deforested the southern reaches of Elofir's realm—the first occurrence of such in two centuries. There is little rest for qaztahl or demahnk."

My guilt spiked, and I winced. "I took you away for hours to pull down wards."

Seretis gave my arm a squeeze. "Not against my will. The discoveries will no doubt prove advantageous in the long run."

Bryce disengaged from Seretis. "Lemme get some blankets to cushion our butts on the concrete," he said then detoured to the laundry room while Seretis and I continued to the nexus.

"What of Mzatal?" I asked.

Seretis's steps faltered and recovered. "He is our driving force. None of us can match his . . . focus." Yet he paled as he spoke, and his eyes grew wary.

I steadied him as we stepped up onto the nexus. "You don't sound happy about that."

"Mzatal does what he must," he said and passed a hand over his face. "None dare shirk responsibilities in attending the flows."

"It must be a lot harder now with him closed off," I said with a wince.

Seretis slipped his arm from mine. "Closed?" He let out a single humorless laugh, harsh and laden with foreboding. "No, Mzatal has not closed."

"But even before McDunn diminished me I could barely feel him," I said in confusion. "He'd walled off except for a pinprick."

Seretis tightened his hands to fists and lowered his head. His aura expanded as if he instinctively raised defenses, like a cat fluffing up at the bark of a dog. "A pinprick remains, and thus he is open yet." Seretis spoke, words heavy and dark, bearing the weight of millennia of experience. "Mzatal commands resolve enough to thrust an entire sun through the span of a single hair. No, Kara Gillian, you have never known him fully closed and merged with his essence blade." He opened his hands slowly, as if it took great force of will. "None can match Mzatal when he is thus. Formidable. Ruthless. Utterly focused."

I tried to comprehend a fully closed Mzatal. "He had his blade at the plantation battle." I paused. "Paul Ortiz almost died there."

Seretis lifted his head, nodded gravely. "He put aside Khatur in the wake of Szerain's exile. Though he reclaimed it to counter Rhyzkahl's machinations against you, he has yet to embrace it fully again. Thus he walks a treacherous line between fury and control, distraction and focus."

Dread settled into a sick coil in my chest. "As long as Khatur exists, Mzatal can't be free."

Seretis met my eyes. "When he created the essence blades, he wed his fate to them. A terrible choice."

The coil tightened. "And now he can't afford to set aside the blade even if he wanted to. Not with the Mraztur craziness and the demon realm falling apart. He needs the power and focus. The world needs it."

"It is a wretched truth, Kara Gillian," he said. "I cannot deny I cherished the respite of the past decade and a half when Khatur lay dormant." His aura resolved to its normal level, and his voice carried a wistful nostalgia. "This last year in particular as he opened more with Idris, and with you."

"He's opened more with you, too," I said.

One side of his mouth lifted. "And with Elofir as well. A welcome echo of times long past. It has been . . ." Seretis angled his head as he searched for the appropriate word. "*Nice*," he finished.

"Nice is good," I said. "But the whole world-going-to-hell thing is getting in the way."

He exhaled. "There is no leisure for 'nice' amidst our current woes. With Szerain exiled, Rhyzkahl crippled, and Jesral weakened, we are hard-pressed." Seretis brought his eyes back to mine, sad in contrast with his quick smile. "Yet

I must confess, I take consolation in Rhyzkahl's plight despite the challenges it poses."

"It couldn't happen to a nicer guy." I grinned, though his words stirred disquiet. The lords carried an unfathomable burden as an essential aspect of their existence—and had done so for thousands of years. Without their constant maintenance, the demon realm would cease to exist. How could *anyone* live with that much responsibility?

Bryce emerged from the house and spread an old quilt at the center of the slab. We settled on it, and Seretis's features relaxed as he connected with the potency reservoir of the nexus.

"How long will Rhyzkahl be out of the game?" I asked.

"I never count him out," Seretis said. "However, he is quite debilitated. He cannot tolerate sunlight, and he has ineffective connection to the flows." He paused, unsettled. "There is no precedent for his condition. We do not know if he will ever recover."

*Without a ptarl*, I added silently. There was no precedent because, in the lords' entire history, no ptarl had ever broken the bond. Though Szerain and Kadir were separated from their ptarls, their bonds remained intact. "As much as I despise Rhyzkahl," I said, "it sucks that he can't help fix the damage he caused."

"His absence requires—" Seretis scrambled to stand then stared down at me with shock and distrust as if I'd turned rabid. "You have connected with him."

Bryce stood, troubled gaze shifting from Seretis to me.

"Connected?" I rose to my feet as well since I didn't like him towering over me—especially when I didn't know what the hell was going on. "Wait, are you talking about the dream thing?"

If anything, his apprehension increased. "Yes. A dream link."

"You don't have to worry," I said defensively. "It wasn't like the other times Rhyzkahl came to my dreams. I wasn't asleep, and I had total control for this one. Why are you so freaked?"

Seretis shook his head, a sharp movement. "Rhyzkahl is the target with this new link." He assessed me with narrowed eyes. "*You* are the initiator."

"Huh?" I blinked, taken aback. "No, I'm not."

"Who wove the link?" Seretis demanded. He advanced toward me, but Bryce thrust a hand between us to stop him.

"What are you talking about?" I demanded right back. As much as I liked Seretis, this confusing third-degree was getting old, fast. "I was about to go to sleep for the night, and the dream-thing just *happened*. I figured it was something Rhyzkahl tried to do that backfired on him."

Seretis glowered. "He cannot create a dream link."

"Sure he can," I insisted. "He used to invade my dreams all the damn time."

Bryce pressed his lips together then shocked me by taking hold of Seretis's chin and forcing the lord to meet his eyes. "Tell her," Bryce said, unflinching.

I planted my hands on my hips. "Tell me what?"

Seretis gave Bryce a look of deep chagrin coupled with unspeakable gratitude. "Rhyzkahl did not forge his previous dream links with you," he said to me, subdued. "I did."

Whoa. That was unexpected. "So *that's* why you wigged out at Pellini's 'dreamer by the sea' comment."

His chagrin deepened. "*Yaghir tahn*," he murmured and looked away. *Forgive me.*

I rubbed the back of my neck. "You owed Rhyzkahl a debt?"

"I am weak," he said, voice low. "I owe *every* qaztahl."

Bryce seized his arm. "Stop that," he ordered.

"Yeah, you need to listen to Bryce," I said. "Just because you're not a raging *asshole* doesn't mean you're weak." Frowning, I tried to piece together his remarks. "I'm lost. If you didn't create the link, and Rhyzkahl can't, who did?"

"I do not know." His mouth bowed into a puzzled frown. "None of the other qaztahl are able to do so, unless they have kept the ability well hidden."

"Could a human have done it?" It was a stretch, but maybe Katashi or Tessa were fucking with me?

The look Seretis gave me said *No, no, and hell no*, but he answered with a more polite, "I do not believe it likely."

All right, so that narrowed my suspect list down to non-humans and non-lords with arcane skills. In other words, most of the demon realm. "Since my abilities are gone, the dream link is too, right?"

"No. Such can be forged in any human, even ones without arcane talent," he said with the authority of experience. "In the days when humans lived in the demon realm, I often linked with them. In this manner, I learned much of humanity." His expression remained free of guilt, unlike when he'd spoken of forming the link to me from Rhyzkahl. Probably because he'd known Rhyzkahl was up to no good.

"Since my arcane loss won't affect the dream link, what should I do if it happens again? Is it dangerous?"

"The danger to you is not physical," he said, yet his tone grew serious. "The danger lies in what you choose to share with Rhyzkahl within the dream connection. It is quite real for him."

"I punched him in the face," I said with a crooked smile. "I'd be happy to share that with him again."

Bryce let out a bark of laughter, but Seretis remained somber as he spoke. "It is up to you to initiate the dream visit. It will not simply happen."

"But I didn't this last time," I said, frowning.

"In that instance, it was initiated by the one who forged the link." Seretis shifted, uneasy. "When did you visit Rhyzkahl's dream?"

I had to think about that one. "Thursday night. Um, four nights ago. I'm not sure of the time. Late."

Seretis dropped to one knee and placed his hands flat on the nexus, closed his eyes. I resumed my seat on the quilt and mulled over the implications of everything he'd revealed. Someone hooked up a dream link to Rhyzkahl where I held the reins. Which meant that Someone had a secret agenda. And I doubted it was simply because Rhyzkahl needed to be socked in the face.

Seretis lifted his head. "There are echoes of Szerain here."

I yanked my wandering thoughts back into place. "Szerain used the nexus on Thursday around midday. He was looking for someone or something that had him scared shitless." I peered at Seretis. "You have any clue on that?"

His mouth pulled into a frown of concentration. "More recent activity distorts Szerain's residuals." He adjusted the position of his hands as if fine-tuning his reception.

"Damn," I said. "Must be from Idris. He uses the nexus a lot. Or Pellini."

Seretis remained in deep concentration. "Not Idris or Vincent Pellini," he murmured as he continued to assess. "Demahnk."

"Szerain took Zack away on Friday," I said, puzzled. "I guess he might have come back here and—"

"Not Zakaar," Seretis said, face ashen. "*Xharbek*."

"Are you fucking kidding me?" Xharbek, Szerain's ptarl, so deep in hiding that even the other demahnk didn't know his whereabouts. "He's on *Earth?*" I asked. "That's good, right? Szerain needs stability."

"Szerain used the nexus to seek Xharbek." Seretis lifted his hands and rubbed them together as though washing them. "Not long after, Xharbek used it to seek Szerain."

The implication crashed through me. "Szerain said that when I disrupted his ritual, it was like sending up a beacon." I gulped. "He was scared shitless. Of *Xharbek*." Szerain was free of his prison, and Xharbek probably wanted to rectify that.

Seretis sucked in a sharp breath and squeezed his eyes shut as agony contorted his features. Bryce let out a curse and shot me a look of frustration and impotent rage that I understood too damn well. We both knew what this was: One of the knifing headaches the lords got when their thoughts strayed into forbidden territory. So, was it anathema to think there might be reason to fear any of the demahnk? It sure as hell fit with my developing theory that the demahnk—a.k.a. the Demahnk Council—were the ones doing the controlling.

Seretis cried out and clutched his head. Bryce put a hand

on Seretis's shoulder, helpless to do more to ease him. An idea for a distraction blinked on in my head, and I surged to my feet. "Sammy!" I shouted, hoping the goofy dog was within earshot. "Sammy! Here, boy!"

To my relief, frantic barks sounded from within the house. "Jill, let him out!" I yelled. Seconds later the back door flew open, and Sammy streaked toward us. He bounded onto the slab then bowled Seretis over in a flurry of enthusiastic face licking and tail wagging. Bryce received a solid tail thwack to the side of the head before he could scramble up and out of the way. Cringing, I watched in trepidation. "Slobber-trampled to death" as a headache cure wasn't quite how I'd envisioned this going, but my concern eased as a laugh burst from Seretis.

The lord rolled into a fetal position and protected his face with his forearms, still laughing and making inarticulate noises of mock-distress. Bryce grinned at me and gave me two thumbs up. I managed a weak smile in response. That could have ended in disaster. *Gee, Mzatal, sorry but Seretis can't come help y'all with your world falling apart. You see, a dog jumped on him and cracked his skull on the nexus.*

Seretis disentangled enough from Happy Dog to sit up. I crouched beside them and scratched Sammy's ears. "You're the best dog ever," I told him. Sammy responded with a big, wet slurp across my face then plopped down next to Seretis and rolled to his back in a clear bid for a belly rub. Seretis obliged with a smile, but after a moment it dissolved.

"It was Xharbek. He used the nexus to set the dream link."

I goggled at that revelation. "Why would a demahnk—a hidden one at that—make a dream link from me to that asshole?"

Seretis pressed his mouth tight. "None can guess the ways of a demahnk."

*Translation: I'm avoiding headache punishment.* My ire flared at the whole situation, but I tamped it down in the face of more urgent considerations.

"Seretis, you said Rhyzkahl can't hurt me in the dream space because I'm the initiator," I said. "Does that mean it's *safe* for me to initiate a visit?"

"He cannot entrap you or harm you physically. However, he can hear and remember your words. Say nothing you do not wish him to know."

"Right. Got it." I engaged in furious thinking. "How many humans are in the demon realm against their will?"

His eyes shadowed. "I only know of six who abide with qaztahl. All brought in by Rhyzkahl this past year."

"*Which* qaztahl?" The eleven lords spanned a vast range of temperaments, from gentle Elofir at one end to vicious Amkir at the other.

"One woman is with Vrizaar, another with Jesral. Two are with Rhyzkahl. Amkir holds one man and one woman." He paused. "Kadir had two men. But they are dead."

A shiver went through me. Kadir relished hunting human quarry.

"It is the mandate of the Council that only humans deserving of punishment by the standards of Earth may be hunted," Seretis said in response to my thoughts.

"You're telling me the demahnk are okay with Kadir's brand of torment?"

"They do not interfere if he abides by the parameters set."

I rubbed my arms, chilled. They'd damn well better not judge Paul to be deserving of punishment. "The rest of the humans are alive?"

"The six captives live, as do the others." His eyes met mine for a heartbeat before he looked down and away. "Michelle Cleland is with Elofir and any others with whom she chooses to spend time. Michael Moran dwells with Rayst and me, and is not unwilling."

Michelle had been a Symbol Man "sacrifice" to Rhyzkahl, and Michael was a brain damaged young man with the ability to shape earth into golems. "I have no problem with the willing ones," I said. "What aren't you telling me?"

His expression grew haunted. "I have failed at negotiations to acquire any humans since coming to agreement with Amkir for Michael." Bryce cursed under his breath and rested a hand on Seretis's shoulder.

"That you tried at all means worlds to me," I said gently. An ugly story lurked behind the confession, I was certain—especially since the brutal Amkir was involved.

Sammy started barking and bolted toward the woods. Seretis leaped to his feet. "An entity has passed through the valve."

"Another demon?" My hand went to my gun as I scrambled up.

"I know not. The Earth flows are too weak for me to read."

Whether it was a demon or an other-worldly mosquito, we needed to be the welcoming committee. I took off toward the path with Seretis and Bryce on my heels. Sammy barked in the woods ahead. "Sammy! Get your stupid ass back here!" I called out. To my surprise the dog bounded back in our direction, which I suspected had far more to do with a silent call from Seretis than my yelling. Bryce and I drew our weapons as we reached the woods and proceeded with caution.

Seretis cursed in demon behind me. "*Kadir.*"

*Oh, shit,* I thought the instant before his aura slithered through me. Even without my arcane senses I felt as if I'd been dipped in cold slime filled with unnamed horrors. Mouth dry, I stumbled to a walk, hand tight on my gun as I moved forward. Didn't matter that the gun would be next to useless against a lord. It made *me* feel better.

Kadir stalked along the trail, anger flowing from him like a noxious cloud. His face and clothing were scored with deep and angry burns, as if he'd been lashed by a whip made of napalm.

Swallowing hard, I lowered my gun and stood my ground. "Why are you here?" I asked.

"I am the one he seeks," Seretis said. He stepped around me with the dog right beside him and took in Kadir's condition. "Fire rain. In your realm?"

The pale lord bared his teeth. "With only Elofir and the demahnk to aid while you dally."

I expected a snappy comeback from Seretis, but instead

he hunched his shoulders like a chastised schoolboy. "Yaghir tahn," he muttered.

I tensed in annoyance. Why was Seretis asking for forgiveness when Kadir was the one who needed the help? Ugh. I *hated* the dynamics between the lords. "Hey, lighten up, Blondie." I lifted my chin. "Seretis came here by accident, not for vay-cay."

Kadir's regard zeroed in on me. Seretis placed his hand on my arm. "He speaks truth, Kara Gillian," he said. "It was my choice to remain. No time for goodbyes now." He gave my arm a squeeze then pulled away, strode past Kadir and down the trail with Sammy at his side. Bryce hesitated then jogged after Seretis. I didn't begrudge his desire for a few more seconds with his friend. He and I both knew that if Kadir decided to do something unpleasant to me there wasn't a damn thing either of us could do about it.

Kadir's expression was a mix of anger, urgency, and strange curiosity as he closed the distance between us. "With or without intent, no qaztahl has the luxury of absence from the demon realm now," he said in a vicious purr, though instead of "the demon realm" he used the hideously unpronounceable demon word for his world.

I offered him a bland smile. "Last I checked, you were a qaztahl. Better get your ass back."

"You must barricade the valve so no others can pass," he went on with clipped urgency as if I hadn't spoken. "It *is* possible to alter a node for permanent passage. Not so for a valve. It is only a matter of time before it gives way with disastrous effect."

"Can't barricade *or* symmetrize your valves now, thanks to your flunky," I said through clenched teeth.

With lightning speed, he gripped my hair near my scalp and dragged my face close to his, violet eyes locked on mine. I sucked in a breath and suppressed the instinct to struggle. He reeked of sulfur and singed hair. *Go on,* I thought at him with a mental snarl. *Assess.*

He released me so abruptly I staggered a step before

finding my balance. New rage smoldered in his eyes. "Katashi." He spoke the name like a curse.

"That's right." I straightened and gave him a sneer. "Your dog is running around biting people, even the ones you don't want bit."

"You yet hold the knowledge of creating a barricade seal. *Find a way*." He sprinted back toward the valve like a nightmarish gazelle to save his realm.

I followed at a jog, but by the time I reached the pond clearing he was gone. Bryce crouched by Sammy several feet from the end of the trail.

"What the hell was that all about?" I asked Bryce. Hopefully, his connection to Seretis could shed some light on the last few minutes of weirdness.

Bryce straightened, sighed. "The only lords who can tolerate the out-of-phaseness of Kadir's realm for more than a few minutes are Elofir and Seretis." He grimaced, scratched the back of his head. "They were able to control one anomaly without Seretis, but a second cropped up that brought fire rain. Kadir *needed* Seretis, and so he came for him."

"Their world has turned into a nightmare!" I said, pairing my words with a hard kick at a rotten stump. "I don't understand why the Mraztur continue to condone Katashi's bullshit with the valves."

Bryce pressed his lips together and spread his hands. "I got nuthin.'"

The rustle of brush and cracking twigs heralded Idris as he sprinted into the clearing. "What happened at the valve?" he asked as he slid to a stop, gaze sweeping the area.

"Kadir came through and took Seretis back," I said. "There was an—" Idris cut me off with an explosive curse and ran for the valve. I stayed out of his way so that he could stabilize it.

Pellini came puffing into the clearing. Since Idris didn't want or need us hanging out and watching him work, the three of us returned to the house. On the way back Bryce and I briefed Pellini on Kadir's bizarre visit. By the time we made it to the kitchen, we had Pellini caught up on the discoveries at my aunt's house and were well into the general state of affairs in the demon realm.

The buzz of the gate intercom halted any further conversation. Bryce peered at the screen on the security panel, and his expression went grave. "Kara, we have a problem."

# Chapter 30

I looked over Bryce's shoulder at the small display. A St. Long Parish Sheriff's Office cruiser and a dark Chevy Impala idled in the driveway beyond the gate. Detective O'Connor stood by the intercom, looking very official in his sunglasses and starched dress shirt.

My stomach lurched. It was really happening. "Oh, well, so much for a restful evening!" I said, being flippant in an attempt to maintain a cool demeanor. Not that anyone bought my act, least of all me. I pressed the intercom button. "Hi, Detective, how can I help you today?"

O'Connor lifted the papers in his hand and glared into the camera. "Kara Gillian, I have a warrant for your arrest. If you refuse to come out and give yourself up, we'll have no choice but to make entry by force."

"I understand, Detective," I said. An arrest warrant gave him legal right to make entry onto my property and into my house if necessary to make the arrest. Thankfully, the aversions discouraged him from coming through the gate to knock on my door with a sledgehammer. However, if I stalled, he was tough-willed enough to bull his way through the arcane barriers. That would spell disaster if he tripped any of the more dangerous protection wards, and I didn't want anyone getting hurt. "I'll be at the gate in less than five minutes."

Protest formed on his face then faded. Good. I'd been

agreeable enough that he lacked sufficient motivation to overcome the aversions. "Five minutes."

I spun away from the display and jogged to my bedroom. Bryce followed and paused in the doorway. "What's the plan?" he asked with a frown as I dug through my dresser drawers.

*Well*, I thought, *first I'll go throw up, and then I'll curl up on the bathroom floor*. "Hiding or running would be pointless and bring heat down on everyone here," I said instead. "My best move is to cooperate." I pulled out a fluffy hooded sweatshirt and slipped it on over my tank top.

Bryce eyed me with bafflement as I fluffed my hair out from beneath the collar. "You do know it's the middle of summer, right?"

"I sure do." I stripped off my watch and emptied my pockets, then reluctantly pulled the damaged ring from my finger and placed it in my jewelry box. "Holding cells are damn cold. Bond won't be set until tomorrow at the earliest, and I don't want to freeze my ass off all night."

Pellini joined Bryce in the doorway and gave a nod of agreement. "I know a lawyer who won't ask a lot of questions. I'll give him a call."

"Thanks." I blew out a breath then squared my shoulders. No sense putting this off any longer. Hell, maybe I could take a nap in jail. Yeah, right. "Now then, who wants to give me a ride to the gate?"

I had to hand it to Detective O'Connor. Though obviously frustrated by my refusal to divulge information relevant to his case, he never once crossed the line into asshole territory. I appreciated that, especially since I sympathized with his plight. He had a job to do and a murder to solve. I couldn't fault him for his commitment to do everything in his power to accomplish that. I, of course, was committed to avoiding prison on Earth or exile in the demon realm.

The deputy with O'Connor was a blond woman with a no-nonsense expression and "Harper" on her nametag. She patted me down and handcuffed me with brisk efficiency. I tried not to think about the number of times I'd done the same to an arrestee—never *ever* thinking I'd one day be on the other side of it. Without a smile or unneeded word, she seatbelted me into the back seat of her car and transported me to the parish jail. I remained silent for the duration of the ride, not because I was stoic, but because I didn't trust myself to speak. I'd convinced myself that I was mentally prepared for this, but the reality was a vicious kick in the gut, and I balanced on the razor edge of control. Ex-cop under arrest was humiliating enough, but ex-cop under arrest who burst into tears on the way to jail would be worse than everything else combined.

Deep breaths and careful control got me through the urge to dissolve into a sobbing meltdown. By the time Harper escorted me to the booking area at the jail I'd regained enough composure to endure being processed in—searched, fingerprinted, photographed, and at last placed in a holding cell.

Concrete benches ran the length of three walls. Near the door a metal toilet and sink were tucked into a shallow alcove that offered zero privacy. The cell was as overly air-conditioned as I'd expected, and I silently applauded my sweatshirt wisdom.

I settled on the bench to my right then took unobtrusive stock of the other five women in the cell and tried to guess what they'd been arrested for. Two in their late thirties or early forties lay curled up on my bench, either asleep or pretending to be. Theft or Issuing Worthless Checks. A girl dressed as if she'd spent the day at the lakefront sniffled on the bench against the back wall. Eighteen if she was a day. Underage Driving Under the Influence, I decided. Across from me, a haggard-faced woman stared at nothing with defeat in her eyes. Possession of a Controlled Substance— no-brainer there. And not far from her, a woman in her mid-twenties sat in a stiff and scowly posture that radiated anger. Aggravated Battery, hands down.

Then again, how was I to know? Maybe every single one of them had been arrested for creating human-animal hybrids. I doubted any of them looked at me and thought, "Homicide."

I leaned my head back against the cinderblock wall, crossed my arms over my chest, closed my eyes, and settled in for a long and boring night. Voices rose and fell in the hallway, and a cart with a clattering wheel rolled past. A door shut with a heavy *clang* followed by a stream of curses. Sweat and piss lurked beneath the acrid tang of industrial cleaner, and above it all drifted the old-cabbage scent of low-quality cafeteria food.

"Hey, Princess!"

Tensing for a confrontation, I opened my eyes to find Angry Chick focused on the sniveling girl. "Stop your fucking whining before I stop it for you," she snapped at Young Thing, which did nothing except make the poor girl cower and cry harder.

Angry Chick rose to her feet. Young Thing's eyes widened in terror, and she let out a thin panicked wail.

"Leave her alone," I said, using the same mild and even tone Bryce used in stress situations. "She's probably never been arrested before. I bet you were scared the first time you got hooked."

Angry Chick rounded on me with a teeth-baring snarl. "You trying to say I'm a habitual offender, bitch?"

So much for being reasonable. Fine. I could play it her way. "Well, you sure are familiar with the term 'habitual offender.'"

Angry Chick let out a growl of rage and took a step toward me, fists clenched.

"That's a bad idea," I said.

She hesitated, no doubt trying to understand why her subconscious told her I was a potential threat when I looked like an easy mark. I continued to regard her steadily. I'd locked gazes with far more powerful creatures than this woman.

To my dismay, instead of backing down as I'd hoped, she narrowed her eyes. "I know you," she said. Dread flickered in my gut at the hatred in her voice. "You're a *cop.*"

*Son of a bitch.* Adrenaline dumped into my system to send my pulse racing, and it took all the willpower I possessed to form a lazy smile.

"Not anymore," I said. "I got a better offer." With any luck her imagination would fill in lurid details. Enforcer for a cartel, or mercenary, or international spy.

Unfortunately, she wasn't that creative. She sneered down her nose at me. "Doesn't matter. Cop or ex-cop, I'll beat you bloody before they pull me off you."

*If* they pulled her off me. The dread roared to life. Even if the guards on duty thought Farouche deserved what he got, I couldn't depend on their support. Far likelier that they regarded me as nothing more than a cop gone bad who deserved whatever might happen. And right now the "whatever might happen" I faced topped me by several inches and outweighed me by at least thirty pounds.

Sweat rolled down my sides despite the chill. My mind raced in search of a tactic to avoid a nasty fight but kept circling back to one ploy. *Shit.*

Heaving a deep sigh, I stood, nice and slowly, maintaining eye contact. When I spoke it was with a quiet and scary intensity that I'd learned from months of dealing with immortal beings of vast power.

"I've survived more pain, more *torture* than you could ever hope to dish out," I said, stupidly pleased that I'd pitched my voice just right to resonate against the walls. With deliberate movements I pulled up my shirts to reveal my collection of scars. A whisper of horror flitted through her eyes. Sure, there were people who were into body modification through scarring, but a primal sense told her these scars were different.

Though my heart pounded like a marching band drumline, I lowered the sweatshirt and adjusted my clothing with steady hands. "Now then, you need to ask yourself if it's worth trying to knock me down and punch me a few times when you *know* I'll get Right. Back. Up." I had no need to pygah to remain calm. Every word I spoke was the absolute truth.

Angry Chick knew it too. She retreated a step then put on the scowl of someone who knows they've been beaten but doesn't want to look like a coward. "You ain't worth my time," she scoffed, but her words had no strength behind them. "Bitch, you lucky I don't want more charges on me right now."

"I am indeed very lucky," I replied as I resumed my seat. I glanced over at the sniveling girl—who wasn't sniveling anymore. She and the three others watched me with wide-eyed awe.

Angry Chick muttered under her breath but plopped back down onto her bench, no less angry than before, although cowed.

Good enough. With that settled, I closed my eyes and went to sleep.

# Chapter 31

I managed an entire hour of sleep before the irate cursing of a newcomer to the holding cell woke me. Mid-to-late thirties, blond and fit in a Cardio Barbie way. Expensive jeans and a rumpled silk blouse over perky and perfect fake tits. Obviously intoxicated, she continued a steady stream of high-volume cursing, even after the guard closed the door and walked off. I glared at her, but her ranting stayed aimed at the door as if she believed her words could carve through the metal. Original gems such as "Don't you know who I am?" and "I'll sue every one of you worthless morons!" and "I'll have your jobs and you'll be cleaning toilets!" — all accompanied by colorful descriptions of parentage and sexual preference.

A growl built in my throat as the tirade continued, but Angry Chick stood before I had a chance to say my piece.

"Sit your ass down and shut your hole!" Her voice cut right through the drunken cursing.

Rich Bitch swung around, tilted her head back to deliver a disparaging look. "Don't you *dare* tell *me* what to do!" she ordered, radiating shocked insult that Angry Chick had spoken to her at all, much less with such disrespect. I knew this kind too well. Mega-Society upper class, entitled and convinced the world existed to serve her. Insulted when anyone had the unmitigated gall to treat her like an ordinary person. Most people swallowed their tongues around her type—myself included, back in the day—because every now and then the "I'll have your job" threat was carried out.

But Angry Chick had nothing Rich Bitch could threaten. I watched with undisguised delight as she closed the distance. Rich Bitch retreated until her fit and trim ass smashed up against the cell door. Inches away, Angry Chick loomed over the wide-eyed woman.

"Sit your ass down and shut your hole," she repeated, slowly but with no less menace.

Tickled, I watched Rich Bitch's face shift from outrage to consternation as she realized she wasn't the most powerful person in the room. Gulping, she hunched her shoulders then scurried to the back of the holding cell to sit beside Young Thing. Angry Chick gave me a satisfied nod as if to say *I got it covered* then resumed her seat. Bemused, I returned the slight nod. Apparently I'd scored a follower. Maybe Angry Chick could be my lieutenant if I ended up staying here for any length of time.

A trustee brought in terrible bologna sandwiches and weak lemonade along with scratchy blankets for each of us. I let Angry Chick have my blanket to use as a pillow. She deserved it.

I ate my lousy sandwich, leaned my head back and closed my eyes once more, but sleep evaded me. My earlier nap had taken the edge off my exhaustion, and worry and tension wound through my thoughts. The women in this holding cell ran the gamut of social classes, as did the women and men enslaved in the demon realm. Amaryllis Castlebrook had been targeted because no one would miss her for a couple of days. What of the others? The captives deserved to go home if they wished, regardless of their backgrounds or how well—or not—they were treated by their captors.

Rhyzkahl was the kingpin on the demon side of the human trafficking. A grim smile tugged at my mouth. I had something he wanted. Perhaps I had enough leverage for what *I* wanted.

Cautious, I relaxed my mind and recalled the feeling of

the dream state visit, as familiar and effortless as if I'd done it a million times. I felt him sleeping, willed myself into his presence.

A terrace of white demon marble shimmered and solidified around me. Beyond the stone balustrade, bright moonlight washed the turquoise sea far below the cliffs, and the leaves of Rhyzkahl's grove glimmered emerald and amethyst a hundred paces away. I'd suspected, and Seretis had confirmed: This was the true demon realm, and in the dreamstate I saw and experienced it like an interactive remote viewing.

My breath caught as the arcane whispered through me, and glints of potency flows greeted me like long lost friends. Barely perceptible, yet I drank it in like licking morning dew off leaves to slake my thirst.

Rhyzkahl sprawled face down on a chaise lounge, an overturned goblet on the tiles beside his dangling hand. A silky white shift hugged the contours of his back, plastered by sweat. Ugh, he'd slept with my *aunt!* Though I dearly wished to confront him about that particular liaison, I restrained the impulse. I wasn't sure if he knew about Idris's parentage, and no way did I want to give him that info. Besides, I already had an agenda in mind.

"Hey, turdbucket!" I gave the couch a hard kick. "Wake up!"

Groaning, he opened his eyes. "Kara," he said, voice thick.

I angled my head. "You feeling any better, puddingkins?"

He pushed himself up to sit, movements unsteady. Pain still creased his features, and though he appeared less hollow than before, it might have simply been a trick of the moonlight. Blinking heavily, he reached toward me as if to determine whether I was a dream or a *dream*. I allowed his fingers to brush my forearm before I backed away.

"Oh no, pookie bear," I said with a fierce smile. "You're going to have to pay for more of that."

"Pay?" He leaned back into the pillows, brows knitted in confusion. "What do you mean, pay?"

Folding my arms over my chest, I regarded him. "I want the captives back."

Though debilitated, he still managed a Rhyzkahl-frown. "What captives?"

My smile turned to ice. "You play stupid with me, I'll leave and never come back."

His frown vanished. "No. Stay." He licked dry lips. "What do you want . . . specifically?"

I paced beside the balustrade, trailed my fingers over the ancient white stone as I took a moment to consider my words. "The people kidnapped on Earth and brought here against their will," I said. "I want them sent to Mzatal to be returned home if they so desire—which *he* will determine."

"What do you offer in exchange?" he asked, wary.

I gave him a sweet smile. "Break your nose again?"

Rhyzkahl shifted in the cushions. "If this is a serious proposition then there must be serious terms." He watched me, eyes not as glazed as during my last visit though they still lacked their usual keen focus. "You care about these humans. Strike a true agreement, and you may recover them. Word games will not serve you."

*Don't forget who you're dealing with*, I reminded myself. The demonic lords were, for all intents and purposes, demigods. Even dazed and feeling like shit, Rhyzkahl still possessed millennia of experience in bargains, negotiations, agreements—and backstabbing.

"Very well," I said. "Let's hammer out details."

"Closer," he said, beckoning with one hand.

My mouth pursed in distrust. I knew from the first dream visit that my proximity gave him clarity and relief. I took a single step toward him, and he shuddered like a jonesing junkie at the sight of a syringe of heroin.

"You want the captives," he said. "Release the syraza, I release one human."

I laughed. "No. That's not going to happen. Eilahn stays with me." It spoke volumes that he named her as his first negotiation point. As long as she remained on Earth, she drained potency from him. He *needed* to be free of the liability. Gee, too fucking bad. No way would I use Eilahn as a pawn.

"Two," he said through gritted teeth. "Release her for two."

"The trade of Eilahn is *not* on the table," I said flatly.

"Then you have no great desire for the release of these humans," he said, lifting one pale eyebrow.

He was going to play *that* lame-ass card? My shoulders lifted in a shrug. "I guess we have nothing more to discuss," I said and thinned the dreamscape slightly as if about to leave.

His eyes widened. "Do not go!"

Yep, called that bluff. I held back a fist pump of triumph. "Why?"

"You know why." Desperation shivered through his words. "I . . . am better able to touch the flows."

*Touch the flows.* I understood his desperation. Zack had diminished Rhyzkahl's existence when he broke the bond. For me, even the whisper-touch of the arcane in the dreamscape offered immeasurable comfort. Far worse for him, being near severed from the flows that had been integral to his life for millennia—and without Zack to support and guide him. I empathized with his plight, but it didn't mean I felt sorry for him.

"Why should I care if you can touch the arcane or not?" I returned the dreamscape to its full texture and took another small step closer. "You're not exactly my favorite person."

Frustration coupled with annoyance flashed across his face. "I do not expect you to *care*," he said. "You brought terms to the table."

Good. Having to actually give a shit would be as much of a deal breaker as trading Eilahn. "All right," I said with a lift of my chin. "Five minutes of basking in my glorious presence for each captive released."

"Thirty."

"Ha! Ten."

"Ten . . ." His eyes dropped to my upper chest, "in contact with my sigil."

Pulse pounding, I recoiled and pressed my hand over the scar—his mark—at the top of my sternum. "No!"

He lounged back in the pillows, pose non-threatening. "Seven, in contact with my sigil."

Fuck. It was clear he knew how very much I wanted the captives released. But what benefit would touching the scar offer him? It wasn't activated—only the twelfth held that dubious honor—yet at the same time I knew that none of the scars were fully quiescent. Or at least they hadn't been before I lost the arcane.

"Two," I said, though my stomach lurched.

"Five," he said, whisper-soft.

Throat dry, I nodded. "Five. Captives to be released to Mzatal within one day of . . . completion of my side of the bargain."

"Agree—"

"No!" I said, heart thundering. "I wasn't finished." A lie, but I'd caught a glint of triumph in his eyes that left me cold. What had I missed? Maybe I should withdraw from the dream to regroup and—

That was it! The dream.

"Far too hasty," I said. "You will release captives to Mzatal within one day of completion of my side of the bargain. This agreement includes all human captives in the demon realm. One captive for each five minutes you have in contact with the sigil scar. *In dreamspace.* Not physically."

His jaw tightened, which was all I needed to confirm I'd caught my error. Sick relief surged through me at the insanely close call. No way would I ever comply with a physical encounter, and with that gaping loophole the captives would never have been released—not without renegotiation from a weaker position. I'd almost betrayed myself with words as Seretis had warned.

"I do not have access to all captives," he said.

I didn't doubt it. In his condition, he'd be hard pressed to recover captives from the likes of Amkir or Jesral. But I'd take what I could get. "Not my problem. It means you have less time with this." I pulled my collar down to show the sigil scar, willed it to glow blue in his dream.

He dropped his head back onto the cushions, looking truly weary and beat down. "Do we have an agreement?"

"Terms as stated before."

"Agreed," he said.

I still wasn't certain I'd covered all possible loopholes, but as long as it stayed in dreamspace nothing bad could happen. To me, at least. "Agreed," I said. "Do you have a captive here ready to release within a day?"

"Yes. Two." He sat up straighter, eyes hungry. "Come close."

I stepped back, came up against the balustrade. "You want it, you come to me." No reason to make this easy for him and, dreamspace or not, I didn't like the idea of sitting on the chaise lounge with him one little bit.

Rhyzkahl hauled himself to his feet, lurched toward me. I turned away and gripped the balustrade. *I control this*, I told myself. *I can end it whenever I choose.* He moved in close behind me, one hand finding support on the stone beside mine while the other snaked over my shoulder to flatten against his scar on my chest.

My arm twitched with the reflexive urge to drive my elbow into his gut, yet that desire faltered as a wave of arcane flowed through me. I sucked in a breath, aware that Rhyzkahl did the same. Othersight leaped to life, and my perception of flows and sigils and warding sprang into vivid clarity. "How? I don't—"

A deafening *riiiiip* drowned out my words and thoughts. High between the terrace and the grove, blazing light as if from a hundred lurid sunsets poured through a gash in the dimensional fabric. An anomaly. A *huge* one. My heart slammed in terror and awe at the sight. "We have to do something!" I gasped.

His breath hissed close to my ear. "We walk in dream, ghosts to the world. We cannot touch it. *I* cannot touch it even waking." Essence-deep frustration infused his words.

Demons bellowed and squawked from the walls of the palace. The leaves of the grove rippled with potency, flaring like glowing gemstones.

Mzatal appeared on the grounds below the terrace, tele-

ported there by his ptarl, Ilana. Immediately, he called his
essence blade, Khatur, to his hand and began to dance the
shikvihr. Ilana launched herself into the air. More demonic
lords blinked in with their demahnk ptarl. Amkir, Vahl, and
Vrizaar, and seconds later Rayst, Seretis, and Elofir. No sign
of Jesral or Kadir. Mzatal shouted directions, orders that I
felt in my essence more than heard. The other lords responded without hesitation to form a large circle and com-
mence dancing their shikvihrs.

Gaps in the circle stood out like jagged defects. Four
missing lords. How could they hope to do what was needed
without a complete pattern? Yet even as I drew understanding through Mzatal, Rhyzkahl spoke. "A shikvihr must
be laid in for each qaztahl, present or not. The lack delays
the anomaly repair."

Jesral and his ptarl appeared. The fox-faced lord looked
pale and drawn, but he moved to fill a gap in the circle.
Seconds later Kadir arrived with Helori and—to my utter
shock—*Paul*. Helori took to the air while Kadir strode to
his place in the wheel with Paul by his side.

Luminescent green clouds boiled into existence in the
sky like an unholy time lapse of radioactive ooze. "No,"
Rhyzkahl whispered, the single word both denial and plea
for mercy.

"What?!" I asked, and the clouds answered.

Droplets of flickering yellow-green fire rained down in a
nightmare torrent of destruction. Though wards protected
the terrace where we stood, the outer surface of the balustrade burned and pitted with the arcane fire. Horrified, I
shrank back against Rhyzkahl even though my head told
me the fire could do me no harm. Yet an instant later I flung
my hand toward the grove as it writhed under the deluge. A
scream-not-a-scream resonated through me, and within a
heartbeat its leaves vanished as if sucked into the branches.
A sob of agonizing loss wrenched from my throat at the
sight of the once-glorious and vibrant grove now standing
eerie, skeletal, and bone white.

Sickened, I dropped my gaze to the lords. Fire laced their
flesh, yet still they danced, igniting their shikvihrs as one on

Mzatal's command. I pressed both hands to my mouth, tears streaming at the destruction. Paul moved in bizarre counter-rhythm beside and with Kadir. Though protective wards flickered around him, charred and blistered scores marked his shoulders and back like those of the lords. The stench of burnt flesh rose in a nauseating tide, driven by the wings of the demahnk ptarls. Their iridescent forms swooped and rose in flight around the anomaly as they wove complex patterns of potency.

*It is not enough.* The thought, not mine, flooded me. Mzatal's assessment. Yet he continued to dance and call out orders, never wavering even as a droplet seared over his face and one eye.

Rhyzkahl gripped me close, shuddering against my back as the anomaly savaged his realm. "Awaken me. Awaken me!"

Perhaps he knew a way to help counter the anomaly, even in his diminished state? Or maybe he simply didn't want to be helpless and asleep on the terrace in the midst of catastrophe. I gave a jerky nod and prepared to withdraw then froze as Mzatal spun and met my eyes, touched me. Through him, I saw what he saw—the ghostly vision of me on the terrace with Rhyzkahl at my back. My heart leaped as I reached for him and connected, gaining in an instant complete awareness of the situation.

A heavy tremor shook the realm and knocked me from my feet. Rhyzkahl sprawled beside me then struggled to rise while keeping his hand pressed to his mark. With single-minded determination, I kept my eyes on Mzatal even as he pulled his attention back to directing the lords and the shikvihr wheel. A *craaack* of stone accompanied the crumbling of a twenty-foot section of the balustrade, and I scrabbled back with Rhyzkahl. "No, I can't wake you yet," I shouted to Rhyzkahl over the din. "I need to stay!" I had no idea *how* I could help, but surely with Mzatal I could—

*"GILLIAN!"* The word ripped through the dreamscape, shredding it to leave me gasping for breath and devoid of the arcane in the chill of a smelly holding cell.

# Chapter 32

Mouth dry and hands shaking, I blinked to focus on the guard who scowled at me from the door of the holding cell.

"Wake up, Sleeping Beauty," he ordered. "You got yourself a visitor."

"Yeah, I'm awake," I said, wobbling as I stood. The jarring shift from hellacious destruction to industrial beige concrete and steel had me reeling, physically and mentally, and it took me several seconds to regain my equilibrium.

A clock high on a wall told me I'd slept less than an hour. The only person who I figured would visit me so soon was Pellini's lawyer guy.

I was wrong. When the guard opened the door of the interview room and escorted me in, it was Boudreaux who occupied the chair on the other side of the table.

*Oh, hell no.* I planted my feet and shook my head. "I'm not speaking to anyone but my lawyer," I told the guard, nicely but firmly.

The guard shrugged. "Makes no difference to me." He took my arm to lead me back out.

Boudreaux stood. "Gillian," he said. "Kara, wait."

"Give me a break, Boudreaux." I shot him a withering look. "I know how this works, and I know how good you are at interrogation. Sorry, not falling for it."

"I'm not here to interrogate you about the case," he insisted. Stress wound through his words, but I'd seen Boudreaux put on that act before.

"Nice try," I said with a smirk. I had no intention of letting the "frazzled cop" information gathering tactic sway me.

"Give me two minutes," he urged before I could move toward the door. "Please."

I regarded him. His bloodshot eyes were shadowed with distress. That much wasn't faked. "Fine," I said. "Two minutes. For *you* to talk."

Boudreaux sat again. I dropped into the chair across from him, remained silent while the guard unlocked the cuff on my left wrist and snapped it closed around a thick eyebolt set into the table.

The guard left and locked the door behind him. Boudreaux fidgeted and rubbed the fingers of one hand together as if he wanted a cigarette in them. He glanced at me then away while his heel tapped a nervous staccato on the floor. I adopted my best bored expression, leaned back and resisted the urge to break the awkward silence—yet another effective interrogation technique. At this rate, the two minutes would be up before he said word one.

"She's gone," he finally said, voice low and strained. "My mom's gone."

Damn. Boudreaux could be sneaky and underhanded when it came to questioning, but I was sure he'd eat broken glass before using his mom as an interrogation trick. I chose my words with care before speaking. "Do you know where she went?"

He jammed a hand through his hair. "I don't know," he said, voice cracking. Uncertainty skimmed over his face. "No one knows. She just . . . vanished." He shot to his feet, sending the chair skittering back several inches with a screech of metal on tile. "There was surveillance on the house," he continued as he began to pace. "They saw her go inside last night, but she wasn't there this morning. No one saw her leave, nothing shows on the videos, and her car is still in the driveway. They even checked for a tunnel!"

Anger roiled my stomach. Catherine McDunn pulled an amazing disappearing act—as if by magic!—and did so *after* she dropped the information that led us to the nature center ambush. Yet my anger fizzled after only a few seconds of consideration. Katashi had coerced McDunn, so why not Catherine as well? My gut told me she was with Katashi, either as his guest or his hostage—an insight I needed to keep to myself or risk opening a godawful can of worms. Boudreaux eyed me with the desperate expectation of a starving dog in a butcher shop. Regardless of his mother's complicity in Katashi's schemes, his distress was genuine. I couldn't remain pissed in the face of it. Even so, I couldn't drop my guard. The interview rooms had video and audio recording, and anything I did or said in here could potentially be used against me. "Why are you telling me all this?" I asked.

He spun to face me. "You talked to her yesterday. What did she say?"

"She told me she was filing for divorce," I said. "She said that she hated McDunn for what he put her and you through, and that she couldn't forgive him. Said that he'd called her wanting money, then again asking her to trust him." Nothing the cops didn't already know. "She told him she hated him and to not call her anymore."

The nervous twitch in his fingers stilled. "You don't believe it."

"Sure I do," I said. "I heard her say she hated him on the recording."

"She cooperated with the police. I know my dad . . . step-dad," he corrected with an unmistakable note of grief, "would never hurt her." He rubbed his hands over his face as if trying to wipe away his unhappiness then sat heavily. "Where is she?"

"Everything isn't always as it seems," I said. Surely Boudreaux deserved a shred of comfort. It sucked to take a hit in a game he didn't know he was playing. "She might have faked everything and gone willingly."

Ice flooded my veins the instant the words left my mouth. Where had *that* come from? It hit too close to a truth I hadn't intended to voice under surveillance or to Boudreaux, and with that one injudicious remark, I'd blundered into a minefield. The last thing I wanted was

Boudreaux sniffing around the Katashi connection. My pulse galloped as I fought to keep my reaction hidden from the camera. Maybe Boudreaux wouldn't use his mom as an interrogation tactic to solve Farouche's murder, but he *would* do anything and everything in his power to find her. He wasn't an ally, and I didn't owe him any information or comfort. How had I forgotten that? "Your two minutes are up," I said, throat dry.

The calm gaze he leveled on me felt as if it penetrated to my essence. "It's my mom, Kara." His voice slid through me, soft and persuasive. "What do you know?"

"I think she's—" Shocked to my core, I clamped down hard on the rest of the sentence. *Son of a bitch.* I yanked my eyes up to the camera. "I refuse to say another word without my lawyer present." Too little, too late. Though I hadn't said much, it was way more than I'd intended.

Boudreaux placed his hands flat on the table. "Kara, please," he said, voice a whisper of desperation. "Help me."

I bit my tongue and shook my head, mentally recited the state capitols and avoided eye contact.

His shoulders slumped, and he blinked as if only now seeing me as a prisoner shackled to the table. "Sorry," he muttered. "I shouldn't have come here."

The heavy clunk of the door's lock saved us both from the minefield. The guard stepped in.

"Hey, Boudreaux," he said, grimacing. "Her lawyer's here and pissed that you're talking to her. I told him she agreed, but you know how it is."

"Yeah, I do." He stood and came around the table. I braced myself for a parting shot, but he simply dropped his eyes to my shackled wrist, exhaled and left the room without a word.

Before the door fully closed behind Boudreaux it opened again. A forty-something black man wearing a green t-shirt, khaki shorts, and sandals strode in, plopped a binder on the table and dropped into the chair.

"Always so much fun when I visit a client and they're talking to a detective," he said, pairing the remark with a sour look.

"I was careful," I said and tried not to squirm. *Not careful enough.*

"I'm sure you were," he said in a tone that put the lie to his words. He began to pull papers out of his binder. "And I'll be requesting a copy of the recording so I know what to brace for." He glanced up and gave me a tight little smile. "Just in case, you understand."

Great. A typical defense lawyer. In other words, a jerk. But a jerk I needed. "Yeah, I understand. Pellini called you?"

"That's right." He stuck a hand out. "Anatoly Gresh. Call me Tolya. You got any objection to me being your lawyer, say it now so I can get out of here in time to see if your arrest made the ten o'clock news."

Suppressing a sigh, I gave his hand a perfunctory shake. "Call me Kara. And I'm cool with you as my lawyer."

"Good, because I've been busting my ass, and I hate doing pointless work." He pulled out a yellow legal pad already covered in scrawled handwriting. "I contacted the judge and filed a motion for an expedited hearing for preliminary examination along with a motion to reduce bond." He tapped his pen against the pad. "And, I asked to have a subpoena issued for Detective O'Connor to appear at your bond hearing. The DA objected, but the judge overruled him." Tolya smiled tightly at that.

"Why do you want O'Connor there?" I asked, perplexed. I'd *never* been to a bond hearing for one of my arrestees.

"It's a chance to poke at his probable cause," Tolya said. "It's shaky, and that might help get you a lower bond." His smile turned vulpine. "More importantly, it's to our advantage to get him on the stand when he isn't fully prepared — because anything he says is locked in as testimony."

Comprehension dawned. "Which you can later use to highlight inconsistencies in his case."

"Precisely," he said. "I also explained to the judge that you're a former law enforcement officer with a sterling record. I threw in that you're the investigator who stopped the most infamous serial killer to ever terrorize this parish." His eyes skimmed over the writing on the pad. "Not to mention you have family roots in this fine community that go back over a century. Lowers the chance that you'd be a flight risk."

I kept my expression immobile. My exile was ready and waiting, and even though it was a last resort, fleeing to another world to live out the rest of my days would still be better than prison. *If* that other world didn't succumb to yet another cataclysm.

"In addition, I pointed out the incredible danger to your person should you be put in the general population of this jail—with so many of the same upstanding citizens that you put here." Tolya's mouth twitched. "I heard about your little altercation with that woman in the holding cell. I confess, a part of me wishes you'd taken a punch," he said. "That would have been a lovely bit of evidence to show the judge, but I completely understand your reluctance to get slugged. Then again, the fact that you actively avoided physical confrontation may work in our favor as well." He leaned back and gave me an appraising look. "I must say, I do wish all my clients were as upstanding as you appear to be."

"Looks can be deceiving," I said. "But thanks. And I have to admit, I'm impressed with everything you've done." He hadn't exaggerated the busting ass part one bit.

Tolya nodded at the compliment. "Vince called me while you were still being handcuffed and gave me the salient points. He knows what info I need and didn't waste time bleating about innocence or guilt. Doesn't matter at this stage of the game anyway." He flipped to the second page of his pad. "That said, I think I have a good shot at getting your bond lowered. I figured you'd appreciate that since the bond for principal to murder usually runs somewhere around a quarter mil."

I blanched. I'd known the bond would be high, but hearing an actual figure made it horribly real. My house and property were *probably* worth that much, but the idea of putting it up as security—and risk losing it—left me queasy. If I used a bail bondsman I'd only have to put up twelve percent, but that was money I'd never get back. Thirty grand, gone. Not that I had thirty grand in the first place. "I'd like a lower bond very much," I said, nice and calm.

Tolya wasn't fooled. "Don't be scared. The majority of their evidence is circumstantial, and I know what I'm doing."

Right. What about terrified? "Who's the judge, and what did he say?"

He gave a dry smile. "Judge Laurent. He knows you. He likes you. That doesn't mean a damn thing, which of course you know. And your hearing is at eight a.m." He straightened then stuffed the pad and his papers back into the binder. "Don't worry about tomorrow. I'll be doing all the talking."

It was tough not to be buoyed by his attitude, especially since it didn't carry the usual taint of bullshit most lawyers spewed when they opened their mouths. "When do we talk about your fee and pesky crap like that?" I asked.

Tolya stood, tucked his binder under one arm. "Pellini called in a favor." He moved to the door buzzer and pressed his thumb against it. "Now you owe *him* one." The guard opened the door. "See you in the morning, Kara. Get some sleep if you can." With that he strode off, sandals squeaking against the tile.

I owed Pellini a favor. And I wasn't running screaming at the thought. How weird was that?

# Chapter 33

My sweatshirt tactic had been perfect for the holding cell, but it bit me in the ass in the unairconditioned van that was used for transport to the bond hearing. Along with the half dozen other prisoners going to the courthouse, my wrists had been cuffed in front of me—and, of course, I didn't think to consider the heat until after the handcuffs made removal of the sweatshirt impossible. Even at seven-thirty in the morning, the temps were high enough to leave me a wilted, stinky, sticky mess by the time we made it to the blessedly cool courtroom.

"You look great," Tolya lied after he pulled me aside for a quick conference. "I doubt you'll need to say anything other than 'Yes, your honor' or 'No, your honor.' Keep doing exactly as you have been, and you'll be fine."

"What have I been doing?" I asked.

"Everything I say," he replied with a wink then strode off to take his seat.

With a sigh, I settled myself on the wooden bench with the others and tried to calm the riot of butterflies in my stomach. No sign of O'Connor, but the unexpected sight of Eilahn sitting on a bench on the far side of the courtroom buoyed my flagging spirits. She met my eyes and gave me a slow nod. *I am ever here for you.*

Reassured, I returned the nod and even managed a weak smile.

More people filtered in. Judge Laurent's law clerk, a

court reporter, a public defender, and various civilian-types who were probably family and friends of the other defendants. The judge had yet to emerge from his chambers, and I clung to the thin reassurance that at least I wasn't a stranger to him. I'd been in his court a number of times to testify, and he'd signed a few warrants for me over the past couple of years. He'd been on the bench as long as I could remember, and had earned a reputation as an irascible, no-nonsense type who didn't like having his time wasted.

A ginger-haired man wearing a brown suit and a confident expression entered, moved to the table on the left and set down a stack of files. He was the assistant district attorney, but he'd been hired less than a month before I was first summoned to the demon realm, and I had to rack my brain for a few seconds to come up with his name. Finley. Colin Finley. He'd worked in New Orleans before coming to St. Long Parish, and cops liked him because he was a hardass. Wonderful.

Finley passed his gaze over the room, settling it briefly on me before he frowned and pulled a file from his stack. He skimmed the information, pointedly glanced at me again, then moved to Tolya. Though he spoke in a voice too low for me to hear, I had no trouble reading the body language. Finley, smug and assured, made a suggestion or an offer, to which Tolya shook his head in a clear negative. Finley smiled and gave a "your loss" shrug and returned to his table.

Another horde of butterflies invaded my stomach. What was *that* all about?

The arrival of the judge cut off my spin cycle of worry. I rose with the others when the bailiff announced, "All rise. The honorable Judge Laurent presiding." I sat when we were given leave to do so, though I kept glancing at Tolya in the hopes of a reassuring look or thumbs up or Morse code or *anything*. But he maintained his attention straight ahead, damn near as impassive as a demonic lord.

Judge Laurent shuffled through the papers before him, raked a glance around the courtroom, then peered over his glasses at the assistant DA. "Mr. Finley, do you happen to know why Detective O'Connor has not yet graced us with his presence?"

Finley sighed and spread his hands. "Your honor, Detective O'Connor couldn't be located to be served with the subpoena."

Crap. If the detective hadn't been served, he couldn't get in trouble for not showing up. So much for Tolya's clever tactic.

However, I had drastically underestimated Judge Laurent. The temperature in the courtroom seemed to drop several degrees as he leveled a frown at Finley. "Couldn't be located?"

"That's correct, your honor."

The judge pursed his lips. "Mr. Finley, I don't believe I've ever had the pleasure of working with you in a courtroom before. Is that correct?"

"That's correct, your honor," Finley said. "I'm usually in Judge Zeller's court."

"Well, Mr. Finley, I've been on the bench twenty years." Laurent pulled his glasses off and used them to point at the assistant DA. "It might surprise you, but I do know how the system works. I bet you *someone* in the sheriff's department can get in touch with Detective O'Connor twenty-four seven."

Finley didn't look as smug anymore. "Your honor," he began, but the judge gave him no chance to continue.

"Bailiff," Laurent said and waited for the deputy to straighten. "Go down to the Sheriff's administrative offices on the first floor. You tell the Sheriff that he or his designee has been summoned by *instanter* subpoena to explain to the court why this detective is not present."

Holy shit. Describing Laurent as irascible was putting it mildly. The bailiff scurried out. Finley stared at the judge in disbelief then sank to sit, clearly trying to get his bearings in this new development. The "couldn't be served" angle would have worked with most other judges, but apparently it was a hot button for Judge Laurent. Damn, I might end up owing Pellini a *big* favor.

Laurent sat back in his chair and slipped his glasses on,

then proceeded to ignore everyone in the courtroom while he flipped through the papers on his desk. Nobody dared talk or move around since he hadn't called a recess, and a bizarre silence reigned while we waited for the arrival of the Sheriff or his designee.

I shot a quick look at Tolya. He held an expression of mild interest, but I couldn't shake the sense he was watching the performance of a play he'd written. Great, my lawyer was clever and manipulative, but I knew this whole scenario was a gamble that could easily backfire. The judge was pissed now, which might carry over into his rulings on my fate.

The butterflies crowded in. More of this stress and I'd be coughing up legs and wings.

Less than ten minutes later the doors opened, and a round-faced man about my height with a bad haircut and a weak chin scrambled in ahead of the bailiff. Not the sheriff, but his second in command—Chief Deputy Ron Pigeon.

Judge Laurent straightened and beckoned the baffled man forward. "Chief Deputy Pigeon, the District Attorney's office informs me that Detective O'Connor could not be located to be served with the subpoena for a hearing in my courtroom this morning."

"Er." Pigeon threw a confused look to Finley—who could only give him a pained one in response. "I'm sorry, your honor," he said, "but, well, I'm sure the detective—"

Laurent cut him off. "This woman is sitting in jail on serious charges," he said, thrusting his hand in my direction. Pigeon cast a bewildered glance toward the bench full of prisoners, but it was obvious he had no idea what was going on, or whether the judge was gesturing to me or Angry Chick. "We're not playing games here," Laurent continued, warming to his topic. "A subpoena isn't an invitation to a party. This is an order of the court—not a request—an *order!*"

"Yes, your honor." Pigeon bobbed his head in a nod.

"I intend to hold a hearing, and I expect Detective O'Connor to testify," Laurent said, color high in his cheeks. He was righteously pissed and enjoying it.

Pigeon shifted his feet. "I understand, your honor, but—"

"Chief Deputy Pigeon," Laurent interrupted, "I know all the detectives have department-issued cell phones that they're expected to answer. Ms. Gillian may not be in jail by the end of this, but someone *else* might be." With that threat hanging in the air, the judge swung his ire to Finley. "As for you, I was once an ADA. I know you have O'Connor's cell phone number. Do you want me to investigate the call records and determine whether you've talked to him since I issued that subpoena?"

Finley paled. "No, your honor!"

Shit. Yeah, it was fun to watch Finley get reamed, but his reaction told me O'Connor knew about the subpoena—which meant he had time to prepare to get on the stand. What if the detective showed up, gave compelling testimony, and the judge set an unaffordable bond? Or no bond?

Perspiration rolled down my sides. If I ever got out of this mess, I was burning this sweatshirt.

"I'm going to recess for fifteen minutes," Laurent announced. "I'd better hear the patter of Detective O'Conner's feet before that time is up." He stood and stormed off the bench, barely giving the bailiff any time to call out the "All rise."

The instant the chamber door closed behind Judge Laurent, Pigeon dove toward Finley. The two engaged in a hushed and intense conversation, and after about half a minute they broke apart and got onto their phones. Calling their bosses? Or tracking down O'Connor? They ended their respective phone conversations and conferred again—with a few dark looks cast Tolya's way and mine. Finley moved to the judge's law clerk and spoke quietly to her before she disappeared into Laurent's chambers. A few minutes later she returned, gave Finley a nod and beckoned to Tolya, and both attorneys headed to the chambers.

More time passed, while the other prisoners looked askance at me. Finally Tolya and Finley exited the chambers and resumed their places. Once again I tried and failed to get any signal of reassurance from Tolya. Laurent resumed his seat and cleared his throat.

"After consultation with the district attorney and the counsel for the defendant it has been agreed that a proper bond pursuant to the Louisiana code of criminal procedure is 25,000 dollars."

I clenched my hands together to control their shaking as relief swam through me. Tolya turned to me with a look of pure triumph. Twenty-five grand was a hefty chunk of cash, but if I used a bondsman I'd only lose about three thousand. Still hurt, but nowhere near as devastating. Judge Laurent rested his sharp gaze on me. "Ms. Gillian?"

I hurried to stand. In my peripheral vision I saw Tolya rise as well. "Yes, your honor?" I said.

"You are not to leave this jurisdiction without permission of the court nor are you to speak to any witnesses. Do you understand?"

"Yes, your honor. I do." The knot of dread began to tease apart. This wasn't over, but I'd regained some ground.

And, more importantly, I could go home and take a damn shower.

It took over three hours to process out and fork over several grand to the bail bondsman. That effectively wiped out my savings, but I'd worry about the future of my finances another day.

"Keep your head down and stay out of trouble," Tolya ordered after he gave me his card with his contact information. "And don't talk to any more detectives. Except Pellini. I'll find out when the next court date is and will be in touch with you before then."

I thanked him effusively and would have hugged him, but I figured that with my current level of stench it would be a mean thing to do.

Eilahn, Idris, and Pellini were waiting in the jail foyer when I finally stepped out of the lockdown area. Carl as well, to my surprise. He gave me a faint smile. "Taking you up on the offer to join your team," he said.

"Thanks," I said fervently. "We sure can use the help."

Tension eased from Eilahn's posture as she passed an

assessing gaze over me, and it hit me how difficult this had been for her. I had little doubt she'd been close by, monitoring and ready. If I'd run into serious trouble, she'd have used all available resources to teleport into the jail and get me out—obviously a last resort for any number of reasons. Her, I hugged. She wouldn't give a crap about my funk. She held me close for several seconds then released with me with a satisfied nod.

"Let us leave this place," she said, and I didn't argue. How the hell could people be repeat offenders? One night in jail was enough to make me want to stay home and take up knitting.

The heat enveloped me as we stepped out, and I finally stripped off the sweatshirt. Even with only the tank top on, I was ready for AC again by the time we reached Pellini's truck. Pellini climbed in and cranked the engine, while Idris took the front passenger seat, and I got into the back of the cab with Carl. Eilahn, of course, zoomed off on her motorcycle.

"Bryce and Jill had a busy night," Pellini said as he pulled a manila envelope off the dash and passed it to me. "They went through all the surveillance footage from outside the Katashi base and established a pattern of when people come and go."

"Sweeeeet," I said and wasted no time checking out the contents. Damn, those two had worked their butts off. Several pages of various camera stills showing cars leaving, clear enough to discern who was in each car with only mild squinting. Another page with exact times cars left and returned during the period we'd been monitoring. "Looks like there are three teams—each with a summoner and a security person."

"Right," Idris said. "Gina Hallsworth and Leo Carter, Tsuneo and Jerry Steiner, Tessa and Angus McDunn."

I scanned through the various departure times. Though at first they seemed random, the data hinted at a bigger pattern. "Idris, do you have the map and valve cycle information with you?"

"Of course," he said in a supercilious tone that I chose to ignore. He dug the papers out of his messenger bag and passed them back to me. I murmured a thanks and spread everything out on the seat between Carl and me. My pulse quickened in excitement as I compared the Katashi info and the valve cycles.

"They work in a rotation," I said, smile widening. "They go to each valve in time for the burps, which means we have a good chance of predicting who's going where and when." My pulse thumped harder as I peered at the schedule for the upcoming emissions. "I need a pencil. A pen. A god-damn crayon." Carl pushed a pen into my hand, and I jotted down correlations. "There are two valves coming up in the next few hours. Tessa's house and the one at Leelan Park. Only a few miles apart." I tightened my grip on the pen. "Tessa's team will almost certainly be coming from the Ga-tor Farm, and it makes sense that she'd take care of the valve at her own house. That gives us a window of opportu-nity to reach her house first and—" I took a deep breath. This was the tricky part— "symmetrize that valve and be out of there before she shows up."

Pellini shot me a baffled look in the rear view mirror. "Did I miss something? Who's going to symmetrize it? I don't have the skills, and Idris doesn't know what to look for." He gave Idris a wince and a shrug. "Sorry, dude."

I expected Idris to snarl, but he merely extended a hand toward the charts and my notes. "Mind if I take a look?"

"Nah, go for it." I handed the lot over to him. Made sense for him to double-check my work.

He skimmed through the schedules, hands tight on the papers. At long last he relaxed and exhaled. "You have a plan for how to symmetrize the valve?" he asked me, ex-pression unreadable.

Grimacing, I shifted in my seat. "I don't know if it could be called a *plan,* but I thought that Pellini could tell you what to do and you'd, um, do it." Crap. It sounded a lot more pathetic when I said it out loud.

But Idris surprised me with a thoughtful nod. "We have nothing to lose by trying."

Wow, had he gone and had a spa day while I was in jail? "Great!" I said. "Let's go take care of that valve!" I'd wonder later why he was so agreeable. Right now I wanted to get to Tessa's house before Idris remembered he was Mr. Grouchy.

# Chapter 34

Pellini did the same drive-by-the-house-twice thing as Bryce, then turned onto a side street to park. I approved of his caution. Katashi's people had been watching my place long enough to know Jill's schedule, which meant they knew Pellini's truck.

He let out a low whistle as we walked up to the house. "Man, this place used to glow like Vegas," he said.

It was weird to think that he'd been able to see the arcane during all the crap of the past year and a half, but I also *completely* understood why he'd kept it so thoroughly to himself. "I know what you mean," I said. "Seretis ripped out the wards and protections like a cleaning lady through cobwebs—and all without alerting the spiders."

I hurried everyone inside on the off chance a nosy neighbor decided to come chat. There were no aversions to keep them away now. Despite my nerves, I grinned at the sudden image of all the neighbors approaching the house like a horde of zombies.

"Carl, will you be our lookout?" I asked after I closed the door.

"Absolutely," he said and positioned himself in the sitting room where he had a view of the street.

Eilahn bounded up the stairs to get a vantage from one of the attic windows or, more likely, the roof. For a fleeting moment I worried that a neighbor or bad guy might spot her, but quickly dismissed it. Eilahn knew how to stay out of sight.

Pellini and I followed Idris to the library. Idris moved straight to the valve and dropped to his knees, but Pellini took two steps in and stopped in shock.

"All of those boxes of books were in this one room?" he asked, incredulous. He made a slow turn, taking in the empty bookshelves and the scant dimensions of the library.

"Every one of them," I said. "I should've taken a picture, because even I can barely comprehend it."

Pellini shook his head in disbelief then leveled a frown toward where Idris knelt on the hardwood floor. "Hang tight," he said and stepped out of the library. Mystified, I waited, and a few seconds later he returned with one of my aunt's sofa cushions. He dropped it a few feet in front of Idris then lowered himself to kneel on it. "I'm a big guy in my mid-forties. I ain't stupid."

Idris flicked a glance to the cushion. I expected a disparaging look but instead it was more *I wish I'd thought of that*. Smothering a laugh, I dashed to the sitting room and grabbed another cushion, which Idris accepted with grace.

With the comfort of knees old and young accomplished, I took up a vantage in the kitchen doorway that gave me a clear view of the back and front doors as well as into the library.

"What first?" Idris asked Pellini.

Pellini leaned forward to examine the valve. "It doesn't look or feel right," he said then winced. "But I don't know how to do what needs to be done."

A whisper of pained frustration flashed across Idris's face. Probably already regretting this. "Well, what do I need to use?"

Pellini stroked his mustache in thought then held his hands up and waved them around in an odd pattern. A few seconds later he made a pushing motion toward Idris. "Put that in."

Frowning, Idris took the invisible-to-me potency construction from Pellini. "But where do I . . ." Idris paused then did his own hand-wiggling.

"Yeah," Pellini said, "but a hair lower." Idris waved his fingers, and Pellini nodded. "Cool. Okay, now the other side." He pushed more Stuff to Idris. Again, Idris placed it, and Pellini told him how to adjust it. The work was tedious, a far cry from my own experience symmetrizing a valve, though to my eyes they knelt over a very unremarkable spot on the floor and fiddled their hands around like idiots.

After the sixth round, the two developed an awkward but effective collaboration with Pellini as the eyes and Idris as the hands. *Higher, left, keep going, right there. Crap, too far, try the other side, yeah, that works.* All while Pellini fed raw material to Idris like an operating room nurse handing instruments to a surgeon.

*Or like the support I used to give Mzatal*, I thought with a wistful pang.

The kitchen clock ticked an aggravating reminder of our limited time. Twenty long minutes passed before Pellini straightened. "There," he said with satisfaction. "Put that last bit closer to the edge, and we're done."

Idris made another little wibbly-wobbly hand move. Pellini glanced my way. "Still clear?"

"Still clear," I said with undisguised relief. "Let's roll."

They rose and moved toward the door, but Idris stopped halfway there. "Wait," he said and spun back toward the valve. "I need to do one more thing."

Pellini frowned at him. "What do you mean? It's balanced."

Idris dropped to his knees and spoke without looking up. "No. They can bypass the symmetrization if they warp the *savinths*," he said. "I need to make adjustments to prevent that."

Pellini turned a questioning gaze to me, but my attention was on Idris. He knew the valves backward, forward, and sideways, and if he said there was a vulnerability, I had no legitimate reason to doubt him. After all, I knew approximately jack shit about the use of savinths. I'd been in the summoning equivalent of "Intro to Calculus" while Idris kicked ass in "Advanced Partial Differential Equations For Really Smart People."

Yet I noted a tremor in his hands, and his shoulders

hunched with tension that I'd *never* seen in him, even during the most rigorous arcane rituals. Suspicion bloomed, bringing with it a buried hope of my own. "Idris, how long do you think this will take?" I asked, pulse quickening.

"Not sure," he said, wiggling his hands over the valve. "Five minutes, maybe ten. But it'll be worth it."

Suspicion gave way to certainty. Five minutes, ten, or however long he needed to stall until Tessa arrived. He wanted to see his birth mother at least once face-to-face.

Going along with his ruse was no doubt a colossal mistake and horrible tactics, but . . . it would be worth it. Idris deserved a shred of satisfaction after everything he'd been through. Who was I to take that away from him? Besides, if I had to be brutally honest with myself, I had plenty of crap I wanted to unload on Tessa. She'd raised me and betrayed me. The desire to know *why* tore at my essence. With the way things were going, Idris and I might never have another chance to confront her.

"It's cool," I told Pellini with a smile that I hoped looked reassuring. "Those savinths can be damn tricky if not positioned right. Wouldn't want to leave a back door." Behind him, Idris snapped his head up, gratitude and relief shining in his eyes.

"All right, then how about I keep watch from the parlor," Pellini suggested with a fatalistic shrug.

"That'd be great," I said and returned to my former spot in the kitchen doorway. Idris ducked his head again and resumed his pretend work. Five minutes passed. Ten. My stress levels climbed higher along with second thoughts and heaps of doubt. *No, this is stupid. I need to tell Idris we can't do this, get everyone out—*

I heard a light thump on the stairs right before Eilahn bounded down them and into the hallway.

"Tessa Pazhel's vehicle approaches," she said.

"Idris," I hissed. He stood, face alight with anxious longing that resonated with my own desperate need for answers. My mind whirled. We still had enough time to cut and run. Idris would comply if I insisted. Except, I completely understood the mute plea in his steady regard.

Pellini stepped out of the parlor. "They're in the drive-way, and she's pissed," he said. "The lack of wards, I'm betting. We'd better scramble out the back, and quick."

"We're staying," I said, dismayed to hear my voice crack. Idris moved to stand beside me and face Pellini.

I expected Pellini to tell us we were a couple of fucking idiots, but he merely blew out his breath. Maybe he'd been expecting it. "Got a plan?"

"Don't I always?" I asked and pretended not to hear his snort. I jabbed fingers at Pellini and Carl. "You two take the parlor. Pellini, as soon as McDunn passes, you draw down. Eilahn, stairs. Idris, library. I'll take the kitchen and will cover as soon as I hear Pellini. Watch the crossfire. Go!"

Everyone scrambled into position like a well-trained SWAT team. Silence fell in the house as the first footfall hit the porch steps. I waited beyond the kitchen doorway and listened to Tessa speak, angry and harsh. Though I couldn't make out her words, I figured it was safe to assume they had to do with the stripped protections. Idris stood a few feet within the library, and when I glanced his way he offered me an uncertain smile and mouthed, *Thank you.* I gave him a wry smile and shrug in reply. We'd find out soon enough how stupid this was.

Tessa's voice grew louder, more strident. A deeper voice answered her. I drew back, kept my breathing slow and quiet as I sent Idris a warning glare on the order of *You stay right where you are until the situation is secure!* I doubted he picked up all the nuances, but it was enough to keep him in place, at least for the moment.

The front door opened. A knot pulled tight in my stomach.

"I have to see—" Tessa let out a gasp. "Oh goodness, it's all gone. Every one of my protections! I never felt a thing from the alarms!" True pain lanced through her voice.

"I'm sorry, ma'am." McDunn, uneasy and cautious.

"Heaven knows what they've done to my valve," she said, tone crisp again. Her shoes clicked over the wood floors toward me, and McDunn's heavier footsteps joined them.

"Lemme see your hands, McDunn!" Pellini shouted. My cue.

Gun raised, I swung around the door. Tessa let out a shocked cry. I ignored her, focused on McDunn. "Weapon down!" I yelled.

He held a gun in one hand, weight balanced as he assessed the threats. Pellini remained in partial cover behind the parlor door, gun steady on the burly security man. "Weapon down *now!*" I ordered.

McDunn flicked a calculating gaze to each of us, then to where Eilahn crouched on the stairs. A low growl throbbed in her throat.

"NOW!" Pellini snapped. "Slow movements!"

"All right," McDunn said, voice calm as he eased into a crouch. "I'm putting my gun down."

"Make one move toward your other gun and I'll drop you," I said. Right ankle. No bulge to give it away, but I noticed the forward shift of that leg as he crouched.

McDunn slowly placed his gun on the floor and stood, keeping his hands out to his sides. Eilahn scooped up the weapon and conducted a brisk and thorough patdown of him. "Backup is already on the way," he said as Eilahn removed assorted knives from his person as well as the pistol in his ankle holster. "I called it in as soon as Miss Pazhel informed me the warding was gone."

He wasn't bluffing. He was too much of a pro not to have made a call to cover their asses. I suspected he'd have preferred to wait until backup arrived before entering the house, but Tessa had no doubt insisted. The backup would almost certainly be Tsuneo and Jerry, but they'd be coming from the Leelan Park valve. Five minutes at least.

"That's fine," I said, pulse racing as I kept my gun trained on him. Even unarmed, he was dangerous. "We don't intend to hurt you or turn you over to the cops. All we need is a few minutes." In my periphery I saw Idris step into the hallway, but he was wise enough to stay well back.

"Kara." Tessa's eyes were wide with shock. Probably not faked, though the reasons for it were debatable. "What in the ninety hells is going on?"

"As corny as it sounds, I've woken up," I said. "You're one of Katashi's lieutenants."

"Lieutenants?" She assumed an annoyed expression, one I knew all too well. "We've been through this before. Isumo is my *mentor*." She gestured around her. "Are you responsible for destroying my protections?"

"Are you responsible for the trap your *mentor* set so that turdface here could take my abilities?"

Tessa threw a glance toward Angus before gracing me with a wonderfully baffled frown. "I don't know what you're talking about, but you need to put the gun down before someone gets hurt."

"Before someone gets hurt?" A harsh laugh escaped me. "Oh, that's fucking rich." Hostility flowed into my words. A lot. "What did you think would happen to me after I got arrested, Auntie dear?"

Her hands flew to her mouth. "Arrested? What were you arrested for? Are you all right?" She raised her arms as if to embrace me and make it all better, but a twitch of my gun stopped that shit. Disconcerted, she dropped her hands back to her sides.

"Littering," I told her with a delightful rush of satisfaction. "I threw your library into the lake."

Her gaze shot to the library door. "What have you *done?*" An undercurrent of deep anger ran through her voice. No more concerned-and-annoyed Tessa. Good. That fake bitch was starting to piss me off.

Idris moved up beside me. "We've been busy," he said, emotionless and controlled. He flicked a hand toward the door. "Care to see?"

Tessa hesitated, but it was obvious her need to see the damage outweighed caution. McDunn tried to follow as she moved to the library door, but Eilahn stopped him with a hand on his shoulder.

I didn't *like* that I took pleasure in Tessa's moan of horror as she took in the empty library, but I reveled in it anyway. "We found the place that your buddy Rhyzkahl warded against me," I said conversationally. "The contents made for nice, light bedtime reading."

Dismay washed over her face as she spun toward me. "Kara, it's not what you think—"

I cut her off. "I also found your notes in the attic, so you can stop lying about your association with Katashi." My hands were starting to ache, and I adjusted my grip on my gun.

Tessa drew a deep breath, and calm settled over her. Pygah. *She just mentally traced a fucking pygah.* Hurt and anger clawed within my chest at the reminder of things she'd never taught me.

"If you know so much," she said, "then you also know I won't tell you anything."

"That's nothing new." My throat clogged. "I *loved* you!" I said, agonized. "You were like a mother to me! How could you throw me to the wolves?"

"I didn't!" Tessa's hands tightened at her sides despite her damn pygah. "I never wanted you to get hurt." She shook her head. "It wasn't supposed to turn out like this, but the situation had reached the point where having Angus diminish you was the best available option."

"Are you going to insist you begged Katashi to show me kindness and mercy?" I said with a sneer.

The cold steel in her eyes took me aback. "You're dangerous," she said with uncompromising certainty. "Harsh measures were on the table. I advocated stripping your abilities, but in the end Isumo and Lord—" She caught herself. "Isumo made the decision without my input."

What the hell? Ever since the nightmare at the Nature Center I'd clung to the fantasy that Tessa had stood between me and a death sentence. *They could have killed me at any time*, I reminded myself. *They took out Steeev easily enough.* I remained of use to the Mraztur, but for what purpose? Especially now that I was diminished. I didn't want to consider the ugly possibilities until I was well armed with wine and chocolate.

"Did you have any input on getting Kara thrown in jail?" Idris demanded, taking up my slack while I recovered from her bombshell. "Do you know what happens to ex-cops in prison?" I wasn't sure whether to be pleased by his support or worried. He'd met his mother, and she was the enemy.

"I wasn't party to that decision," she said with a lift of her chin, then she cast a righteous glare at me. "Your own actions set you up for that."

"But you're a key member of Katashi's organization, and you stood by and let it happen," I countered. "Guess what? If I get killed in prison, you might as well have murdered me with your own hands."

She paled, but it only took her a second to rally. "You believe your allies are so admirable and without reproach?" she shot back. "Mzatal? *Szerain?*" Her voice dripped with venom on the second name.

"*Your* allies' methods suck!" I yelled. "And you're a horrible, lying, conniving bitch who never deserved my love!"

Tessa recoiled a step and stared at me, color high in her cheeks. "You're my *niece*. I did the best I could for you given the circumstances. You can't possibly think—"

Carl stepped out of the parlor. "Their backup is here. Two men," he said, no more perturbed than if reporting that the morning paper had landed on the doorstep.

I took a deep breath and found my center. I didn't need a pygah. Getting that crap off my chest worked just as well, and she could keep her lame excuses about *circumstances*. "Let them in," I said. "We're done."

I lowered my gun enough that it wasn't a direct threat but didn't holster it. Carl swung the door open and stepped back to reveal Jerry Steiner easing across the porch toward the door with his gun tucked close to his body, and Tsuneo on the walkway behind him.

Jerry leaped nimbly aside to get out of the potential line of fire from a shooter within, while Tsuneo did the same in the opposite direction. When no hail of bullets materialized, Jerry made a tactical peek around the door frame. Satisfied he wasn't about to get his head blown off, he leaned out for a more thorough inspection.

"You cool?" he asked McDunn.

"Like the ice planet Hoth," McDunn replied as chill as ever. Some of the tension left Jerry's stance at the answer, which told me it was a code phrase.

Jerry entered the house, shut the door behind him and

put his back to it. Fine by me. No sense letting the neighbors
see if things went to shit in here. His eyes darted this way
and that as he took note of threats and tried to figure out
what was going on. At the sight of Idris he paled and went
still as a rabbit beneath a circling hawk. Idris regarded him
with seething malevolence that radiated danger and a
promise of death. Didn't matter that fifteen feet separated
the two. Jerry was *terrified* of Idris, and for damn good reason considering what he'd done to Idris's sister.

Though McDunn surely felt the tension, he remained
placid as he turned to me. "Unless you have any objections,
I'd like to take my people and go now."

"None whatsoever," I said cheerfully.

He looked over at Eilahn. "Could I have my weapons
back?" he asked, polite and respectful.

She gave him a tight smile and thrust a plastic grocery
bag containing heavy, angular items into his hands. Wary,
McDunn peered into it, then let out a sigh and withdrew
what I recognized as the spring and barrel for his handgun.
While Tessa and I had shouted at each other, my boldly
clever guardian had slipped away to unload and disassem-
ble McDunn's weapons. I wasn't sure, but I thought I detected a trace of not-so-grudging respect in his expression
as he dropped the items back into the bag and tied it shut.

Jerry shifted, uneasy. "C'mon, let's roll out," he urged.

McDunn shot him a quelling glance then touched Tessa's
shoulder. "Miss Pazhel, we need to leave."

Eyes on me, Tessa began to speak then stopped. Maybe
she realized it was too late for mere words to undo the damage. Or maybe she understood that nothing could undo or
repair it. Whatever part of our relationship had been based
in truth was as dead as ash. She dropped her gaze and
turned away without another word.

Idris took a lurching step forward. "Did you know?" he
blurted to Tessa's back. Distress rose in his face when she
failed to reply or react. "Did you *know?*" Before I could
stop him he reached and caught her arm, swung her around
to face him. "Tell me! Did you know about me and just not
give a shit?"

Tessa hissed in a breath, eyes wide. She pulled away, and Jerry yanked his gun up to cover Idris. "Get the fuck away from her, asshole!" he yelled.

Idris turned a look of utter menace onto Jerry, intense enough to make his lord-daddy proud. With Jerry already on a hair-trigger, the air crackled with stress. *Idris* was Jerry's greatest foe. Kill Idris, and he wouldn't have to live in fear anymore.

McDunn yanked Tessa behind him, damn near squishing her against the wall to shield her from both Idris and Jerry's overreaction. "Steiner! Stand down!" he roared, but Jerry gave no sign he heard McDunn. His attention stayed riveted onto Idris. I took careful aim at Jerry as Pellini did the same, tightened my finger on the trigger—

The heavy grocery bag flew across the room to smack into Jerry's head with an ugly *thwock*. A gunshot slammed through the hallway as Jerry staggered back, and it took me several heart-pounding seconds to realize it hadn't come from my gun.

I spun toward Idris, but he stood unscathed, eyes wide and breathing hard. I looked around to see McDunn glaring big scary daggers at Jerry, who leaned against the door with the bag of gun pieces at his feet and one hand pressed to his forehead. Blood trickled down his face, and his gun dangled from the fingers of his other hand.

Snarling, Pellini yanked the gun from Jerry's grasp. He appeared unhurt as well, but my heart dropped as I continued my hurried scan.

"Eilahn!" She sat on the stairs, hands clamped onto her thigh and an aggravated expression on her face. My stomach did a horrible flip at the blood that stained her jeans though I told myself there'd be a lot more if the bullet had hit her artery. I sprinted to the kitchen and grabbed a dishtowel, ran back and pressed it to her wound.

"Leave. Now," I growled to McDunn.

McDunn didn't have to be told twice. Chances were low that a single gunshot would draw undue attention, especially so soon after the Fourth of July when people still let off the occasional firecracker. But he had a host of other reasons to get the fuck out of the house. He hustled Tessa toward the front door so fast her feet barely touched the floor. Dazed and bleeding, Jerry staggered with an unfocused gaze in a futile search for his gun.

McDunn yanked the door open and came face-to-face with a startled Tsuneo. "Get her in the car," he ordered and shoved Tessa into the summoner's arms. He scooped up the bag of gun parts and moved to grab Jerry.

"No!" The shout of rage burst from Idris. Fists clenched, he started forward in long strides with Jerry as his clear goal. I didn't need othersight to know potency rippled over his hands. "No! You're not taking him," Idris snarled. "He doesn't get to hurt anyone else!"

Shiiiiiiiiit. As much as I agreed with Idris's bloodlust, this was *not* the time for it. I pushed away from the stairs and lunged after him, though I knew I had slim chance of closing the distance in time to stop him. As Idris charged, McDunn settled his weight and balled his hands, ready to defend his man, fucktard though Jerry was. Idris was young, strong, and determined, but even with an arcane edge he was no match for McDunn's training, experience, and size—and his ability to eradicate arcane ability.

Without warning, Carl stepped from the sitting room, grabbed Idris's forearm and smoothly blocked him several feet from McDunn and Jerry. "You need to get a hold of yourself or more people will get hurt," he murmured. Quiet and calm. Typical Carl.

Pulse pounding, I stuttered to a halt behind Idris, braced for him to shove Carl aside and bull forward. Instead, Idris dropped his eyes to Carl's hand on his arm then turned his gaze to Eilahn and the blood-soaked towel pressed to her thigh.

The vengeful rage left Idris like air from a burst balloon. Utter chagrin filled his face as it hit home how close he'd come to putting us all in a disastrous situation. Maybe Carl had a calming touch like Sonny? Either way, he'd stopped a disaster.

"I'm sorry." Regret swam in Idris's eyes. He started to say more, but I lifted a hand to stop him.

"Hold that thought," I said, more snappishly than I meant to, but I *was* kind of on edge. I shifted my attention to the pair by the door. McDunn had relaxed his hands and nothing else. Jerry's head continued to bleed. "Get out."

McDunn grabbed Jerry by the back of the collar, hauled him out and closed the door hard behind him. Heavy footsteps on the porch mingled with a querulous whine from Jerry about how "the fat asshole" had his gun. A sharp *smack* followed that I suspected was McDunn's way of telling Jerry how little he gave a fuck. I silently willed him to hit Jerry a few dozen more times—hard. The "fat asshole" had turned out to be one of the best people I knew.

A few seconds later two cars started and left. "Clear," Pellini announced.

"Thanks." I turned to Idris. "I need to talk to you in the kitchen." He winced but went without protest. "Do what you can for Eilahn, please," I said to Carl and Pellini. "I need a few minutes."

"Got it covered," Pellini said. He unloaded Jerry's pistol and tucked it into his waistband, then crouched by Eilahn as Carl fetched towels. Tessa's favorites, I noted with dark amusement.

Idris stood at the sink, back to me as he gazed out the window at the lake. I closed the door and moved to him.

"I screwed up," he said, voice thick. "I let my emotions get the best of me and put us all in danger."

"Yeah, you did." I leaned against the counter beside him. "You were provoked, and Jerry is a worthless piece of shit. And that was a terrific apology, but that's not why I wanted to talk to you."

He gave me a baffled look. "What then?"

My heart began to thud unsteadily. I leaned close and spoke low. "I need you to send Eilahn back to the demon realm."

He drew back in surprise. "Dismiss her?"

"It's best this way," I said, unable to keep my voice as steady and assured as I'd hoped. "I can't bear the thought of her getting killed for real." I didn't say *and I'm not worth guarding anymore*. Even though that was a factor in the amalgam of crap that brought me to this point, the decision was far more complicated. I knew Eilahn would never abandon me, whether I was a summoner or not. She was willing to die to protect me. But I was no longer willing to lose her.

Idris searched my face. "Are you sure?"

I swiped at a few pesky tears. "I wasn't before she got shot. But . . ." Gooseflesh rippled over my skin. I'd watched her die once before. That was enough.

"I get it," he said quietly.

A sick ache spread through my chest as the full import of my decision hit home. She'd been with me for the better part of a year, watching my back and perching on my damn roof and decorating my house with outrageous enthusiasm for every holiday. "She won't want to go," I told him. "You're going to have to catch her off guard."

He exhaled. "Right."

I returned to Eilahn and sat beside her on the stair. A fluffy yellow towel with embroidered roses swathed her thigh. "How is it?"

"It is a mere flesh wound," she said. Pellini let out a cough that sounded like laughter though I had no idea why.

"I hate seeing you hurt." I wrapped my arms around her.

She smiled and leaned her head against mine. "I am not certain I would associate with you if you enjoyed it."

I laughed, but it felt strange and weak. "This was a flesh wound," I said, "but what if the bullet had hit something more vital?" I let out a shuddering breath. *Stop it, Kara.* I didn't need to convince her or myself. Eilahn opened her mouth to reply, but I cut her off. "I love you. You are very dear to me." Releasing her, I stood and backed away as grief surged up to drown me. "I'm sorry," I gasped. "I have to do this."

Eilahn's forehead wrinkled in confusion but only for a second. Through the open kitchen door, Idris worked the dismissal, formed and readied in this last minute I'd spent with her.

Heedless of her injury, she shot to her feet as the flows wrapped around her. "Dahn. *Dahn!*" She flung a hand out toward me, pleading and furious. A stench of rotten eggs filled the air, and an unseen wind whipped around us. "Jhivral, dahn!" *Please, no!*

I stepped back, tears streaming. "I'm sorry!" I cried out. "I'll send Fuzzykins and the kittens as soon as I can. I promise!"

Eilahn let out an inhuman screech as a rent of blinding white light opened in the fabric of the universe behind her. A sharp *crack* rattled the house, and she and the light vanished.

# Chapter 35

We got out of there as fast as possible. I didn't trust Mc-Dunn—or Tessa, for that matter—not to call the cops on us once they were clear, but we made it to Pellini's truck with no issues.

"Eilahn's motorcycle." I scanned the area in dismay. "We need to get it back to the house, and I don't know how to ride one." I finally spied it further down the street, tucked between two cars.

"On the truck?" Idris suggested.

"Would be tough to get it loaded up without a ramp," Pellini said. "Plus, we'd need straps to keep it from falling over." But then he shrugged. "I can ride it. Always wanted to try out a Ducati."

"Perfect!" I said and decided not to ask how skilled he was. At this point it didn't matter since he couldn't be worse than Idris or me. Pellini was turning out to have one hell of an eclectic skill set. I handed him the spare key from my key ring while he gave me the truck's.

"It's too bad you can't take the bike home, Kara," Idris said with a grimace. "That way Pellini and I could go symmetrize the node in the Kreeger River."

"I'll tag along with y'all," I said. "That's an hour wasted if you take me home first." The itchy crawly feel of my un-showered skin ramped up a notch, but I plastered on an accommodating smile. "Y'all can put up with my stench."

Pellini let out a bark of laughter. "Nah, *Idris* can put up with it. I'll be on the bike."

"You owe me one," Idris said to Pellini with a *hint* of a smile. "You up for talking me through another symmetrization?"

"Sure, but if anyone has to dangle from a rope this time, it sure as hell ain't gonna be me."

Pellini hadn't lied about knowing how to ride a bike. He crammed Eilahn's helmet onto his head then zoomed off with damn near as much panache as the syraza. After a block he slowed to let us catch up then led the way out of town. To add to Pellini's streak of being handy in a variety of ways, he also knew a place not far from the bridge where we could rent a boat, which scratched the need for anyone to dangle from the bridge. After anchoring near the node, Idris and Pellini symmetrized while I leaned back, closed my eyes, and thought as little as possible. I especially didn't think about how I'd lost both my aunt and a dear friend less than an hour earlier. Nope, not one bit.

Despite the added challenge of working with a valve node in a river, Pellini and Idris managed to finish up in under thirty minutes. As we motored back to the boat rental place I considered how good it would feel to jump into the water and rinse off the surface grime. However, the sight of a water moccasin as thick as my forearm slithering into the river put a hard stop to that line of thinking. We'd be home in under an hour, and my shower was blissfully free of snakes—venomous or otherwise.

Pellini mounted the Ducati and fell in behind us for the drive home. Idris was broody and quiet, which I understood, but just could *not* handle right now. In an effort to save what was left of my sanity, I launched into the tale of Angry Chick, Young Thing, Rich Bitch, and the rest of my inmate experience. Much more fun to relate now that it wasn't an immediate threat, and Idris appeared to enjoy hearing it. He needed the mental break as much as I did. In return he told me about the hijinks that ensued when he and Bryce retrieved the camera from the tree near the

Katashi base and ran afoul of a furious squirrel. I wasn't sure how much of it was true, but it made me laugh, which I sorely needed.

I started to tell him about Tolya Gresh but sucked in a sharp gasp as an achingly familiar presence washed through me. *Mzatal! But how . . . ?* He was deeply worried or upset. Had something happened in the demon realm? Maybe strong emotions could bridge the distance in our bond.

"Kara? You okay?" Idris peered at me in concern.

"Yeah, I—" My phone rang. Bryce. "Hang on," I said then hit the answer button for the hands-free. "Hey, Bryce."

"Mzatal is *here*," Bryce said over the car speakers, voice low and strained. "Where are you?"

"Wait, *what?*" I blurted before my brain could get into gear. "Here where? There? At the house?" *Well, that explains why I can feel him!* I thought in shock.

Idris stared at me with wide-eyed dismay. *The valve?* he mouthed. I could only reply with a helpless shrug. Surely Mzatal wouldn't risk destabilizing the pond valve by passing through it? Yet I couldn't think of any other explanation for how he could be here on Earth.

The next voice we heard was Mzatal's. "Zharkat. Where are you?"

Idris flapped his hands and then grabbed his head in a *What the holy crapping hell is going on, and is he insane???* gesture that I had no trouble translating. I'd have done the same thing if not for the pesky fact that I was driving.

"I'm less than a minute away!" I said as I punched the gas. "You used the valve?"

"To reach you. I await you on the nexus."

I clamped down on colorful language as I sped along the highway. "Stay put right there!" I jammed the button to hang up in order to better pay attention to driving.

The instant I disconnected Idris let out a strangled noise. "He must have felt it was worth the risk to stress the valve like that," he said, aghast as he fought to rationalize Mzatal's actions. He gulped and shook his head. "I guess he really needs you for something?"

A lump of unease took up residence in my stomach.

What could have driven Mzatal to such an extreme? "We need to barricade that valve," I said. "And by 'we' I mean you and Pellini. I'm going to have to try and explain what needs to be done based on what Kadir taught me at the plantation about creating a barricade seal. As soon as Mzatal leaves we can do that. Otherwise we're going to have lords dropping in right and left until the damn thing ruptures. Kadir said it would be disastrous, and we don't need any more—" I cut off my stream of babbling as I punched the remote for the gate, cursing as the thing swung open at a snail's pace. The instant I had sufficient clearance I zoomed through then remembered Pellini on the bike behind me. "Crap. Pellini has no clue why I'm driving like a maniac," I said as I raced up the driveway. "Will you explain?"

Idris said something I assumed was a yes, but it was drowned out by the spray of gravel as I careened to a stop in front of the house. I threw off my seatbelt, jumped out of the truck and took off toward the backyard at a run.

Mzatal stood on the nexus, feet planted wide and hands clasped behind his back. His eyes locked onto me as I came into sight. He looked glorious and badass, dressed in black silk trousers and tunic with shimmering patterns of blood red. I wanted to be angry and demand a reason for why the hell he'd risked the valve, but instead I ran to the center of the nexus and threw my arms around him with a sob.

The smell of smoke and sulfur surrounded him like a cologne of Badass as he swept me into an embrace. Abruptly aware of my own far less sexy aroma, I tried to pull away, but he held me close, his mouth finding mine. Our connection flared into full presence, and my petty worries about my unwashed state dropped away. I held him close and kissed him with desperate passion, lost myself in it and in him. The bond engulfed me, and I opened fully, sharing with him all the despair and pain of the days since I'd seen him last. His love met mine, merged into a joyous union as we held each other close.

After an eternity I broke the kiss, pulled back enough to

search his face. "Boss," I said, speaking the word as the endearment it was. "Why are you here?"

"Eilahn came to me but moments ago as I engaged an anomaly in Rhyzkahl's realm," Mzatal said, voice low but no less intense. "She told me of your grievous plight—the sundering of your arcane senses." His eyes remained on mine as he stroked the backs of his fingers over my cheek then pushed a strand of hair from my temple. "I saw you in shadow form on Rhyzkahl's terrace not a full day ago, and within hours he sent a woman to me with no explanation." Deep concern darkened his eyes as he read the details from me. "You have an agreement with him." His tone held no jealousy or accusation, only worry and a desire to protect me.

"I do what I must," I said with a slight quaver.

"I cannot restore your abilities, zharkat," he said. Frustration and deep regret filled the bond. "Perhaps later I will be able to—"

"It's all right," I said. Strangely enough, it was. My abilities weren't a priority at the moment. I caressed him through our bond and cupped his cheek in one hand. "Beloved." I drew a shuddering breath. "You shouldn't have come here." He'd abandoned the other lords during a crisis and traveled through an unstable valve because he was worried about me. In the scope of one wavelength of light, the act was a priceless, romantic gesture. But within the full spectrum, it bordered on self-serving madness. During the plantation battle, Rhyzkahl had taunted Mzatal that I would be his downfall. I hadn't wanted to believe it, but now I understood.

Pain deepened the shadows in his face. "How could I not when you are at such risk?" His awareness of his folly resonated through the bond, as did more: He didn't want to be the Mzatal who could set aside worry for me—or others. That Mzatal was closed to such petty distractions. Closed to all but that which served to achieve his goals.

Tears spilled down my cheeks. "Your world is at greater risk than I am. Both our worlds are." I placed my hands on his chest, gathered the silk of his tunic into my fingers. "Oh,

Mzatal," I breathed. "I saw you. I watched you engage the anomaly and lead the other lords. You were *brilliant,* and I have never loved you more or been more proud." I clung to him, held him close by my grip on the silk. My throat clogged to where I could barely speak. "That's who you need to be, for the sake of our worlds. Without distractions." He drew breath to protest, but I rushed to continue. "Because of the love we hold for each other, we must both fully commit to our causes, or else all will be lost, and that love will be for nothing." My heart screamed at me to stop at that and speak no more, but I plunged on. "You can't hope to succeed in this without your blade." Essence-deep agony flared with my words. "You *must* call Khatur and . . . fully commit." I wept openly as he wrapped his arms around me and held me close.

"Zharkat, I cannot." A shiver passed through him, of denial, of horror. *Fully commit.* Terrible implications echoed within the two words. "I *cannot.*" His voice broke. Closing off was a desolate and isolated prison of his own making, near as dire as the submersion Szerain endured.

And I had to convince him to step into the cell and lock the door behind him. "We fight a war on two different fronts." I reached for the thick rope of his braid, drew it over his shoulder and gave it a tug. Desperate emotion twisted his face at the simple gesture that meant so much to us. A secret and wicked joy, a shared passion. Dying inside, I released the braid. "We . . . we had our time in the sun, but we dare not indulge any longer. Not if our worlds are to stand a chance of survival."

"Zharkat—"

"You *always* do what is needed, beloved," I said in little more than a whisper. I tipped my head up to his. "You must do this. *We* must do this." I swallowed. "Together we can do anything." *Even if we aren't together.*

A long sigh shuddered from him. He cradled my head to his chest and remained still for a long moment. When he spoke, the words flowed through the connection and resonated through my skull.

"It is the only way."

I slid my arms around him, beneath his shirt to the skin of his back. I memorized the feel of him, his body against mine, the steady beat of his heart against my cheek. I drank him in, knowing it would never be enough.

*And now we must each go to our own distant battles.* My hand went to the back of his neck, and I drew him down for a kiss. Our parting kiss, perhaps our last one. He knew it as much as I, and we joined with all the desperation and pain and love and grief and joy that had brought us to this point. He broke the kiss, cradled my face, and rested his forehead against mine. The world retreated and we simply Were. *United. Timeless. Infinite.*

And now I *knew.* The first time we'd made love, Mzatal had shared the universe with me like this, forehead to forehead. *That* was when he'd instinctually forged our essence bond.

Mzatal's confirmation enveloped me. In the vastness of the void, he asked if I regretted the union. Asked if I wished to sunder it. In answer I drew our consciousness higher, entwined, reveled in the freedom and the expansion. Though our bond would be silenced, it would remain for eternity.

Eventually, I covered his hands with mine, forced myself to pull away, kissed his palms, stepped back. "Go, beloved," I murmured. "Unleash hell."

Resolve settled over him. He squeezed my hands and released them. "*Tah zhar lahn, eturnik.*" *I love you, eternally.*

"*Tah zhar lahn, eturnik,*" I echoed as my heart broke into a million pieces.

His hands closed into fists to call potency as anger kindled at the *injustice* of our situation. Rage crackled through our bond, and his breath hissed through clenched teeth.

Dread and grief flooded me as his fury escalated toward a flare—an arcane burst potent enough to reduce my entire property to ash. This was the toll he paid for daring to be open *and* maintain his essence blade—uncontrolled fury that now only affirmed our decision.

His eyes sought mine through the rage, and I felt his essence call to me. He wavered on the brink of the terrible sacrifice—to give up all that was the true Mzatal. Love.

Laughter. Joy. To silence and sequester our bond. He couldn't do it on his own, needed me to urge him into the prison he'd created. To save both worlds, it was my *duty* to lock down a weapon of uncontrollable intensity and release a new one of ruthless precision. Nausea rose as his anguish and fury whirled higher. My duty *sucked*.

"Boss." I called to him on all levels. "Mzatal. Do it. You have to close off *now*." I backed to the far edge of the nexus. "*CALL THE GODDAMN BLADE!*" I screamed at him. "*DO IT NOW!*"

A terrifying cry ripped from his throat. He thrust his hand up, gripped the hilt of Khatur as the blade answered his call.

"*So alone*." His words shivered through our bond.

"*Never*," I answered.

"*Tah zhar lahn*."

"*Eturnik*."

Eyes on mine, he swept Khatur in a vicious arc. The barriers slammed shut like impenetrable walls of tungsten steel, and our connection shattered into icy silence. His face transformed to an unreadable, glacial mask as he retreated within. His eyes went last, radiating boundless wrath that hardened to terrifying, flint-grey vehemence. A wave of black malevolence roiled from him and through me.

Shocked to my bones, I staggered back and off the nexus. Expectation didn't hold a candle to reality.

The concrete of the nexus slab beneath his feet blackened. Heart hammering, I retreated farther as the blight spread, and within seconds the whole of the platform succumbed and glistened like obsidian. Strands of silvery metal writhed across its surface and settled into intricate patterns. Unnamed dread rose within me as the last strand slithered into place.

Dangerously silent and forbidding, Mzatal turned his back on me as if I held no more importance than a worm in the dirt. He strode off the nexus toward the wooded path that led to the pond valve, and I sank to my knees to watch his departure in numb horror. With each step, the grass charred and smoldered beneath his boots. The trees shivered as he passed between them and then went still.

Silence. Not a whisper of wind through leaves. Not the call of a bird or the buzz of an insect. And nothing of our connection.

In another heartbeat he was gone, leaving only aching emptiness and the stench of sulfur in his wake.

*Mzatal. Beloved. What have we wrought?*

# Chapter 36

A crow cawed, harsh and merciless and, as if it had broken a spell, normal sound rushed in. The rustle of leaves, the chatter of squirrels, the hum of a mosquito. Ordinary sounds of my backyard.

I swallowed and licked my lips, pulled myself to my feet and edged closer to the slab of the nexus. Not concrete anymore, that was for sure. Wary, I extended a hand toward the glassy blacker-than-black surface, touched a finger to it and yanked it back as if testing a hot stove. Emboldened, I touched it again for an instant longer, and when I failed to die or turn into a newt, placed my hand flat on its surface. Cool and smooth, and even without arcane senses I could *feel* that it was powerful.

The silvery threads had formed an intricate filigree, like a perfect and symmetrical fractal snowflake. Silver-white and so shiny they practically glowed.

I straightened and took in the whole of it. If I focused on its amazing beauty, I didn't have to think about everything else that had happened here. Didn't have to think about what Mzatal had become, and what we'd sacrificed.

I shook myself, blew out a gusty breath. Yep, the nexus was frickin' incredible. Idris would shit himself when he saw it.

Speaking of Idris, where the hell was he? I looked around, frowning. Surely he and Pellini had felt Mzatal after he'd changed. Why hadn't they come outside? Even Sammy was mysteriously absent, and no one was peeking out the kitchen window.

Worried thoughts tumbled over each other as I hurried to the house, each theory more outlandish than the last. By the time I hit the back door I'd progressed to the certainty that Mzatal had sent a secret invisible Pulse of Dire Doom through the house and Pellini and Idris were—

—poring over maps at the kitchen table with Sammy asleep on the throw rug. Idris glanced up as I burst in.

"Hey, Kara, I brought your phone in from the truck." Casual nonchalance, as if he didn't give a single fuck that Mzatal had been in the backyard moments earlier.

"Yeah, Sarge called you a minute ago," Pellini added, and then he and Idris returned their attention to the maps.

Comprehension dawned. Mzatal must have set aversions or done some manipulation on the two to make sure that he and I wouldn't be disturbed. Relieved, I scooped up my phone and noted Cory Crawford as a missed call. "Where's Bryce?" I asked.

"In the mobile home with Jill," Pellini said. "Something about Christmas cookies in July. Apparently Jill bakes when she's stressed."

"We're going to need a longer obstacle course at this rate," I said with a snort then called Cory back. He answered on the first ring.

"Kara, thanks for calling back."

"Sure thing. What's up?"

"There are people on that spot in the parking lot again," he said. "Three of them this time: the same redhead as before, a young Japanese guy—Tsuneo, it looks like from the pics you sent me—and the old guy."

My mind snapped to attention. I spun back toward the others and covered the phone. "Katashi's at the PD!" Idris let out a curse, folded the maps and grabbed his bag. Pellini pushed up from his chair then hurried to his room. "Isumo Katashi," I said to Cory. "We're on our way."

"Kara, if they're up to serious shit, why don't I go slap cuffs on them?" Cory asked. "I can trump up a charge in a flash."

"No! They may not look all that dangerous, but they are, *especially* the old guy. And they'll have other people nearby whose job it is to make sure no one fucks with them. It won't be as simple as slapping cuffs on." As I spoke I grabbed an empty shopping bag and loaded it with beef jerky, snacks, and bottled water. I hadn't eaten since a rubbery sausage biscuit in jail before my hearing.

"All right," Cory said, but it was obvious he didn't like sitting on his hands while people were doing weird stuff around the PD. "Is there anything I *can* do?"

"Keep your people clear of the area. I don't want to scare off the baddies."

"Got it," he said. "See you when you get here."

I ran to my bedroom and grabbed my gun and a box of ammo along with clean underwear, bra, shirt, and tactical pants. Arms full, I dashed out to Pellini's truck only a few steps behind Idris. He moved toward the back as if to be nice and let me have a chance at riding shotgun, but I shook my head. "No, you take the front."

Idris complied without argument. I dove into the back seat with my bundle of stuff. Pellini climbed in and started the engine, and I yanked off my stinky shirt and bra. Idris gave me a startled look then jerked his gaze away, ears pinking.

I shucked off my jeans and undies next. "Both of you have already seen me naked, so what difference does it make?"

Pellini glanced at me in the rear view mirror and quirked a smile. Idris stared straight ahead as I set a world record getting into my clean clothing. By the time we passed through the gate, I was dressed and seatbelted and ready to kick some Katashi butt.

While Pellini drove like a bat out of hell, I called Bryce to let him know why we'd streaked out of there. He replied with the expected, "Be careful and keep me posted," then added, "Do you have extra ammunition?"

"I grabbed a box on my way out," I said then glanced at Pellini. "You have spare ammo?"

"Thousand rounds of .45 under your seat," he said, and

while I goggled at that he continued, "along with two hundred fifty rounds of double-aught buckshot, a twelve gauge shotgun, five hundred rounds of nine millimeter, and a Glock 19."

"Uh, I think we're good," I told Bryce.

He laughed. "So I heard. A man after my own heart!"

Pellini caught my eye in the mirror as I hung up. "When things started getting weird, I figured I needed to be prepared."

"I am *beyond* impressed," I said fervently.

He took a hard turn onto Serenity Road and gunned it. "Also have a Smith 642 and a box of .38 in the glove box." He slid a look to Idris. "You know how to shoot a gun?"

To my surprise a flush crept up Idris's cheeks. "I know which end to point at the bad guys," he said, "but I've only shot BB guns."

"That's a start," Pellini said without a hint of disdain. "I'm a certified firearms instructor. When this shit is over I'll give you a few lessons. If you want, that is."

Idris blinked in astonishment, then his face lit up. "Yeah, I'd like that a lot."

"Good deal. I try to get out to the range at least once a week to practice. Only way to keep skills sharp."

I ate beef jerky and pretended I wasn't paying attention while inwardly I writhed in embarrassment. I couldn't remember the last time I'd been to the range, and even when I was a cop I'd gone every few months at most. I'd always told myself it was more important that I study the arcane. Ugh. Excuses. Thankfully neither of them queried me about my own firearm skills, and the conversation devolved to occasional colorful commentary from Pellini on the general lack of competence of other drivers.

I tapped Idris on the shoulder. "The PD valve isn't supposed to burp until tomorrow afternoon. You think Katashi guessed we were planning to symmetrize it in the morning and moved up his timetable?"

His jaw tightened. "He's up to no good, that's for sure. He only makes field trips for alterations, not research."

Wonderful. I closed my eyes and readied myself to face

whatever Katashi might throw our way, steeled myself to set my feelings about my encounter with Mzatal aside until I had private time to fully deal with them. We fought the same war, worlds apart, and now I was on my way to *my* battle, *my* front line. I couldn't close off as Mzatal had, but I sure as shit could concentrate on this and do what needed to be done.

After a speedy drive of shortcuts and blown stop signs, Pellini made a sharp turn into the PD detectives' parking lot. Orange construction cones and caution tape still created a physical boundary around the valve. No sign of Katashi or any of his people.

Pellini parked well away from the valve, and we all climbed out. Everything seemed normal to me, but the dismay on the faces of Pellini and Idris told me how very wrong my perception was.

"That looks really . . . weird," Pellini muttered. Idris said something under his breath that didn't sound biologically possible and set off toward the orange cones.

"Idris, what can you tell me?" I asked but he responded with only a slight headshake, attention locked onto the valve. So much for my fantasy that we could symmetrize this one and go.

Cory stepped out of the door to Investigations and gestured me over. I jogged to him while giving the valve area a wide berth. "Those people didn't do anything," he told me when I reached him. "I poked around after they left but didn't see anything out of the ordinary."

"Nothing that *you* can see." I looked around, disturbed. "I have a feeling they did plenty." As I watched, Idris approached the valve as cautiously as if it was a sleeping tiger. Pellini remained a few feet behind him, smart enough to trust Idris's judgment. "I know you hated twiddling your thumbs, but it was better not to confront them."

"I don't get it," Cory said, pained and bewildered at the same time. He knew there was trouble, but it bugged him that he saw no evidence of it. "Is there something dangerous out there?" He lifted his chin toward the parking lot.

I didn't follow his gaze. "There's a damn good chance of it,"

I murmured, pulse quickening as I watched the wall behind him. The shadows near the corner of the building were deeper than the rest, and . . . they'd moved. Nothing obvious—a slight oily shift that anyone else would dismiss as a trick of the light or a passing cloud. I no longer had othersight, but I still had my cop senses along with a shitload of experience with demons. That darker shadow concealed a *zhurn*—a winged demon that was only visible as an absence of light save for rare glimpses of burning red eyes.

"I don't like the look on your face," Cory said, keeping his tone mild. "I also want to turn and see what you're staring at." Luckily he was smart enough to know that jerking around to gape might spook whatever I had my eye on.

"You can, but keep your movements slow," I said, nice and conversational. He complied while I kept my eyes glued to the zhurn. If I glanced away and it moved I might not find it again. "The shadows at the corner," I told him. "The dark ones. Watch them." My heart pounded as I ran through my various options. None of them were ideal or subtle.

"What the hell is it?" His hand drifted to his gun.

I'd never told Cory about the demons. He knew I did weird stuff, but he hadn't wanted specifics. And now was not the time to drop a charged word like *demon* on him. "It's a creature from another dimension," I said. The zhurn could hear me but wasn't likely to care what I said. After all, there was little if anything I could do to it.

The door to Investigations flew open, and Boudreaux raced out. He passed Cory and me without a glance, blocking my view of the zhurn for an instant, but it was all the demon needed.

"It's gone!" I wheeled around in an instinctive search. Boudreaux ran to his car, either oblivious or not caring that Idris and Pellini crouched within the caution tape. Pellini lifted his head in surprise and called out to him, but Boudreaux dove into his car and pulled out of the parking lot with a shriek of tires on asphalt.

It took me a few seconds to realize that the vibration in the ground wasn't from the speeding car or a heavy truck driving by. "Oh, shit," I breathed even as it faded.

"Was that an *earthquake?*" Cory asked in disbelief, still looking around uneasily for the demon.

Before I could answer him, Idris's voice resonated across the parking lot, tense and angry. "Kara. Katashi has rigged the valve to destroy it."

My gut went cold. An arcane blast strong enough to destroy a valve would do a terrible amount of damage to the physical world as well from the shock wave alone. "*Why?*"

"Eliminates an outlet. Shunts potency to the node and makes it a 'supernode,' but I don't know how he plans to use it."

"How big an area of effect? Can you stop it? Oh, and there's a zhurn lurking around."

"Mile. Two. Maybe more." Clinical and abrupt. "The charges are set but not activated, so I can't be sure." Idris continued to work in all-out super-summoner mode. "I need time to disarm them. Keep the zhurn off of us."

*Miles?* I crushed the panic and clung to my faith in his half-demonic lordliness. "Got it," I said then turned to Cory who stared in open disbelief. "You need to evacuate the PD and as much as you can around this area," I told him. "People need to drop everything and *go*." He opened his mouth to argue then shut it as another, stronger tremor hit. It only lasted a couple of seconds, but no way could anyone mistake that for a big truck.

"Evacuate," he said crisply. "I'm on it." He might have been out of his element with my kind of weirdness, but handling disaster was right in his wheelhouse. Calm certainty settled over him as he ran into the building and started shouting orders. The honking of the fire alarm cut through the air, followed by a steady flow of people exiting. I held my gun behind my leg and out of sight. Anyone who recognized me would know about my arrest, and now was *not* the time to deal with questions about why I was in the PD lot with a loaded gun.

For a horrifying instant I thought the people would scurry into the parking lot and onto the valve, but I'd underestimated Cory. An officer I didn't recognize stepped in front of the crowd, directed them away from Idris and Pellini and to the lot on the far side of the building. I remained halfway between the building and the valve and scanned for the zhurn and other threats. Fortunately, with all the commotion, I only racked up a dozen or so curious looks.

As the PD emptied, officers ran to nearby buildings to facilitate evacuation. I shifted from foot to foot, uneasy as tremors continued in a slow cycle, yet grateful for them at the same time. No way would we be able to convince people to get the hell outside in the middle of July otherwise. *But the danger isn't truly earthquakes,* I thought with worry. Were they safer out in the open?

A wave of shrieks and shouts rolled from the street. Officers drew their guns, attention riveted on the roof of the PD. *The zhurn?* I held my gun at the ready and watched the edge of the roof, poised to fire at the first hint of a moving shadow.

No, not the zhurn. A big ass reyza. *Son of a fucking bitch.* To the bystanders he surely looked like a true demon from hell—manlike in form with skin the color of bronze, huge bat-like wings, and wicked clawed hands. He leaped off the roof and took flight. I yelped out a curse and got two quick shots off, missing with both. "Pellini!" I yelled, pivoting as the demon flew over me and swooped toward the valve. "Idris! Watch out!" I didn't dare fire again for fear of hitting one of them.

In a flash Pellini drew, aimed, and fired three shots at the rapidly approaching reyza. Clearly he hadn't been blowing smoke up our asses about weekly firearms practice. The reyza bellowed as blood sprayed from his left bicep, but the injury didn't slow him. Pellini grabbed Idris by his collar to pull him back, but the demon seized Idris by the wrist and delivered a kick to Pellini's chest that sent him sprawling.

"*Kel gor mraz,* Alavik!" Idris yelled as the reyza vaulted into the air and climbed with heavy beats of his wings. Though I didn't know a lot of demon words, I was pretty sure *kel gor mraz* meant *You're a fucking piece of shit assface* or a similar sentiment. Alavik was no doubt a reyza Idris had spent time with during his months as a captive of the Mraztur.

I had no clear shot, but I kept my gun trained on the reyza in case an opening appeared. Idris kept his head even as he dangled in Alavik's grip. Before he was more than a half dozen feet from the ground, Idris yanked his folding knife off his belt, flicked it open, and slashed the razor sharp blade across the demon's forearm.

Alavik keened in pain as blood sprayed and tendons parted. His clawed hand spasmed, and Idris dropped to the asphalt and rolled, teeth bared in defiance. With Idris clear, I opened fire, and Pellini did the same while still on his back. At least two bullets pierced Alavik's wings, but even when other officers joined the shoot-the-demon game, he remained aloft. Unburdened, the reyza rose quickly then veered away over buildings and out of sight.

Idris scrambled up and ran back to the valve. "He has arcane shielding on his head and torso," he called out to us. Pellini climbed to his feet and staggered toward Idris. I dropped my empty magazine, yanked a fresh one from my pocket and slapped it in.

"What the fuck was that thing?" a familiar voice said from behind me. I spun to see my favorite road sergeant, Scott Glassman, gun drawn and ready. Beside him, a wide-eyed Asian woman—likely his trainee—held her weapon in a death grip. Bet she hadn't counted on anything like this when she signed up.

"Long story!" I shouted back over the rising din of people pouring into the street from nearby buildings. "But if you see it again, shoot it. Aim for the wings." Shit. And the zhurn was still around somewhere. And who knew how many other demons had been stationed to keep us from undoing Katashi's work. Out in the street, people milled or watched the sky or peered at cell phones and tablets. Videos of Alavik's dramatic attack on Idris were about to go viral. *The times they are a-changin'.* But no sense worrying about what I couldn't control.

"Get those people as far away from here as you can," I told Scott. With any luck that would ensure he and his trainee were also far away if the worst happened. He gave me a sharp nod, and the two turned and yelled at people to move down the street. The woman had an impressive set of lungs and a commanding presence, both of which had everyone cowering and scurrying to obey her.

Alert and ready, I continued a survey of the area as Idris and Pellini worked furiously. Movement grabbed my attention. "Pellini! Behind you!" I yelled. "Under the red car!"

I expected the zhurn to go still and hide again, but to my dismay it streaked from the shadow and darted straight for the valve. Pellini shot at it one-handed, while I squeezed my trigger as fast as I could until the slide locked back. The demon squealed as bits of shadow flew from it, but kept moving. A dozen feet from the caution tape it launched itself toward the valve, wings and tail and body elongating as it dove into the dead center of the circle of cones and disappeared as if the asphalt had sucked it in.

A heavy tremor rocked the parking lot. Idris fell back with a cry of horror. "No. No!"

I ran toward him. "What? What happened?"

He scrambled to his feet then stared down at the asphalt, aghast. "The zhurn. It activated the charges."

I yanked my gaze to the ground as if I could miraculously see what he meant. "That's bad, right?"

Idris swallowed, paling. "The countdown started."

Yeah, bad. "How long do we have?"

"Five minutes." Sweat beaded on his upper lip. "Maybe ten if I can slow it." He hauled his gaze up. "You two. Go, get clear."

Pellini spoke up before I could tell Idris to get stuffed. "Can you stop it?" he asked.

Idris wiped sweat from his face. "Maybe. It'll be a lot harder now." For the first time, doubt and fear flickered in his eyes. "I . . . I don't know. I might make it worse, or set it off sooner—"

I seized his shoulders. "You're the son of a demonic lord!" I yelled and gave him a hard shake.

"A horrible one!" He shoved my hands away. To my dismay his uncertainty deepened. "I don't want to be like him! He's a manipulative asshole, and maybe that's the reason my own mother never wanted me!"

My breath caught as his agony poured out, and I realized why his confidence had locked up. "Idris, you're *not* him, and—"

"How do you know?" he demanded in what was perilously close to a sob. "I have the blood of one of the Mraztur, and I'll be just as bad as them if I mess up this valve, and I—"

A *crack* echoed through the parking lot as I backhanded him hard enough to send him staggering. Hell, in the past year I'd punched and slapped enough demonic lords that a mere *son* of one didn't stand a chance. And, best of all, his look of bewildered outrage told me I'd succeeded in shocking him out of his death spiral of irrational angsty crap. And I knew all about irrational angsty crap.

I seized the front of his shirt with both hands and pulled him close so only a few inches separated our faces. "Listen to me. You are the most amazing and gifted summoner I've ever known. You're NOT Rhyzkahl, and I'm an authority on that subject. I'm cool as shit, and you're my cousin. *That's* the bloodline you need to be concerned about. Now straighten up, be the brilliant and kind and awesome cousin I love, and Fix. That. Valve."

I released his shirt and stepped back. He blinked, then squared his shoulders and turned to the valve while I trembled in relief. We were probably still going to eat it, but at least we'd go down fighting. Pellini gave me a nod of approval that warmed me to my toes then settled in to work next to Idris.

"I'll watch your backs," I announced then let out a yelp as Jill appeared beside me out of nowhere. She swayed, eyes unfocused, and I threw my arms around her. "Jill! Fucking hell, woman!" My heart slammed. She'd teleported here. Or rather, the bean had. But why would the bean bring her *here* when our community fortune cookie read *You will be blown to bits in the near future*?

I steadied her and discarded the notion of finding a safe place to stash her. No such thing at the moment. On to the next wild idea. I bent close to Jill's belly. "Hey! Listen up! It's not safe! You got her here, you can get her out! Do it! NOW!"

"Kara?" Jill mumbled. "What are you doing?"

Damn. She was still here talking to me, which meant the bean wasn't listening. Or was being willfully disobedient. Brat. "Um. Nothing important." I straightened. "Let's find a place for you to sit."

She put a hand to her temple. "Yeah. I don't feel so hot."

"You can sit in Pellini's truck. That'll be nice and safe." What a nightmare. The only way this could be any worse would be if—

"Kara?" Jill lifted her head and gave me a woozy smile. "I think my water just broke."

# Chapter 37

"What do you mean your water just broke?" I demanded in horror. I looked down at the growing pool of I-did-not-want-to-know-what-kind-of-liquid on the asphalt between her feet.

She shook off the dazed look and scalded me with a glare. "It means my kiddie pool has a crack," she snapped, but she couldn't hide the shaking in her voice.

"I've only been to one class," I said and would have gone on in that vein, but her fear finally penetrated my thick skull. "Aaand it was more than enough!" I finished gamely.

She clutched my arm. "Why am I at the station?" she asked, confusion making her words shrill. "Goddammit, it happened again!" She swung her gaze around while I groped for a reassuring answer. I had a feeling the truth would *not* suffice.

My phone buzzed on my belt with Bryce's ringtone. Shit, he had to be freaking out. I hit the answer button, but he spoke over me in a rush before I could say word one. "She's gone! Disappeared from right in front of me," he gabbled in the closest to outright panic I'd ever heard in him. "I saw it this time. Kara, I swear to God I—"

"She's here," I yelled to make sure he heard me. "Jill's right here beside me," I said at a more normal volume.

"Tell me," he ordered, all trace of panic gone.

"We're in the PD parking lot. The valve is going to blow

at any minute." That pretty much covered it. He wanted a situation report, not story time.

"On my way." The line went dead.

The ground swayed in a tremor. Across the street a window ledge detached from City Hall and crashed to the sidewalk.

Jill let out a little moan, and her grip tightened on my arm. "Let's get you into Pellini's truck," I said. That was the best option at the moment. I slung an arm around her waist, force-marched her to the truck and managed to shove her up into the backseat. She flopped onto her left side while I half-knelt on the floor and steadied myself with one foot on the running board.

"I can't believe this is happening," she said in a combination of fear and annoyance.

"You just wanted to be the center of attention," I said with a shaky laugh to cover my own fear. "I can't believe I'm going to have to deliver your kid!"

Jill managed to hold a brave face for approximately two seconds before she writhed and bit down on a squeal. "You'd better have learned something in that class!"

"First, we'd better get your pants off." That wasn't from class—that was basic logistics. I reached for her waistband then gulped as her belly did a weird lurch and ripple that looked *nothing* like the instructional videos.

Jill seized my hand in a crushing grip. "Something's not right!" she cried out, eyes wide in panic. "This . . . this isn't right!" She let out a howl of pain as her tummy rippled weirdly again.

"Uh. Shit. Breathe!" I wasn't going to tell her I agreed. This was *not* normal labor. "One and two and three—"

"You breathe!" she snarled and even balled her free hand into a fist right before her head lolled and her hand went limp.

Terror spasmed. "Jill!" I checked her pulse. Still strong, and she was breathing, but—

I yelped as a clawed hand grabbed my ankle, and I instinctively shook my leg in an effort to get free of whatever demon had me. I scrabbled for my gun and twisted around, shocked to see a grotesque scaly frog-thing no bigger than Fuzzykins dangling from my ankle by one long-fingered hand.

I let out a strangled cry of disgust, gave it a solid shove with my free foot and ripped my gun from its holster. It gave a piercing shriek but dug its claws harder into my ankle. It writhed into the form of a blue-furred crocodile then a dragon-ish thing with pearly white scales and wet wobbly wings. The shit? I brought my gun to bear on it then registered the blob that dangled from it by a cord of flesh—a blob that dripped blood and had remained constant during the shapeshifting.

Aghast, I gaped at the creature, then snapped my gaze to Jill—and her not-pregnant belly—then back to the creature. As I stared, it caught up its umbilical cord, bit through it then let the placenta splat to the asphalt. No, not a creature. The *bean.* Blinking up at me with huge violet eyes. Hanging onto my ankle. After biting off her cord. Which wasn't bleeding.

"Kara?" Jill, out of it. "What . . . I don't—"

"Hey, Jill! Just relax, okay?" I said, super brightly and *super* freaked. "Everything's *great!*" Nope, wasn't going to say, *Oh, by the way, your baby just* teleported *out of you.*

Instinct surfaced and pushed my gibbering what-the-fuck shock out of the way. I holstered my gun and reached for the bean where she clung to my leg. "You can't *do* that!" I sputtered to her in horror. What if she lost her grip and fell on the hard asphalt? "Come here!" I needed to get her into the truck where she'd be safe, right? Nothing else made sense, but taking care of a newborn had certain inviolate rules.

Apparently the bean didn't give squat about rules for babies. She ducked away from my grab and dropped neatly to the ground then swiveled her head toward the valve. *Like a miniature dragon.* Holy shit.

"Jill I'll be right back everything's fine you stay put okay?" I babbled then climbed out of the truck and crouched by the bean. "Is that why you brought your mama here?" I asked. "So you could get to the valve?"

She focused her luminescent eyes on me. A nictitating membrane flicked over them, then she hop-climbed onto my knee. I thought maybe she wanted to be held, but before I could move to do so she clambered awkwardly around to my back, clung to my shoulders, hooked her back claws onto my bra and wound her sinuous tail around my waist.

Gulping, I stood with caution. In our reflection in the truck window I saw her extend and wave wings that still dripped with baby-ooze. "You do know this is really creepy weird, right?" I muttered then started toward the valve. A shower. If I didn't die in this crap, I was going to get a shower if I had to use a garden hose in the middle of town.

I heard Jill call my name from the truck, questioning at first then with more urgency. Yep, she'd just seen the drag-on-demon thing clinging to my back. *Please please please,* I silently prayed, *don't let her realize it's her baby yet!* "Jill, it's okay!" I called back to her. "I promise!" I gave the bean the side-eye. "Can't you make her take a nap or something?" I muttered.

The bean extended her neck until her wickedly horned head was jaw to jaw with mine. She tick-growled softly, gaze riveted on the valve as we approached. Idris and Pellini continued to work feverishly. I had no idea how much progress they'd made, but their expressions told me things were bad.

"Um, guys?" I said. "I brought help."

Pellini flicked a quick glance up then did a double-take, eyes widening. Idris kept his attention glued to the patch of asphalt. Katashi's arm lay beside him, mostly covered by the cloth with only the fingers sticking out.

"Can't defuse it," Idris said voice strained. "People need to get clear. We're holding as best we can."

"No, seriously," I said. "We got a ringer." Damn, but this was surreal. I glanced to the bean and let out a weak laugh. "Okay, kid. Do your thing."

Her claws tightened on my shoulders as she told me to get closer. Not in words, spoken or otherwise, but there was no mistaking her desire. Much closer. On the valve itself.

"Shit." Heart pounding, I stepped cautiously forward.

Eyes still on the ground, Idris sucked in a breath, probably because of the reaction of the flows to the bean's presence. He jerked his gaze up at me.

"Kara! No! You need to get back—" The rest of his sentence died away as he stared at my piggyback passenger.

A strangled laugh escaped me. "Hey, guys. Meet the bean." Then I took a hurried step forward as the bean gave me a clear *Get your butt on the valve before I have to do it for you!* nudge. Pushy kid.

Pellini stood, eyes on the not-a-baby, then flicked a glance at his truck. The bean's back claws strained my bra band as she shifted her weight and flapped her wings. Her grip on my shoulders tightened, and she brought her wings in close as I stepped into position on the center of the valve. A vibration ran through her, all the way down to the tip of her tail. I startled as she let out a long, piercing wail.

The arcane blazed into life around me, and I gasped. The valve appeared as a bottomless shaft of coruscating blue beneath us, unlike any view of a valve I'd experienced before. I saw the charges attached near the lip—eleven grey, egg-shaped lumps embedded in the blue, like tumors.

Concepts flowed through my thoughts. "Green. Stripes?" I asked the bean, trying to understand her instructions. An image flashed in my mind. "Green stripes. Got it." Too weird. "Pellini. There's going to be some green potency spewing out in a minute. Catch it and shape it into strands. Idris. You connect each strand to an egg-thing, then run it straight down the shaft. Uh . . . straight into the valve. Like candy striping the walls."

Pellini remained silent, acknowledged with a nod.

Idris looked up in grief and dismay. "Kara, it's going to blow! I can't hold it."

"I know," I said calmly. "It's all right. Just do what I tell you, okay?"

The bean shifted, and her tail snaked under the waistband of my jeans and over my lower back. The twelfth sigil ignited in a blaze of peacock blue that dominated my senses as if someone had shoved a blue filter in front of the sun. Gooseflesh raced over my skin in waves of hot and cold.

"Be careful, kid," I said under my breath. "That thing is dangerous."

Emerald green potency fountained from the valve. Pellini seized it, worked it into strands which he passed to Idris. Jaw set, Idris gingerly attached the strands to eggs and ran them down the shaft as directed, fluorescent green stripes against the blue. *To dampen the blast through the valve system.* This was one brilliant baby. Dragon. Demon. Whatever she was.

"This isn't going to work," Idris said. His expression showed exasperation, but aching fear shone from his eyes. He swallowed. "I should've tried dis—"

"It's not going to stop the blast, but it will dampen it," I insisted. "It *will.* Just finish the last one and trust me."

Idris flicked his eyes to the demon-dragon-baby on my shoulder then back to the ugly eggs. He pulled a trembling hand over his mouth, hesitating as doubt flared, in himself, in the plan. It was up to him, one way or another. Up to him to save everyone.

He took the last strand from Pellini and brought it to the last egg, but before he could attach it another tremor shook the valve. The strand slipped from his grasp, flailed like a time-lapse of ivy seeking purchase and slapped against the egg.

Cracks fissured over the egg's surface, and black light spewed forth while the other ten egg things radiated soft green.

The impending explosion of the one egg built as pressure in my chest until I was certain my heart would stop beating. "Stay close," I called out to anyone within earshot. "Everyone. Get close. And stay that way."

Idris sat back on his heels. Shock and disbelief radiated from him. *I failed everyone.* His thoughts flowed through me like water. *I'm not supposed to die this way! It's too soon.*

The pressure in my chest squeezed my breath away. Blue-green snakes of potency whipped outward from beneath my feet like wriggling spokes from a hub.

Pellini put his hands to his head. *Fuck. Bryce'll take care of Sammy, right? God, I hope so. Shit. At least Boudreaux's clear.* More thoughts that I couldn't shut out.

The twelfth sigil cooled. The blue-green spokes of potency continued to lengthen. Twenty feet. Icy. Fifty feet. Burning cold. Another foot. No more.

Silent words and impressions tumbled over me from people farther away. *It's probably that damn fracking. The prisoners. Gotta do something. Jesus, I'm sweating my ass off. Ugh, I left my cigarettes in my desk.* How could the lords stand the constant barrage?

The bean shrieked by my ear, a terrible sound of frustration. The spokes melted into a blue-green carpet and a sensation like being submerged in water closed in.

A protective cocoon. It was all the bean could do.

*I'm so sorry, Amber. I couldn't avenge you.*

*Will I go to hell?*

And then silence. A flash of ruddy light beneath me. Tame, then not. Beyond the perimeter of the blue-green sanctuary, everything blurred, vibrated. The cocoon dissolved, and with it my arcane sense. Surroundings snapped into sharp focus. Sound crashed in. Screams. The crack of concrete. The shriek of twisting steel. The crash of glass. Horror clawed within me as a portion of the station collapsed in upon itself. The entire front half of City Hall disintegrated into rubble. And then buildings beyond it. Trembling, crumbling. And more beyond those. Like a five minute earthquake compressed into the span of a heartbeat. Nightmare. Impossible. And real.

# Chapter 38

Smoke and gas and blood. Shouts and orders and screams. Panic and fear and determination.

Dust choked the air, and water fountained from a broken hydrant. Concrete and rebar groaned and creaked as it settled into ungainly piles. The entire front of the three-story City Hall lay in the street. More than two thirds of the PD had collapsed, and tears sprang to my eyes as I took in the sight. Surely everyone had made it out? They were still my people even if I didn't work there anymore. The station would always be special to me—a place I'd called home.

I tore my eyes away from the ruin. "How is it?" I asked Idris.

"Don't know yet," he said, hands shaking as he worked them over the valve.

I didn't want to think about the number of casualties in the blast radius—*couldn't* think about it if I wanted to keep going. But without the bean's intervention it would have been much worse.

She scuttled around to cling to my chest, her back claws hooked on the waistband of my jeans. She spread her wings and brought her scaly snout to within an inch of my nose, her eyes fixed on mine. I steeled myself for a baby dragon-demon surprise of who-knew-what instructions, but instead she stretched her fanged jaws wide in an almighty yawn. Aww, she was a tired baby.

I cradled her close in an awkward wingy sort of way.

"You did damn good, kiddo," I murmured, then sighed. Crap. Not half an hour old, and she'd heard me curse. Oh, well, best for her to get used to it. "Y'think you can give your poor mama a break and look human when she first sees you?" I said with a soft smile. "She's been through a lot for you."

She let out an adorable little burble and made an unsettling shift that left me feeling as if I held a bag full of wiggly kittens. White scales transformed to soft skin, and her tail shrank to a stub. She waved her wings once before they quivered and morphed into smooth skin on her back. The dragon face shifted into something humanish—except it swiveled on the end of a disturbingly long neck. I stooped and picked up the red silk that had wrapped Katashi's arm and tucked it around her.

"C'mon, sweetie, all the way human," I urged. "Do it for your mommy." I glanced at said mommy. Bedraggled and dazed, Jill slid down from the backseat, staggered a few steps then collapsed to sit against the rear wheel of the truck with one hand on her belly. "She deserves a break," I went on, "and she needs your help right now."

The bean tick-growled, but she adjusted her neck to a reasonable human baby length and shrank the stub of her tail away. She was still a lot bigger than a typical newborn, but at least she looked like a baby now—mostly. She yawned, a bit too wide, revealing several rows of pointy teeth. And the blink of her inner eyelids was way weirder on a baby than a dragon. I tried to wrap her in a Kara version of a swaddle but, when claws emerged from her fingertips, I got the message and left the cloth loose around her. "Put the claws *away*," I murmured as I held her close and hurried over to Jill.

"Hey, chick," I said with a smile. "Got someone who wants to say Hi."

Jill lifted her head as I crouched. The distress vanished from her face at the sight of the bundle in my arms, and she took the bean from me with a choked gasp.

"She's pretty kickass," I said with a warm smile as Jill made cooing noises at her baby. "Just like her mom."

Jill brushed her lips over the bean's head, made more mommy-to-baby noises then finally looked up at me. "What happened? I was ready to whack you for doing that counting thing . . . and the rest is hazy." She bit her lip. "Something really bad happened, but I don't remember." Worry swept over her face, and she held the bean closer, mama instinct in full force. Already I saw her fretting over how to get her daughter to safety.

"Would've been a lot worse if not for your kid." I stroked the back of my fingers over the bean's cheek. Jill spared me a questioning look. "Seems she has a few tricks up her sleeve," I said. "She's special—the best of you and her daddy." That didn't explain a damn thing, but thankfully she was distracted by her baby and still dazed enough that she didn't feel her usual urge to press for more answers. I knew I needed to get up and make sure the valve was safe and start helping with rescue and recovery, but I wanted to drink in another few seconds of the amazing creature in Jill's arms.

"She is pretty special, isn't she?" Jill glowed with adoration and pride, bent her head to nuzzle her daughter. "Look at her. She's awesome."

"She's beautiful," I agreed with a smile. If Jill had indeed seen the winged thing on my back earlier she wasn't letting herself think it might have been her newborn. I stroked the tiny fingers, hardly able to believe they'd been claws only a few minutes earlier.

A change in air pressure hit me an instant before a palpable and familiar aura washed over me. Jill jerked in shock even as I whirled to see Zack and Szerain standing a few feet away. Eyes wary and stance tense, Szerain remained in the guise of Ryan and wielded his essence blade in front of him like a shield. Zack swayed and caught himself on Szerain's shoulder. I wanted to be relieved and elated at their arrival, but a base instinct kept my guard up.

"Oh my god, Zack!" Jill cried out then gave him a watery smile and pulled the silk back from the bean's face. "She's beautiful, isn't she? Oh god, I can't believe you're here."

Zack closed on Jill, his movements deliberate as if he required the utmost concentration simply to keep his cells from flying apart. He crouched, unsmiling. A warning sounded in the back of my head.

"I've come for Ashava," Zack said as he reached for the baby.

Jill drew back and clutched her daughter closer to her chest. *"Ashava?"* she echoed with the tiniest shiver in her voice. "Don't I get a say in naming her?" It was more than the name that had her on guard. I'd always known Jill to have good instincts, and it was clear she felt a weird vibe. I settled my weight, poised to intervene if needed, for however much good that would do. Szerain darted his eyes around as if expecting the bogeyman to leap out at any instant. His breath hissed in and out, short and sharp, and the hand that held the blade Vsuhl trembled.

"What's going on, Zack?" I demanded.

Zack shuddered. "Give her to me *now,*" he gritted out, hands still extended, though he didn't try to forcibly take her—yet.

"No!" Aghast, Jill turned her body to shield the bean from him. "You're *not* taking my baby from me!"

"Zakaar!" Alarm threaded Szerain's voice, and sweat beaded his face. "Xharbek is near!"

Xharbek, Szerain's long lost ptarl—who had commandeered my nexus to hunt Szerain and create the dream link to Rhyzkahl. I shoved myself between Jill and Zack then let out a hiss of pain as the twelfth sigil flared with searing heat across my lower back. In the same instant, a naked baby appeared in Zack's arms.

Jill let out an anguished scream, stared in horror at the empty cloth in her arms and then at Zack with her baby. "No! Give her back!"

*She teleported to daddy,* I realized in shock and dismay. Ashava shifted in a heartbeat to the pearlescent dragon-demon form and clung to Zack's neck. Szerain gripped Zack's arm and dragged him to his feet. Jill scrambled up with my help, though I had a sick feeling we'd already lost this battle.

"Give me back my baby!" she screamed, agonized as

Zack stepped back. She didn't care about wings or claws or luminous eyes. That was her daughter. "Zack, no, please. Don't take her away!"

Szerain caught Zack's arm and moved in close. Zack met Jill's eyes. "I'm sorry," he murmured.

"Take me with you!" She reached out, pleading.

And then Zack and Szerain and Ashava vanished.

Jill let out a terrible cry of rage and grief. "You *asshole!*" she shrieked into the empty air then collapsed against me, shaking. I wrapped her in a hug while I fought to make sense of it all.

I'd barely closed my arms around her when Carl materialized where Zack had stood seconds earlier. *Carl.* I gaped in shock as Szerain's words jangled through my head. *Xharbek is near.*

Before I had a chance to react, he seized Jill by the upper arms and pulled her from my grasp. "Where did they take her?" he asked, inches from her face, each word clear, precise and powerful.

"I don't know!" She tried to squirm from his grasp with zero success.

"Hey, get off her!" I shoved at him but I might as well have tried to budge a mountain. "Don't you dare hurt her!" *Carl is Xharbek!* There was nothing laid back and calm about him now.

"Let me go!" Jill's voice shook. She didn't know all the details about Xharbek, but she'd grasped that this was *not* good ol' Carl, even beyond the whole teleporting trick. Carl's gaze flicked to me for an instant, reading everything from Jill and me and probably everyone else in the vicinity.

He released Jill and disappeared.

I grabbed her as she staggered. "Oh, shit," I breathed, gulping. "Oh, shit shit shit shit." *Carl is Xharbek.* He'd been a part of our lives. Hidden. A lie. Like Zack was before I discovered he was Zakaar. *Nobody is truly who they appear to be.*

And Xharbek wanted Jill's baby. That had to be why Zack and Szerain took her away. To protect Ashava? Or was Xharbek the good guy in this scenario? My gut told me no, but that didn't mean a damn thing. Nothing was black or white anymore.

Jill breathed raggedly, eyes wide, swallowed and went quiet. Then my dear friend—the one who was strong and fierce and rolled with the punches like no one's business, who was teleported from her home, gave bizarre birth to a demon-baby, survived a major disaster, had her baby stolen by the baby daddy, and then was shaken like a ragdoll by the mild-mannered morgue tech—leaned on my shoulder and burst into tears.

I hugged her close and let her sob, even as I tried to think of a place I could stash her where she'd be safe. Everything was a godawful mess, but I couldn't just leave her, not in her condition.

Idris stumbled up from the valve. "Kara! We have a problem."

Seriously? How much more could go wrong?

"Kara!"

Not Idris. I turned to see Bryce clambering over a pile of rubble, face set in utter determination. Dirty, sweaty, and with a long scrape down one arm, to me he looked like an angel sent from above.

He jumped down and moved straight to us, shoulders set with purpose as he took in the sight of a no-longer-pregnant Jill sobbing on my shoulder. Without a word he gently took her from me and lifted her in his arms. Jill buried her head against his neck, let out a shuddering sigh and went quiet. His eyes met mine. "I got this."

I gave him a look of pure gratitude. I could trust him to protect her and give her the care she needed. I jogged over to Idris. "What is it?" I asked him.

Worry creased his brow. He raked a hand over his hair. "The other ten charges—the ones that didn't go off—are still a threat."

My stomach dropped a few miles. "Explain?" I managed.

"The, um, bean's strands deactivated all of the charges but the one that blew. The one I fucked up," he said, words hurried. "It's like she clipped the wires on a bomb for ten of them, but the bombs themselves are still intact." Stark dread filled his eyes. "Kara, it's like nothing I've ever seen. More charges mean more intensity, not just a wider area. If they all go off, there'll be nothing left but dust."

A surreal calm settled over me. "First off, you didn't fuck up. It was pure shit luck that a tremor hit at the wrong time. Second off, you're going to dismantle those remaining ten to where they can't possibly blow, right?"

"Yeah." He nodded, firm and sure. "But it's going to take some time." He surveyed the area, paled at the amount of destruction. I saw it in his eyes as he envisioned it reduced to dust. "We need to evacuate, a couple of miles radius at least, and—"

"Idris." I stopped him, spoke quietly but firmly. "All rescue operations would have to stop. There is no perfect answer here. Either way we risk lives."

He drew a breath and blew it out. "Got it." He met my eyes steadily. He didn't need a Kara-brand pep talk this time at least.

"Yes, you do," I said. "Do I need to watch for zhurn again?"

He grimaced. "*Anything* that could reactivate the charges."

I caught his arm as he turned away. "Zack and Szerain kidnapped the bean—Ashava. Carl is Xharbek. He teleported in, pissed, looking for Szerain and Ashava."

Idris took it in then settled into his super serious summoner demeanor. "We'll deal with it. Later." With that, he ran back to the valve, dropped to his knees, and he and Pellini began their waggly hand dance.

First order of business, Get Dangerous. I dashed to Pellini's truck. Bryce sat in the back with all the windows rolled down, his left arm draped protectively over Jill who sat curled up against him, her eyes closed. His free hand held the Sig P227 on his lap. I didn't see his Glock but I was certain it was within easy reach. A long, hard-plastic box lay open on the floorboard. Pellini's arsenal.

"She had the baby," I said, "and—"

"She told me everything," he said quietly then resumed scanning for potential danger, as vigilant and ready for action as a robot sentry. My throat tightened with gratitude for his presence. He'd have a better tactical position outside the truck, but tactics were only one consideration for him at the moment. He sat with Jill because it was what she *needed*. He intended to protect her—in every way—and I had absolute faith in his ability to balance it all.

I reloaded my empty magazines and grabbed all the extras Pellini had—grimly pleased to find a half dozen high capacity Glock 9mm magazines loaded and ready to go. I tucked three into each side pocket of my pants, then took Pellini's Glock 19 and clipped the holster into place at the small of my back. Probably didn't need anything more.

"Take the shotgun," Bryce murmured, scanning. "And zipties."

I didn't argue. He outstripped me in Being Dangerous by about a zillion percent which meant I followed his advice. The shotgun had a strap that held a dozen shells. I slung it across my back and divided another half dozen shells between my two side pockets. I grabbed a bundle of zipties and shoved them into a front pocket. They made an uncomfortable bulge, but it felt good to have them. No two ways about it—Pellini was forever on my zombie apocalypse team.

Armed and ready, I closed the door gently then raced back to the valve. With a gun in each hand, I proceeded to stalk around Idris and Pellini and watch for any and all not-normal twitches of movement.

Easier said than done. *Nothing* was normal. Rubble choked the street in front of the PD, with some chunks as large as Pellini's truck. First responders mobilized with careful haste. Police and air ambulance helicopters thumped overhead. The first generator fired up with a throaty roar. Cops and emergency personnel shouted orders, and their radios crackled, turned up high to be heard over background noise. Civilian survivors pitched in to help, and a woman with a crew cut and a megaphone organized the volunteers into task groups with brutal efficiency. A bald man in maintenance coveralls and with shoulders as wide as my bed carried supplies beside a woman in a pencil skirt and Louboutin heels.

*All of this mayhem, for no reason other than to further the Mraztur's irresponsible scheme to create a permanent gateway.* It didn't bode well for what they'd do on Earth if they succeeded.

Sweat plastered my shirt to my torso, and I licked dry lips, ignored the wary or accusing stares from people who surely wondered why we made no move to help with rescue operations. Every scream of pain and sob for help sliced through me, but I clung to the fact that thousands more would die if Katashi found a way to reactivate the charges.

A shadow passed over the lot. I dropped to one knee and brought both guns up, and only ingrained trigger discipline kept me from shooting at a helicopter.

Yet providence was on my side, for a change. The helicopter veered off, allowing me to see a kehza as it streaked down in a dive. Adrenaline surged. I leaped up and set my feet in a strong stance, breathed deeply and waited for the kehza to get closer. No wild and panicked shooting this time. *It's not going to get past me. That's all there is to it.* I held both guns close together, sighted down the one in my right hand then squeezed the triggers as fast as possible while maintaining control.

The kehza shrieked as bullets pierced its wings and leg, and it fell in an awkward tumble to the street, sending rescue workers scrambling away. I resisted the urge to do a fist pump. Instead I dropped empty mags and slapped in fresh ones, then positioned myself between the kehza and the valve. *It's not going to get past me*, I silently repeated like a mantra. The kehza flapped into a crouch, let out a metal-curling screech as it swung its head toward the valve. Too late, I remembered the shotgun. I growled a curse as I held both guns on the demon. Double-aught at close range would do a shitload more to slow it than 9mm, but I had no time left to unsling the shotgun and bring it to bear.

The kehza's muscles bunched, but instead of leaping forward it flailed and flung itself to the side. It wasn't until the demon spasmed again that I registered the boom of a gun amidst the other noise. Scott Glassman moved into view with a shotgun hugged up tight against his shoulder. He fired once more into the thrashing demon, then backpedaled in surprise as white light streamed from a hundred fissures in its body. An instant later a *crack* split the din, and the kehza was gone.

Scott cursed and swung his gaze around as if expecting the demon to reappear behind him.

"You killed it!" I yelled at him. He looked over at me and sagged with relief, apparently willing to trust my judgment on such matters.

"Any more of these things around?" he shouted back.

"Probably! Shoot anything that doesn't look like it belongs on Earth!" I hated labeling all demons as shoot-to-kill, but if *I* couldn't distinguish enemy from ally in this situation, there was no way to explain it to a newbie.

He racked his shotgun one-handed. "Ten-four. I'll pass the word. Deer slugs brought that thing down. Kelli has the assault rifle. She's former marine and kicks ass." He jogged back up the street, pulling out his radio as he moved. A few seconds later I heard his voice from the radio of every cop in the area with the directive to "shoot the hell out of the monsters."

From the far side of the PD came the *pop-pop-pop* of multiple gunfire along with the *blat* of an automatic weapon—soon followed by the lovely music of a ripping *crack*.

*Rednecks vs. Demons.* I grinned. The tide had turned in our favor.

I kept the shotgun unslung and took out a *zrila* in three shots, hating every second of it. The zrila were brilliant artisans, and my only consolation was that it was highly unlikely this demon had ever died on Earth before. Half a minute later I blew two legs off a scuttling graa. While it scrabbled, I closed the distance and put a hole in its midsection. Though my shoulder whimpered with every shot, the shotgun was damn effective against the warding that shielded the demons. *Thank you, Bryce!*

A shadow passed over. Not a helicopter this time. *Wings!*

Alavik—bleeding, right hand hanging limp, and still a dire threat. Though he flew beyond the range of my shotgun, I didn't switch weapons. I guarded what he wanted. He'd come to me in due time, and I'd be ready for him.

Wings beating strong, he soared over the ruined PD then wheeled in a tight and fast turn. He intended to come in hard and hot. I shoved the butt of the shotgun against my aching shoulder and sighted down the barrel. Just like shooting skeet. So what if I'd shot skeet only twice in my life. Badly.

"Pull, motherfucker," I muttered.

I didn't get the chance to test my demon-skeet skills. Before my finger could touch the trigger, Alavik jerked in midair as the boom of another shotgun echoed across the rubble. I dropped my shotgun a few inches to better see how this played out. I sucked at skeet, but someone else out here didn't. The reyza beat hard to climb out of range, then screamed as buckshot shredded one wing. Two more powerful shots hit him, one right after the other. Cracks flared over his body as he tumbled down, and he vanished with a *crack* while in midair.

A chorus of cheers arose. I looked across the partially collapsed PD to see a tall black man in a business suit lowering a shotgun as he balanced atop a pile of rubble. My former captain and current Chief of Police, Robert Turnham. He scanned the skies then clambered nimbly down and disappeared from sight.

Though I harbored the cautious hope that we'd dispatched all the demons, I didn't let my guard down. It would only take one to destroy us all. Aggravation flared as I shot a quick glance toward Idris and Pellini. Without my arcane senses I had zero idea if they were making progress and was forced to guess from their expressions. Sweaty and tired and intense. Yeah, that told me nothing.

A twitch of movement next to Idris sent my heart racing. A demon? How did it get past me?

My knees shook with relief. Not a demon—only the

creepy-as-hell Katashi arm, fingers jerking and twitching. I resumed my watch of the area then hauled my gaze back to the arm. My eyes narrowed. At least ten minutes had passed since the last gunshots, but I knew there was no fucking way Katashi would give up simply because he ran out of demons. He wanted those charges reactivated, and he was determined, clever, and unafraid to do his own dirty work. But he also wasn't stupid enough to stroll up without a disguise. Or wards to hide in.

The twitching grew more intense.

I dropped the shotgun by Idris and snatched up the arm. My pulse galloped like a herd of wild horses as I swung the thing in a slow arc, using it like a Geiger counter. The twitching grew stronger when I pointed it toward the side street. It made sense. The buildings there were less damaged, and two huge downed oak trees blocked passage. No mayhem or emergency crews, so a logical approach avenue for Katashi. *Please let me be right about having no more demons,* I silently prayed as I took off in a low run away from the valve. I didn't dare wait for Katashi to come to us. Too much chance that he could reactivate the charges by tossing a sigil at the valve, or some other brilliant and improbable action that would spell our doom.

A line of cars along the edge of the parking lot provided concealment. The twitching increased as I ducked from car to car. I dashed across the sidewalk and edged between two cars parked by the curb. The arm spasmed non-stop in my grasp. Staying low, I peeked out, on the lookout for any movement. Across the street, my favorite café stood dark—Grounds for Arrest, its windows shattered into sparkling fragments on the sidewalk, and its sign in the gutter. A shard of glass bounced against the fallen sign. *Damn, I could use a coffee right now.* The barista, David, knew exactly how I liked it: Enough cream and sugar to make my pancreas beg for mercy. Hunger tugged at my stomach to go with thoughts of coffee. A chocolate donut would rock. Grounds for Arrest didn't sell them, but maybe—

Mouth dry, I heaved my thoughts back on track. Aversion. A strong one. I knew the feel of them all too well. As soon as I got myself a coffee I'd figure out what was causing—

*Focus!* Aversions were tests of will. I'd been through too fucking much in the last year and a half to die because of coffee or donuts. Gritting my teeth, I resisted the hunger and cravings and scrutinized the street. The shard of glass that struck the café sign. Focus on that. It was important. The glass was important. It had been in the street, then bounced to hit the sign. *Like someone kicked it while walking.*

My fingers dug into the flesh of Katashi's arm. I had the will, and now I saw what didn't want to be seen: a ripple of not-right between the sign and me. I couldn't see details, but I didn't need them. I knew where he was, and that was enough.

I dug my foot into the asphalt and launched myself forward like an Olympic sprinter, zeroed in on that not-right-don't-look-at-me and bodyslammed Katashi's bony ass into the pavement.

He went down with a choked cry of pain and the *snap* of at least one broken bone. The aversions shattered, and I realized I still gripped the arm. I dropped it and yanked a ziptie from my pocket, then needed my full concentration to subdue and restrain the asshole as he struggled. He was a tough and wiry old fuck, and managed to clock me in the side of the head with the back of his fist. I tightened one loop onto a wrist then had to knee him hard in the guts to stun him long enough to allow me to yank his arms behind him and get the second loop on and tightened.

He wheezed out a pained cough then snarled out a torrent of curses in English and Japanese. His fingers moved as if knitting in the air.

"Oh, fuck no!" I grabbed the index and middle fingers of his right hand and twisted them hard to fracture the bones. He didn't scream, but he paled and let out a strangled noise. Just in case, I ziptied the fingers of both hands together. "You even wiggle your nose funny, and I'll—"

A gunshot split the air from close by. I flinched and

ducked, then twisted toward a strangled cry of pain and lifted my weapon. Jerry Steiner stood in the street in front of the café. Blood spilled over the hand he pressed to his belly. I didn't have time to wonder who shot him, not when his other hand held a gun that he lifted toward me. *Fuck this piece of shit.*

I squeezed my trigger. *Click.*

My stomach dropped. Misfire. I knew the drill for this, right? Slap, rack, ready. A drill I hadn't practiced since the Academy. I slapped the magazine to seat it, racked the slide to eject the misfired cartridge. Not fast enough to get a shot off before he took his. No place to take cover. He took a staggering step closer. His eyes met mine over his gun. From this vantage the barrel looked big enough to climb into.

I threw myself down and to the side, bit back a yelp at the gunshot. Steiner's knee exploded in blood and bone. He let out a hoarse scream and dropped like a felled tree, gun tumbling from his grasp.

*Not me. I'm not hit.* I scrambled up and put my back against the rear fender of a car. Bryce climbed over a tilted slab of sidewalk and shoved through branches of a fallen oak, face like stone and eyes locked onto Steiner. My hands shook from the excess adrenaline, but I finished clearing my weapon and chambered a fresh round.

Katashi tensed, gaze arrowing toward the valve, though cars blocked his view. Rage suffused his face. I shifted position in case it was a ploy, then risked a tactical peek over the trunk of the car—long enough to see Idris and Pellini on their feet and wearing matching expressions of relief.

A laugh bubbled up. "They dismantled your charges. You lose, you dried up turd."

Katashi glared up at me in fury and hissed a phrase in Japanese. I had no clue what he'd just called me, but doubted it was a compliment. Erring on the side of caution, I went ahead and kneed him in his old shriveled balls. He purpled and curled in on himself. *Asshole.*

Steiner screamed as Bryce dragged him by one arm into the shadow of a car not far from me. Bryce shoved the dropped gun into his waistband, then pulled a wallet from Steiner's back pocket and tucked it into his own. Steiner breathed in shallow rapid breaths and scream-gasped, "God, please, please," over and over, a cry lost in the midst of other screams and riotous background noise.

"Thanks for the save," I said to Bryce with a crooked smile.

His face relaxed, no longer the stone mask. "Anytime." He dropped his gaze to Steiner, sighed. "I'm going to get Idris," he said.

I wasn't sure if he was speaking to me or Steiner, but I nodded anyway. He retraced his steps through debris to the parking lot. Pellini emerged from a gap between cars and helped me hustle Katashi into the shadow of fallen oak branches, sitting him behind a car crushed down the middle by an iron lamp post. Despite his grey pallor and shallow panting, Katashi's eyes were as keen as ever, missing nothing, assessing, calculating.

Fuck him. He could scheme all he wanted. As soon as we got home we were sending the piece of shit to the demon realm for a cozy stay with Mzatal.

Pellini tugged on his mustache. "We need to vacate before his people come looking for him."

"Not until Idris has dealt with Steiner," I said, resolved. "He deserves whatever measure of justice he can get out of this." I understood the indecision in Pellini's eyes. Serve and protect. Even the scum. I touched his arm, lifted my chin toward Steiner. "He'll die before a medical team can get to him," I said quietly. "They're swamped, and we can't help him." I paused. "Remember Amber Palatino."

Pellini gave a stiff nod, jaw tight.

Idris strode to Steiner with Bryce right behind him. He crouched and spoke to the wounded man, though I couldn't hear the words. Bryce retreated a few steps. This was Idris's moment.

Steiner turned his head toward Idris. His agonized words cut through the other noise. "Help me. Oh god. I'm sorry. Please." His whole body spasmed. Panic contorted his face. "Pleeeeease."

Idris drew his knife from his belt, flicked it open. My heart dropped. Steiner deserved whatever Idris gave him, but I'd hoped the mortal wounds would keep Idris from a darker path of vengeance.

Steiner eyed the knife with terror that melted into desperate hope. "Mercy. Please . . . yes, please. End it. Please."

Idris trailed the flat of the blade over Steiner's throat and down his chest. "No," he said, face set in icy hatred. With his free hand he gripped Steiner's ruined knee, twisted. Steiner's scream speared through my essence. This was worse than killing him.

Idris watched his face with eerie intensity as Steiner begged for mercy between weak, labored breaths. I retrieved Katashi's arm from the street, then Pellini and I kept a watchful guard and tried to block out screams and moans and sobs—and didn't intervene.

We both sighed in deep relief when Steiner took his last rattling breath. Idris stood, knife in hand, and turned his back on the corpse. He strode toward us and, for an instant, I saw the stamp of Rhyzkahl in his bearing and intensity. At least the blade in his hand wasn't an essence blade.

Pellini hauled Katashi to his feet and leaned him up against the car. "Stay right there," he ordered and left the unspoken "or else" hanging. But Katashi's attention was solely on Idris.

"Idris, we have to go," I said.

I might as well have been a mosquito a mile away for all the effect my words had. Idris squared off in front of Katashi. "It's over. You're done." His voice carried quiet promise.

Katashi met his eyes, unflinching. "You enjoyed watching a man die and adding to his pain."

"He deserved more," Idris said through clenched teeth.

"It is a shame you were robbed of time to go further," Katashi said, voice low but rich. "Blood rituals are in your essence." He smiled. "There is nothing as sweet as building potency through the parting of flesh beneath your blade. And the screams." His eyes half-closed in rapture, and a shiver of pleasure went through him. "Your sister's were like celestial music."

Idris spat a curse in demon and stepped toward him, face contorted in fury.

"Shut the fuck up!" I yelled at Katashi. Was he insane? Taunting a pissed off Idris while bound hand and foot had to be near the top of the Stupidest Things To Do list. I grabbed Idris's arm to pull him away, but he shrugged me off, his eyes locked on the old summoner. Pellini grabbed a scrap of newspaper from the ground and tried to shove it in Katashi's mouth, even as Bryce swooped in to intervene.

A shock like the jolt from a Taser went through me, and everyone but Idris staggered back from Katashi. Son of a bitch. That had to have been one of Katashi's force field wards.

"Idris!" I gasped. "Look for wards!"

Idris shook with tension. Bryce reached for him then yanked his hand back with a hiss of pain.

Katashi stood straighter, regarding Idris with undisguised elation. "Her rape and sodomy were spectacular, yes? A shame I needed her blood for the ritual. I miss her talented mouth around my cock."

Idris leaped at Katashi with a primal scream of rage. He slashed the knife out. Once. Twice. Katashi's throat gaped red as blood sprayed out. He crumpled to the ground, breath bubbling from the gash. I swore the old man was laughing.

Idris stood tall, nostrils flaring, knife clenched in his hand as he watched Katashi gurgle his last breath.

Pellini and Bryce looked on, expressions grim. My hands trembled as I grappled for an explanation. Katashi wasn't stupid. *We* were. He'd baited Idris on purpose. *Why?* To protect the valve information?

I wiped a hand over my face and caught Pellini's eye. "Let's get the body out of sight. This one would be hard to ex—"

Blinding light blossomed on Katashi's chest and spread in deep channels over his body. The arm I held shuddered and flared, and I dropped it like a hot poker. Before it hit the ground, the light engulfed Katashi, and he and the arm disappeared with a ripping *crack*.

We all stared in shocked silence at the empty and discolored patch of asphalt.

I found my voice first. "What the *fuck* just happened?"

# Chapter 39

I stared at the place where Katashi most certainly was *not* anymore. Even his blood had vanished. "He was a *demon?*"

"No way," Idris croaked. *"No."* He held up a hand in denial. "That makes no sense. Has to be something else."

"An implant," I said, groping for any possible explanation. "Like . . . like one of the lords' recall implants. Maybe a self-destruct implant set to activate when he dies." I liked that theory a lot more than one that had him passing through the void and waking up with his allies in the demon realm. So what if my theory had more holes than a colander.

Idris dropped his gaze to the knife in his hand, expression stricken. "We needed him."

"He's gone, Idris," I snapped. "And he'd be just as gone if his ass hadn't burned up, thanks to a certain slit throat."

He glared at me, then gave a strangled cry and slammed the knife closed. "I let him taunt me into ruining *everything!*"

He wasn't processing info very well. Neither was I, for that matter. Overload much? "Nothing we can do about that now," I said, striving for calm. "We have to prioritize the shit we *can* do."

"We need to get out of here," Bryce said. He glanced toward Pellini's truck where Jill remained tucked away in the back seat. "They've cleared the main street enough to get emergency vehicles in, which means we can get *out* once we move the debris blocking the truck into the lot."

Without a word, Pellini took Idris by the arm and marched
him toward the parking lot entrance. I used my shirt to mop
sweat from my face. "Good. He'll center Idris with manual
labor." Emergency workers were starting to set up floodlights
in preparation for a long night. "Am I a bad person for wanting to leave when there's so much to be done here?"

"You're exhausted," Bryce said without hesitation.
"You've had a huge day and are on the verge of collapse.
The mass casualty teams have it. You're more of a detri-
ment than a help at this point."

I smiled weakly. "Gee, thanks." But it was true. Every
joint and muscle in my body ached, and I felt as if I'd been
on sensory overload since morning. My brain was mush.

"What the hell is that?" Bryce said as he crouched and
examined a pinkish lump on the pavement.

I bent for a closer look, then prodded it with the toe of
my shoe to flip it over. Wrinkly skin and a layer of underly-
ing tissue about the size of my palm. "Oh. Ew." I shuddered.
"I can't see the arcane part of this, but I bet my sweet dim-
pled ass that Mzatal's mark is on that thing, which blocked
it from discorporeating with the rest of the arm." I picked it
up with two fingers and then didn't know what to do with it.

"Souvenir," Bryce said.

"Maybe it'll still be useful," I scooped up a scrap of paper and wrapped the skin in it before sticking the bundle in
a side pocket. "Easier to carry around than an arm."

"Not as much pizazz though." He squeezed my shoulder.
"You keep an eye on things, and I'll go help with the heavy
lifting. We won't be long." With that he headed off toward
the parking lot entrance where Pellini and Idris shifted rubble. My unassuming hero.

My phone rang, and I snatched it from my belt. Boudreaux. "Hey!"

"Kara! Thank god," he said, agitated. "You all right? Is
Vince?" The connection warbled and clicked, but I could
make out his words. "I haven't been able to get through to
*anyone*."

"I'm okay. So is Pellini. Cory evacuated the station." I
paused. "It's a mess down here."

"I should've been there." Whatever else he said was lost in a burst of crackling in the connection.

"Where'd you go?"

"My mom called from a phone booth," he said, voice thin and stressed. "Begged me to come for her. Told me she was at Mighty Mort's, and I had to be there in ten minutes."

The truck stop was a good five miles away. With or without permission, she'd called to make sure her son was out of the danger zone. "She wasn't there?"

"No! She left a note in the phone booth. Said she and my dad were okay." Anger and frustration and exhaustion laced his voice. "They knew, but—"

Poor guy. "Boudreaux?" Nothing. "Boudreaux?" No signal either. Arcane residue interference. At this rate it would end up with its own acronym. *Sorry, honey. Couldn't call to tell you I'd be late. ARI is bad tonight.*

I hiked myself onto the hood of a puke green Buick that sported four flat tires and watched emergency crews work with amazing efficiency around me. There were pockets of confusion and misdirection, but that was to be expected when dealing with the inconceivable. As far as I could tell, the workers were all locals from Beaulac and St. Long parish. Made me proud to be a native. They'd done plenty of training, but I doubted if more than a handful had ever worked a mass casualty incident.

Doubt surged through me. Should I have let Cory try to arrest Katashi and his people? If he'd intervened, would disaster have been averted, or would Cory be dead now?

No. I could play the What If game until the end of time, but it wouldn't change a damn thing. I'd made a decision based on available information. I never could have guessed how high the stakes truly were.

My attention drifted to the triage crews as they moved through the area with rolls of colored tape clipped to their belts. I didn't envy them. They had to make hard life and death decisions to prioritize the use of available resources.

Green tags were easy. Ambulatory. Those victims could walk themselves to the designated field treatment area.

Yellow. Delayed treatment. That was for victims who

couldn't walk out on their own but didn't need immediate emergency care. Serious but not life-threatening, such as a broken leg.

The assignment of Red and Black tags was where it got hard. Red meant top priority needing immediate emergency care. Salvageable given the resources available. Black meant lowest priority. For deceased, a black tag was a no-brainer. A lowest priority black tag on a live victim was another matter. The victim was alive but, in the judgment of the emergency worker and an impartial algorithm, too injured to survive given the available personnel and equipment.

I watched as a crew member crouched by Jerry Steiner's body, checked to see if he was breathing, then placed a strip of black and white striped tape on his shoulder before striding off to check the next victim. "Buh-bye, asshole," I muttered.

A familiar voice cut through other racket. Marco Knight. "I'm fine! Leave me alone."

What the hell was he doing here? His clairvoyance must not have warned him of a Giant Arcane Disaster. I pushed off the car and ran out into the street to see the NOPD detective, pale with concrete dust, sitting on a hunk of granite that used to be part of the City Hall façade. A first responder wrapped a red strip around his wrist and trotted away. Blood matted Knight's hair and darkened the side of his face. He tried to stand, but swayed and sat again.

"Marco, you need to stay put," I told him.

"I'm fine. Shit." Knight struggled to fix his gaze on me. "Kara? It's time. The place I took Pellini. The place I showed you by Ruthie's Smoothies. It's *time*."

"Something's happening there?" Fucking hell, like we didn't have enough to deal with already.

"Right now." He grabbed my wrist, and his eyes went wide and wild. "Now!"

"All right," I said and patted his hand. "As soon as we can—"

Nausea struck, accompanied by a freaky low-level buzz in my bones. In the parking lot, Idris tumbled to his side and curled in a fetal position while Bryce doubled over. A few emergency workers staggered or puked or clutched their bellies. Pellini stood straight and alert as if listening for a sound as quiet as the whisper of butterfly wings.

Right before I was first summoned to the demon realm, an arcane gate destabilized, causing ten minutes of headaches, nausea, or vertigo for anyone in Beaulac with even a touch of arcane talent. Clearly something similarly big was happening at Ruthie's—and Pellini with his Kadir imprint didn't seem to be affected. *Can't we get a break for five lousy minutes?*

The nausea stopped as if a switch had been thrown. The buzzing in my bones remained, but retreated to the edge of perception within seconds.

Knight used his grip on my wrist to haul himself upright but collapsed to the pavement before he could fully straighten. I knelt beside him, only now seeing that his right foot was twisted at an unnatural angle. "Don't move," I ordered and cast a frantic look around for *anyone*. "I'm going to get help."

His fingers dug into my wrist. "The twelfth," he gasped with an edge of desperation. "The twelfth!"

My heart thudded. "Is something about to happen with the sigil?" I groped my lower back with my free hand. Unremarkable. I hadn't felt anything with the sigil since the bean tapped it.

"I needed to see her. To talk to her." Knight tried to look beyond me, toward the valve. Frantic. Distressed. "She was *here*."

*She?* "Hang on. You mean Jill's baby? The *bean* is the twelfth?" I tried to make that fit into the larger picture but my brain had put up the No Vacancy sign.

His head lolled. "Tried . . . to get here."

Four men approached carrying a litter, and I quietly died of relief. "You did good, Marco. Real good." I gently disengaged from his grip and stepped back to give the pros room to work. "These guys are going to take good care of you now."

Near the collapsed section of the police station, workers

wrestled a rescue litter up through a hole in the rubble. *Who didn't make it out?* I mustered energy and clambered over minivan-sized chunks of concrete toward them. Scott Glassman grabbed hold of the litter along with two others and heaved it to the surface. My breath caught. *Cory.* Strapped to a backboard, head immobilized, and too much blood.

I looked to Scott in horror as they carried him away. "Is he . . . ?"

Scott dragged a hand over his face, smearing soot and grime. "They don't know. Head injury, and his legs were pinned."

Acid filled my mouth. This was too real, too close to home. "He cleared the building! I saw him."

"He and Dustin went back to get the prisoners out. Dustin's trapped but says he's okay."

Throat tight, I nodded. "I have to take care of some stuff. Can you keep me posted? Please."

"No problem." His eyes flicked toward the valve then back to me. Now that slaying demons wasn't a priority, he had questions. Lots.

"Glassman!" the chief called from the still-standing corner of the building. "We need your help."

"Duty bellows," Scott said with a *We'll talk later* look, then jogged that way. He could ask me all the questions he wanted *after* I showered and slept for a million years.

"Hey, Kara!" Tim Daniels climbed over a fallen light pole, uniform filthy and face scraped. "I don't know if you heard." His face was sad and serious. Aching fatigue settled on me like a lead blanket. I couldn't handle any more bad news. "It's your aunt's shop," he said with a sympathetic wince. "Everyone got out safely, but the place was completely destroyed. I'm so sorry."

The lead blanket lifted to be replaced by a chorus of sparkly singing birdies. I slapped both hands over my mouth and did my best to make my hysterical laughter look like sobs. Tim gave me an awkward pat on the shoulder.

"Thanks, Tim," I finally managed. "She'll be so upset. I'll have to think of the right way to break the news to her." Stripper-gram?

I left the wreckage of the station and made my way back to the truck. Idris gulped water from a bottle, pale but appearing more grounded. Bryce passed the Malibu key to Pellini and pointed down the side street. "It's parked by the Kwik-E Mart. Can't miss it." He looked to me. "We're good to go."

"Works for me." I glanced at Pellini, dismayed to see how bloodshot his eyes were. "According to Knight, something big happened near Ruthie's Smoothies."

Pellini straightened. "That's where Knight and I went the day I left you at the diner." He winced and shuddered. "Maybe that's why my bones are itching like crazy."

"Mine too," I said, "though not as bad as earlier."

Bryce shrugged. "Not me," he said. Idris nodded in agreement with Bryce.

Just Pellini and me. Weird. I pulled my hands over my face, sighed. "As much as I hate to say it, we need to go check it out."

Pellini held up the key. "Idris and I can handle it. We have to check the node for this valve anyway, and Ruthie's is on the way to the warehouse. Bryce is heading home in my truck with Jill." He made a shooing motion with one hand. "You should go with them."

Bryce spoke before I could argue that Pellini needed a break as much as I did. "Good plan," he said. "Jill needs the support." He graciously didn't add, *and Kara is an exhausted mess who'll be more trouble than she's worth.*

Fine. I knew when I was beaten. "Let's get out of here."

Idris slung his messenger bag over his shoulder and headed off through the rubble with Pellini.

"I'll drive," I said to Bryce when he opened the back door for me. "I need the distraction. That is, if you're okay with sitting by Jill."

He hesitated, no doubt wondering if I was up to it, then climbed in the back. "Get us home in one piece."

I rolled my eyes. "Yeah yeah yeah."

My cockiness aside, it took every remaining shred of my focus to navigate through the affected area. Debris was everywhere, and gaping fissures split the pavement in places.

I gave emergency vehicles right of way and spent minutes at a time waiting to drive the next leg After a three block drive that felt as if it took an eternity, we rolled out of the devastated area. Like night and day. No gradual dissipation of energy and destruction as in an explosion. A sharp line of demarcation. Even some buildings were half wrecked and half pristine. Un-fucking real.

I flicked on the headlights though it was only dusk. Too many distracted drivers on the street. *What the hell will we wake up to tomorrow?* The same scenario played out in at least one driveway of every street—families cramming belongings into vehicles, piling in, and getting the hell away from demonic monsters and bizarre destruction. Panic. Common sense. I couldn't blame them.

I glanced in the rearview mirror, and a measure of my dark mood lifted. Bryce had his arm around Jill as she dozed against his chest. She needed the attention and consideration that Zack wouldn't or couldn't give. Bryce *cared*.

I found classical music in Pellini's collection and let the soothing strains of Mozart accompany us home.

# Chapter 40

I parked the truck, got out, and opened the door for Bryce. He gave me a nod of thanks then slid out with Jill in his arms and carried her toward her mobile home. No more need for her to stay in the house. She'd stopped being a target the instant the bean—Ashava—was born.

I watched them go, grateful again to have Bryce with us. He would give Jill the care she desperately needed right now. I had zero worry that he'd push anything with her. He was being *there* for her, and that was enough for him because he loved her, and it wasn't about what he could get out of the situation. I wasn't even sure if *he* knew he loved her, but I did. I wasn't blind.

The door to the mobile home closed softly behind the two. My own home beckoned, and I hauled myself up the steps and inside. My phone rang with Pellini's ringtone seconds after I kicked the door shut behind me. "Hey," I answered. "Just made it home."

"Good, fire up the laptop," he said, tense and rushed and with an underlayer of essence-deep weariness. "I'm emailing you a bunch of pictures. You are going to straight up shit a cat sideways. Idris did."

"Idris shit a cat?" I flopped onto the sofa and opened the laptop. "Where are you?"

"Sideways. We're in the Ruthie's Smoothies parking lot. You remember the bone itch we got when Knight grabbed you?"

"More of a buzz for me, but yeah," I said. "Definitely caused by something by Ruthie's? What is it?"

"I don't know *what* we have. Pics are in the first email I just sent you. A couple of big crystal things with Kadir's symbol on them. Force field or wards won't let anyone close. Except me."

I opened the email. "Holy . . . shit." Big? More like humongous. Two clear crystal shards, jagged at the top, six feet in diameter and fifteen feet tall. One in front of the dry cleaners, and the other in the parking lot in front of Ruthie's with a Subaru wagon perched precariously atop it. "Sounds like the bone buzz has something to do with our connection with Kadir." That was *not* a pleasant thought.

"Seems so," Pellini said. "But that's the tame news. Check out the video in the next email."

I watched it all the way through, then again. Watched it a third time as cold lead filled my bowels. Four feet off the ground to the right of the crystals, a crack of white light widened into an anomaly the size of a Frisbee. People screamed, talked, shouted near the camera. Between one frame and the next, Carl—*Xharbek*—blinked in, worked his hands around it. Shrank it, sealed it, vanished. End video.

No wonder Idris shit a cat sideways "An anomaly." My voice quavered. "On Earth." The first, as far as I knew. I had an ugly feeling it wouldn't be the last.

"Idris said we were lucky it was a small one." Pellini didn't sound like a man who felt lucky. "We're heading out to the node. Nothing else we can do here."

"I'll keep my phone on me," I said. With a weary goodbye, he hung up.

I clicked on his third email—an aerial view of downtown Beaulac—then stared at the impossible image. The area of devastation wasn't roughly circular or any other shape the mind could accept as possible through natural means. The police department and its valve sat smack dab in the middle of an eleven-pointed star a half mile across, with lines of destruction as clear as if they'd been stamped out with a cookie cutter.

Heartsick, I closed the laptop. There'd be time the next day . . . or the next . . . to see what the media, doomsayers, and government did with *this*. Demons. Arcane bombs. Untouchable crystals. Star-shaped earthquakes. Anomalies. Teleporting people. Baby dragons.

Baby. *Shit*. Knight and the twelfth. Ashava, not the sigil on my back. I'd forgotten all about that. Seemed trivial compared to everything else. I retrieved my journal from the bedroom, sat at the kitchen table, and flipped to the dog-eared page with Knight's warning.

*Twelve. The twelfth is a radical game changer. Spawned of fierce cunning. Beauty and power exemplified. Beware the twelfth.*

My heart pounded as I read it. It took on a whole different meaning when referring to a person rather than my sigil. But Ashava *had* connected to the twelfth sigil at the PD. I found the page with the invocation Szerain spoke when he created the twelfth sigil on my lower back the night of the plantation battle. It had been part of saving me from becoming Rowan—weaponized summoner and thrall of the Mraztur. But clearly there was more to it.

*Vdat koh akiri qaztehl.*

Infinite resources to the all-powerful demonic lord unfettered.

I flipped back and forth between the two pages as I drew the clues together. Trembling, I slammed the journal closed and shoved it across the table.

*Eleven plus one is twelve.*
*All-powerful demonic lord.*
*Not the sigil. Not Szerain. Eleven lords. Plus one.*
*The twelfth lord.*

"And her name is Ashava," I murmured.

Ramifications jangled in terrifying cacophony. Ashava was the child of a demahnk and a human. Did the same hold true for the other lords? Eleven demahnk. Ptarls. Guardians. Advisors.

Parents?

*Demonic lord unfettered*. Ashava. Perhaps she'd be able to think what she wished without fear of excruciating headaches. I already knew she could shapeshift. My heart lurched. Were all of the lords shapeshifters bound to a single form? And, if so, was it the Demahnk Council who had crippled them? Their own offspring? I brought my hand to my mouth, sickened.

And Szerain. He had to have known when he forged the sigil on my lower back that Ashava was a demonic lord. Was the sigil to help him, to help her, or to bind her into an alliance before she was even born? If he knew what she was, that meant he also knew his own parentage—which seemed impossible in light of the headache punishment for forbidden knowledge. But . . . maybe that was part of the reason the demahnk exiled and imprisoned him on Earth. Uncontrollable.

Too much to think about, and no sure answers at hand. I went to the sink and ran cold water, splashed my face and pressed cool fingers over my eyes. *Let it go for now. Take a hot shower. Get some sleep. Lay it all out tomorrow.* Yeah, deal with it later. Along with everything else.

Exhaustion gripped me as I dried my face and hands, so much that I almost missed the glow in the backyard. Frowning, I peered out the window. It emanated from the nexus—which had *never* glowed before. That much I was sure of.

I slipped out the back door and down the steps. The silvery pattern in the obsidian emitted a soft and natural radiance, like a myriad of luminous fish at the surface of a dark sea. A dozen feet from the slab, I halted and looked down, skin prickling. A five-foot wide swath of trampled grass ringed the nexus, with yet another five feet of untouched grass between slab and swath—as if someone had paced around and around the nexus for hours in a defined orbit, never straying from it.

My pulse quickened as I looked toward the far side of the slab. Standing with his back to me was a barefoot figure wearing nothing but a simple white shift. Tall. Broad-shouldered. White-blond hair.

*Rhyzkahl.* Like I needed this shit. Baring my teeth, I drew my gun. Not a pointless gesture with him diminished.

*If he's still diminished*, I silently warned myself. "What the *fuck* are you doing here?"

Tensing, he spun as if startled—which made no sense considering the lordly mind-reading talent. He eased as he took in the sight of me then *sauntered* in my direction with the unhurried pace of a second hand around a clock. Yet I didn't miss how he maintained his distance from the nexus and never stepped out of the band of trampled grass. Wary but curious, I backed away from the swath and kept my gun trained on him.

With a quarter of the circle remaining between us, he stopped and glared at me. Potency burns marred the left side of his face and hand, and the glow from the nexus revealed soot and grass stains on his silky white robe, along with a few streaks that appeared to be dried blood. His hair was still finger-length, but more sexy-tousled than bed-head now. Though my own attraction to him was non-existent to the point of revulsion, I could appreciate that he would always have that God Of Sex vibe to him.

"You have been industrious," Rhyzkahl said with a disdainful flick of his fingers toward the new and improved nexus.

"You like?" I said, smile tight. "I'm taking an art class at the Vo-Tech. That's my senior project." I angled my head. "Why are you tromping around my backyard like a homeless romance-novel cover model?"

Frustration skimmed over his face, but he schooled it into a haughty sneer. "Why should I not? I find this mockery of a nexus amusing."

I lowered my gun and holstered it. "You want to take it for a spin?" I asked, watching him. "Be my guest. Go ahead and hop on up there."

His lifted his right hand as though he wanted to strangle me with it, fingers stiff, and palm marred by a deep burn. "I choose not to."

"Pussy," I said.

Rhyzkahl dropped his hand as he grappled for a response. "I cannot," he finally said through gritted teeth.

I folded my arms over my chest and paced beside the

swath toward where he stood. Two planets in different or-
bits. "You can't touch the nexus," I stated, "but you can't
leave it either." I stopped and regarded him as a theory coalesced. "Mzatal trapped you."

Rhyzkahl put on his scowly-haughty mask, but his eyes
betrayed his fear. "He is anathema," he spat.

"To you, yes." I looked toward the woods and the pond
trail then back to the orbit of trampled grass. "Mzatal's
gone hard core and kicked you out of the demon realm." I
said, piecing clues together. Rhyzkahl's shoulders stiffened,
confirming my hunch. Tapping my chin with one finger, I
considered. "Because you weren't pulling your weight?" I
shook my head. "No. You were fucking up the balance.
*That's* why your realm kept getting more than its share of
anomalies." I chuckled as a muscle worked in his jaw. "You
were like a black hole warping the fabric of space and time
with no Zakaar to stabilize you, so Mzatal drove you to the
valve," I gestured to the potency burns on his face and hand,
"and chained you here." Not only that, Rhyzkahl couldn't
read me. Of that, I was certain. "Do I have it right? Mzatal
gave me a pet lord?"

Rhyzkahl took a threatening stride to the edge of his
orbit. "I am *not* your pet," he snarled, vein throbbing in his
forehead when I didn't flinch.

"You just need to be tamed, that's all," I said with a soft
laugh, delighted at the outrage and denial that bristled in
his stance. I was probably enjoying this *way* too much, but I
needed it after the day I'd endured. I glanced up at the sky.
"It's supposed to rain later tonight. If you're a good boy, I
might give you a blanket."

Rhyzkahl made an inarticulate sound as I walked away,
but I didn't look back. As soon as Idris and Pellini came
home, we were going to barricade that damn valve by the
pond. I didn't care how exhausted we were. No more surprise guests.

I continued inside and to the bathroom, stripped off my
clothing and, *finally*, indulged in the searing hot shower I'd
longed for since my arrest. I shampooed my hair three
times, scrubbed every inch of my body with the loofah, then

closed my eyes, stood under the spray, and let my mind empty.

Eventually, I felt clean and renewed on a number of levels. After drying, I wrapped a towel around me and padded to my room, pulled on shorts and a plain t-shirt then descended into my basement.

Idris's duffle lay in a crumpled heap on the floor beside the futon, along with a pile of dirty clothing. Ryan's belongings occupied the dresser and table, but I had a feeling they'd never be retrieved. Szerain still maintained the Ryan persona, but for how long? A pang of loss whispered through me. The Ryan I'd laughed and cried with was gone forever. *I never got the chance to say goodbye.*

The cigar box that held my summoning implements rested on the oak table. I opened the lid, let the comforting scents wash over me, then lifted the knife out. Edge keen and bright, hilt as familiar as my own hand. For over a decade my identity had been wrapped up in the contents of this box and everything it represented.

Summoner. Arcane practitioner. Powerful. Special.

I replaced the knife in the box, closed it and carried it upstairs. In the laundry room, Fuzzykins lay on her side in a nest of towels while her kittens eagerly nursed. She gave me a soft *brrrump* and only one dubious look when I pulled down the ladder to the attic. As soon as things settled a bit I'd coordinate with Idris to send the cats to the demon realm.

Though my last trip to the attic had been several years ago, the single light bulb still worked and filled the dusty space with clear, white light. My attic had a sturdy floor and shelves that held a miscellany of items once deemed worth saving and mostly never touched again. I found an empty spot next to a stack of old board games with missing pieces and tucked the cigar box into it. No grief or regret or sadness welled. The box and its contents were mementos worth treasuring, but I was more than a mere summoner or arcane practitioner. I had skills and savvy and experience. Powerful. Special. I was *Kara Gillian*, damn it.

A few minutes of searching turned up the pop-up hiking

tent I'd bought on a whim half a decade ago and used exactly zero times. I climbed down the ladder and headed to the kitchen, dropped fruit and cheese into a resealable plastic bag, grabbed a bottled water, retrieved two blankets from the linen closet, then carried everything to the backyard.

Rhyzkahl frowned as I chucked the food, water, and blankets onto the trampled grass near him. I pulled the tent out of its bag—relieved when it popped into shape as advertised—then slid that into his "orbit" as well.

"You might want to put the blankets in the tent so it doesn't blow away," I said, calm and settled. "Oh, and don't mistake my mercy for weakness."

He regarded the tent with scorn and barely hidden uncertainty. "I do not mistake your *weakness* for mercy."

"You can be an ass if you want, but be aware there's no one else here who would show you a fraction of this *weakness*."

"You expect me to ingratiate myself to you?" His mouth twisted in a sneer, but I sensed that he clung by his fingernails to what little stability he had.

"No," I said. "I gave you food, water, and shelter because I have no desire to make anyone suffer." I paused. "Even you. But I want to be sure you understand that, if you fuck with me or anyone I care about, you're going to be sleeping in the rain and eating bugs."

He turned his back to me and stalked off. Good. Glad that was settled. As soon as he was a quarter of the circle away, I looked toward the nexus. The glow rippled as if beckoning me forward, and I was happy to oblige.

Unfortunately, I'd underestimated Rhyzkahl's desperation. The instant I reached the middle of the trampled grass, he spun and charged me, face vicious. Though his powers were diminished, his lordly speed was not, and before my brain registered the danger, he'd closed half the distance.

*I'm fucked.* The thought flashed through my head as my human-slow reflexes kicked into gear. Rhyzkahl reached a hand toward me like a claw, ten feet away, five, two—

Blue-white lightning lanced from the edge of the slab to

Rhyzkahl, spiderwebbing over his body in an instant. He cried out in agony and fell back, writhing as the arcane power crawled over him.

I drew a shaky breath. *Of course* Mzatal would think of everything. "Thanks, Boss," I murmured. As soon as my pulse slowed to a less frenetic pace, I continued to the slab. The moment my foot touched the stone, the lightning vanished, leaving Rhyzkahl twitching on the grass. I ignored him and gave the nexus my full attention.

The surface appeared smooth as glass, the silvery strands perfectly flush with the obsidian. I froze at the edge of the slab as nightmarish memories stirred.

*Endless black glass plane. Tilting. Rhyzkahl's voice. Elinor. Identity slipping. Confusion. Rowan. Fear. Cold. So cold.*

*No.* I shook my head to dispel the memories. Warmth. Solid footing. Wholeness. Rhyzkahl, bound.

Mzatal's silvery mark repeated in uncountable fractal patterns in the black glass. I smiled a smile that began in my core and worked its way out to fill my entire being. "Kara Gillian." My name, rich and full on the night air.

Like balmy beach sand, the nexus called to me. I stripped off my shoes and tossed them to the grass, breath catching as pleasant warmth radiated through my bare feet to my knees. The silvery filigree of the sigils shimmered like liquid starlight, and in the center of the nexus the delicate outline of a circle flared a brighter silver-white, captivating. I took a step toward it then flinched in surprise as the strands within the six foot circle went dark. No. More than dark.

Gooseflesh shivered over my skin as I approached the circle. I knew that utter darkness. What seemed like a lifetime ago, I faced the maw of the void atop the basalt column in Mzatal's realm and clung to the stone like a lost kitten in the rain.

*The void can consume the resolve of even the most stalwart.* Mzatal's words.

I swallowed. The darkness whispered to me, tugged at my essence. Unknown. Unfathomable.

"Turn away. There is no shame in it." Rhyzkahl's voice rippled through me like gossamer silk. Gentle. Persuasive.

Wise to flee the black. Easy to turn away.

"No." My voice rang out clear and strong. Sweat pricked my armpits. Mzatal's sigils warmed the soles of my feet. I sank to my knees beside the circle, leaned over and gazed into the lightless void. No frightened kitten this time. I extended both hands, lowered them toward the surface.

"Kara! Do not touch it."

I hesitated an inch from the black, trembled. "You will not consume my resolve," I told the darkness. "I am *Kara Gillian!*" My palms met warm obsidian. Pitch black gave way to the shine of stone.

Rhyzkahl made a strangled sound behind me.

Silver-white filigree sprang into glowing life within the circle. A multitude of Mzatal's sigils and . . .

I scrambled to my feet for a better vantage. Barely discernible contours of a human figure spread-eagled like Da Vinci's Vitruvian Man—except with the curves of a woman. The interweave of a *different* sigil defined her subtle shape. As I took it in, her sigils shimmered brighter. Her sigils. *My* sigil. I honed in on one, followed its lines with my eyes, felt it resonate with my essence.

Laughter. Mine.

I stepped into the circle, lay on my back, aligned with the figure. Arms stretched out to my sides, hands at the level of my crown. Legs straight, feet wide apart.

The starry canopy of the night sky swam above, and the nexus floated me in its lustrous glow. The weariness of the day slipped away. The vibration in my bones eased to a soft hum. Rhyzkahl's scar at the top of my sternum cooled. A tingle rose from below, surged through me, and the world burst into colors too vivid to be real. Potency flows like rivers of subtle light. Energy that flickered through the treetops and swirled in the air.

Sitting up, I stared in wonder as every plant, every insect, every creature—*everything* shone with its own signature of potency.

Rhyzkahl cursed in demon. I grinned and called potency to my hand, gathered it into a searing ball on my palm. I understood the first layer of what Mzatal had wrought. On the nexus, the arcane was mine. And more than othersight—*lord*sight. A lord's powers, with Rhyzkahl as my battery. An ingenious ritual tethered him to me, and I laughed in delight as I took in the whole of it. Rhyzkahl had insisted on connecting with his sigil scar while in dreamspace, and now he was bound to that very sigil.

Mzatal had more use for him. I could *feeeeel* it, but the reason evaded me. Revenge with purpose.

Rhyzkahl stood in his orbit, posture rigid, and wearing his best pissed-off face. I spun the potency in my hand and smiled at him. "It must kill you that Mzatal outwitted you to this extent."

He drew breath to respond, but I raised a barrier of potency between us and cut him off. My own brand of privacy fence. I dissipated the charge in my hand into a thousand iridescent sparks, then eased onto my back again and gazed up at the night sky. It didn't bother me one bit that I had the arcane only on the nexus. I'd take it as the precious gift it was.

And, off the nexus, I'd kick ass in all other ways. Kara Gillian style.

The moon skimmed the trees, full save for a slim crescent of shadow. To the north, stars shimmered through the muggy night in defiance of the moon's intrusion. Lightning flashed to the south and rumbled the promise of a coming storm. My gaze drifted between stars and moon, to the potency that danced through the atmosphere, and I reveled in the moment.

A meteor speared across the sky and vaporized in a flash above me. In the shadow of its absence, a trick of light and imagination floated for a heartbeat—a dragon black as the void, with wings outstretched and eyes of silver starlight.

# Glossary

## Terms Related to the Demonic Lords

**Demon Realm and demon language:** The world of the demons and demonic lords. The demon language has never been fully mastered by a human because of the verbal complexity and telepathic component. The same sound may have a multitude of different meaning depending on the telepathic pattern behind it. The demon word for their world is heavily telepathic and seventeen syllables.

**Demahnk Council/Demon Council:** Comprised of the demahnk ptarl/advisors of the lords. Holds power and influence that Kara is still discovering. Enforcers of Szerain's exile.

**Eleven:** A significant number in the demon realm in rituals, architecture, and managing potency. Also, the number of demonic lords.

**Manipulation:** The altering of memories or controlling of actions through telepathic means. Utilized by demonic lords and demahnk.

**Mraztur:** Derogatory demon word used by Kara and her allies to refer to the demonic lords unified against her personal interests and those of Earth. Rhyzkahl, Jesral, Amkir, and Kadir. Rough translation: motherfucking asshole dick-wad defilers.

**Nexus:** A confluence of potency streams harnessed as a focal point of power in each lord's realm. Universally marked by a platform of stone, wood, or crystal surrounded by eleven columns. Foundation for the most powerful rituals.

**Plexus:** The chamber in each lord's realm where the arcane potency flows of the planet can be monitored, manipulated, and adjusted by a demonic lord. Used daily, often for many hours at a time. Most are furnished for comfort during long work sessions. Kara's rough translation: *a demonic lord's man-cave.*

**Ptarl:** The demahnk counselor/advisor of a demonic lord.

**Qaztahl:** Demon word for demonic lord. Both singular and plural. The lords are human in general appearance, but have a palpable energy aura and are able to shape and wield potency. Mind readers. Fully responsible for maintaining the potency stability of the planet. It is the one matter they agree on without question.

**The Conclave:** An annual meeting of all qaztahl where global issues are addressed and plexus schedules for the upcoming year are confirmed. Outward hostility is frowned upon. Intrigue is rife.

**The Groves:** Clusters of white-trunked trees that form a network of organic teleportation nodes, with one in each realm of the eleven qaztahl and a dozen or so more scattered across the planet. Animate and sentient. Kara has a unique relationship with the groves. Teleportation can only be activated by a lord, demahnk, or Kara. Each grove has a *mehnta* as its caretaker—a lifelong commitment.

## The Demonic Lords—The Qaztahl

*Names of ptarl and other details are included if they have been revealed to Kara through* Vengeance of the Demon.

**Amkir** (AHM-keer) One of the Mraztur. Light olive complexion, short dark hair. Anger issues. Unsmiling. Asshole. Got totally punched out by Kara.

**Elofir** (EL-oh-fear) Ptarl: *Greeyer*. Short sandy-blond hair. Slim, athletic build. Friendly, gentle, deeply caring. Enjoys the quiet of his wooded realm. Lover to Michelle Cleland. Pacifist by nature but will totally fuck up anyone who messes with her.

**Jesral** (JEZ-rahl) One of the Mraztur. Slim, brown hair, keen gaze, impeccably styled and graceful. Smiling, outwardly friendly. In reality a backstabbing slimy bastard. Seriously, this guy is a dick. Cold and calculating. Hates that he doesn't have an essence blade of his very own. I mean, it totally sticks in his craw that he's not one of the "elite three" who got blades.

**Kadir** (kuh-DEER) Ptarl: *Helori*, estranged. One of the Mraztur. Slender, blond, androgynous. Cold, psychopathic, chaotic, vicious. Utterly brilliant. Lives slightly "out of phase" with the rest of the demon realm. Nicknamed "Creepshow" by Kara. Associated demon: *Sehkeril* (reyza)

**Mzatal** (muh-ZAH-tull) Ptarl: *Ilana*. Essence Blade: *Khatur*. Tall and elegant, keen silver-grey eyes, Asian features, very long jet black hair worn in a braid. Powerful and focused. Creator of the essence blades. Has a bond with Kara. Associated demons: *Gestamar, Safar, Juntihr* (reyza). *Jekki, Faruk* (faas). *Dakdak, Tata, Krum, Wuki* (ilius). *Lazul* (mehnta). *Juke* (kehza). *Anak* (zrila). *Steeev* (syraza)

**Rayst** (rayst) Partner of Seretis. Swarthy. Stocky build, but moves with grace. Kind and friendly, but not a pushover. Pays attention to the dynamics between others.

**Rhyzkahl** (REEZ-call) Ptarl: *None* (formerly Zakaar/ Zack). One of the Mraztur. Essence Blade: *Xhan* (last known to be in the possession of Jesral). Long white-blond hair, ice-blue eyes, tall, muscled, utterly beautiful. Seductive and charming. Betrayed and tortured the hell out of Kara. Associated demons: *Eilahn, Olihr* (syraza). *Pyrenth* (deceased, reyza). *Kehlirik* (reyza). *Rega* (faas).

**Seretis** (SAIR-uh-tis) Ptarl: *Lannist*. Partner of Rayst. Chiseled cheekbones, and shoulder length dark, wavy hair. Looks like a Spanish soap opera star. Bisexual. Loves being around humans, and has gone to extreme lengths to protect humans in the demon realm from other lords.

**Szerain** (szair-RAIN) Ptarl: *Xharbek* (in hiding/presumed dead by most). Essence Blade: *Vsuhl*. Utterly brilliant artist. Smart and inquisitive and very patient when his plans call for it. Is called a kiraknikahl—oathbreaker. Diminished and exiled to Earth as Ryan Kristoff. Associated demon: *Turek* (savik)

**Vahl** (pronounced like the first syllable of volume) Tall, black, just the right amount of muscle, and oh-so-sexy. Seriously, the dude is yummy. Too bad he tends to make rash decisions that cause him to be indebted to the other lords. He's like that dude in college who was probably a decent guy but got so caught up in wearing the right clothes and driving the right car and living in the right neighborhood that he maxed out all his credit cards, and when the economy took a dip, and he got laid off, everything got repossessed, and he had to declare bankruptcy. But, still, not a bad guy and fun to hang out with, and when he had money he'd totally buy a round for everyone.

**Vrizaar** (vree-ZAR) Dark-skinned, bald, with a goatee and no mustache. Dresses like a biblical king, with gold and jewels that are awesome and just shy of gaudy. As cautious and prudent as Vahl isn't when it comes to dealings with the other lords, but not so staid that he doesn't enjoy the thrill of adventure. Loves to sail.

### Summoners Known to Kara

**Aaron Asher:** (30s) Katashi's student and associate. Former student of Rasha Hassan Jalal Al-Khouri. Associated with J.M. Farouche and the Mraztur.

**Anton Beck:** (40s) Katashi's student and associate. Recruited Idris for Katashi.

**Cherie and Keveen Bergeron:** (deceased) Grandparents of Raymond Bergeron A.K.A. Tracy Gordon. Killed by Rhyzkahl in the Bloodbath Summoning.

**Frank McCreary:** (deceased) Killed by Rhyzkahl in the Bloodbath Summoning.

**Gina Hallsworth:** (30s) Katashi's student and associate.

**Graciella "Gracie" Therese Pazhel:** Tessa's mother. Kara's maternal grandmother. Sworn summoner of Szerain. Killed by Rhyzkahl in the Boodbath Summoning.

**Idris Palatino:** (20) Student of Katashi and Mzatal. Kara's cousin. Son of Tessa and Rhyzkahl. Gifted summoner. Adopted as a baby, and then again as a young teen after his first adoptive parents were killed. Innocence stripped by the Mraztur. Forced to watch his sister raped and ritually tortured and killed.

**Isumo Katashi:** (100+) Master summoner. Tessa's mentor. Conducted the very first summoning after the arcane ways reopened post-cataclysm. Was once a sworn summoner of Mzatal but betrayed him. Associated with the Mraztur. Every living summoner has been trained by him or one of his students.

**Peter Cerise/Chief Eddie Morse:** (deceased in his 60s) Organized the summoning of Szerain three decades ago that ended in a bloodbath with his wife and five other summoners slain by Rhyzkahl. Sworn summoner of Szerain. Became the serial killer known as the Symbol Man. Killed by Rhyzkahl when he attempted to summon and bind the lord.

**Rasha Hassan Jalal Al-Khouri:** (80s) Katashi's student. Retired. Associated with J.M. Farouche. Antagonistic relationship with Aaron Asher.

**Robert Lamothe:** (deceased) Killed by Rhyzkahl in the Bloodbath Summoning.

**Tessa Pazhel:** (late 40s) Kara's aunt and mentor. Student of Katashi. Frizzy blond hair and eclectic fashion sense. Raised Kara from age eleven.

**Tracy Gordon/Raymond Bergeron:** (deceased in his late 20s) Grandson of two of the summoners killed by Rhyzkahl in the Bloodbath Summoning of Szerain.

**Tsuneo Oshiro:** (late 20s) Student of Katashi. Bears a tattoo of Jesral's sigil. Associated with the Mraztur.

**William Slavin:** (50s) Katashi's student and associate.

### Humans Who Know Kara Is a Summoner

**Angus McDunn:** (mid 50s) Broad-shouldered, big and stocky. Red and grey hair. Was J.M. Farouche's right hand man. Husband of Catherine McDunn and stepfather to Detective Marcel Boudreaux. Lost a young son over twenty years ago to abduction and murder.

**Bryce Thatcher:** (40ish) Ex-hitman. Was a veterinary student when he accidentally shot and killed his roommate, Pete Nelson. Recruited by J.M. Farouche shortly thereafter. Paul Ortiz's bodyguard. Part of Kara's posse.

**Carl:** (mid 40s) Morgue tech. Quiet and unflappable with an unspeakably dry sense of humor. Tessa's boyfriend. Immune to the arcane for reasons unknown.

**James Macklin Farouche:** (deceased late 50s) Businessman, philanthropist, and vigilante-gone-wrong. Became obsessed with finding missing children and punishing those responsible after his five-year-old daughter was abducted nearly twenty years ago. Involved with Rhyzkahl and human trafficking. Arcane talent of influencing people. Executed by Bryce Thatcher.

**Jerry Steiner:** (late 30s) Hitman who enjoys his work. Very nondescript appearance. Easily blends in. Rapist and sociopath. Was one of the men who participated in the rape, torture, and murder of Amber Palatino Gavin.

**Jill Faciane:** (late 20s) Red hair, blue eyes, petite, athletic. Kara's best friend. Crime scene tech. Smart and sarcastic. Pregnant with Zack's child ("the bean"). Former gymnast who'd been favored to make the Olympic team before a bad fall.

**Leo Carter:** (mid 50s) Black. Close-cropped hair. Farouche's head of security. Trained sniper—preferred weapon a Bergara tactical rifle with a Schmidt and Bender scope.

**Michael Moran:** (early 20s) Brain damaged in an accident. Brilliant pianist. Has the ability to form golems out of dirt. Taken to the demon realm by Rhyzkahl and given to Amkir. Paid for in blood and pain by Seretis, and lives in the realm of Seretis and Rayst. Can sometimes clairvoyantly see the lords' locations.

**Michelle Cleland:** (24) Physics major turned drug addict and prostitute on Earth. Taken to the demon realm by Rhyzkahl after the Symbol Man ritual. Empath. Flourished with Vahl as she came to understand her gift. Willing courtesan of the qaztahl. Beloved of Elofir.

**Paul Ortiz:** (22) Computer genius. Former captive employee of J.M. Farouche. Uses potency flows in tandem with computer networks to find information and accomplish hacker tasks. Beaten nearly to death by his cop dad because of his sexual orientation. Hispanic. Like a brother to Bryce. Critically injured by Mzatal. Currently resides in the demon realm.

### Humans Who Do Not Know Kara Is a Summoner

**Chief Robert Turnham:** (50s) Beaulac PD. Tall, slender, black man. Meticulous, quiet, efficient. 25 years law enforcement experience.

**Sergeant Cory Crawford:** (early 40s) Dyed brown hair and mustache, brown eyes, stout. Chooses drab brown clothing and wild-colored ties. Good leader. Knows Kara is involved in paranormal activities but prefers not knowing details.

**Sergeant Scott Glassman:** (late 30s) Patrol training officer. Acts like a hick, but savvy. Stout, bald, ruddy complexion.

**Detective Vincent Pellini:** (early 40s) Often antagonistic toward Kara. Greasy black hair, mustache, overweight. Boudreaux's work partner.

**Detective Marcel Boudreaux:** (early 30s) Often antagonistic toward Kara. Small and wiry. Chain smoker. Pellini's work partner.

**Detective Marco Knight:** (mid 30s) NOPD. Clairvoyant or similarly gifted. Loner. Chain smoker.

**Officer Tim Daniels:** (mid 20s) Open, friendly, and helpful. Found a stray cat that Eilahn adopted as Fuzzykins.

**Dr. Jonathan Lanza (Doc):** (mid 40s) St. Long Parish pathologist. Easy-going manner.

**Catherine McDunn:** (early 50s) Head trainer for Farouche's thoroughbreds. Wife of Angus McDunn and mother of Detective Marcel Boudreaux.

**Lenny Brewster:** (late 60s) Hale, sharp-minded, and soft-spoken. Lanky black man. Barn manager for Farouche's thoroughbred farm.

**The Rest of the World:** Blissfully oblivious to Kara's dabblings in the arcane.

### Demon Types — Summonable
*Demons named in the books are in italics.*

**Faas** (faahz) 6th Level. Resembles a six-legged furry lizard with a body approximately three feet long and a sinuous tail at least twice that length. Bright blue jewel-colored iridescent fur, brilliant golden eyes slitted like a reptile's. *Jekki, Faruk, Zhergalet, Rega.*

**Graa** (grah-ah) 8th Level. Spider-like with wings like roaches and heads like crabs. Can have anywhere from four to eight multi-jointed legs that end in strange hands that consist of a thumb and two fingers, each tipped with curved claws.

**Ilius** (ILL-ee-us) 3rd Level. A coil of smoke and teeth and shifting colors. Feeds on animal essence. *Tata, Wuki, Dakdak, Krum.*

**Kehza** (KAY-za) 7th Level. Human-sized, winged, face like a Chinese dragon, skin of iridescent red and purple, and plenty of sharp teeth and claws. Can tell if a human has the ability to be a summoner. *Juke.*

**Luhrek** (LURE-eck) 4th Level. Resembling a cross between a goat and a dog with the hindquarters of a lion. Often a good source for unusual or esoteric information. *Rhysel.*

**Mehnta** (MEN-tah) 9th Level. Appearing like a human female with long flowing hair, segmented wings like a beetles, clawed hands and feet, and dozens of snake-like strands coming out of their mouths. *Lazul.*

**Nyssor** (NIGH-sore) 5th Level. Looks almost exactly like a human child, often beautiful with angelic faces. Features a little *too* perfect, and eyes a little too large and having sideways-slit pupils. Hundreds of sharp teeth. Many humans find them creepy as fuck. *Votevha.*

**Reyza** (RAY-za) 12th Level. Three meters tall, leathery wings, long sinuous tail, skin the color of burnished copper, horns, clawed hands, bestial face, and curved fangs. *Kehlirik, Gestamar, Juntihr, Pyrenth, Safar, Sehkeril.*

**Savik** (SAH-vick) 2nd Level. Immature savik: two foot long dog-lizard kind of thing with six legs. Mature savik: Over seven feet tall, reptilian with dark and smooth bellies, and translucent glittery scales elsewhere. Head like a cross between and wolf and a crocodile. *Turek.*

**Syraza** (sih-RAH-za) 11th Level. Slender, almost birdlike, long and graceful limbs. Pearlescent white skin, hairless. Large and slanted violet eyes in a delicate, almost human, face. Wings that look as fragile as tissue paper but most assuredly are not. Shapeshifter. *Eilahn, Steeev, Olihr, Marr.*

**Zhurn** (zurn) 10th Level. Black, oily, shifting darkness. Winged. Burning red eyes. Voice like a blast furnace. Sharp claws. *Skalz.*

**Zrila** (ZRIL-uh) 1st Level. About the size of a bobcat, looks like a six-legged newt with skin that shifts in hues of red and blue. Head like a hairless koala. Brilliant artisans who make the majority of the clothing and textiles in the demon realm. *Anak.*

## Demon Types—Not Summonable

**Demahnk** (de-MAHNK) Unknown if summonable. Look like large syraza with ridges on the torso and skull. Sometimes called "Elder syraza."

**Hriss** (h'RIS, huh-RIS) Pixie-like essence eaters. "Mosquitos from hell."

**Kzak** (k'ZAK, kuh-ZAK) Vicious, black, and dog-like. Rows of teeth and sinuous movement. *Kuktok.*

**Luhnk** (lunk) Mammoth-like. Six-legged. Huge females. German shepherd-sized males.

**Nehkil** (neh-KILL) Akin to a flying basking shark or living dirigible. Feeds on stray potency in the form of "ethereal spores."

**Skarl** (SCAR-ul) Hyena-like in form, but friendly as a socialized house cat. Musky. Gives off a comforting vibe when sleeping in a pack.

## Named Demons
*and associated demonic lord (if revealed)*

**Anak** *zrila*: Mzatal. Textile artisan. Made one of Mzatal's neckties.

**Dakdak** *ilius*: Mzatal. Never far from Mzatal in his palace. Dubbed as a "Mzatal Early Warning System" by Idris because he often arrives in a room shortly before the lord.

**Eilahn** *syraza*: Rhyzkahl. Multiethnic beautiful in human form. Assigned by Rhyzkahl as bodyguard for Kara. Takes her job seriously. Adores holiday decorations and her cat, Fuzzykins.

**Faruk** *faas*: Mzatal. Jekki's mate. Delights in styling hair. Maintains Mzatal's intricate braid.

**Gestamar** *reyza*: Mzatal (essence bound). One of the oldest reyza. Sense of humor and scary all at the same time.

**Helori** *demahnk*: Kadir (ptarl, estranged). Supported Kara after Rhyzkahl's torture. Spurned by Kadir. Prefers human form. Is a nudist at heart.

**Ilana** *demahnk*: Mzatal (ptarl). Quietly influential.

**Jekki** *faas*: Mzatal. Spry and energetic personal attendant of Mzatal. Loves to cook. Faruk's mate.

**Juke** *kehza*: Mzatal. Summoned by Kara to assess a human for summoning ability. Loves pistachios.

**Kehlirik** *reyza*: Rhyzkahl. Often summoned by Kara. Skilled with wards. Loves popcorn and human books.

**Krum** *ilius*: Mzatal. Sometimes mistaken for Wuki.

**Lannist** *demahnk*: Seretis. Wise and creative. Has a thing for unicorns.

**Lazul** *mehnta*: Mzatal. Keeper of Mzatal's grove.

**Marr** *reyza*: First syraza Kara ever summoned.

**Olihr** *syraza*: Rhyzkahl. Struck down by an anomaly in Szerain's realm. Saved by Safar and Ilana.

**Pyrenth** *reyza*: Rhyzkahl. Killed by Kara using an essence blade.

**Rhyzel** *luhrek*: The demon Kara was trying to summon when Rhyzkahl came through instead.

**Rega** *faas*: Rhyzkahl. One of Rhyzkahl's personal attendants.

**Safar** *reyza*: Mzatal. Escorted Kara in Szerain's realm when she first arrived. Crashed into the grove while carrying her.

**Sehkeril** *reyza*: Kadir. A lanky demon with a cruel streak. Eviscerated Kara during the Symbol Man's final ritual.

**Skalz** *zhurn*: unknown. Prefers to communicate telepathically.

**Steeev** *syraza*: Mzatal. Recruited by Kara as a bodyguard for the very pregnant Jill.

**Tata** *ilius*: Mzatal. That other ilius.

**Turek** *savik*: Szerain (essence bound). Ancient demon. Has known Szerain for thousands of years.

**Votevha** *nyssor*: unknown. Summoned by Kara to assess a human for summoning ability. Likes bacon. Creepy.

**Wuki** *ilius*: Mzatal. Sometimes mistaken for Krum.

**Xharbek** *demahnk*: Szerain (ptarl—missing/dead) Whereabouts and circumstances unknown. Helori implied that he is not dead.

**Zakaar** *demahnk*: Recently broke ptarl bond with Rhyzkahl. Currently lives as FBI Agent Zack Garner on Earth. Guard and guardian of Ryan/Szerain.

**Zhergalet** *faas*: Expert with wards.

### Demon Words

**Chak** (like chalk without the L) Hot beverage without an Earth equivalent.

**Chekkunden** (cheh-KUN-din) Derogatory. Rough translation: *honorless scum*.

**Chikdah** (CHICK-daa) Derogatory. Rough translation: *cunt*

**Dahn** (dahn) No

**Ekiri** (ih-KEER-ee) Per Kehlirik: Race that lived amongst the demons long ago, but departed for a new realm thousands of years past. Taught the demons mastery of the arcane. Built stone pavilions the demons call "gateways."

**Iliok** (ILL-ee-ock) The three essence blades created by Mzatal. *Khatur* (Mzatal), *Xhan* (Rhyzkahl), *Vsuhl* (Szerain)

**Jhivral** (j'HIV-rall) A true plea. Not the casually polite usage of "please" in English.

**Jontari** (zjon-TAR-ee, jon-TAR-ee) Demons who do not associate directly with the demonic lords. The vast majority of the demon population. Cities and enclaves are far from the palaces of the lords.

**Kiraknikahl** (keh-RAK-nee-call) Oathbreaker

**Kri** (kree) Yes

**Ptarl** (puhTAR-ul) Demahnk advisor and counselor to a qaztahl. Bound by ancient oaths.

**Pygah** (PIE-gah) An arcane sigil used for calm, focus, and centering. A foundational teaching for summoners (though Kara was not taught it until she met Mzatal). Most effective when traced as a floating sigil, but may be done mentally.

**Qazlek**: Demons who closely associate with the lords.

**Qaztahl** (KAHZ-tall) A demonic lord or the demonic lords as a group.

**Rakkuhr** (rah-KOOR) A disruptive red potency alien to the demon realm. Rhyzkahl, Jesral, and Szerain are known to use it.

**Saarn** (sarn) A human or other creature who feeds on essence. Does not apply to species like the ilius or hriss whose natural food is essence.

**Shik-natahr** (SHICK-nahTAR) Rough translation: *born of the eleven*. An honoring designation. Spoken to Kara by Kadir.

**Shikvihr** (SHICK-veer) Rough translation: *potency of the eleven*. An eleven-circle ritual that offers a power base to other rituals and enhances a summoner or lord's abilities. Completion of all eleven circles/rings gives a summoner the ability to trace floating sigils on Earth.

**Syraza** (sih-RAH-za) Shapechanger.

**Tah sesekur dih lahn** (tah seh-seh-KUR dee lon) Rough translation: *I understand and feel for/with you.*

**Yaghir tahn** (YAH-gear tahn) Forgive me.

**Zharkat** (ZAR-cat) Beloved.

### Other

**Amber Palatino Gavin:** Ritually raped, tortured, and murdered by Asher, Katashi, and Steiner as a control measure for her brother Idris, and to set a trap for Kara. Body left in an eighteen wheeler in Beaulac.

**Aria Farouche:** Amicably divorced J.M. Farouche after their five-year-old daughter Madelaine was abducted and Farouche became obsessed with finding her.

**Bloodbath Summoning**: An attempt over thirty years ago by Peter Cerise and five other summoners to summon Szerain.

**Elinor:** 17th century summoner. Trained in the demon realm with Mzatal, Rhyzkahl, and Szerain. Killed by Szerain during a ritual that precipitated the Cataclysm. A part of her essence is said to be tacked onto Kara's. Possibly involved with Giovanni.

**Fuzzykins:** Eilahn's calico manx cat. Kittens: Bumper, Squig, Granger, Fillion, Dire, Cake.

**Giovanni Racchelli:** 17th century associate and art student of Szerain. Named by Gestamar as one of Szerain's favorite humans. Possibly involved with Elinor. Died young.

**Jade:** Rasha's granddaughter. Abandoned Rasha to be with Aaron Asher.

**Pete Nelson:** Bryce Thatcher's vet school housemate. Accidentally shot and killed by Bryce.

**Rowan:** As yet enigmatic personality Rhyzkahl intended to transform Kara into. Demonstrated arrogance and sense of invulnerability. Seems to be familiar with Szerain.

**StarFire Security:** Legitimate high-end security company owned by J.M. Farouche.

**Symbol Man:** Peter Cerise. Serial killer who used blood and death magic. Tried to summon and bind Rhyzkahl. Killed by Rhyzkahl.

**The Cataclysm:** Demon realm disaster that began in the 17th century and lasted nearly a century. Earthquakes, floods, fire rain, and rifts in the dimensional fabric. Started by a ritual performed by Szerain and Elinor.

**The Child Find League:** Non-profit organization founded by J.M. Farouche to help find missing children. Impressive track record.

**The Others:** The vague designation given by Zack for ones he cannot speak of who, along with the Demahnk Council, hold and enforce ancient oaths.

**The Three:** Mzatal, Rhyzkahl, and Szerain. Bearers of the three essence blades. Dominated the demon realm unchallenged and unchallengeable for centuries.

# Diana Rowland

### *My Life as a White Trash Zombie*
978-0-7564-0675-2

### *Even White Trash Zombies Get the Blues*
978-0-7564-0750-6

### *White Trash Zombie Apocalypse*
978-0-7564-0803-9

### *How the White Trash Zombie Got Her Groove Back*
978-0-7564-0822-0

To Order Call: 1-800-788-6262
www.dawbooks.com

# Seanan McGuire

## *The October Daye* Novels

"...will surely appeal to readers who enjoy my books, or those of Patricia Briggs." —*Charlaine Harris*

"I am so invested in the world building and the characters now.... Of all the 'Faerie' urban fantasy series out there, I enjoy this one the most."—*Felicia Day*

### ROSEMARY AND RUE
978-0-7564-0571-7

### A LOCAL HABITATION
978-0-7564-0596-0

### AN ARTIFICIAL NIGHT
978-0-7564-0626-4

### LATE ECLIPSES
978-0-7564-0666-0

### ONE SALT SEA
978-0-7564-0683-7

### ASHES OF HONOR
978-0-7564-0749-0

### CHIMES AT MIDNIGHT
978-0-7564-0814-5

### THE WINTER LONG
978-0-7564-0808-4

To Order Call: 1-800-788-6262
www.dawbooks.com

DAW 142

## Necromancer is such an ugly word
#### ...but it's a title Eric Carter is stuck with.

He sees ghosts, talks to the dead. He's turned it into a
lucrative career putting troublesome spirits to rest,
sometimes taking on even more dangerous things. For
a fee, of course.

When he left L.A. fifteen years ago he thought he'd
never go back. Too many bad memories. Too many
people trying to kill him.

But now his sister's been brutally murdered and Carter
wants to find out why.

Was it the gangster looking to settle a score? The ghost
of a mage he killed the night he left town? Maybe it's
the patron saint of violent death herself, Santa Muerte,
who's taken an unusually keen interest in him.

Carter's going to find out who did it and he's going to
make them pay.

As long as they don't kill him first.

---

# Dead Things
## by Stephen Blackmoore
978-0-7564-0774-2

---